THE KING'S OWN

Lorna Freeman

A ROC BOOK

ROC
Published by New American Library, a division of
Penguin Group (USA) Inc., 375 Hudson Street,
New York, New York 10014, USA
Penguin Group (Canada), 90 Eglinton Avenue East, Suite 700, Toronto,
Ontario M4P 2Y3, Canada (a division of Pearson Penguin Canada Inc.)
Penguin Books Ltd., 80 Strand, London WC2R 0RL, England
Penguin Ireland, 25 St. Stephen's Green, Dublin 2,
Ireland (a division of Penguin Books Ltd.)
Penguin Group (Australia), 250 Camberwell Road, Camberwell, Victoria 3124,
Australia (a division of Pearson Australia Group Pty. Ltd.)
Penguin Books India Pvt. Ltd., 11 Community Centre, Panchsheel Park,
New Delhi - 110 017, India
Penguin Group (NZ), cnr Airborne and Rosedale Roads, Albany,
Auckland 1310, New Zealand (a division of Pearson New Zealand Ltd.)
Penguin Books (South Africa) (Pty.) Ltd., 24 Sturdee Avenue,
Rosebank, Johannesburg 2196, South Africa

Penguin Books Ltd., Registered Offices:
80 Strand, London WC2R 0RL, England

First published by Roc, an imprint of New American Library,
a division of Penguin Group (USA) Inc.

First Printing, February 2006
10 9 8 7 6 5 4 3 2

An Unfortunate Display

I felt the touch return even through the fire and wind, and I batted at it but it flitted away, only to return again. Lightning crackled, grounding itself in my staff and then arcing into the fire tracery around me, turning into sheets of flame in the sudden downpour.

"Damn it, Rabbit, stop!" shouted Arlis over the howling wind, the pounding rain, and the screams and shrieks of the people in the square.

The touch evaded my attempt to knock it away, and moved to my forehead, paused, then slipped over my eyes, nose and mouth, to stroke down my throat and rest over my pounding heart. Snarling, I feinted and then, coming back the other way, managed to grab what felt like a hand. I squeezed, twisting, and in the middle of my private storm heard the crack of bones and a faint cry of pain. Immediately, the phantom hand dissolved in my grip. Teeth still bared, I waited a moment or two, but whoever was making free with my person did not return.

Breathing as if I'd just gone fifteen rounds with the village strongman, I let the wind, rain, and fire die, and looked around. And winced. Jeff, Arlis, and I stood in the middle of an almost empty square. What Harvest decorations remained were torn and dripping, branches were ripped off of trees, and windows broken.

"Don't stop now," Arlis said, his voice acid as he wiped the rain from his eyes. "You left out earthquakes, lava flows, and tidal waves."

Praise for *Covenants*

"An extraordinary debut . . . takes us to a world brimming with fantastical possibilities and intrigues."   —Rambles

"Rabbit's self-development and knowledge are particularly satisfying."   —*KLIATT*

"Stands out for its complexity, its compassion, and its meticulous world building. . . . The author's vivid descriptions make every passage a joy to read."
      —The Internet Review of Science Fiction

Also by Lorna Freeman

COVENANTS

To my sisters:
Marcia, Joy, Halleigh, Sandra, and Adia.
All y'all are brats, but I
love you anyway.

ACKNOWLEDGMENTS

Again, this was not a solitary effort. Eileen Austen, Trai Cartwright, David Delbourgh, Chris Kern, and Teresa Rhyne all had a hand in this. As did Tod Goldberg, who patiently corrected my bearings until I found my footing and my way. Thank you, everyone, for the insights, support, and bops on the head when needed.

Prologue

When I was a child, my father was asked to head the trade council in our Weald—a great honor as humans were viewed with deep suspicion in the Border. (We were thought light-fingered as we'd pilfered one kingdom already.) Despite his drawbacks, however, Da not only managed to guide the council in developing a well-considered plan, but also in implementing it in a reasoned manner, to the benefit of all in the Weald. As the Weald's general council had a hard time agreeing on the placement of privies, it was considered a resounding success.

Da's reward was more councils.

One

"Alas," Lady Alys cried, her long blond braids spilling about her as she turned from her mirror and collapsed on her daybed. Her nurse thrust past the messenger to clump to her side and start chafing her hand. "Alas and alack," Alys cried again, allowing the just-delivered letter clasped in her other hand to fall to the floor. The messenger, stumbling from the nurse's push, dropped his carrypouch with a hollow thump and tinkle as his possessions burst from it. He fell to his hands and knees to gather them up, his backside waving high in the air.

Alys tried once more, raising her voice. "Alas! My sweet Dillem has answered his liege's summons to help fight the wicked Lord Morul."

The nurse, still rubbing Alys' hand, leaned forward and made soothing noises of sweet Dillem's fighting prowess, saying that he would soon return safe and sound to wed m'lady.

"No, no," Alys loudly moaned, moving so that she could see around her nurse. "You don't understand." She tried to lift her hand but the nurse still had it. After a brief tug of war, Alys regained possession and pressed the back of her wrist against her brow. "Morul has entreated the northern darkness—"

The crowd around the street players' makeshift stage

stirred, casting uneasy looks our way. Lady Alys, sensing that she was losing her audience, began to shout.

> *"The northern darkness,*
> *born of myth, magic and rune,*
> *bell and blood, candle and book,*
> *binds hell to its bidding—"* .

Lady Alys broke off in mid-declaim as the crowd shifted once more, opening a path between her and us. Her eyes flitted over Troopers Jeffen and Arlis' more regular appearance to alight briefly on my tabard, with its new lieutenant's insignia, before moving on to my waist-length braid with my feather attached to it, the butterflies on my shoulder and finally coming to rest on the plain, tall ash staff I carried. All of it reeking of the myth, magic and rune that made up the kingdom of Iversterre's northern neighbor, the Border. Wanting in on the act, the wind eddied around me for a moment, fluttering the feather and the butterflies' wings.

The life of a street player was a hard one. Besides the ever-present threats of overripe vegetables and small dead animals, official tolerance was always chancy, and to insult those in power was to live very dangerously. Alys shrank back on her daybed, while the nurse and messenger decided that there was no need for them to be there as this was really m'lady's scene. They exited stage left. A moment later the curtain rang down and an announcement came from behind it that, due to unforeseen circumstances, the remainder of the morning's performance was canceled.

"Lieutenant Lord Rabbit," Jeffen said, sighing. "Drama-bane and play-killer." Tucking his cloak about him, he turned from the stage. Arlis and I followed, heading for one of the streets leading from what the town's aldermen, in a burst of grandiosity, named Theater Square. It boasted one playhouse.

I said nothing, more concerned with what new rumors would arise to join the thousands of others that whirled around Freston. We had arrived yesterday afternoon, returning from the Border accompanied by folk most in Iversterre believed only existed in children's stories and dramas like the one that had just so abruptly ended. Add to the mix the arrival and determined stay of King Jusson IV, and the small town was rocking and reeling like one of the fire peaks in the Upper Reaches.

The wind, however, whipped around me, bringing with it the fragrance of harvest. It was going to be a good one; the fields were full to bursting and fall fruit hung heavy on trees. Harvestide was fast approaching, the celebration of the last gathering of the year. The wind murmured, telling me of acorn stashes and birds flying south, before taking off to flutter ribbons tied around lampposts and romp among the people in the square. My face eased into a smile as I watched, taking in the familiar sights, sounds and smells.

Home.

At least, home for the last five years.

I was born and raised in the Border, a loose association of fae, fantastic beasts and other like persons, existing in contentious unity to the north of the kingdom of Iversterre. Once the People were spread down to the southern seas in a network of city-states, small fiefdoms, territories, factions, tribes and clans, all gleefully crossing and double-crossing each other as they played the fae version of king of the hill. It was a golden age of shifting alliances, treachery and betrayal. Then one day humans appeared and began their own game of push—sometimes by guile, sometimes by bloody force—and the People were displaced bit by bit, until they looked up to find that not only had they been shoved off the hill, but they'd been thrust to the edge of what was once all theirs. More than a little upset, they set aside their differences during the last war of acquisition started by the human kingdom and, for the first time, the humans faced a united opponent. Iversterre's Royal Army was beaten silly, with the Border Army doing a victory dance on the remains.

However, lost wars and the People's dislike of humans didn't deter my parents, Lord Rafe ibn Chause and Lady Hilga eso Flavan, from leaving the land of their birth and settling in a Border back province. Changing their names to Two Trees and Lark, they turned farmers and weavers, and bore eight children in between crops, all the while believing that if they left the fae alone, the fae would leave them alone. They were right. But that was mainly because my ma and da had the good fortune to settle in Dragoness Moraina's territory—and honored Moraina did *not* like fuss and botheration. Unless she herself was causing it.

Despite being named Rabbit, I am human. And, while human, I grew up surrounded by the fae. I had my share of chores—plowing fields, mucking out barns, and all the other things that made farm life interesting—but I also spent spring afternoons learning forest craft from a tree sprite, summer days swimming with river otters, winter nights listening to guesting bards' tales of swords and sorcery. It was my golden age of childhood.

But when I entered my adolescence it became apparent that I was mage-born and my parents apprenticed me to Magus Kareste. A short time later, I ran away to Iversterre and became a horse soldier in the Royal Army of King Jusson IV. I never looked back—until last spring, when my past caught up with me with all the finesse of a bull in rut.

It was during a routine patrol last spring that my troop became lost in the mountains above Freston. Scouting for a way back to the garrison, I came upon Laurel, a mountain cat and head of the Faena. Next I knew, I had the feather I now wore in my braid, the symbol of a covenant that swept me and my troop out of Freston to the Royal City of Iversly, and then to the Border and the court of His Grace, Loran the Fyrst.

I came into my full power last spring with all four aspects: air, earth, fire and water. Most mages only have one.

Laurel drew the truth rune on my palm last spring. The same rune that was lifted against Iversterre's Royal Army in the last war with such devastating results.

King Jusson claimed me as cousin and heir last spring— which caused several assassination attempts by Lord Gherat of Dru, his kinsman, Lieutenant Slevoic ibn Dru, and my cousin, Lord Teram ibn Flavan. When I proved hard to kill, they rebelled.

We uncovered a massive smuggling and slavery ring last spring, which Dru and Flavan were using to finance their attempt to overthrow King Jusson.

It was last spring that His Grace Loran claimed me as *cyhn*, which triggered a rebellion in *his* court.

And it was last spring that I acquired the butterflies, courtiers of the Faery Queen.

Now, however, I snuggled down in my cloak, content. Against all the happenings of last spring, I was home. It was a perfect fall morning. The mountains surrounding Freston were a sharp outline of peaks and splashes of vivid autumn colors against a deep blue sky; the air was crisp, with a hint of spice as the goodwives of the town began their Harvestide baking. I was with my mates, I'd just been paid lieutenant's wages for the first time and my Nameday was fast approaching. I looked up, judging the sun's position. We had more than enough time for a meal at the Hart's Leap before I'd be missed at the garrison. Underneath the cover of my cloak, I hefted my purse, satisfaction filling me at its weight.

"I think Lady Alys was just upset because Rabbit's plait was longer and prettier than any of hers," Arlis said, his voice carrying the languid grace of the southern part of the kingdom. A little older than Jeff and me, he sported a trim goatee that he thought made him look dashing. Trouble was, he was right. Arlie cast a glance at the feather and then at the butterflies idly fanning their wings in the weak morning sun. "He has better baubles, too."

Arlie was a decent sort, despite his goatee and southie accent. He was also a King's Road patroller, but I didn't hold that against him since his particular troop had suffered the same trials and tribulations ours did as they accompanied us on the journeys to and from the Border. Even so, I wasn't about to let that pass. "Enjoy it while you can, old man," I said, "because, as you age into decrepitude, this is the closest you'll ever get to beauty—"

There was a distant call of trumpets and I stopped, turning my head in the direction of the Kingsgate.

"How many is that?" Jeff asked, as he and Arlie stopped with me. "Eight?"

"Yeah," I said, reaching underneath my scarf to rub a faint tickle on the back of my neck. "I think number seven arrived last night." I felt a tingle across the truth rune on my palm, then my hand went numb and I wondered if my newly unearthed winter gloves had shrunk over the summer. I stretched out my fingers and the feeling slowly returned, filling my hand with pins and needles.

"Lord Beollan of Fellmark," Arlis said. He saw our looks of surprise and gave a twisted smile. "One of the King's Road North lads was telling me at mess this morning how they had to double up to make room for his lordship's armsmen as the town is full." He sighed. "I supposed this lot will be bunking with *us*."

Jeff and I shared a smirk. Unlike Arlie's pampered King's Road patrol, our Mountain Patrol troop was the lowest of the low in a garrison filled to the brim with the inept, the suspect, the patronless, the disgraced. We pulled the worst patrols, were given the dregs and pickovers, and ac-

tually had to go into the mountains and fight bandits instead
of prancing about on showy horses with accoutrements
gleaming, posing for merchants, farmer's wives and
cowherds. As no one wanted to be associated with us if they
could help it, we probably would manage to keep our barracks to ourselves. Even in the face of the rapidly dimin-
ishing space in town.

Arlie saw our grins. "Laugh all you want, lads, but as
fast as they're arriving, Lord Stick-up-the-Backside's
equally tight-arsed armsmen will soon be sharing your
quarters."

King Jusson Golden Eye's Great Lords and nobles *were*
following him to Freston in droves—partly because he was
the king and wherever he was immediately became the center of the universe, partly because they wanted to find out
what had happened during our travels to and from the Border, but mainly because they wanted to make sure that no
one else gained an advantage—including me, even though
(or especially since) I was the king's cousin and heir. I
didn't feel at all slighted, as the aristos' dance for position
reminded me of disasters and accidents, fascinating to
watch as long as one was a safe distance away. Which was
why I was lurking in Theater Square, instead of going with
Captains Suiden and Javes to their audience with Jusson.
The fact that I was also playing hooky from the garrison
had nothing to do with it. Much.

"Ah, but you forget, aged one," I said. "We have Ryson."

Jeff's smirk broadened. "Too right. M'Lord Snoot's men
will camp in an open field during a snowstorm before sharing a room with *him*—" He broke off at another trumpet
blast.

"Hah. Nine," Arlie said. "And I wouldn't count on
Ryson. I ran into him in the baths this morning. He was actually in the water, using soap, *scrubbing*—"

"My lord!"

At first I didn't pay any attention as I was lost in the wonderment of Trooper Ryson voluntarily going near soap and water. Jeff, however, touched my arm and I turned around to see a thin stick of a man wearing a cape of motley hurrying towards us. Behind him was Lady Alys, minus her stage makeup, costume and blond braids. Her real hair was a glorious red, catching fire in the morning sun as it tumbled past high, firm breasts that rose out of her bodice, and flowing to a tiny waist, the ends caressing rounded hips. I blinked, dazzled. Man and woman both skidded to a halt in front of us, bowing and curtseying.

"My lord, gracious sirs," the man repeated as he finished his bow. "Please forgive us, we meant no offense. We chose the play thinking only of how well it was received last time we staged it."

Alys raised her head as she completed her curtsey, revealing soft green eyes set under delicate russet brows in an oval face with skin like peaches in cream. She saw us looking and her pink lips curved in a smile, parting enough to hint at white, even teeth. She cast her gaze down and bobbed another curtsey, holding her skirts just high enough for us to get a glimpse of dainty ankles above small, arched feet.

There was a collective intake of breath, and then Jeff, Arlis and I all took a quick step towards her, jostling each other. "No offense taken, Lady Alys," I said quickly.

She gave a gurgle of laughter, peeping up at us through thick eyelashes. "No lady I, my lord, but a simple player. If it pleases you, my name is Rosea."

"Lieutenant Lord Rabbit ibn Chause e Flavan," I said, clicking my heels together and bowing, hand over my heart. "Of his Majesty's Royal Army, Freston garrison, Mountain Patrol, Horse—"

"And the high lord of prissydom," Jeff said as he shoved me aside. He also made a soldier's bow. "Trooper Jeffen, gentle maid. A *real* soldier." He jerked a thumb at me. "Don't let his dandified clothes and high-sounding titles fool you. I taught him everything he knows. Unfortunately, it didn't take."

"Or perhaps you just know less than a dead gnat," Arlie said, stepping in front of Jeff. His elegant bow revealed a dancing master somewhere in his past. "Trooper Arlis of the King's Road Patrol, South, Horse. Stay with me, Fair Rose, and I will show you the treasures of the world—"

"At least those housed at the Copper Pig," I said, naming a notorious tavern just outside the town walls. I thrust both of them back and stood in front of the two lowly troopers, spread eagle. "*Lieutenant* Lord Chause, at your service." I smiled at Rosea, ignoring the cold tingle that coursed down my spine. "My friends call me Rabbit."

"What friends?" Arlie muttered, while Jeff blew a muted raspberry.

Rosea pretended not to hear them as she gave another gurgle, eyeing the butterflies. "Rabbit? Such a funny name, my lord." She started as her companion thumped her side. "But so charming!" she added quickly.

"And I, my lord, gracious sirs, am her brother, Rodolfo," the skinny man said. He gave a flourish of his many-colored cape as he bowed again and, for a moment, his dark brown eyes seemed to flash blue in the autumn sunlight. I blinked at how suddenly familiar the master player looked.

"Have we met?" I asked, frowning.

"I don't believe so, my lord," Rodolfo said. "Perhaps you've seen us perform before. This is my traveling troupe, Rodolfo's Players. I bear full blame for our choice of play."

I doubted that I'd seen any play he'd mounted—I would've remembered Rosea. "There's no blame to you, Master Rodolfo. However, as two important visitors from the Border are in Freston, maybe we should discuss what material would be appropriate." I smiled at his sister. "The Hart's Leap sets an excellent morning table."

Rodolfo gave a sigh of regret. "I cannot at present, my lord, due to my press of duties. But my sister knows our book as well as I. Perhaps you could take her?"

Grinning in triumph, I offered my arm. "With pleasure—" There was a cold touch on the back of my neck. Scowling, I straightened.

"My lord?" Rosea asked, her hand hovering where my arm was a moment ago.

I bowed once more. "Beg pardon—"

There was another touch and my hand shot up to my nape, catching a hint of fingers. That was too much. I glared over my shoulder.

"What?" Jeff asked as Arlie innocently blinked at me.

"Is everything all right, my lord?" Rodolfo asked.

I pasted a smile on my face and turned back to the players. "Yes, of course—"

This time the touch ran down my spine, and I spun completely around. "Not funny, lads."

"What'd we do?" Arlie asked, his hands tucked into his cloak against the nipping autumnal chill. Jeff shrugged at me, his own hands resting on his sword belt.

"Truly, my lord," Rodolfo said, puzzled, "they've not moved."

Wondering if one of the butterflies had managed to fall down my tabard, I squinted down at them on my shoulder. However, all were present and accounted for, and they looked back at me, also puzzled. Deciding that maybe it was just the itch of my new winter woolens, I took a deep breath—and let it out again in a whoosh as I felt the touch again, a cold lingering brush that started at my neck and once more followed my spine. At the same time, the truth rune on my palm went numb again.

"Pox-rotted damnation!" I jerked away from the unwanted caress. Snatching off my glove, I traced fire as the wind began to swirl around me, lifting the butterflies' wings.

"Bones and bloody ashes, Rabbit!" Jeff said, dancing back as Arlie made shocked noises. "What the sodding hell are you doing?"

"If this isn't convenient, my lord," Rodolfo said, "we can meet another day." He grabbed Rosea by the arm and started edging away. "Perhaps tomorrow. Or even next time we come through town."

I felt the touch return even through the fire and wind, and I batted at it but it flitted away, only to return again. The butterflies leapt up and began fluttering in agitation about my head as the wind swirled faster, starting to howl. At the same time, dark clouds rapidly filled the sky and thunder boomed. Lightning crackled, grounding itself in my staff and then arcing into the fire tracery around me, turning into sheets of flame in the sudden downpour. The deadness in my rune began to creep up my arm.

"Damn it, Rabbit, stop!" shouted Arlis over the howling wind, pounding rain, and the screams and shrieks of the people in the square. Another bolt of lightning split the sky, drowning out the rest of his words.

The touch evaded my attempt to knock it away, and moved to my forehead, paused, then slipped over my eyes, nose and mouth, to stroke down my throat and rest over my pounding heart. Snarling, I feinted and then, coming back the other way, managed to grab hold of what felt like a hand. I squeezed, twisting, and in the middle of my private storm heard the crack of bones and a faint cry of pain. Immediately, the phantom hand dissolved in my grip. Teeth still bared, I waited a moment or two, but whoever was making free with my person did not return. The numbness faded and my own hand was suddenly filled with prickling heat.

Breathing as if I'd just gone fifteen rounds with the village strongman, I let the wind, rain and fire die, and looked around. And winced. Jeff, Arlis and I stood in the middle of an almost empty square, with no trace of Rodolfo or Rosea anywhere. What Harvest decorations remained were torn and dripping, branches were ripped off of trees, windows broken. And among the dropped packages, baskets, cloaks and other soggy belongings, were people who'd been knocked down and trampled by the fleeing.

"Don't stop now," Arlis said, his voice acid as he wiped the rain from his eyes. "You left out earthquakes, lava flows and tidal waves."

Jeff said nothing, glowering through the wet hair plastered against his face. Beyond him, down one of the streets, I could see several of the town Watch moving towards us at a fast trot, their faces grim. Off in the distance another trumpet blare sounded as the dark clouds scudded away. More aristos arriving to add to the crowding of both Freston proper and its garrison.

I, though, wouldn't have to worry about sharing my bunk with some snooty lord's armsman. I closed my eyes as the watchmen surrounded us, the wind gently murmuring as the butterflies settled down on my shoulder. I was going to new quarters—the town's jail.

TWO

Freston is a small town nestled in a bowl-like valley at the junction of the King's Road and two mountain trade routes. Its garrison's official duty is to protect merchants' caravans from those desperate enough to descend to banditry in the northern marches. Which was why several units patrolled the King's Road, but only one patrolled the mountains, even though it was in the mountains that the bandits had their strongholds. (One of the lads at the garrison called this army intelligence. Remembering my da's experience with our Weald, I told him governing councils had the same disease.)

Only the hardiest and most determined of merchants came as far as Freston, as our sister town, Cosdale, was the more favored stop. South and east of us, Cosdale sat lower in the mountain ranges and so its winters weren't as harsh and long. It was also larger, with more shops, inns, taverns and a Theater Square with two playhouses, all of which the troopers garrisoned there never failed to point out whenever we couldn't avoid them.

However, both Freston and Cosdale were cast into deep shade by Gresh, to the southwest. Gresh was a true city, sprawling at the nexus of six trade routes, one of which was the Banson River that flowed the length of Iversterre down to the sea. Trade traffic converged on Gresh to ride the river

boats to the Royal City of Iversly and its port, allowing
Gresh to bill itself as the gateway to civilization.

Which Freston was not. While the Marcher Lords' forti-
fied manors, keeps, compounds and small villages were
spread throughout the north, the only significant settlement
beyond us was the garrison town of Veldecke, set on the
border between Iversterre and, well, the Border. Freston
was truly the last real town in the northern wilderness.

The buildings in Freston reflected its modest claims.
Even the homes of its leading citizens were minuscule
compared to the sprawling mansions that took up city
blocks in Iversly. But then, most Freston inhabitants were
more concerned with winter heating—unlike Royal City
dwellers to whom open rooms, interior courtyards and high
ceilings meant staying cool in that city's hot and humid cli-
mate.

The jail was built along the same lines of conservation as
its fellow buildings. It was tucked away on a small street
leading from the main square, the insides of the narrow
stone edifice just like the outside. However, this did not en-
gender any sense of coziness. Instead, it had the disposition
of all jails: cold, damp and miserable.

And the jailhouse guards had the same dispositions as
their fellows everywhere. After playing the time-honored
game of pound on the prisoners, they relieved Jeff, Arlis
and me of our cloaks, swords, belts, knives, boots and
purses. (They didn't try for my ashwood staff, sneering at
the plain wood as fit only for firewood.) I now stood at the
far wall of one of the jail's two common cells, dividing my
attention between the bruises blooming under what was left
of my clothing and my breath misting out before me in the
flickering light from the torches. From the smell, they had
been dipped in tallow and their burning added to the rich
aromas that filled the cell—competing for space with whatever rustled in the rank straw on the cell floor.

I heard the sound of boots coming down the stone steps that led to the cells just as the church bells rang the late hour. I didn't bother to look up. I knew the sergeants who were sent to retrieve soldiers from jail and I'd almost rather stay where I was. Though there were worse liberators. Captain Suiden could show up. At that thought I shivered.

"Here they are, your honor, safe and sound," the head jailer said. A key rattled in the lock and hinges gave a rusty screech as the cell door opened.

Without raising my head, I could see Jeff and Arlis stand from where they had huddled together for warmth, giving both me and any flea that dared hop their way the evil eye. As I watched, they snapped to attention. A sergeant, then. Holding in a sigh, I raised my head—only to jump to attention myself as I met the Lord Commander's gaze.

He was tall, broad across the shoulders, and looking as a commander of the Royal Army and Royal Guard should. Lord Commander Thadro's blue-gray eyes were filled with frost as he stared into the cell. Behind him several royal guards lurked, the plumes in their helms almost brushing the ceiling, the griffins on their tabards seeming to shimmer in the torchlight. Thadro took in our bruises and Jeff's swollen eye before turning to the head jailer. "Release them."

The jailer tucked his hands into his belt, a genial leer on his face. "Well, now, I can't just go doing that on your say-so. There's serious charges, your honor. Very serious charges. Good honest folk injured. Damage to property. Merchants losing custom. Why"—his beard-stubbled face fell into lines of leering astonishment—"they even scared some poor street players so badly that the play was stopped cold. *Before* the hat was passed." His eyes dipped to Thadro's purse. "I would imagine it'll be quite a while before they could be released, your honor. Quite a while."

Despite the well-deserved reputation of Freston's garrison, I'd never been in the town's jail before. (Having Suiden as a captain helped—any of his troop who went before the magistrate then had to go before *him*.) But I'd heard about Menck from other temporary inhabitants and I held still at his attempted shakedown. However, Thadro merely produced a sheaf of papers.

"By the town council, magistrate, mayor and the king's order," Thadro said.

Menck gingerly took the papers, shuffling through them to come to the royal order. His eyes first went down to the bottom of the sheet where, in the dim light, the king's seal dully gleamed. He then started at the top, his lips moving as he used a finger to work his way through. Finally, he lowered the papers, his mouth a flat line as all dreams of extorted largesse winked out.

"Return all their belongings and release them," Thadro said. "Now."

A short while later, Jeff, Arlis and I walked out into the chill afternoon, once more fully clothed and armed. (Menck's eyes were shiny with tears when he handed over our still-full purses. Apparently he and his mates hadn't the chance to divvy up the spoils.) We followed Thadro into the town square, the royal guards bringing up the rear, and I looked around, surprised at how normal everything looked. The sinking sun cast a warm glow on the town hall and gilded the silver-and-crystal spire of the church on the opposite side of the square. The butterflies, lying still and quiet on my shoulder, suddenly erupted into flight, winging their way towards the garrison. They must have not enjoyed their first experience of a human jail.

Thadro watched the butterflies fly away. He then stopped and faced me, his eyes gone from frosty to ice-cold. "Is it asking too much for you to restrain yourself, Lieutenant Rabbit?"

"I had nothing to do with them leaving, sir."

"And I suppose this morning you were just an innocent bystander."

I winced at Thadro's sarcasm. "No sir—I mean— Someone was touching me, sir."

I could feel Jeff and Arlie's incredulous glares boring into my back.

"Touching you?" Arlie said, his voice once more acid. "Oh, la! The horror!"

"Probably wouldn't stay on his side of the square, either," Jeff said.

"I don't care if all the ladies of Larsk are stroking you up one side and down the other as they dance the saraband around you," Thadro said. "There will be no more displays, understand?"

"But sir," I said, "nobody was *there*—"

"It's the witch!"

Startled, I looked around and saw a crowd gathering by the square's fountain. Albe the blacksmith pushed to the fore, still wearing his leather apron and carrying his smith's hammer. He raised his hammer and slammed it down on a paving stone, and eager hands reached down to snatch up the pieces. I was shoved back by Thadro and quickly surrounded by the guards, and a moment later pieces of paving stone hit the guards' raised shields with solid thunks.

"What?" I asked wide-eyed, stunned that people I knew were trying to stone me. I tried to see past the guard and the crowd howled as they caught sight of my face.

"Damn it, Rabbit!" Jeff grabbed me by my tabard, yanking me away. A second volley was thrown and a high lob fell past the guards' circling shields, striking Jeff in the back. "Hellfire!" he swore.

At Thadro's signal, the guards pulled their swords from their scabbards and the shouting and catcalls of the swelling crowd died. But only for a moment.

"Kill the witch!" Kresyl the baker shrieked.

Another volley hit the shields, with more high lobs
falling past them, and in between the guards I could see that
people with pitchforks, scythes and torches were running to
join the crowd. But before Thadro could order his men to
attack, there was a loud clatter of horses' hooves and a large
group of armsmen rode into the square from behind the
crowd. They immediately began applying the flats of their
swords to folks' heads. Several horsemen broke off and
came our way, led by a man wearing a plumed hat. I got a
flash of silver eyes before he and his fellows turned their
horses, becoming a barrier between us and the mob. At the
same time the town hall doors banged open and the Keeper
of the King's Peace ran down the steps of the hall. The
Watch that had remained safely on the town hall steps first
jumped to attention, then fell in behind her. Peacekeeper
Chadde ignored them as she raced to where we stood.

Lord Commander Thadro slapped the rump of the horse
in front of him. "Move."

Silver eyes again looked down at us, then the man smiled
and gave a flourishing salute with his sword before shifting
his horse. Holding his own sword, Thadro stepped to the
front, where he was joined by Peacekeeper Chadde. I went
to stand with them, but Jeff caught my arm once more.

"Don't. You'll set everyone off again."

He was right. Despite the presence of the horsemen, the
Lord Commander and the Keeper of the King's Peace, a
rock flew out from the back of the mob, landing at
Chadde's feet. The peacekeeper looked at it, then raised her
head. "I saw you, Danel."

I blinked. I *knew* Danny, a postilion at the Hart's Leap.
Peering between Thadro and Chadde, I almost didn't recognize him, the way his face was twisted.

"He threw it at the witch, Chadde," Albe called out before
Danny could respond. The mob growled as their attention
shifted back to me.

"Who? Rabbit?" Chadde asked. "Rabbit's no witch. He was at Eveningsong last night. As he often is. Just as he also attends the morning and midday services as his duties allow." She smiled at the blacksmith. "You'd know that, Albe, if you went to church as often as you go to the Copper Pig."

Even in the fading light I could see the flush that swept over Albe's face. He glared around as someone behind him snickered.

"Though I don't know if you'll be able to do either once his honor the mayor sees what's happened to his square," Chadde continued, her gray eyes hardening. "There are laws about inciting to riot and the willful destruction of town property. Just as the king has laws regarding the murder of his kin, officers and agents."

It was kind of hard to tell which weighed more—the threat of the king's justice or the wrath of the mayor. Or maybe it was that people started factoring in the armed and mounted men in their midst. Suddenly, there was the patter of stones hitting the ground, while Albe stared at his hammer with mild astonishment, as if wondering how in the world it got into his hand. He tucked it into his belt and loped off with the air of a man who'd just remembered that he had important things to do. Others also apparently thought of chores not done and started slipping away, torches quickly doused in the square's fountain, pitchforks and scythes lowered.

"That was a bit of excitement," the plume-hatted man on horseback said. He looked down again at us, giving a bow. "Lord Beollan of Fellmark, milords and gracious sirs. We were returning from a tour of the countryside and happened upon you." He lifted his head to scan the by now mostly empty square, noting the chunks of paving stone, stout sticks, chains and what looked like a length of wrought iron littering the ground. "Good thing we did."

Thadro sighed as he shoved his sword into his scabbard. "Yes, a very good thing." At his gesture, the royal guards sheathed their own swords and shifted so that they were once more behind Jeff, Arlie and me. Thadro looked us over, checking for injuries. "You were hit, Trooper Jeffen?"

Jeff glanced at Chadde's expressionless face. "Only a love tap, sir."

"I see. Good." Thadro sighed and looked at me. "Let's get you away from here, Lieutenant Rabbit, before you cause another riot."

Three

After the town square, our walk to Jusson's residence was uneventful, with everyone sunk in their own thoughts. I huddled down into my cloak, a chill seeping into my bones, while Arlis and Jeff walked quietly beside me, all of our movements somewhat stiff from our playtime with the jailhouse guards. Up ahead were Lord Beollan and two of his armsmen a-horse, followed by Peacekeeper Chadde and the Lord Commander. I didn't know the peacekeeper well, having made a habit of not coming to the attention of the town constabulary. Besides, she was someone who tended to blend into the background—brown hair, gray eyes, medium height, slender build. She wore a plain tabard over an equally plain shirt, leather breeks, and boots. The only thing that stood out was the ceremonial truncheon hanging at her side, the silver and wood gleaming in the light from the street lamps. Chadde's face was calm and closed; however, as we rounded a corner, she turned her head and met my gaze, and I felt as though all the secrets I ever had were laid bare. Then she faced forward again, leaving me to wonder what the hell had just happened.

Upon our reaching the king's residence, Lord Beollan smiled, his eyes speculative as they rested on me. "I'll leave you here, though I'm sure I'll be seeing you shortly. Grace."

He bowed and then rode off with his armsmen to stable their horses. I looked after them, yearning.

"Rabbit," Thadro said and, legs leaden, I slowly climbed the front steps with the others. The King's Own standing guard on either side of the door saluted, one opening it. We stepped through and it shut behind us with a thud that echoed through me.

Thadro quickly led us down a hallway to where more King's Own were once again guarding a door. And once again, one flung it open, revealing an elegant study. It was furnished with long, austere lines and muted colors, though the lack of fuss and furbelows was somewhat made up for by the Harvest wreath that hung on the clean plaster wall. A fire blazed in the brickwork fireplace, while an ornamental pot simmered on a brazier, scenting the air with a king's ransom of vanilla, nutmeg and orange peel that mingled with the smell of beeswax from lit candles. The curtains were flung back to show a twilight-shrouded pleasure garden that was surely a riot of fall colors in the daytime.

It was a far cry from the jail.

And the person seated behind the desk was a far, far cry from the head jailer.

"Come in," King Jusson said.

I was a small child when word reached my parents' farm that Jusson had succeeded his queen mother, and he had been grown then. But instead of looking like someone in his middle years, a decade and a half into his rule, he appeared my age. Tall and slender, with a mass of black hair, winged brows and tilted eyes with a gold ring etched around black irises, he also looked like a dark elf from one of the Border city-states. He wore a simple gold circlet on his head and his raiment matched the austere elegance of his study. As did his expression.

When in doubt, try obeisance. "Your Majesty," I said, bowing.

Jusson's expression didn't change. "Everyone come in," he said. "Thadro, shut the door."

Closing the door with a quiet snick, Thadro walked to stand behind the king.

"Sit, Rabbit," Jusson said, nodding at a single chair set before his desk. I hesitated. In the warmth of the room a pungent reminder of jail was rising off Arlie, Jeff and me, and the candlelight showed every smear and smudge we had.

"The chair will clean," Jusson said. "Sit."

I sat.

Jusson's gaze went behind me. "Peacekeeper Chadde, is it?"

"There was a riot, sire," Thadro said as Chadde bowed. "We were attacked by a mob and Peacekeeper Chadde not only helped us withstand it, but joined our escort here."

Jusson's gaze came back to me, noting my bruises before going to Jeff and Arlie's own scrapes and discolorations, and Jeff's black eye. The king frowned. "They were injured?"

"That was done before the riot," Thadro said. "While they were in jail."

"We see," Jusson said, the frown remaining. He leaned back in his chair and, steepling his hands, considered me over them. "You've been very busy, Rabbit."

I shifted and, realizing that I held my staff in a death grip, I carefully leaned it against my chair. "Yes, Your Majesty. You see, there was this hand—"

Jusson held up a hand of his own, and I stopped. "How long ago did Ambassador Laurel arrive in Iversterre, Thadro?" he asked his Lord Commander.

I blinked, wondering what Laurel had to do with the groping hand.

"About six months, Your Majesty," Thadro replied.

"Six months," Jusson repeated. He saw my puzzled expression and gave a sharp-edged smile. "Ambassador

Laurel wasn't careful with his . . . speculations, cousin. Nor was anyone else he told them to. Especially when said speculations turned out to be true."

When I'd accidentally translated my troop mates into animals and fantastic beasts last spring, Laurel had theorized that living where the People had once lived, growing crops, raising livestock, birthing children on the very land that contained fae bones and ashes, had made the human population of Iversterre fae too. Whatever that was true or not, our very substance *had* been altered—and Jusson was right; none who'd been translated were anywhere near discreet about it. Captain Javes was very fond of telling anyone who'd listen of how he became a wolf.

Lowering my gaze, I plucked at the stain near my knee as the implications sunk in. I just had a taste of the townsfolk's reaction to talent at work around them. I could imagine what their reaction would be to it working inside them.

Jusson tapped on the desk, reclaiming my attention. "Ask us about our journey here, cousin. Ask us how we had to fight to keep our kingdom from descending into hysteria and chaos." Gold leached into the king's eyes. "One poor mother came to us, her simple son accused of being a changeling. But we were too late and the child had already been hanged and burned. His father made the noose, then lit the fire."

Realizing that my mouth hung open, I shut it and bit my lip to keep it closed.

Jusson's brow raised. "You don't ask us, Rabbit."

I unbit my lip and tasted blood. "Sire, I—" I faltered, not knowing what to say.

"Three months of progression," Jusson said. "Stopping in every city, town, village and crossroads we happened upon. Soothing, bribing, quelling, punishing, while my lords buzzed about like hornets, seeking any chance to sting. Still, it was working. The accusations, the stonings and burnings waning as our people stopped trying to rend themselves in pieces. We achieved, if not peace, then at least a sort of calm." He shifted, resting his elbow on the chair arm and placing his chin on his fist. "And you destroy it in less than one hour."

"But, sire—"

"Do you think that what happened this morning isn't spreading through the region?" Jusson asked. "To the rest of the kingdom? On eagle's wings, cousin, as fast as it can."

"But the hand—"

Jusson's own hand slammed down on the desk and I jumped. "I don't give a pox-rotted damn if a thousand hands are crawling all over you! You do *not* put your own in harm's way." His eyes were almost solid gold in his anger. "Shall I tell you how many were injured? The damage done to not only property but to people?"

Apparently the leering head jailer hadn't been exaggerating about the aftermath of my morning battle.

"Damage also to reputations, sire," Thadro put in. "Yours and Rabbit's."

"Indeed, yes," Jusson said. "To my word as king that there is nothing among us that would cause hurt. What do you think those hornets are doing with *that?*"

I said nothing, my stomach in knots, my spine tight.

"I had many people in here today, Rabbit," Jusson said. "Each demanding your head, though Doyen Dyfrig did blame pernicious magical influences instead of you. Even so, he joined the others in insisting that I purge the land of anything that even hints of the Border. As a town elder said, 'Send them all back to hell where they came from.' " The king shook his head, his eyes steady on mine. "Three months of work gone, and my kingdom once more sliding towards the abyss."

I looked down again to see that my hands were shaking.

"Nothing to say?" Jusson asked, his light voice mild.

I shook my head. "No, sire."

"Ah," Jusson said. "A sign of intelligence." He shifted again in his chair. "Sometimes, when things go wrong, there's nothing to do but to start over. I will *not* allow my people to destroy each other in their superstitions and fears. Nor will I allow purchase to those who seek to use this for their own ends, whether within the kingdom or without. So I'll begin anew, even here in this bump of a place on the backside of the mountains. Begin anew, even with you, cousin. Lord Commander Thadro lost his second in the rebellion last spring and hasn't had time to choose another. So I'm choosing for him. You are assigned as his lieutenant. Effective immediately."

That got my attention. I sat upright, my eyes wide. "Sire, Captain Suiden—"

"Suiden already has a second," Jusson said.

That was true. Lieutenant Groskin had been Suiden's second longer than I'd been in the army. I tried again. "Sire, my mage lessons—"

"Ambassador Laurel will still teach you, cousin, with a sharper emphasis on self-control."

Backed into a corner, I opened my mouth anyway. "Sire—"

"No argument, Rabbit," Jusson said. "I've only a small complement of my Own with me and can't spare any for you, so Troopers Jeffen and Arlis are assigned as your personal guards."

All small sounds behind me ceased, including that of breathing.

"However, they also will report to Thadro. Until I decide otherwise."

Thadro's blue-gray eyes were gleaming with satisfaction as he reached down behind the desk and came up with a bundle. Humming, he opened it to reveal a royal guard's uniform, complete with a royal blue-and-white tabard with dark blue piping.

"Thirty-two lines through Chause," Jusson mused. "Forty through Flavan. How many total is that?"

I said nothing—Jusson knew damn well how many degrees I had to his throne. In a land that counted nobility by how many direct descendants a House had of Iver, the first king of Iversterre, it was why he *could* call me cousin and name me his heir.

"Rabbit has sixty-four lines, sire," Thadro said, stepping into the breach. "There's some duplication between Chause and Flavan." He shook out the tabard with a snap and I could see the griffin on the front, along with a lieutenant's insignia on the shoulder. My finger rose to my collar and I gave it a swift tug, swallowing hard.

"So there is," Jusson said. "My nobles do tend to intermarry, don't they?" He didn't wait for an answer. "Of all the Houses, you're second only to me, Rabbit. It's time that you learn what it means to be my heir. So you will." The king's razor smile returned. "As you say, fiat."

Four

Apparently not trusting me not to bolt, Jusson handed me, Jeff and Arlis over to his majordomo. The king's most senior servant looked the same as when I last saw him in the palace at Iversly—short, thin, his white hair thick upon his round head. His face was impassive as he accepted us into his care, ushering us out of the king's study with a bow. As we left, I heard Jusson invite Peacekeeper Chadde to pull up a fresh chair and tell him about the larcenous head jailer.

"Menck's a kinsman of Mayor Gawell, your Majesty," Chadde said, her voice unruffled. "We've had problems with him and his men before. This time, though—"

The study door shut, cutting off the rest.

The majordomo led us up the back stairs to a bedchamber on the second level. It had a large four-poster bed, a tall clothespress, a small table with chairs around it and a mirrored washstand, all illuminated by a fire crackling in the stone fireplace and an abundance of lit candles. With the influx of nobles into town, I was surprised that such a spacious chamber hadn't been snapped up. Then my gaze fell on the three tubs in the middle of the room, and all thoughts of new assignments, invisible hands and appropriating aristos disappeared.

"Baths," Jeff breathed. "Ones we don't have to draw ourselves."

We watched with greedy eyes as servants poured hot water from copper cans into the tubs while another servant added sweet herbs, turning the steam fragrant. More servants stood at attention holding towels, soap and long-handled brushes, and an august person stood next to a straight-backed chair holding a tray of razors, combs, scissors and other tools of a barber.

A dry smile curved the majordomo's thin lips. "If my lord and sirs will remove their clothes?"

Before we could undo the first lacing, the servants swarmed us, stripping us naked and dumping us in the tubs. Those with the soap and brushes then descended and set to work.

"Hey, watch where you put that— Ow!" Jeff yelped.

"Sorry, sir," the servant said, not stopping his scrubbing.

"There are dead fleas in my water," Arlie remarked, looking down.

I said nothing, distracted by how my skin was glowing bright red. But the knots and kinks were starting to loosen and I slid down into the tub as far as I could go, allowing the heat to envelop me. Through the curling steam I watched servants buzzing around the chamber, laying out smalls, shirts and winter hosen, buffing our boots (one servant reverently picked up mine—Habbs, for city wear), and opening bundles that revealed two more Royal Guard uniforms, minus the officer's insignia. Over by his chair, the barber used tongs to turn his hot towels as he poured something over them from an unstoppered bottle, and more fragrant steam rose to add its spice to the room. As the king's study was a far cry from jail, this was as far as the moon from my life as a farmer's son turned horse soldier.

I stopped a servant's attempt to scrub me by taking the bath brush myself. Foiled, he turned to my hair and started to undo the tie, plucking the feather from it first. Without thought, my hand flew up, catching his wrist. Still holding the brush in my other hand, I twisted around, sending the water in the tub sloshing.

"There he goes again," Arlie said, sinking down into his bath.

"Rabbit," Jeff said, sighing.

Everyone else in the room went still, all eyes fastened on me.

All except the king's majordomo. "Give me the feather, Finn," he said as he walked up to the tub, and Finn released the feather into his outstretched hand. The majordomo then placed it on the edge of the washstand where I could easily see it. "It'll be here until you're ready to wear it again, my lord."

Realizing I still gripped Finn's wrist, I released it to rub my hand over my face. "I'm sorry, Master Finn." I tried a smile and it came out crooked. "It's that—" I stopped and gave my own sigh. "I'm sorry."

"He is just 'Finn,' Lord Rabbit," the majordomo said over Finn's murmured acceptance of my apology. He moved aside the other servant and finished undoing my braid. "As I am merely Cais." Picking up a copper can, he carefully wetted my hair. "That is the feather Ambassador Laurel gave you, correct?"

"Yes, Master—yes, Cais."

"We understand that it is very important to you."

"Yes," I murmured. "I suppose it's important." Making myself relax, I sat back and allowed Cais to wash my hair. However, throughout the remainder of my bath and while I was shaved, my eyes kept drifting to the washstand, the feather bright red against the white of the porcelain top— and as soon as my hair was braided once again, I nonchalantly snatched it up again. Tucking the feather back into my braid, I let out a breath I didn't know I was holding.

Then, taking my staff from where it was propped against the wall, I turned to face the mirror. The cut, drape and fit of my tabard and trousers were excellent, indicating that they were made specifically for my tall, rangy frame. Wondering how long Jusson had planned my annexation by the Royal Guards, I reached up to straighten my braid, but Cais beat me to it. Startled, I met his bland gaze before he turned to give Jeff's tabard a smoothing tug and to adjust Arlie's sword belt. He then stepped back. "Very good. If my lord and sirs would follow me."

Cais led us to the front stair and, as we descended, I looked around. Having been hustled through earlier by Thadro, I hadn't been able to see much. The staircase swept down to the black-and-white-checkered marble foyer floor, while above a huge crystal chandelier rained light on us. It was as austerely elegant as the king's study and, reaching the first landing, I craned my neck, trying to see more of the house. Just then, though, a gong sounded and both Jeff and I froze. Cais and Arlis continued a couple of steps, then turned to stare back up at us, surprised. Then Arlie's mouth quirked.

"That was the dinner gong, lads." His teeth flashed white in his freshly trimmed and oiled beard. "Food's on."

Jeff's face flushed and I felt my own face heat once more. "I know what a dinner gong is—" I broke off, hearing someone walking quickly over the marble floor. A moment later, Thadro came into view.

"Good," he said as we finished descending. "I was just coming to get you. Cais, if you would take Arlis and Jeffen to the guards' mess."

With a bow, Cais led Arlie and Jeff away. I caught Jeff's sympathetic glance over his shoulder, then they were gone, leaving the Lord Commander and me alone in the marble-and-crystal foyer. I could feel the weight of his stare as the silence stretched out.

"Lieutenant Lord Rabbit ibn Chause e Flavan, second to the Lord Commander of the Royal Army and Royal Guard, and heir to his Majesty, King Jusson IV. Pretty high up in the world for someone who was just plain Trooper Rabbit in the Freston Mountain Patrol a few months ago." Thadro paused, but having been plain Trooper Rabbit, I knew better than to fall into that trap. I kept silent.

"Do you think that you're now in clover, Lord Rabbit? That you've had a honey fall?"

I also knew when to answer. "No, sir."

" 'No' is right," Thadro said. "You were assigned this post only because His Majesty's acknowledged heir shouldn't be in a back-mountain troop made up of the disgraced." He stepped closer and I resisted the urge to move away. "But this is not a plum to be eaten at your leisure. As the king said, you are his, and now you're also mine. You *will* learn what it means to be both."

Thadro paused again, but I once more stayed quiet. I wasn't about to point out that Jusson had no problem with me being in that same troop since my coming to Iversterre. Nor was I going to tell him that I had absolutely no desire to be a royal guard and even less in being the king's heir. But even more than my recent past and present inclinations, what held me mute was that, while serving under Suiden had never been easy, I'd never doubted my worth to my captain. This was the first time I'd ever had a commanding officer look at me as though I was something he'd found wiggling in a mud puddle. I felt my gut tighten with the beginnings of anger.

The silence lengthened, then Thadro's mouth twisted into a smile. "However, as Guardsman Arlis pointed out, it is now time for evening meal." Turning around, he headed out of the foyer. I fell in behind him, my stomach rumbling as it reminded me that I hadn't eaten since that morning. "You are dining with His Majesty and his guests tonight,"

Thadro said over his shoulder as he led down the hallway to another guarded door. The Own on either side stiffened to attention and one reached for the doorknob. Thadro, though, stopped the guard and faced me, his smile fading. "His Majesty is holding this dinner in part to undo the damage you caused this morning. I will not have you unraveling what he is working hard to knit together. You are to follow my lead and direction, and when in doubt you will shut up and smile. Understand?"

"Yes, sir," I murmured.

"Good." At Thadro's signal, the guard flung open the door, revealing not the dining hall I'd expected, but a salon. There was a lit fireplace at one end with a large wreath made of fall grasses woven with oak leaves and acorns hung over the mantelpiece, and bundled wheat stalks stood on either side of the hearth. Fat candles surrounded by colorful gourds and leaves decorated several low tables that were strategically placed by couches and chairs. The drapes were thrown back and the candlelight cast bright squares out the windows, catching passersby's faces as they looked up in brief wonder before hurrying on in the cold night.

However, there wasn't any wonder inside the salon. The royal guests knew exactly who I was and what they thought about it. I was met at the doorway with a wall of hostile stares and I came to a full halt. Thadro, though, plunged into the crowd without pause, and I knew that one too. Taking a deep breath, I dived in after the Lord Commander, and we worked our way through town officials and local gentry standing cheek by jowl with the Great Lords who had followed Jusson to Freston. Some of the lords sported the dark hair and olive complexions of the southern aristos, while others had the blond paleness of the northern Marcher Lords.

There weren't any women, though. As Jusson was unmarried—and as he'd apparently left whatever female

relative acted as royal hostess back in Iversly—none of the
men brought wives, daughters or sisters. And that wasn't
the only lack. Following the Lord Commander, I searched
the room to see if Lord Esclaur ibn Dhawn e Jas was present, the lordling having been part of the delegation Jusson
had sent to the Border last spring. However, I realized that
not only was he missing, but there weren't any of the
younger sons that made up Jusson's bachelor's court. Except for his royal guard, his Lord Commander and his servants, the king had come to Freston alone.

Arriving at a trio of comfortable-looking chairs placed
against the far wall opposite the fireplace, Thadro slipped
behind one while I did the same on the other end and, side
by side, we faced the room—and I immediately became
aware of other missing folk. There was no one from the garrison, not even the garrison commander.

"Are Captain Suiden and Captain Javes coming, sir?" I
asked, my voice low.

"That's not your concern, Lieutenant," Thadro said, just
as softly. "Your ties with the garrison have been severed."

Fighting against a scowl, I turned back to the room—and
met Doyen Dyfrig's eyes. Though my attending Eveningsong was good enough for Peacekeeper Chadde, it seemed
that it didn't carry much weight with the head of the Freston church. My gaze skittered away from his expression,
only to land on Mayor Gawell. His honor looked even more
unhappy and I flinched from him, to find myself looking at
Lord Beollan of Fellmark. He smiled and I grinned back in
relief at finding a friendly face. And there was one female
presence in this solid mass of maleness. Behind Beollan
stood Chadde, showing her customary calm. Apparently
she'd made a very good impression on King Jusson as she
was the only petty town official present. She had taken the
time to go home and change her breeks for a plain gray
gown. Then she met my gaze, and I realized that it wasn't

so plain—it matched her eyes, making them seem to glow in the candlelight.

"By the king, Thadro?" A Great Lord shoved his way through to stand in front of us, his legs braced apart, his hands resting on his hips. "He works witchery and you have him next to His Majesty?"

I glanced down. He was right. The middle chair had a crown carved into its back. I looked up at the lord and met cold eyes. I glared back and felt a thump in my side.

"Lieutenant Lord Rabbit is not a witch, Ranulf," Thadro said, the bony point of his elbow digging into my ribs.

"I know Captain Suiden's lads," Mayor Gawell said, "and this pagan is *not* Rabbit." He pushed his way through the crowd to stand next to Lord Ranulf. Gawell wore a black velvet robe with scarlet slashes in the sleeves that were echoed not only in its embroidered collar and cuffs, but also in his leggings. But what might've been fashionable on a smaller frame was overwhelming because of Gawell's girth. Even his chain of office didn't hang straight, but rather rested at an angle on the upper curve of his belly so that its seven-pointed starburst medallion flashed up into the face of anyone standing before him.

Gawell's jowly cheeks were tinged red as he glared at me. "Destroy my town, will you? Demon spawn!"

The muttering swelled and several of the locals made warding signs against evil, while the aristos allowed their hands to drift towards sword hilts and daggers. I felt a tingle in my fingers as my rune began to itch, my own hand twitching over my sword—and behind the cover of the chairs Thadro grabbed my sleeve, holding my arm still.

"Of course that's Rabbit, Gawell," Doyen Dyfrig said. He didn't have to push—the crowd opened up to allow him to stand by the mayor. "He was at church last night, staying through the last hymn and prayer, and Chadde tells me that he was in Theater Square bright and early this morning, doing his best to chat up one of the players." He sighed and a wry look came over his worn face, his faded blue eyes twinkling a bit. "Who else would it be?"

The heat returned to my cheekbones as snickers arose along with conjectures about the fair Rosea—and the tension eased.

Lord Ranulf, however, took a step closer, peering at me. "But did Lord Rabbit have blue eyes? I remember them being brown when we met in Iversly last spring."

The Great Lord was right again—my eyes had been brown from birth until they changed last Midsummer's Day during my fight with Kareste. Right or not, though, the man before me was a stranger. Wearing a gray tunic and leggings, he was a somber contrast to the more vivid mayor. Except for his hair. It was a fiery red that reminded me of Rosea's, and was done in the Marcher style of warrior braids that hung from his temples, woven with ribbons in his House colors, while the rest was loose. But instead of Rosea's creamy smooth skin, Ranulf had freckles across his nose and cheekbones, disappearing into his mustache and beard. And instead of her neat figure and green eyes, he was tall and brawny, with dark brown eyes that seemed as deep as a cave. While my time in the Royal City had been rather chaotic, I thought I would've remembered such a determinedly northern lord.

"We've met—?" I began, but Thadro stepped on my foot.

"Rabbit's eyes *were* brown, not blue like this creature's," Mayor Gawell said, not noticing my smothered yelp. His honor made another warding gesture. "Cut off its hair and burn its staff, and then we will see what really stands before us."

Mayor Gawell was a congenial sort, more inclined to good food and company than belligerence (unless town property was damaged). Now, however, his eyes were bulging out in his ire, his heavy face twisted in a way that reminded me of the mob that afternoon.

"Shear the witch!" someone called out from behind the crowd, and the same guests who'd been snickering and making lewd comments just a moment ago actually growled, one even starting to draw his sword.

At that moment, though, Dyfrig moved to stand next to me. "Will you start an affray in His Majesty's house, messirs?" He glanced around, his eyes not so twinkly anymore, and the guests paused, the mayor even taking a step back.

"But he *is* a witch," Gawell said, his voice almost plaintive. He fluttered his hands at me. "I mean, look at him!"

I opened my mouth to say that I wasn't a witch, but Thadro's elbow dug into my side once more.

"What he is or isn't," Dyfrig said sternly, "is not for you to decide—"

A breeze suddenly swept through, rustling both the grasses in the wreath and the tops of the bundled wheat stalks, bringing with it the autumnal smell of fallen leaves and ripe fruit. Softly murmuring, the wind tugged on my hair tie and braid before romping around the room, rippling the drapes, flapping coats, lifting tunics and robes, and showing more of Mayor Gawell's leggings than anyone really needed to see.

"Rabbit," Thadro said.

"It isn't me, sir," I said. My rune started to itch again and I scratched at it. "The wind does as it wills."

At least it did with me. As also did my earth and water aspects. Only my fire aspect seemed content to wait for my command. Then again, maybe not. I eyed the candle flames dancing in the wind, hoping that no one would notice how they leapt up completely from their wicks to spin around before coming down again.

"As it wills?" Dyfrig asked, his stern look changing to one of curiosity. "It's not just a force, then?"

"No, Your Reverence," I said. "The wind is very much aware. As are all the other aspects." Including Lady Gaia—

the fertile earth—and her consort the Moon who were both considered deity in the Border. However, *that* tidbit I figured I'd keep to myself.

Dyfrig stared at me, astonished. "'Aware'—" He stopped as the wind swirled around him, catching at his robes, and his eyes widened, gleaming. "Oh, my," he said softly.

"So you'll seduce the Church with your magics?" Lord Ranulf asked, grabbing at his tunic to hold it still. He looked at Thadro. "This is what you'll have us accept as the king's heir?"

I expected the room to erupt again at Lord Ranulf's words, but this time the guests looked at me with the same weighing calculation I saw on Lord Beollan's face after the riot. Feeling like exhibited goods at a horse fair, I also turned to look at the Lord Commander. Who merely looked back as he said, "Ask it nicely to stop, Lieutenant Rabbit."

Before I could say anything, though, the wind gave a soft chuckle and, ruffling the doyen's hair, died down. "Oh, my," Dyfrig said again. Then the gleam in his eyes faded and he gave me a deep frown. At that moment, though, the door was flung open and servants poured into the room, carrying plates, silverware, crystal goblets and napkins, followed by more servants with platters, bowls and tureens of food, and pitchers of hot mulled wine. Everyone turned to watch the procession, a reverent hush falling as Jusson's cook, in a white apron, entered with his own entourage, all carrying trays of tarts, meringues, creams, custards and jellies. The head cook himself walked in solitary splendor holding a spectacular multitiered cake, the smell of apples and spice wafting from it.

"Well, that was provident," someone said.

I glanced over to see Lord Beollan and Peacekeeper Chadde standing next to me. Unlike Lord Ranulf, the Lord of Fellmark was dressed in the southern fashion of lace on his shirt, a brocaded vest, a close-fitting, fine wool coat and trousers. With his plumed hat gone, though, I could see that his hair was pale northern blond, and while he was clean-shaven, he too had warrior braids woven with ribbons in the colors of his House. But instead of hanging on either side of his narrow face, they were pulled back to join a neat queue on the back of his head. Unconscious (or uncaring) of his startling juxtaposition of northern barbarism and southern foppery, Beollan turned his attention to Lord Ranulf, who had drifted to where a couple of southern lords stood in front of the fireplace.

"Yes, it was," Thadro said, following Lord Fellmark's gaze. "Very provident." He gave me his mud-puddle look. "*Think* for once, Rabbit."

"Yes, sir," I said. "But what's going on?"

Lord Beollan shifted his attention to the Lord Commander. "You haven't told him, Thadro? Is that wise?"

"Told me what, sir?"

Thadro's expression became frosty. "Captain Suiden may've allowed you license to question and demand, Lieutenant Rabbit, but that is not the case in the King's Own."

I goggled as my brain froze at the thought of Suiden allowing anyone any sort of license whatsoever. Before I could speak, though, Chadde moved closer to me.

"You've been rubbing your hand as though it pains you, Lord Rabbit," she said. "Did you injure it in jail?"

I took my gaze off the Lord Commander to shake my head at the peacekeeper. "No, ma'am," I said. "It's flea-bitten and it itches like the blazes." Opening my hand, I looked for the tell-tale red bumps—and blinked once again as the rune on my palm shone brightly back at me. The rune's light bathed Chadde's face and she did her own blinking, then her expression grew intent as she leaned closer.

"Hell's ballocks, Rabbit!" Thadro moved, shielding both

me and the rune from the rest of room. "People here know what that is."

So they did. Unlike the southern part of the kingdom, the memory of the last war with the Border was still fresh in the north, especially the part where the truth rune was lifted against the Royal Army and every soldier saw the truth not only about himself, but also his friends, family and loved ones. Most ran screaming.

I quickly lowered my hand as Chadde straightened and took a step back, her expression once more dropping into the calm. I looked past the Lord Commander at Lord Ranulf. His gaze went from my hand to Chadde, and then he opened his mouth. However, the door opened once more and Cais walked in. After a swift glance around the room, the majordomo stepped to the side.

"His Majesty, King Jusson IV," he politely bellowed.

Five

I'd seen more dramatic entrances. At Cais' announcement, Jusson walked in, wearing the same elegant clothes he had on earlier, the same simple circlet of gold on his head. He did have a couple of King's Own behind him, but they peeled off to stand just inside the salon on either side of the door. As we all bowed, the king ambled over to the groaning sideboard. Casting an approving eye over the array of foods and drink, Jusson beckoned to Doyen Dyfrig.

"If you would please bless the table, Your Reverence," Jusson said.

Dyfrig said a (mercifully) short prayer and, when he was done, Jusson nodded at his guests. "Let's eat."

Leaving the majordomo to work the logistics, Jusson sauntered to his chair. The king's gold-rimmed black eyes flicked to Beollan and Chadde, and they both moved away, joining the rest of the guests mobbing the food. I impatiently waited to be released to get my own dinner and a slice of the magnificent cake, but neither Thadro nor Jusson said anything. Jusson settled himself into his chair, and a moment later Cais emerged from the melee bearing a filled plate and goblet on a tray for His Majesty. As the majordomo set the king's food and drink on a table next to him, Jusson murmured something to him and he returned to the fray. Moments later he emerged again, this time with Mayor

Gawell and Master Ednoth. Jusson invited the mayor to sit on one side of him, while directing the head of Freston's merchants' guild to the other side. The thin merchant easily folded himself into his chair and immediately tucked into his plate. Mayor Gawell, however, hovered as the chair Jusson indicated for him was the one that I stood behind.

"Is there a problem, Mayor?" Jusson asked as he took a sip from his goblet full of gently steaming wine.

Apparently it was one thing to accuse me of being demon spawn in front of the town elders and nobles of the land. It was another to do it before the king. "No, Your Majesty." The mayor cast me an apprehensive look, then gingerly sat, balancing his plate on his diminished lap. Jusson gestured and a servant appeared to move one of the small tables for his honor's plate and cup.

Smiling, Jusson took another sip of wine, then set his goblet down. "How is the town, Mayor Gawell? Has it calmed down?"

Gawell, busy checking over his take, lifted his head enough for me to see him blink owlishly at the king. "Yes, Your Majesty. It has, for now." He gave a jowly smile that didn't touch the rest of his face. "The threat of the king's justice was very effective. However, we still have people injured and property damaged."

Ednoth nodded in agreement, seeming more interested in his food. However, his chair was angled so that I could see his eyes narrow shrewdly as he chewed.

Jusson set his goblet down and picked up his plate. "Yes, you've told me. And as I told you, recompense will be made to all who have suffered injury to person or home or business."

"That's good, Your Majesty," Gawell said, "but we are more concerned about, ah, future occurrences."

"I have spoken to my cousin," Jusson said, "and he's

given me his assurance that what happened this morning will not happen again. Isn't that right, Rabbit?"

Recognizing my cue, I gave a small bow, trying to look repentant. "Yes, sire."

"Huh," grunted Mayor Gawell. "And why should we believe you?"

"Rabbit has the truth rune on his palm," Jusson said before I could respond. "He can't lie."

So much for keeping my rune a secret. I cast Thadro a glance but the Lord Commander was busy scanning the room.

"Can't lie?" Gawell asked, wide-eyed. "God ha' mercy."

Well, actually I could, but the rune made it incredibly painful to do so. Doing my best to look honest and trustworthy, I cautiously lifted my hand to show the rune; fortunately it was now quiescent. Both the mayor and the head merchant stared at it with fascinated horror.

"Why, that's on the church altar," Gawell said, peering closer.

"So it is," Jusson said. "It's also on my throne room floor in Iversly, and a part of several noble Houses' devices. A familiar symbol, messirs, one that we ourselves revere."

"Indeed," Ednoth murmured, his eyes narrowing once more. "So, what *did* happen this morning, young lord?"

My mind raced as I figured Jusson wouldn't want me blurting out about a phantom hand taking liberties with my person. "I was using my talent, Master Ednoth, and wasn't paying attention to what was happening around me." I braced myself, but it seemed that I'd stayed to the truth as my rune remained quiet.

"Showing off, eh?" Ednoth asked. He didn't wait for my answer, which was good. "Well, the street player *is* a toothsome lass."

"I've heard that," Jusson said, his voice easy. He turned

his head to the mayor. "Bring me a list of damages tomorrow, your honor, and I'll make them whole."

It was a scene that was repeated over and over. Whether sitting with chosen victims, or walking around hunting them down, the king worked the room. With both the Freston folk and the Great Lords, he had me apologize and promise it wouldn't happen again, and then he'd confirm compensation for any losses. To anyone who doubted my veracity, Jusson pointed to the truth rune on my palm. And despite Thadro's worries, there wasn't any hissing or shrieking in terror when I displayed the rune. If anything, most once more wore Lord Beollan's look of weighing speculation. The exception was Lord Ranulf. And it was with Lord Ranulf that Jusson veered from his charted course for the first and only time that evening.

For a while it seemed that they'd never meet as, wherever Jusson was in the salon, Ranulf seemed to always be on the opposite side. But finally they came face-to-face in the middle, though whether through design or accident, I couldn't tell. Both were a study in happenstance.

"Your Majesty," Lord Ranulf said.

"Lord Ranulf," Jusson said, his face grave. "Our condolences on the death of your father. Leofric was a true friend and advisor to us after our ascension to the throne."

I was startled at Jusson's first use of the royal "we" all evening. Then Thadro bumped me with his elbow and I shifted my gaze beyond the king to the fireplace, intent on the flames. They crackled back merrily at me, happy to have my attention.

Ranulf gave a small bow. "Thank you, Your Majesty. I received your kind letter."

"Do you know our cousin, Lord Rabbit ibn Chause e Flavan?" Jusson asked. He didn't wait for Ranulf's answer. "Rabbit, this is Lord Ranulf ibn—no," the king corrected himself, smiling. "He is Lord of Bainswyr now."

I bowed, offering a polite smile despite his slams earlier that evening. "Grace to you, Lord Bainswyr."

I got a nod and an abrupt "Lord Rabbit" in return.

I did my best to sound affable anyway. "You said we'd met in Iversly," I asked, "but I don't recall—"

"It was some function," Ranulf said. "I don't remember where." He turned so that his back was to me. "Your Majesty, forgive my presumption, but is it wise to have him so close to you? Not only has he caused harm in town, I have heard of the—the changes he has wrought in his troop."

So much for affability. Figuring to save myself another elbowing from Thadro, I made my face blank as I stared at the back of Ranulf's very red head.

"Where else should we have our heir, Lord Bainswyr?" Jusson asked, mildly interested. "Up in the mountains chasing bandits? Or perhaps back in the Border with the magicals?"

"Back in the Border is not a bad idea, sire," Ranulf said. "He has seven brothers and sisters, all with the same number of lines to the throne, yet you've not brought them to Iversterre, claiming them as kin. Let him rejoin his family and choose one of us for your heir. That way, everyone is where they should be, for he has proven that he does not belong here."

"Three times sworn to that same throne, and a fourth time sworn—to me," Jusson said, dropping the royal talk. "*I* hold his fealty, Lord Ranulf. Would you have me violate it by sending Rabbit back to the fairies?" His brow rose. "What would they do with such a repudiation? And what would breaking my oath do to *me?*"

There was silence while conversation continued all around us, some of it mirthful as Jusson's guests were mellowed by the good food and wine. I could see Doyen Dyfrig shake his shaggy white head and Mayor Gawell's paunch

jiggle as they both roared with laughter at some jest against
Master Ednoth, the head merchant's hands raised in mock
supplication. Then Ranulf spoke, his face once more expressionless.

"Please forgive me, Your Majesty. It's only that I am
concerned for your welfare."

Jusson smiled again. "There is nothing to forgive, son of
my friend," he said, and he shifted the conversation to problems that Ranulf had encountered stepping into his father's
stead as head of his House.

"Very soft words, sire," Thadro said as we stalked the
next group of guests.

"Soft words can always be replaced with hard ones,
while hard ones are almost always impossible to soften.
Let's see if I can win Leofric's son gently." Maintaining a
pleasant expression, Jusson nodded at Beollan, who was
watching us openly from across the room. "It is not remarkable that he would have reservations about anything
that tastes of the Border," he continued. "I can afford to let
those reservations remain—for now."

I must've looked puzzled for the king turned his pleasant
expression on me. "Bainswyr's principal holdings are near
the Border, Rabbit. They suffered a great deal of damage
during the last war. Damage that still continues."

In the last war with the Border, the Royal Army had
marched towards the lone mountain pass into their northern
neighbor, thinking to overwhelm any resistance. As they'd
successfully done before. However, that time the Border
Militia was waiting for them—a militia that contained not
only the regulation horse and foot soldiers, but also mages,
enchanters and other talent wielders; elementals, sprites
and other spirits of the land; and dragons, winged lions and
other fantastic beasts. Even the trees got in on the act. And,
of course, there was the Truth rune. The Royal Army was

slapped back into the northern marches, where it was destroyed in a single battle.

And with all the spells, enchantments and brute talent force used, it wasn't surprising that effects still lingered. I had heard stories of places where crops grew strangely and animals didn't breed quite right. Places where human births were closely watched by the local doyen and the midwife carried a sharp knife. Just in case.

"Yes, sire," I murmured. Wondering what nightmares he had to deal with, I glanced over at the Lord of Bainswyr, now standing with some of the local landowners—and found him looking at me, his brown eyes cold and dark.

The fare on the sideboard had been reduced to scraps, the magnificent cake was gone and the wine pitchers were empty when Jusson gave the signal that the dinner was over. It ended as simply as it started—he had Doyen Dyfrig say a closing prayer, then without any fanfare left, as casually as he'd entered, the royal guards standing at the door falling in behind him. I started to follow but Thadro stopped me and led me back to the crowned chair, where we resumed our sentry duty, watching the guests file out. As the salon emptied, Cais gave directions for cleanup to the servants. Then he also left, shutting the door behind him.

"Was there any part of my orders that you didn't understand, Lieutenant Rabbit?" Thadro asked.

I'd been wistfully watching the servants stack the serving bowls and platters, telling myself that I could raid the kitchen for leftovers as soon as I was released. At the Lord Commander's words, though, I jerked my head around. "Sir?"

"No provocation, Lieutenant," Thadro said. "Nothing to make a bad situation worse. Yet, every time I looked around, you were doing your best to undermine His Majesty's efforts. Efforts that he was making on your behalf."

I stared at Thadro, distantly thinking that Jusson wasn't

being all that altruistic. The king had another purpose than my reinstatement in the kingdom's good graces, a purpose that everyone seemed to know—except me. What was foremost in my mind, though, was how much I disliked being looked at as though I was pond scum.

"Arguing with Lord Ranulf, conjuring the wind, questioning me and waving about that damned glowing rune," Thadro said, listing my transgressions. "Loose and easy interpretations of orders may have happened in your last posting, but I will not tolerate it here. Do you understand *that?*"

Sod you, I thought. "Yes, sir," I said, aiming my gaze over his shoulder at the servants, who were very obviously not looking in our direction. Then the door opened and Cais reappeared, giving Thadro a discreet signal.

"With me, Lieutenant," the Lord Commander said.

I followed Thadro as he slipped out from behind the chairs, dimly hoping that I was finally being dismissed to eat and then sleep. But, to my hungry and tired dismay, Cais led us down the empty hall to a familiar portal: Jusson's study. At the majordomo's knock the door opened and I met Jeff's gaze. One eye was lost in black and puffy folds, but the other imitated a fish's eye, round and blank before he moved aside to reveal Jusson once more seated at his desk, a neat stack of papers in front of him. And sitting in one of the three guest chairs drawn up in front of the king was Laurel Faena. The mountain cat slued around in his chair, his amber eyes glowing in the candlelight as they met mine.

"Come in, cousin," Jusson said. "Come in and sit down. Thadro, shut the door."

Six

Laurel looked the same as he had the last I'd seen him—which wasn't surprising as that was yesterday eve. He also looked quite at home as he lounged in his chair. Standing on his back legs, Laurel was a little taller than me; seated he was about the same height as Jusson. His tawny winter fur was coming in full and thick, but as a concession to both the season's chill and the royal audience, he wore a padded coat of autumnal gold, brown and red, embroidered with gold thread. By his side was his oak staff, as elaborately carved as mine was plain, and adorned with strips of woven cloth, beads and feathers. Beads and feathers also hung from his ears and were worked into his head fur, the feathers as red as the one in my queue. But then, he did give me mine.

Laurel whiskers twitched back in a smile that showed his eyeteeth as he watched me approach. "I give you good evening, Rabbit."

"Honored Laurel," I said, just as politely, wondering what the hell was going on. Despite Jeffen standing there, Thadro had shut the door and was now going to his usual post at the king's back. I started to follow, but Jusson stopped me before I could join the Lord Commander.

"No, cousin." Jusson pointed at the remaining guest chairs. "Have a seat, if you please." He waited for me to arrange myself on the opposite end from Laurel, then he sat back. "Our apologies for the late hour, Ambassador Laurel. But events have intervened and this is the first free time we have."

"I understand, honored king," Laurel rumbled. "Will we be joined by Captains Suiden and Javes? The Enchanter Wyln?"

I stirred, my wondering turning to panic at the thought that Laurel didn't know where anyone was. But Jusson ignored my squirming. "Not the captains," he said. "The town seems to have eased back from its earlier bloodlust, but after their assault on our cousin, our Lord Commander and our guards, we were concerned that they might go after anyone in uniform, so the garrison is under lockdown." His voice turned dry. "We don't want anyone else injured— even someone foolhardy enough to attack Suiden."

Laurel gave a small chuff of a laugh. "I truly understand."

Jusson tapped the papers that were before him on his desk. "However, both Suiden and Javes have sent reports, and though the injuries Lord Esclaur incurred while in the Borderlands have him recuperating at his family's estate, he too wrote a very detailed report. As did Vice Admiral Lord Havram ibn Chause. We even received one from Doyen Allwyn, forwarded to us by His Holiness, Patriarch Pietr. Imagine our surprise when we read in all of them that there was another reason why you came to Iversterre. One that had nothing to do with smuggling rings and threatened wars."

Laurel had been sent by the Border High Council to protest the smuggling ring—the same ring that had been formed by the Council cabal and the House of Dru to foment unrest between Iversterre and the Border. However, he'd also been sent to retrieve a runaway apprentice mage. Me.

"Yes, honored king," Laurel agreed. "There was another reason."

"And you didn't see fit to inform us?" Jusson asked, mildly interested.

"The success of the one rested upon the other," Laurel said. "If I hadn't returned with Rabbit, Magus Kareste's friends on the High Council would've declared war because of the smuggling. It seemed that remaining silent was the best way of accomplishing peace."

"I see," Jusson said. "Tell us, how did Rabbit react when he discovered that you'd delivered him to Kareste?"

"He was upset," Laurel admitted.

Upset? I'd done my damnedest to take Laurel apart. But he was bigger, heavier and had a longer reach. Shifting in my chair again, my gaze met Thadro's. To my surprise, there was nothing of the mud puddle in it.

"Was he?" Jusson asked, his voice still mild. "Well, that's understandable, seeing as you'd given him back to a man he'd fled in horror—after swearing that you'd keep him safe."

"The law governing the apprenticing of the talent-born is strictly enforced, honored king," Laurel said, his voice just as mild. "You had a very potent demonstration of why with Rabbit's inadvertent translation of his fellows while in Iversly, and the chaos that followed."

The changing of my troop mates into animals and fantastic beasts did happen on the morning of the rebellion. However, the one had nothing—or very little—to do with the other, as the conspirators, my cousin Lord Teram ibn Flavan and Lord Gherat of Dru, had been planning their coup for years. I slid forward in my chair, ready to explain how the aspects did as they willed and a lot of a mage's training was on how to keep from being consumed by his own talent. Only to again meet Thadro's stare as it once more turned very muddy.

"It *was* an eventful spring, wasn't it?" Jusson marveled. "Full of magic and rebellion, both here and in the Border. But we survived and now you're back."

Laurel nodded. "Yes, honored king. With Rabbit safe—and my oaths honored. However, I'm no longer the Council's representative. The new ambassador should arrive shortly."

"So we've read," Jusson said. A brow rose. "More politics, Master Laurel?"

"The Council felt that it would be better for me to focus just on one task," Laurel said.

"Which is"—Jusson's eyes dropped to the sheets in front of him— " 'teacher in the talent' to our cousin. As is this Enchanter Wyln, who is brother-in-law to the Fyrst of Elanwryfindyll."

Laurel nodded once more. "Yes. While Rabbit has had enough training for the Council to declare that he doesn't have to be apprenticed again, he will still need many more years of study for him to become a full mage. Wyln and I are here to see this through."

"How magnaminous, this giving of your time and efforts to someone who has no claim on you!"

"Not really, honored king," Laurel said. "As I said, someone untrained in the talent, especially someone with Rabbit's strength, would invite all sorts of havoc, and no one sane wants that, fae or human."

"So you say. But we remember you had a hidden agenda once before and we can't help wondering if there are any other reasons for your return." Jusson's brow rose. "Are there?"

Laurel lifted his paw, the truth rune softly shining. "I give my word that I'm here to teach Rabbit."

Jusson smiled again. "Such a solemn avowal, complete with signs and wonders! However, we've seen our cousin dance very nimbly around that rune just a little while ago and, from what we've seen and read, you are even more graceful in your steps, Master Cat."

"We want the same thing—Rabbit strong and capable, no?" This time Laurel didn't raise his paw, but took his staff, the beads on it rattling as he held it in front of him. "By the Lady, this I will achieve. Fiat."

Want the same thing? A sneaking suspicion flashed across my mind and I frowned.

"Strong and capable *and* ours?" Jusson asked. "We've also read about Loran the Fyrst's claims on our cousin."

My suspicion grew stronger. "Sire?" I asked. Jusson, intent on Laurel, once again ignored me, but Thadro added a frown to his mud-puddle stare.

"Yes, honored king," Laurel said. "His Grace Loran has declared Rabbit *cyhn*—"

" 'Kin'?" Jusson interrupted.

"Close," Laurel said. "It's an elfin term meaning fosterage, among other things."

My suspicion deepening, I opened my mouth. But Thadro, glaring, shook his head and I closed it again, fighting not to glare back. Apparently I was to have no say in how my future was divvied up.

Jusson kept his gaze on Laurel. "Another thing I've read. But Rabbit has been a soldier going on six years. He does not need to be fostered."

"Elves have a different idea of adulthood, honored king," Laurel said. "But rest assured that Rabbit's *cyhn* to the Fyrst's lineage will not affect his fealty to you." He also smiled, his eyeteeth gleaming. "Besides, interfering in your oaths would not be wise. You *are* king, no? And your pledges bind the very land. Tampering with any part of that could unleash a strong, hrmm, backlash."

Hell. My gaze snapped away from Thadro to Laurel at the cat's reference to Jusson's conversation with Lord Ranulf. A conversation where Laurel hadn't been present, at least not bodily. I waited for the royal explosion, but Jusson just looked irritated. "I thought you learned how to block your thoughts from being scried, cousin," he said.

When I'd come into my full power, one of the talents that manifested was the ability to thought-scry. I was a strong sender and it had seemed that those who could would stroll through my thoughts at whim—as Laurel and others had demonstrated on several occasions. I spent most of last summer learning to keep my thoughts to myself. So I thought. Apparently, I thought wrong.

"I had, Your Majesty," I said, also irritated.

"You've had a very full day, Rabbit," Laurel said. "And you're tired and hungry. It's understandable that your control would falter." He looked back at Jusson. "However, the fact that it had, honored king, and that I was able to take advantage of it, shows that Rabbit isn't ready to be left on his own—" He stopped, his ears swiveling back. A moment later there was a knock at the door.

"Our other guest, Lord Wyln, has finally arrived," Jusson said, still annoyed.

Thadro nodded at Jeff, who opened the door. But instead of the Enchanter Wyln, it was the Keeper of the King's Peace who stood in the doorway. Before either Jusson or Thadro could react, Chadde came into the room and bowed, her gray eyes sweeping over both me and Laurel as she straightened. "I beg pardon for my intrusion, Your Majesty," he said, "but there's been a murder."

Seven

The head jailer was as unprepossessing dead as he'd been alive.

I stood in the town's charnel house looking down at Menck's naked body occupying one of four waist-high stone slabs. Torches were in sconces on the gray stone walls, casting flickering shadows over the room, while steadier light was provided by lanterns placed at the head and feet of the corpse. The tallow-dipped torches reeked here as they did in jail, competing with the rushes and dried herbs strewn on the floors. And underneath it all was a lingering stink of corruption mixed with a more pungent aroma normally found in privies and jakes. I tugged the borrowed cloak further around me, very glad for the smell-dampening cold.

Menck's eyes stared up at the dark ceiling in leering horror, his mouth gaping open to show missing and decayed teeth, his beard-stubbled cheeks pasty white. I was not a stranger to violent death, having caused my share of it in the course of my army career. But I'd never seen anything like the stab wounds on the jailer's torso—so many of them, and all a bright, glittering red. Then I realized that the glittering was because the blood was frozen, and I frowned. While cold, it hadn't dropped to freezing yet. I reached out a gloved hand to a hairy and somewhat grimy arm to see if the rest of the jailer was frozen as well.

"Lieutenant," Thadro said.

Holding in a sigh, I dropped my hand. Beside me, Jeff slid a glance at the Lord Commander before meeting my gaze, then we both turned back to watch Laurel as he gently poked and pried at the corpse, Peacekeeper Chadde at his side. When we first arrived, Thadro had tried to preserve Chadde's modesty by covering Mencke's delicate parts with a kerchief. However, the peacekeeper gave the Lord Commander a calm stare and, quirking a smile, he removed it again. She now followed Laurel's every move.

"What's the witch doing here? And what the hell is *that?*"

I quickly turned. Standing in the doorway was Lord Ranulf, covered in a cloak made entirely of fur. For a moment it was if a great bear stood there. Then Ranulf strode into the room, reaching for his sword, his gaze on Laurel. As he did, Thadro stood in front of me and Jeff stepped next to the Lord Commander.

"Easy, Ranulf," Thadro said, shifting so that he blocked the Marcher Lord from Laurel as well. Laurel, however, didn't pause in his examination of the jailer's earthly remains.

"His Majesty sent him, my lord," Chadde said, moving to the other side of Thadro.

Feeling trapped against the corpse-containing slab, I tried to move out from behind the wall of backs. But Thadro cast me a muddy glance over his shoulder and I stopped. Laurel glanced up, his eyes going to the Lord Commander and then to me, before returning to his examination. He rumbled softly, his brows knit as he lifted Menck's arm—and I noticed that it moved easily, with no signs of stiffening. Freshly killed, then. My gaze went back to the frozen wounds. Maybe.

"He did? How interesting," Lord Beollan said, entering the room behind Ranulf. The Lord of Fellmark wore his plumed hat and was also wrapped in a cloak, but his was soft wool lined with fur and fastened at his neck by a silver pin in the shape of a dragon. Studded with tiny jewels, the pin winked in the flickering light, making the dragon seem alive. "Any particular reason His Majesty sent his Lord Commander, his cousin, and"—Beollan's gaze traveled over Jeff's Own uniform to rest on Laurel—"a very big cat?"

"Lords Beollan and Ranulf were the ones who found Menck's body," Chadde said to Thadro before turning to answer Beollan. "Master Laurel is a famed thieftaker in his own land, my lord." She cast a look over her shoulder at Laurel, for the first time appearing a bit uncertain. "His Majesty felt that he could help."

So Jusson did. But then, the king often poured all sorts of oddments into a boiling pot just to see what would bubble up to the surface.

"The head jailer killed," Jusson had said when Chadde finished her telling. "After beating, robbing and generally misusing our cousin and his fellows. And now you've come to make sure that Rabbit hadn't taken his revenge?" He didn't wait for Chadde's answer. "Thadro, take Guardsman Jeffen and accompany our cousin and the peacekeeper while I wait here for my other guest. Find out all you can about this murder and report back to me." Still radiating annoyance even as he smiled, the king looked at Laurel. "Perhaps you'd like to go with them, Master Faena. It's a chance to practice your craft. At least one part of it."

Laurel hadn't argued and, when we arrived in the charnel house, he handed me his coat and staff and immediately began examining the corpse. Now, done with Menck's hands, he moved to the other end of the slab. "Not a thieftaker, honored Chadde," he said, gently lifting Menck's leg to peer closely at his ankle. "Thieftakers hunt down the

guilty for a fee. We are more of a cross between your office
and a magistrate's, with the power of the High Council behind us."

"Indeed?" Beollan asked. "And who are 'we'?"

Laurel looked up at the Marcher Lord, his amber eyes
glowing. "The Faena."

Faena came from all the Border races. Justicers, priests
and intercessors, they were the warp woven into the woof
of the Border, filling in the empty spaces between its citizens and making them whole. But as it was the Faena
who'd lifted the truth rune during the last war with Iversterre with such devastating effectiveness, I waited for an
explosion of outrage from the two Marcher Lords.

Beollan, though, merely shrugged. "Oh. You're *that* cat."
He turned his attention on Laurel's elaborate staff. "The
head of the Faena, correct?"

Returning to his examination, Laurel gave an absent
rumble. "Yes."

"You're a little far afield, aren't you?"

Laurel gave another rumble. "As you said, I'm a cat. We
tend to do that, wander far and wide." Setting the leg down,
he moved to the head jailer's clothes. He picked up the
jailer's shirt and spread it open near one of lanterns. Though
I narrowed my eyes against the smell of overflowing privies, I could see that the shirt had been sliced from laces to
hem. And while it was stained with other substances, there
was no blood, or even corresponding holes for the knife
wounds. Someone had carefully cut open Menck's shirt before stabbing him to death.

"I've heard about him," Lord Ranulf said as he pushed
past Chadde to the slab to glare impartially at the corpse,
Laurel and me. "Not only that he's one of the damned
Faena, but how he's also some pagan priest of a demon goddess."

Laurel *was* a shaman of Lady Gaia—and so presided

over all her rituals of fertility, birth, healing and death. But even my da, as faithful a son of the Church as there ever was, would never have dared to call the earth deity a demoness. And I, baptized, catechized and diligently following the same Church, shifted a couple of steps to put a little more distance between me and the Lord of Bainswyr. Then I realized what he had said and I turned my frown upon him.

" 'Heard about,' my lord?" I asked. "Didn't you meet Laurel in Iversly?"

Thadro, judging the threat had passed, had started to turn to face the dead jailer. At my question, though, he stopped, shooting me an annoyed look.

"No," Ranulf said abruptly.

"No, we have not met before," Laurel said. Setting aside the shirt, he moved to a patched leather jerkin. Checking the pockets first, he turned it inside out. He then frowned and began to examine it more closely.

"Does it matter?" Lord Beollan said. "Surely you and, ah, Master Laurel weren't joined at the hip during your time in the Royal City."

Well, no, we hadn't been. In fact, there was one social event that Laurel definitely had not attended. One where all the guests wore costumes from a children's pantomime and remained hidden behind masks while poisoned wine had been served and I fought for my life against five in a darkened courtyard. I eyed Lord Ranulf, wondering if he'd been a guest at my cousin, Lord Teram ibn Flavan e Dru's masque. "No," I said slowly, "Laurel and I weren't together all the time in Iversly."

"It was probably at one of those functions that you met, then," Beollan said. "If you don't tease yourself, I'm sure you'll remember." He came to stand at the foot of the slab and stared down at the head jailer's body. "Poor bastard."

Chadde turned her head to Beollan, her gaze suddenly intent.

"Ranulf and I found him out by the jakes at this tavern that I discovered earlier today in my rambles," Beollan said, oblivious to the peacekeeper's attention. "We've just come back from the mayor's, telling him about his kinsman. His honor said that he was going to break the news to the man's wife before coming here."

"I thought you went to your bedchamber, my lord," I said, curious. I was certain I had heard his voice as he went up the main staircase at the king's house. I'd also heard Ranulf's, but didn't ask him as I figured I'd save Thadro wear and tear on his boots from having to step on my foot.

"Only to get my cloak, hat and gloves, Lord Rabbit," Beollan said. He gave a tired smile. "Despite the king's hospitality, I'd no wish for bed yet"—his smile changed—"at least not an empty one. I thought the Copper Pig would satisfy my desire for, ah, adventure."

"'Struth." Lord Ranulf also looked down on the naked corpse, fleeting sympathy crossing his face. "The tavern had good sport, but was a rough-and-tumble place. He was probably killed for his purse. Such as it was."

While the Copper Pig's reputation was unsavory, it was more for the gambling, prostitutes and bad ale it offered than for violence. I was about to say so when I caught Thadro's gelid eye.

"The Pig's not a place of bloodshed," Chadde said, filling the gap. "Whoring, petty thievery and weighted dice, but not murder. The whole valley isn't—the last killing was close to fifteen years ago, and that involved a jealous wife, a pretty serving girl and a roving husband. Not robbery." The peacekeeper's brows knitted together. "Though Menck's purse *is* missing, and knowing of his various dealings, it was probably more substantial than it should've been. As are the number of those who wished him ill." She watched Laurel set the jerkin down and pick up the leather breeks. "But if robbery was the motive, then why so many stab wounds?" Her gaze dropped to the corpse. "And wounds like that?"

"Revenge perhaps?" Ranulf suggested. "Someone who didn't care for the treatment he received in jail?"

"When Rabbit was released from jail, the head jailer was very much alive," Thadro said mildly, "and the lieutenant's time has been accounted for since."

"The jailer could've been killed from a distance," Ranulf persisted. "By magic."

"No," Laurel said. "It was done up close, with a knife." He put the breeks down and looked around. "Was there a coat or cloak, honored peacekeeper? Or shoes?"

Chadde shook her head. "He had just what you see, Master Laurel. Though whoever took Menck's purse could've also taken his cloak and shoon."

Laurel poked at some gray and greasy-looking hosen and smalls, then returned to the jerkin. "His purse wasn't stolen either. Or if it was, what was in it wasn't significant." Using his claw, he ripped open a seam at the bottom and pulled out what looked like wool wadding. Then, lifting the jerkin up, he poured out a stream of gold coins.

There was a long moment of silence as the coins continued to fall onto the slab with a tinkle. "Who knew strong-arming was so lucrative?" Beollan murmured.

Lord Ranulf gave a short laugh. "Would that my treasure box held that much."

"That's at least twenty years' pay," I said, gaping.

"More," Jeff whispered, his eyes wide. "At officer rates."

"No officer in His Majesty's army earns that much gold," Thadro said. "Not even I."

While I didn't know what Lord Commanders earned, I did know that when I was promoted to lieutenant, my pay was upped to a half gold a year. Staring down at the coins on the slab, I saw an awful lot of gold.

Shaking out the last of the coins, Laurel set the jerkin down and picked up the breeks. We remained silent as he once again ripped open a seam to reveal a hidden pocket. But instead of coins, there was a leather pouch. Laurel untied and upended it, and another stream fell onto the slab—this one of gemstones, the gems' facets adding their sparkle to the coins.

"Rabbit," Laurel said

I jerked my gaze away from the dazzling display.

"Your dagger," Laurel said, putting the empty pouch down.

Reaching under my cloak, I pulled my knife from its sheath at the small of my back and handed it to the Faena, who used it to stir through the gems. As he did, the hair on the back of my neck rose.

"What is it?" Ranulf asked, watching Laurel closely. But then all of us were. All except Beollan, who stared unwinkingly at the gold and jewels. His dragon pin's tiny gemstone eyes seemed to blaze with their own fire.

"The head jailer was murdered," Laurel said. "And a knife was used in the killing. However, robbery was not the motive. Nor was revenge or jealousy, or any other mundane reason." He started to run a paw over his head, then remembering that he'd been touching both Menck and the jailer's privy-invested clothes, lowered it—and Chadde's eyes widened slightly as she caught sight of the truth rune on the middle pad.

"So why was he killed?" Thadro asked, beating out everyone else.

"*Dauthiwaesp*," Laurel said, his tail lashing. "You'd call it death magic."

Eight

The silence that had fallen after Laurel's pronouncement was broken by a familiar sibilance and, looking around, I saw Lord Ranulf's sword gleam as he drew it from his scabbard. But before Laurel—or any of the rest of us—could react, Peacekeeper Chadde grabbed Ranulf's wrist. Ranulf tried to dislodge Chadde's grip, shaking his arm. "Damn you, let me go!"

"My town, Lord Bainswyr," Chadde said. "My rules. Rule number one, no drawing on His Majesty's kin, his agents or his guests."

"The magical admitted it!" Ranulf roared. "Foul sorcery!"

"Master Laurel said dark magic had been done, not that he'd done it," Chadde said. Her grip tightened. "Put the sword away, my lord."

"Ranulf," Beollan said, looking up from his contemplation of the coins and jewels. "Do as the peacekeeper says."

"Who else could it be? The demon lord and his familiar," Ranulf said, panting as he struggled against Chadde.

"The Border is not the only land with talent-born, Lord Ranulf," I said, distantly marveling at the peacekeeper's strength in subduing the brawny Marcher Lord. "There are Turalian wizards, adepts in Caepisma, and a magician-priest caste in Svlet. I'd even heard tell that each Line in the

Qarant Trade Consortium has its own prescriber. Something about keeping their fellow merchants honest. In fact, Iversterre may be the only kingdom that does *not* have any official talent-workers." I gave a humorless smile, thinking on the earlier discussion between Jusson and Laurel. "Until now."

"Very good, Lord Rabbit," Beollan said. "Figured that out, did you? Or did his Majesty tell you?"

"That's neither here nor there," Thadro said before I could answer. He looked at the Lord of Bainswyr and made an annoyed sound. "I'd tell Chadde to let you attack the Faena, Ranulf, but I don't want to have to explain to the king how you'd come to be smeared across the floor. Put your sword away before you get hurt."

Laurel hadn't paid any attention to Lord Ranulf's belligerence, but had gone to a bowl of water set on one of the three empty slabs. Picking up the small bag he'd placed there before he began his examination, he poured its contents into the bowl. Using my dagger to stir, he then set aside the knife and plunged his paws into the water. I shivered again, thinking that the water had to be very cold as it had been drawn from a pump in the tiny courtyard of the charnel house.

"I assure Ranulf Leofric'son that neither I nor Rabbit had anything to do with the unfortunate's death," Laurel said, vigorously scrubbing. An astringent scent filled the air, competing with the tallow and privy aromas. "And just because there aren't any other official talent-workers in your kingdom doesn't mean that there aren't any at all. But that's not what we ought to be concerned about. At least, not right now."

"All right, I'll bite," Beollan said. "What *should* we be concerned about?"

"Death magic has been worked, honored lord," Laurel said. "To what purpose?"

The room grew quiet again and I was distracted from

Laurel knowing Ranulf's father's name by the memory of
that morning's attack of the phantom hand. But Menck had
been alive and extorting then, so that meant that dark sorcery was probably waiting, like a cocked crossbow. Or
maybe the bolt had already been shot and was even now flying towards its target. My shiver this time had nothing to do
with anything so ordinary as the cold.

Ranulf shook his arm again. "Let go. I'm not attacking
anyone."

Chadde released Ranulf's wrist, and Ranulf slid his
sword back into its scabbard, his mouth a thin line bracketed by his beard as he scowled. Chadde turned to the
corpse, her own frown returning. "So these stab wounds are
caused by the casting of the spell?"

"Yes." Finished scrubbing, Laurel shook the water from
his paws. "The pattern of the wounds is the spell; the death
of the unfortunate the empowering of it." He walked over to
me and, with a sigh, I offered a corner my cloak. "The fact
that the wounds are frozen tells two things," Laurel continued, drying his paws. "First, the caster of the spell has the
water aspect."

Lord Ranulf's dark eyes rested on me as he snarled.

"If Rabbit had cast the spell, he wouldn't have needed
the death to complete it," Laurel said, his voice as mild as
Thadro's. "He's more than powerful enough not to need
any, hrmm, outside help."

"Really?" Beollan asked, interested. "More powerful
than you?"

"Yes," Laurel said. Done with my cloak, he dropped it
and I handed him his coat.

"What's the second thing, Master Laurel?" Chadde
asked, still staring down at the corpse.

"That the unfortunate was kept alive until the last stab.
The freezing of the wounds kept him from bleeding out,
no?" Laurel picked up my dagger again. "Here—" He

pointed with the dagger tip to a wound. "This one was the final one, piercing the heart." Still using the dagger, Laurel lifted Menck's wrist, and we could see abrasions and bruising. "He has the same marks on his other wrist and both ankles. He was tied down as he was slowly killed. It was someplace private, honored folk, where no one would hear his screams. Then they dumped the body where it was found, not bothering to bring the unfortunate's cloak or shoes. Why should they? He certainly had no need of them."

"What's wrong with the money and jewels?" Beollan asked abruptly. His thin face was all angles and sharp planes as he returned his attention to the minihoard on the body slab. The rest of us did too, attracted by the glitter of sudden, intense wealth.

Laurel dropped my dagger back in the bowl and, extending a claw, he swished the water. "Certain metals and stones have an affinity for the talent, honored Beollan. The more precious they are, the greater the affinity." He glanced at the pile of the certainly precious metal and gems. "Whoever killed the jailer didn't realize that he had them with him or they would've made certain to remove them first."

"Why?" Ranulf asked, also studying the stones and coins. Despite the spark and twinkle of the gems and gold, they seemed duller than they should've been, as though a coating of dust lay over them. The Marcher Lord reached for a coin to examine it more closely.

"Because both Menck's extended death and whatever was conjured with it have left their mark on them," Laurel said. "I suppose you could say that they're cursed."

Ranulf stopped midreach, and everyone took a collective step back from the slab.

"Permanently?" Beollan asked from his new vantage point.

"That remains to be seen," Laurel said. "Sometimes

curses can be lifted. Sometimes, no." Finished cleansing my knife, he handed it dripping to me, taking his staff back at the same time. "However, right now we need to discuss the disposition of the unfortunate's body."

" 'Disposition'?" Thadro asked.

"It should be burned with the appropriate death rituals," Laurel began, but Chadde, Beollan and Ranulf all started talking at once.

"No," Chadde said.

"Impossible," Beollan stated.

"Sacrilege!" Ranulf growled.

"They're right, Laurel," I said, drying my dagger on my cloak. "You can't do that here."

Laurel's brows crooked. "There was no problem burning honored Basel's body."

Trooper Basel had been the Mountain Patrol's cook. He had turned into a White Stag when the troop had translated in the Royal City—and was then murdered by Lieutenant Slevoic ibn Dru because he had witnessed one of the Vicious' attempts against my life. We built a funeral pyre for Basel, as Laurel had then pointed out that to have the Stag's body parts ending up in apothecaries' potions or other places would not have been good. And now Laurel was saying that bad things were associated with Menck's death, too. But, however true that was, in the northern marches folk had very strong ideas about burying their dead.

"That was in Iversly," I said as Jeff nodded in agreement. "It's very different here. The only ones burned are those convicted of witchcraft or other, like depravity. Not burying him in hallowed ground would not only declare him anathema, but also would taint his family and even the town."

"That is true," Chadde said. "And while he was most definitely criminally corrupt, we have no proof that in this instance Menck was anything more than a victim—" The peacekeeper broke off as Laurel flung up a paw, his ears swiveling. The cat snatched my dagger from me and used it to pick up Menck's clothes, covering the coins and jewels with them.

We stared at him in surprise, then steps sounded outside in the small courtyard. All of us turned and a few moments later the mayor walked in, accompanied by the head of the town's merchant guild, Master Ednoth. I felt my spine relax and beside me Jeff let out a small breath of relief. Menck's gruesome corpse and the talk of curses and death magic were making us jumpy.

"My lords and—" Mayor Gawell's gaze went to Laurel. "Laurel Faena, right?" He didn't wait for an answer. "His Majesty was kind enough to send a messenger to tell me that he'd asked you to aid our peacekeeper."

I frowned at how Gawell, having accused me of being hell's spawn, seemed to take Laurel—the talking and upright-walking mountain cat—in stride. There was also a very slight crease between Thadro's brows as he looked at the mayor. Then the Lord Commander's face went politically blank.

"We need all the help we can get," Ednoth said, his fringe of hair a little mussed as though he'd just gotten out of bed and had hurriedly smoothed it down. "Murder's not something that we're accustomed to; the last one we had was so long ago."

I glanced at Chadde to see how she felt about Master Ednoth's dismissal of her abilities, but the peacekeeper appeared her usual calm self.

"Very true." Gawell gave a massive sigh that seemed to suck most of the air from the room. He expelled it with a cough, though, as he also had sucked in the acrid aromas still emanating from Menck's clothes. The mayor walked over to the slab that contained the head jailer's body and looked down at his kinsman, his face in the flickering torch-light seeming more irritated than sorrowful. "However, I am not surprised that Menck was killed. Grieved, but not surprised." He shook his head, looking even more irritated as his mouth tightened, his eyes going over the pile of clothes. "Do you have any idea what happened?"

"His purse was missing, your honor," Chadde said, her voice matching her calm face.

I started at Chadde's statement, then, before I could be elbowed by Thadro, became still. Beside me Jeff began to turn his head to stare at the peacekeeper, then checked himself. Fortunately, both Mayor Gawell and Master Ednoth were focused on Menck's remains, so they didn't see either of us. Nor did they see the long look Laurel gave Chadde before putting down my dagger and becoming busy making sure everything was put away properly in his carrypouch. Ranulf managed to keep his attention on the corpse, but his fingers drummed on his sword belt. The only ones who didn't respond to Chadde's misdirection were Lord Beollan and the Lord Commander. Beollan turned his head to survey the mayor and merchant, while Thadro simply remained as he was before, expression, body stance and all.

"I went to question Lord Rabbit," Chadde continued, "as he and his friends had been Menck's latest victims. But his lordship had either been in the king's, the Lord Commander's, or the king's majordomo's presence all evening." She gave a slight smile. "Besides, I'm sure Lord Rabbit has no need for Menck's purse and, as the king's cousin, has other ways of taking revenge."

Even with my lieutenant's wages, my purse wasn't all that fat. But if it held nothing but air, I still wouldn't have wanted anything the head jailer had. At the peacekeeper's words, I tried to look prosperous and disdainful at the same time.

Mayor Gawell nodded. "Unfortunately, Menck had many enemies." He gestured at the pile of unappetizing clothing, the stained shirt on top. "Is this all he had with him?"

"Yes, your honor," Chadde said. "His cloak and shoon are also missing. Whoever took his purse probably has those too."

Gawell sighed again, and let loose with a fit of coughing. He took a step back from the noxious garments, his eyes watering. "Hell," his honor said, pulling a scented handkerchief from his sleeve and covering his nose.

So much for the grieving relative.

"Hell is right," Master Ednoth said, aiming a sour look at the unfortunate Menck. "I'm not surprised that he ended facedown in a privy."

And so much for the supportive friend.

"*By* the jakes, not *in* them," Beollan murmured, his silver eyes gleaming. "Though apparently the tavern's patrons do consider a miss as good as a hit."

Chadde reached over to one of the other unoccupied slabs, picked up a folded cloth and, shaking it open, revealed a shroud. Gently moving aside the mayor and the merchant, she tossed it over Menck's body, also covering the clothes and the loot underneath. "Master Laurel and I are done here, your honor, Master Ednoth. But come daylight I will go out to the Copper Pig to look around and question the taverner and the regulars. Maybe they've seen something—and maybe they'll even tell me." The shroud arranged to her satisfaction, she turned to the mayor. "Have you spoken with Menck's wife regarding his funeral?"

Handkerchief still clamped to his nose, Mayor Gawell nodded. "Yes," he said, his voice muffled. "I told her not to worry; I'll take care of everything. Though I suppose that too can wait until the morrow. No reason to get Dyfrig up in the middle of the night." The mayor cast one last, disgusted look at Menck's shrouded form before turning and marching for the door, Ednoth with him. "You will keep me informed of your progress, Chadde," he said over his shoulder. "I want whoever did this caught and justice done."

"Yes, your honor," Chadde said, her gray eyes watching the mayor and head merchant's retreat. "I will."

Nine

Laurel insisted on warding Menck's body, and the coins and gemstones, before we left the charnel house. He also insisted that I help him.

"A violent death, dark arts, and cursed goods that were probably ill-gotten to begin with," Laurel said. "It wouldn't be wise to leave it all unguarded, honored folk. It'll only take a few moments."

No one argued, not even Ranulf. Instead, he helped Chadde by taking one of the two lanterns and, with the others, moved to the doorway to watch Laurel draw the wards of earth over the slab. When he was done, the Faena stepped back and looked at me. "Fire, Rabbit."

Feeling as though Menck was leering at me through his shroud, I touched a shimmering green earth line and thought on fire in battle—in burning pitch and in flaming arrows. Flames sprung from my fingertips to run alongside earth until it too enclosed the slab, white-hot in the room's gloom. Done, I bowed my head and, despite my bruises, Arlie's fleas and Jeffen's black eye, said a quick prayer for Menck's soul, everyone bowing their heads with me, even Laurel. Even Ranulf.

"So be it," Chadde said, she and the others blessing themselves at my fiat. Ushering us out of the death house, Chadde took the lantern from Ranulf, hanging both on hooks on either side of the doorway. She then closed and locked the door, placing the key back on her belt. With the iron bands imbedded in the door's thick wood and iron grilles in the high, horizontal windows, the charnel house was near as secure as the king's treasury (the north took their dead very seriously). And with the lanterns burning outside, people would soon know that someone had died and send to family and friends to see if it was one of their own.

Everyone waited once more as Laurel and I again drew warding lines, this time on the doors and windows. Ranulf frowned as he watched us, while Beollan followed our movements as if he could see the lines. Chadde and Thadro also watched, their expressions betraying nothing, while Jeff faced outward scanning the courtyard, a faint frown between his brows.

"Will that keep out thieves, Master Laurel?" Beollan asked when we finished.

Laurel shook his head, his beads rattling. "No, these wards won't stop anything physical. We've stout doors, locks, and iron bars to do that. But something that wasn't so physical, then perhaps this will hinder it."

On that heartening comment, we followed Chadde out of the small courtyard, our steps quick as the peacekeeper led us down a small side street to the town's square. There, amid the broken paving stones of that afternoon's riot, she stopped. "We part here, my lords and gracious sirs—"

"Wait a damn moment," Lord Ranulf began.

"Not now, Ranulf," Thadro said, his voice very soft. "And definitely not here."

Damn right, I thought. A sense of being watched stole over me and I joined Jeff in scanning our surroundings. For a moment I thought I saw a flash of red across the square in the dim light from the streetlamps. I stared, straining my eyes, but if there had been something—or someone—it had faded back into the shadows.

Lord Ranulf's mouth flattened once more into a thin line as he glared at the Lord Commander from under his brows, but he fell silent.

"No sulking, Ranulf," Beollan said lightly. "I'm sure that the peacekeeper will keep us informed of her progress."

I tried not to gawk as the Lord of Fellmark tucked a hand under Ranulf's arm. They hadn't seemed to know each other *that* well during the king's dinner. Jeff and I looked at each other, then away again.

Ranulf rubbed his face, tension easing from his shoulders. "Yeah, sure. I'll wait."

"I would also say not here, honored folk," Laurel said, also very softly. "In fact, I would ask that we remain quiet on what we've seen until those responsible are caught." Six pairs of eyes focused on him. "Of course, that doesn't mean that your king shouldn't be told," he added blandly.

"That is probably wise, Master Cat," Beollan said as the rest of us nodded.

"It's a knotty problem, my lords and gracious sirs," Chadde said in a normal tone that seemed to carry to the square's four corners and back again, "given that Menck had a long list of enemies. But I'm sure if we find who has his purse, we'll find his murderer." The peacekeeper looked at the Faena, her brows raised. "Will you be able accompany me to the Copper Pig, Master Laurel?"

"Yes, honored Chadde," Laurel said, uncaring of the sharp glance Thadro gave him.

"I will come for you, then." Chadde gave a bow. "Goodnight all."

The waxing moon was a merry grin that beamed down on us as we walked back to the king's residence. The feeling of being watched had faded after we left the square, but I remained firmly planted between Thadro and Laurel, very glad that Jeff was walking behind us. Beollan and Ranulf were in front, having pulled away from us a bit. As I sleepily wondered on their friendship, they passed under a street-lamp—and I caught the flash of . . . something. I strained harder trying to see, but whatever it was had disappeared. If it was there in the first place. Probably just my overtired imagination, I thought as I stumbled over a cobblestone.

Laurel caught my arm. "Are you all right, Rabbit?"

"Yeah," I said. "I'm just tired."

Thadro gave me a faintly derisive look. He looked as though he could go on a week's march and then fight both sides of a war all by himself.

Laurel tucked his paw in the crook of my arm. "Considering your adventures today, it's not surprising that you're exhausted."

Murmuring agreement, I gratefully leaned on the Faena. The hot bath I had earlier had long since worn off, and my body was sore and stiff, my head beginning to throb.

Upon arriving at the king's residence, we found Cais waiting for us in the foyer. I eyed the majordomo, worried that he was going to herd us once more to Jusson's study. But the king had apparently decided that he could wait for Thadro's report, as Cais bowed and indicated the stairs.

"My lords, gracious sirs. Allow me to see you to your rooms."

That was more than fine by me. It had been a very long day, full of incident, and I wanted food, then my bed. We followed the majordomo up to the second floor, where Beollan and Ranulf immediately disappeared into their rooms, Beollan with a murmured goodnight, Ranulf with a grunt and a decisive snap of his bedroom door. Down the hall beyond my room I could see King's Own standing outside what I assumed was the royal chamber. Vaguely wondering on how Jusson and Wyln's meeting had gone, I went to my own door—and continued past my door as the Lord Commander did not stop. However, Cais did.

"Lord Thadro," the majordomo said.

I stumbled to a halt as Thadro paused, turning around to look at Cais.

"His Majesty specifically asked to see you alone when you returned," Cais said, his voice pitched low.

Frowning a bit, Thadro looked at me and then Laurel.

"Let me see to Rabbit," Laurel said softly, before Thadro could speak. "Then, if the king wishes, I will join you as you give your report."

Thadro's frown abruptly deepened. "Lord Rabbit is a lieutenant in the King's Own, not a child to be put to bed with warm milk." He cast me a disapproving stare. "Though perhaps that's what's wrong with him—too much coddling."

I was too tired to work up much astonishment at hearing my boyhood on a farm and my subsequent time in Suiden's troop described as coddling. However, Jeff's eyes narrowed as he gazed at some point in the distance.

Laurel opened his mouth to respond, but Thadro held up his hand, concern mixing in with the contempt. "Spare me the excuses, Master Laurel. I can see he's about to fall over." He dropped his hand. "Go to bed, Lieutenant. I will see you in the morning."

"Yes, sir," I muttered as he continued down the hall to the king's chamber. I started to walk back to my bedroom, but apparently I wasn't moving fast enough. Laurel grabbed one arm while Jeff took the other, and they both hustled me through the door just as Cais opened it. The majordomo shut it behind me, and I heard a bolt turning.

Laurel rumbled as he propped his staff against the wall. "I don't remember the honored commander being quite so testy last time we met."

Jeff, Cais and I all looked at him blank-faced. We were *not* discussing the king's Lord Commander with the Faena.

"Right," Laurel said with a short chuff. He walked over to an ewer on the washstand and sniffed at the water in it.

"It has not been a good day, Laurel," I said, as I also leaned my staff against the wall. Pulling off my gloves, I undid the the frogs on my borrowed cloak—and Cais was there to take it and the gloves away. As he did, I noticed that the room was empty except for us. "Where's Arlie?" I asked.

"He went to get Lord Wyln," Jeff said, also undoing his cloak. He blinked a little when Cais took his too.

"He did?" I asked. "Why wasn't Wyln with you, Laurel?"

"The garrison commander put us in different quarters," Laurel said, looking underneath the washstand. "Apparently Commander Ebner's grandsire fought in the last war and passed down tales about the Faena. Honored Ebner was not about to have me in the middle of his soldiers, so I was lodged as close to the gate as possible—with guards to take care of my every need."

"Yeah," Jeff said. "And Ebner wasn't having an elf enchanter so close to the full-of-unsuspecting-humans town, so he put Lord Wyln at the other end of the garrison. Even though Arlie knew the guards posted at Lord Wyln's quarters, they still wouldn't let him pass without Ebner's permission. He had to go to the commander's office to get it."

I had been so glad to get to my familiar cot in my familiar barracks when we'd arrived back in Freston yesterday afternoon, that I'd not paid much attention to the disposition of my teachers in the talent, nor did I question the ease with which I slipped their leashes this morning. Now, however, I was worried. While Laurel seemed to shrug off his treatment in the garrison, I had a hard time believing that Wyln had been so sanguine about not only being separated from both Laurel and me, but also having human guards set upon him. Frowning, I sat down to take off my boots, and Cais was immediately there with slippers.

"Allow me, my lord."

"Uh, sure," I said.

"Arlie's probably with the king and Lord Wyln, and now the Lord Commander too," Jeff said as he walked over to the fire to warm his hands. He gave a twisted grin at my expression. "I know, but at least he didn't have to go see magicked dead bodies—" He stopped and cast a glance at Cais, biting his lip.

"Don't worry, Jeffen," Laurel said as he rummaged in the clothespress. "I'm sure honored Cais is very deep in Jusson Iver'son's confidence."

"My family has served the House of Iver since its founding, Master Laurel," Cais agreed, standing to help me remove my tabard and shirt. "You've met my nephew, Lord Rabbit."

"I have?" I asked, pausing in my undressing.

"Finn," Cais replied.

"Oh," I said. I thought back to my time in Iversly. "You have other kin in service with you, don't you? In the palace and in the guard?"

"Brothers." Cais gave his dry smile. "Don't worry, my lord. We've had several centuries to learn how to keep secrets."

Thinking that Cais and family must've known some whoppers, I glanced down to see the majordomo holding out a dressing robe. *My* dressing robe, full of purples, reds and blues. I looked over by the clothespress and found three trunks pushed against the wall. While the garrison may've been in lockdown and guarded to the hilt, someone managed to liberate Jeff's, Arlie's and my footlockers. I started to ask if whoever retrieved our trunks had spoken with Suiden or Javes, but at that moment there was a tap at the door, and I turned, tensing.

"It's all right, my lord," Cais soothed. Tucking the robe around my unresisting body, he went to the door and opened it to reveal Nephew Finn with a cart—and I felt stupid with relief that it wasn't Thadro. Then I got a whiff and every thought fled.

"You have had a very busy day," Cais said as he stood aside to let Finn in. "And it occurred to me that you've not had time to eat." He closed the door and locked it again with a definite click.

My stomach gave a weary growl as Finn pushed his wonderful cart past me, hoping that finally someone would listen.

Laurel had joined Jeff at the fire and he now looked up from rummaging in his carrypouch. "Haven't eaten today?" he asked. "Rabbit, is this true?"

"I had breakfast this morning," I said, following close behind Finn. He stopped the cart by a small table with a couple of chairs. Cais joined him and they began to unload it.

"Porridge and tea," Jeff said. "Very early this morning." He frowned at me. "You didn't go to supper when Lord Commander Thadro came and got you?"

"No," I said, pulling out a chair and sitting. "I was on display and I guess Thadro felt having me stuff my face wouldn't present a good image."

"Yeah, but—" Jeff started, then pressed his lips together as if something might slip out.

"It was an oversight, my lord," Cais said. "One that we will now rectify." He lifted the lid off a tureen and stirred with a ladle, and heavenly aromas filled the room. "No meat, correct?"

That was correct. Having grown up in the Border, where forest boars greeted you with shouts of good morrow, I had different ideas on what constituted food. But I was more than happy with what was set before me—thick fish soup served with warm bread and butter that hit my stomach like a healing balm. I quickly scraped my bowl clean and Finn filled it several more times, while Jeff sat at the table with me and told me about the guards' mess. Finally full, I set my spoon down with a sigh of repletion. Murmuring thanks to Finn, I started to push my chair back. Finn, however, deftly replaced my empty soup bowl with a covered dish. "Dessert, my lord."

I shook my head, wistful. "No, thank you. I'm full—"

Finn removed the cover to reveal a slice of the magnificent cake. "I had Cook put aside a piece for you."

I relaxed back into my seat. Maybe there was room, a little corner somewhere that was crying out to be filled. I sure as hell was going to try to find it. But before I could take a bite, the cake was snatched away.

"Hey!"

Laurel put a paw on my shoulder to hold me down as he plunked a large cup in front of me. "Drink this, then you'll get your sweet."

I didn't need the fumes rising from the cup to recognize it—it was the same vile tea that Laurel had dosed me with after I'd battled the djinn storm during our voyage to the Border last spring. I glared around, seeing a kettle hanging on the fireplace hob. The Faena had been busy.

Laurel put a honey jar on the table. "The Lord Commander was right—you look like you're about to fall on your face. What happened this morning?"

Scowling, I picked up the honey jar and spooned heaping amounts into the tea. "Someone was touching me." Picking up the cup, I quickly chugged the tea down, but the bitterness still hit hard. "Poxy hell," I said, shuddering.

Laurel took the teakettle off the hob. "So you used the talent against this person? That's a little extreme, no?"

"Yeah, well, when I looked, nobody was there," I said, my scowl deepening as he poured a second cup.

Laurel stopped midpour, his amber eyes suddenly intent on mine. "Nobody was there," he repeated. "Where did this nobody touch you?"

My face heated as I remembered the forced intimacy of

the touches. "Neck, back, forehead, throat and chest," I muttered. "But I stopped him there. Broke the goat-tupping deviant's hand."

"Broke his hand," Laurel echoed.

"Well, more probably his wrist, the way I twisted it."

"His," Laurel repeated once more. "This invisible no-body was a he?"

"It felt like a man's hand," I said. "Large and sort of square." I frowned. "But it was soft and smooth, like a girl's." Thinking on the kind of man that had no calluses—even the king had some from sword work and handling the reins—my frown deepened. "Freaking pervert."

"Scholars have soft hands," Laurel said absently. "As do mages." Realizing that my cup was half full, he resumed pouring. After lacing it with honey, I swigged that too, with a shudder. Unfortunately, he refilled my cup once more, the kettle emptying with a gurgle. Scraping the rest of the honey jar into it, I drank the last of the tea—and the tiny hammers that had been beating against my forehead eased, then stopped. Not that I was going to admit it.

Laurel slid my cake back in front of me, but my attention was on his worried expression as he returned the kettle to the hearth, and I didn't pick up my fork.

"Mages?" I asked. "Why would a mage be after me?"

"Have you told anyone about this, Rabbit?" Laurel asked in return.

"Part of it," I began.

Laurel gave me a sharp look. "Why not the whole?"

"Because no one was pox-rotted interested," I said, just as sharp.

"That's true, honored Laurel," Jeff said. "When he tried to tell the Lord Commander, he was reprimanded, and His Majesty cut him off and wouldn't let him finish. Even Arlie and I didn't listen—we were kind of mad that he landed us in jail." He shrugged. "I guess everyone was more concerned about the consequences and not why he'd done it in the first place."

"I see," Laurel said. Coming back from the fireplace, he placed a paw on my forehead; checking, I supposed, for fever. "And how do you feel now, Rabbit?"

"Very tired and extremely cranky," I said, my voice still sharp as I batted his paw away. "What the hell is going on?"

"Someone tried to bind you," Laurel said, evading my hand to place his paw once more on my forehead.

Cais didn't react to Laurel's statement, but Finn, loading dishes on the cart, allowed them to tilt, dropping a knife onto the rug. It bounced a couple of times and Cais glanced down at it, then at his nephew. Turning bright red, Finn ducked down to pick the knife up.

I pulled away from Laurel's paw again to stare at him blankly. "Bind me?"

"Yes," Laurel said. "As a mage does an apprentice."

"But why?" I asked, my voice rising.

"For control. To control you."

"Against my will? People can do that?"

"Of course they can," Laurel said. "When you arrived in Elanwryfindyll, did Magus Kareste ask your permission when he and his fellows tried to bind you again?"

The memory arose of how Kareste met me with nine other mages in Loran the Fyrst's throne room—and the metallic taste that filled my mouth as they tried to slip a talent-made leash on me.

"But I was Kareste's apprentice and was bound to him once before." A sudden worry struck me. "Do you think the Magus has escaped?"

"No," Laurel said. "He's still imprisoned by the Lady, else I would know it. Whoever is trying to bind you doesn't need prior workings; he just has to be close enough to see you. It's by line of sight, the closer the better."

My eyes widened so much that I thought they were

going to fall out. Jeff looked similarly affected. "That's *all?*" I gasped. "Just give me the eye and snatch me?"

"In the Age of Legends this kind of abducting was common. It was why many of the leagues, guilds and unions came into being. As mutual protection societies." Laurel once more placed a paw on my forehead. "Societes that Iversterre does not have."

I thought on the morning in Theater Square and the crowd that had pressed about us. "But it could've been anybody," I said. "The square was full of people."

"So the invisible sorcerer was hidden among many," Laurel said. His paw sliding down from my forehead, he lifted my face and I found myself staring into his amber gaze as the warmth of his rune filled me. "Still, just as Kareste underestimated you, so did this other, and you stopped the working." His ears went back against his skull. "For now."

Ten

Laurel waited until I was tucked into bed before leaving to join Jusson's meeting. I had offered to go with him—I didn't know which motivated me more, Thadro's sarcasm or the fact that I'd been stalked by a faceless sorcerer—but Laurel refused.

"No. You can barely stand. Go to bed."

I thought I was doing a pretty good job of staying upright, though the room did seem to be swaying a bit. I didn't argue, though. Cais produced a new flannel nightshirt (despite my colorful robes, I usually slept in my smalls; to do otherwise would've invited nocturnal mischief from my troop mates) and helped me into it while Finn passed a warming pan between the sheets. However, as the major-domo gathered up my dirty clothes, I stopped him and plucked my knife and sheath from the bundle, sliding them under my pillow. Finn paused in his efforts to stare at me and I gave Cais' nephew a tired smile.

"An old habit." One that I'd developed living in close quarters with Slevoic.

"But it was your boot knife, not that big gut-ripper," Jeff remarked.

I shrugged. "Lost it at the Fyrst's court." When I'd been taken captive and placed in chains during the attempted coup by the Border High Council cabal, I had my weapons stripped from me. I got every one back except for my boot knife. That I'd last seen in the hands of a would-be assassin creeping up on the unprotected back of Loran the Fyrst. I'd stopped the assassin, but lost track of the knife, not even really thinking about it as other issues had occupied my mind. "Figured I'd get another one when we returned to Freston," I said, yawning.

Catching Cais' eye, Finn went back to his task of making sure no chill remained on the sheets. Done, he stepped back and I climbed into the bed, sinking down into the bedding and sighing at the soothing heat. I was vaguely aware of Laurel walking about my bed, leaving shimmering lines of warding in his wake. There was a murmured discussion between the Faena, Cais and Jeff, then the door opened and closed. Rolling onto my side, I felt the feather still in my braid tickle my face. I removed it, tucking it under my pillow next to my knife, and stared into the fire until the flames blurred, then went dark.

"Well, you *are* a handsome one, aren't you? Even with the braid and feather."

I was in what appeared to be a lord's council chamber. A large table with a map spread out on it took up the middle of the room, while a somewhat smaller table with what looked like a half globe of softly glowing alabaster in the center was in a corner. There were shelves neatly filled with scrolls and books, and a banner hanging on one wall, its device one I'd not seen before. On the opposite wall was a full-length mirror, though the glass was cloudy and dark. It was an unfamiliar room but I paid it scant attention as I was much more interested in who stood before me.

"Fair Rosea, or should I say Lady Alys?" I said, grinning and performing my soldier's bow, my uniform fresh and crisp.

The street player's fiery red hair seemed darker and shone with its own light. Instead of tumbling free as it had

that morning when I'd met her in Theater Square, it was up
in an elaborate concoction of braids and pearls. Her plain
skirt and blouse had been changed for a light green silk un-
derslip with a dark green overdress of velvet, tiny seed
pearls dotting the bodice. Pearls also hung from her ears
and were twisted around her neck, all shimmering in the
gentle candlelight of the council chamber. Rosea moved
nearer, her perfume light and elusive. "It is your dream, my
lord." She curtseyed, her gentle pink mouth curved in a
smile. "I am whatever you wish me to be."

Heigh-*ho*. While I supposed I'd had the typical adoles-
cent dreams of most boys, I didn't remember having one
quite so aggressively accommodating. I glanced down and
saw that instead of wearing shoes her feet were bare, her
toenails also a soft pink, a strand of pearls twined about one
ankle. I fought to get a breath into suddenly constricted
lungs. "Uh," I said.

Rising from her curtsey, Rosea laughed, stepping close
enough that I could feel the heat from her body. " 'Seize the
chance.' Isn't that the House of Chause's motto?" Her green
gaze glinted up at me. "Seize it then, Lord Rabbit ibn
Chause e Flavan."

I was already reaching for her, but my hands bumped up
against a barrier and I became aware of the lines of warding woven about me. I ran a finger along one, trying to recall why they were there.

"Oh, those." Rosea shrugged, doing interesting things to
her bodice. "They are such a bother, my lord. Perhaps if you
were to take off the feather, they would go away."

Feather?

"In your braid, my lord."

Oh. That feather. My hand went to it—and jerked away
again as my hand started to tingle. Looking down, I saw
that the markings on my palm were alight just like the lines.

"My lord."

Blinking, I looked up again. And caught the flash of something in Rosea's hand. I shifted, trying to see it more clearly, but she moved, blocking my view.

"The feather, my lord," Rosea insisted. "Remove it and we can be together. Always." She pressed closer to the bright lines, her green eyes seeming to glow, and my thoughts slowed, my hand lifting to my feather. Then I became conscious of a distant roaring. I hesitated, listening.

"Don't stop, my lord," Rosea said urgently. "If you don't do it now, all will be lost. You will lose *me*."

The roaring was like the ocean during a storm. A howling, shore-pounding, shipwrecking storm that was fast approaching. I started to turn to look.

"No!" Rage flashed across Rosea's face and she tried to reach through the warding lines. She snatched her hand back, though, as if burned. She then leaned forward, and I could feel her breath through the lines, warm and sweet on my face. "Hurry, my lord. Remove the feather—!"

There was a short scream as the sea broke over us and I was swept from the council room. Pulled under the storm-driven waves, I fought to reach the surface, twisting and turning as my chest burned, but the sea pressed me down, down, down.

Not winter yet.

I sat up in bed gasping, my flannel nightshirt soaked. I stared down at it, straining to see in the dark, but caught only the scent of my own sweat. Not seawater then. Bringing my knees up, I rested my forehead against them, taking deep breaths as I waited for my heart to calm down.

"Rabbit?" Jeff asked.

"Yeah," I said. The nightshirt was clammy against my skin. I thrust back the covers and started to get out—and came face-to-face with Laurel's warding lines. I paused, deciding that I didn't want to go beyond their set boundary.

"Are you all right?"

Other than a very realistic nightmare about drowning, I was fine. "Yeah," I said again. Kneeling on the bed, I pulled off my sweat-soaked nightshirt and tossed it at the foot of the bed. "Just some strange dreams." Underneath my knees I could feel that the bedding was also damp. Waiting a moment for my body to dry some in the tepid air, I then crawled across the bed to the other side, sliding down under the covers, shivering a bit at the cold sheets against my bare skin.

"Oh," Jeff said. "Well, I guess that's not surprising, considering everything."

"Yeah," I said a third time, profound in the small hours of the morning. I realized that I wasn't hearing any other nighttime noises. "Where's everyone?" I asked.

I could hear Jeff shift and, by the faint light from the fireplace, I could just make out two trundle beds, one of which looked empty. "Laurel's with Thadro," Jeff said.

"Still?" I asked. I gave a sudden yawn, the sheets warming up from my body heat. "That's one long meeting."

"There wasn't any meeting," Jeff said. "Wyln and Arlie didn't show. Laurel and the Lord Commander are out looking for them."

I choked midyawn, sitting straight up. "What?"

"Thadro did stop by here first to take you with him," Jeff said, "but you were out like a snuffed candle and Laurel said Thadro mustn't disturb the warding lines around your bed."

"Laurel said— He didn't stop the commander, did he?" I asked, worried.

"No," Jeff said with a soft laugh. "Cais did."

"Cais," I repeated. I flopped back against my pillows, wishing I'd been awake to see.

"The majordomo was very polite," Jeff said. He shifted on his bed again. "Weird stuff is happening, and not just Menck's murder."

"Well, that's weird enough," I began.

"Yeah, but with all that he had been involved in, it's surprising that he hadn't been skinned, gutted and left hanging in the town square before now," Jeff said.

That was true. Even the garrison commander had complained to the town elders about how soldiers who'd become a little too merry while in the town were waking up in jail plucked like chickens. "Mayor Gawell protected him," I said.

"There's protecting," Jeff said, "and there's aiding and abetting. And it wasn't just shaking down people in jail. One of the serving lasses at the Hart's Leap told me that Menck used to pester the girls there something fierce. They complained to the innkeeper, who barred Menck from coming in. Then the innkeeper's son was set upon and beaten. The lass said that Menck swaggered into the Hart the following day. The innkeeper didn't stop him."

I recalled the son's beating—and the rumors that it was because of a gambling debt owed to one of the garrison's soldiers. "Commander Ebner got all worked up about that," I said. "Told Gawell that all his men were accounted for, and for Gawell to look to his own House."

"And Ebner was right," Jeff said. He sat up and clasped his arms loosely around his knees. "But don't you see? It was Mayor Gawell who came to see Ebner, not Chadde. Why would the mayor be involved in that? That's Chadde's job."

"Hell," I said, as I remembered both Gawell's and Ednoth's annoyance at Menck's murder—and the look Chadde had given them as they walked out of the charnel house. I pulled the covers up to my chin, their weight comforting.

"Now Chadde is keeping stuff from the mayor," Jeff said. "And Thadro let her get away with it. Just as he let

Cais gainsay him over you, even though he treats you like you're something he scraped off the bottom of his boots."

"I noticed," I said. "But I'm more worried about Wyln being missing. Ebner had him locked up and under guard, Jeff. That's bad enough. But what if he got out and went to look for me? I'm not at the same place I was yesterday." I thought about the powerful dark elf enchanter—angry, offended and maybe worried, crossing paths with the same riotous people who greeted me when I got out of jail. My spine tightened. "And where's Arlie? Is he with Wyln? If so, why hasn't he brought Wyln here?"

"I wouldn't worry about Arlis," Jeff said, his voice a little distant. "I'm sure he's fine wherever he is, whoever he's with—"

The bedroom door suddenly opened and the majordomo walked in, carrying a tray. "I heard you talking," Cais said, shutting the door behind him before going to the small table, a candle on the tray lighting the way. "Master Laurel left instructions if you were to awaken."

As he came closer, I could see the teapot on the tray and I slid further down in the covers. "Laurel said the wardings aren't to be disturbed," I tried.

"Master Laurel assured me that a teacup will fit between the lines," Cais said, pouring the tea. "After which you are to go back to sleep, my lord."

The cup did fit easily through the wardings, though I could've sworn the lines shifted to make room. The majordomo stood over me until the last bitter drop. He then somehow got my nightshirt through the wards and, taking the tray and candle with him, murmured a very pointed goodnight as he firmly shut the door, leaving us once more in the dark.

There was a moment of silence, then Jeff gave another soft laugh. "Lord Commanders and now us. Sort of makes you wonder who's the servant and who's the master." He settled down in his bed. "I guess we better do as he said. Goodnight."

"Goodnight," I echoed. I could feel the tea at work within me, once more easing the pains and aches that had awakened with me from my nightmare. However, though Jeff's soft snores soon filled the room, I lay on my back staring up towards the ceiling, where I could see Laurel's warding lines of earth crisscrossing above me. I touched one where it came down at the side of the bed—and smelled sweet grass and earth that took me back to my days of plowing fields on my parents' farm. My dream was now in fragments, a jumble of Rosea, waves and a voice booming that it wasn't winter yet, all of it nonsense. Figuring that Jeff had been right in that it wasn't surprising that I had weird dreams, I still slid one hand under my pillow to find my feather. Then, turning on my side, I curled my other hand about a warding line. Watching the line glow through my fingers, my eyelids drooped until I slipped into sleep once more, the feather clasped to my chest.

This time I did not dream.

Eleven

"Two Trees'son."

My eyes cracked open, noting the predawn gloom. I closed them again—wake up hadn't sounded yet and I was going to sleep until the sergeants yelled me out of bed.

"Two Trees'son."

That did not sound like any sergeant I knew. My eyes opened once more and, rolling on my back, I rose up on my elbows to look around. The memory of the previous day's events flooded back and I blinked sleepily at Jeff, sprawled in his trundle bed. The voice, though familiar, hadn't sounded like him either. Besides, he was still snoring. I started to lie down again, figuring that I'd been hearing things in my sleep.

"Two Trees'son."

I paused midsnuggle to stare at the fireplace. It was full of fire even though last night's fuel was gray ash. Seeing that they had my attention, the flames started leaping up the chimney.

"By the Lady, Two Trees'son, will you get over here?"

Pushing back my covers, I sat up and looked at the wardings. But even as I considered how to get past them, and if I really wanted to, they shimmered brightly before coalescing into a slowly spinning sphere of swirling browns and

greens. It bobbed after me as I stumbled over to the fireplace.

"Honored *Cyhn*?" I asked, trying to make out a face in
the fire. However, I saw nothing but flames.

"You are *not* your best in the morning," Wyln said.

"Yesterday was eventful, honored *Cyhn*," I said. My
braid was half undone and I pushed my hair out of my eyes.
As I did, something brushed my face and I looked down at
my hand to see that I still clasped my feather.

"So it was," Wyln said. "I need you here, Two Trees'son."

"'Here'?" I asked. "Where's here?" I crossed my arms,
hugging myself. The room was cold. "Everyone's looking
for you, honored *Cyhn*."

"Are they?" Wyln sounded amused. A tendril of flame
shot out, forming into its own sphere that hovered in front
of me. "This will bring you. Quickly, Two Trees'son." The
fire started to die down. "And put some clothes on."

"Wait," I began. But the fire winked out, leaving the gray
ashes on the hearth.

"More oddities," Jeff said behind me, his voice thick
with sleep.

"That was Wyln," I said. "He wants me to join him."

Jeff sat up, scrubbing his hair and yawning. "Are you?"

"Have to," I said, looking around for my robe. I found it
hanging in the clothespress with the rest of my clothes and
I slipped it on. "An elder has summoned." There were stories of those who refused to obey their *cyhn*—and the dire
things that happened to them, from banishments to behead-
ings. Great stuff for bards' songs but I'd no desire to be
known through the ages as Rabbit Lackhead.

"Huh." Jeff stood and stretched, rising on his toes, yawning again. "You're going to tell Thadro?"

Damn and blast. I blinked at Jeff, my early morning
grogginess clearing fast. The Lord Commander had made
it very clear yesterday that I wasn't to scratch without

permission. I didn't think he'd wink at me taking off without his say-so. Or let me go even if I did ask.

"Wyln's still out there, so Thadro's probably not back yet," I said, hoping furiously.

"Probably not," Jeff said. He went over to his footlocker and began sorting through it. "So, you're going to tell His Majesty?"

Jusson, though, was very much at home, and not only would he be less happy than Thadro about me disappearing to join Wyln, but kings were even more liberal with a headsman's axe. "Maybe I can go and come back before Jusson misses us," I said.

"Think so?" Holding fresh clothes, Jeff straightened and cast an expert glance at the light leaking around the curtains. "Then you better leave now before everyone else gets up."

Sheep-biting, fornicating weasels. I ran my hands over my face again, once more brushing the feather against it. I stared at it a moment, then at the fireball waiting patiently beside the earth sphere. I thrust the feather into my robe pocket. "I'll tell Thadro if he's around, or Jusson if he's not."

Jeff nodded. "And if they say no?"

"Then I'll have to convince them otherwise," I said, ignoring the hollowness in my gut. I walked over to the washstand and poured water into the bowl from the ewer. I then realized what Jeff was doing. "You don't have to go."

"Yes, I do." Jeff carried his clothes to his bed, dropping them on the tumbled bedclothes. Shucking yesterday's smalls, he quickly began to dress. "I'm not explaining to either Thadro or His Majesty how I was ready to let you go off on your own." He glanced at the window again, the light around the curtains brighter. "If you wait any longer, Finn will be here to help you with your drawers."

With a couple of suggestions of what Jeff could do with

said drawers, I too began to dress. In a very short time we were buckling on sword belts and tucking knives away. Though Cais had taken my Habbs the night before, I still had my standard-issue boots—which was just as well as I didn't know what I would be wading through if I met up with Wyln.

No, not if. When.

Attaching the feather to my reworked braid, I took my cloak and gloves from the clothespress, putting them on before grabbing my staff. "Ready?" I asked.

Jeff nodded and, taking a deep breath, I opened the door. To my surprise, Thadro had managed to scrounge up a couple of King's Own to guard me during my slumbers. Both jumped to attention as I walked out. I returned their salutes before taking off down the hall to the king's chamber, where the same thing happened, one flinging the door open without inquiring first to see if I were to be admitted. Just like I'd been expected. I paused at the threshold, suddenly wary.

"Come in, cousin," Jusson said.

I was starting to dislike that phrase. I walked in and found myself in a sitting room with doorways leading off to side chambers. Through one opening I could see a narrow bed, where I assumed either Thadro or Cais slept to be close at hand for the king. It didn't look as though it had been used as the covers were still neatly made. But then, so was the bedding on the massive four-poster that I glimpsed through another door. A wall hanging with the royal crest was over the bed's headboard.

Jusson, fully dressed, sat at a table where he'd apparently just finished eating breakfast, with Cais at his shoulder, ready to replenish an empty cup at a moment's notice. Both looked fresh, as if they'd had a full night's rest after a week of holiday, while I, with my interrupted night, felt rather brown around the edges. "Don't either of you ever *sleep*, sire?" I asked.

"On occasion," Jusson said. He pointed at a chair. "Sit."

"Yes, sire," I said, trying not to fidget. "However, there's this errand I have to run—"

"We will go see this elusive elf together, cousin. After you eat."

My fidgets disappeared. "You know?"

"Magic—no, talent you call it, right?" Jusson waved a hand, encompassing the fire and earth spheres floating over each of my shoulders. "Whatever, it was worked in my house. Of course I know."

There was no "of course" about it. I knew that Jusson was able to detect the use of the talent around him. But that wouldn't have allowed him to overhear my conversation with Wyln—unless he was eavesdropping on *me*. Just as Laurel had the night before. Feeling as private as a public highway, I held off yielding my cloak and gloves to Cais. "Beg pardon, Your Majesty, but Wyln said that I was to hurry."

"Did he? Well, I'm disinclined to bustle about for someone who has no problem keeping *me* waiting." The king once more pointed. "Sit, Rabbit." He glanced behind me at Jeff. "You too, Guardsman. As your lieutenant is in a hurry, we won't have time for you to eat in the guards' mess."

"Your Majesty," Jeff said, his eyes wide. "It's not proper."

"I won't tell if you won't." Jusson's brow rose at me. "Cousin?"

We sat, Jeff gingerly, as if his chair (and the world) might collapse under him. I scowled as the majordomo produced a steaming pot of Laurel's brew. Just for me. I used the whole honey jar to sweeten the tea, drinking it between bites of warm rolls with butter, fruit, porridge, and poached eggs with cheese, all served by Cais. Despite last night's late meal, the food set before me disappeared fast, with Cais slipping me a second, and then a third helping. Finally having enough, I set my fork down with a sigh. I felt much better, which was surprising since I hadn't known that I had been feeling bad. That hollow feeling in my gut had been more than worry, for now that I was full, it was mostly gone.

Smiling, Jusson pushed back his chair and stood. "Very good, cousin. Let's go see my lord elf."

My gut tightened again.

Leaving the table, I remember the long stretch between meals yesterday and nicked some fruit and rolls, putting them in my pocket. Then, wrapped up against the early morning elements, Jeff and I followed Jusson out the room. Out in the hallway, Jusson had shed the night guards but had picked up several daytime ones, none of whom looked surprised at the king going traveling—though I did catch a couple of side glances at the spheres floating next to me. Cais had followed us downstairs and whipped around to open the front door to bow us out. Reaching the street, I looked down it to see if the horses were coming.

"We're not riding, cousin," Jusson said. "It's such a fine day that we will walk." He glanced at the blazing sphere. "Which way?"

I also looked at the fireball and it darted off down the street. "Uhm, that way, Your Majesty."

It *was* a fine day. The mountains were waking up in the early morning sun, the brightening sky once more promising to be that crisp fall blue. And while the chill of the night still lingered, more than enough warmth was generated by the brisk pace Jusson set. There were no complaints, though. It felt good to stretch my legs and apparently the guards thought so too. There was an easy looseness about their movements, their eyes bright as they looked about them. Even Jusson was enjoying himself, his cheeks slightly flushed, his own black eyes sparkling. Just another king out for his morning constitutional. For the most part we had the streets to ourselves, though we did encounter the occasional early riser, most with baskets on their arms, heading for market. They sleepily glanced at us as we approached, then their heads snapped back around as they realized that King Jusson IV, surrounded by his royal guard, was striding towards them following after a ball of flame. Hasty curtseys were dropped and bows made as we went past, heads respectfully lowered. However I did get upward glances, eyes wide as they took in my braid, feather and staff before shifting to the earth sphere that remained floating at my shoulder. More than one blessed themselves.

The fire sphere bypassed the town square and skirted around both the market and Theater Squares, before entering into a less affluent section. Tiny as it was, Freston—like most cities and towns, I supposed—had parts where those afflicted by poverty, vice, laziness or just monumental bad fortune subsisted. The streets turned first a little shabby, then neglected and finally derelict. We went by alleyways piled with rubbish, broken streetlamps, broken railings and missing roof tiles. And, except for the skittering of four-legged animals, the streets were completely empty, though I did notice flickers in windows and cracked doors. We were being watched, and our hands went to our swords, all easiness gone.

However, we continued unmolested and we soon came to the southeast edge of Freston. The town's wall rose over us and we could see the different colors where the old Eastgate had been bricked up. "I noticed that when I arrived here," Jusson said, staring up at the two-tone stones. "Why was it closed?"

"I don't know, Your Majesty," I said. "It was done before I came here." I glanced at Jeff, but he shook his head—he didn't know either. The rundown houses had given way to boarded-up shops and padlocked warehouses, and I shifted my gaze to them. "But from what everyone says, this used to be a busy place."

Remnants of the section's former glory remained in the broad streets and large buildings, including the old posting inn—which had smoke rising from its several chimneys and its gates open, its yard neat and clean. Startled, I turned my head to stare—the last I knew, it too had been boarded up— but at that moment the fire sphere made an abrupt turn down a smaller street, plunging us into the shadow of the town's wall. We worked our way through the abandoned commercial district in a series of twists and turns that brought us to what looked like a derelict warehouse. The sphere darted over the gated wall and we all came to a halt.

"A strange place for lord elf to fetch up in," Jusson said, his brow creased.

"Yes, Your Majesty," I agreed as I eyed the cracked and crumbling wall, before lifting my gaze to the building that hulked beyond. "Very strange."

"Well, we can stand out here and speculate or go in and find out." Jusson reached out his hand—and as one all the guards moved in front of him. "Oh, all right." He waved at the gate. "Open it."

The gate opened easily. Too easily. Instead of the screech of neglected hinges, it swung silently into a still, dark yard. Someone had been busy with a grease rag.

"Bones and bloody ashes," Jeff murmured.

Profoundly glad that Wyln's summons hadn't come at night, I peered beyond the gate and saw the fire sphere, a bright spot in the gloom. It must've seen us too, for it darted off again. A couple of King's Own entered the courtyard first, followed by Jusson and me, Jeff and the rest of the guards on our heels. We had to step carefully—weeds sprouted up through the paving stones, hiding chunks of the wall that had fallen out, broken glass and other debris. The sphere crossed the yard to the warehouse and once more waited. That door also opened silently and we stared into a cavernous space with columns pacing down it, their tops disappearing in the murk that hid the ceiling. There were high horizontal windows, but scant light came through the grime-encrusted panes. What illumination there was came from the open door and from the fire sphere hovering just inside, which darted away again, this time into the interior. Without thought, my hand came up and formed its own fireball, and it immediately rose to hover next to the earth sphere, casting our shadows before us.

"Two Trees'son," a voice called out.

We shifted en masse to see the first fireball, a bright spark in the middle of the warehouse, and we carefully walked towards it, our boot steps echoing. But though the outside was a study in disrepair, the inside floor was clear, free of dust and any other signs of disuse. My unease increased—if I had Laurel's tail, it would've been lashing.

A slender figure emerged from the gloom as we drew nearer, his back to us as he looked down at the floor. We slowed, stopping a short distance away as we also looked. The darkness in the rest of the building seemed the usual reaction to the absence of light. However, there— I leaned forward trying to see, while my boots remained firmly planted, going no further. While both fire spheres cast enough light to see the faint cracking in the floor around us, I couldn't see where the person stood at all. And what I could see looked ragged—as if the dark had been folded over on itself again and again, and held there until something burst out of it, leaving it lying about in tatters like a pile of ripped and torn clothes.

"Don't worry, it's safe." The figure turned, both fire spheres illuminating his features. "For now."

There wasn't anything as dramatic as a collective gasp,

but a stillness came over everyone, including Jusson, as they stared. The dark elf smiled and the stillness grew.

"I give you good day, Jusson Iver'son. I am the Enchanter Wyln."

Twelve

Like Laurel, Wyln looked as he had when I last saw him. He did have flames leaping in his eyes, but that just denoted his aspect—fire. However, it wasn't the flames that had the royal contingent staring in shock. As Jusson had once told me, he knew that he had elfin blood. I supposed, though, that he'd never expected to have it so emphatically confirmed. For though he and Wyln weren't exactly twins—Wyln's cheekbones were a shade sharper, his chin a tad pointier, and his hair much longer—they looked enough alike to be brothers.

Or, more accurately, uncle and nephew. A very much great uncle and his many-times-grandnephew, true, but still related by blood. And elves were very big on blood ties, as they proved by glomming onto me with my sixty-four lines to the throne of a dark elf king.

Jusson quickly recovered his wits, which may've been because royalty learned very early not to stand about slack-jawed, though I suspected it was more because of Wyln's air of amusement. "Grace to you, Lord Wyln," the king said. "I—" He stopped again, and for the first time ever I saw him at a loss for words.

I shifted closer to Jusson, the guards moving with me. "Sire?" I asked, worried.

Shaking his head, Jusson tore his gaze from the enchanter only to have it fall back to the floor. "What *is* this?"

"Remnants, Jusson Iver'son," Wyln said, his light voice lilting. "Something was worked here. Something very dark, very wicked."

"Something," Jusson repeated.

"We'll have to discover exactly what," Wyln said. "Which is why I brought Two Trees'son here."

At Wyln's words, I forgot about Jusson's fumbling and blinked at the enchanter. "Honored *Cyhn*?"

Wyln smiled gently at me, the flames in his eyes bright in the cavernous murk. "It is a learning opportunity, Two Trees'son. A chance for you to gain knowledge and experience."

If it meant getting close and personal with what was on the floor, I would've just as soon remained ignorant. I took a step back, now worrying about myself. "Maybe we should send for Laurel—"

"Good, you've found it," Laurel said from behind us. "And you've brought Rabbit."

We all turned to see Laurel come through the open door into the warehouse, followed by Thadro and more royal guards, including Arlis. Laurel and Thadro hurried to join us, the Lord Commander going to stand behind Jusson while the guards swelled the ranks of their fellows. Thadro glanced over Jusson's shoulder at the raggedy dark, then shot me a glare, apparently for letting His Majesty get near it. I, though, paid little attention to the Lord Commander's silent carping as I was fixed on Laurel heading towards me, the Faena's rune bright enough to cast shadows.

What the hell?

I took another step back, this time away from Laurel. That, however, took me closer to Wyln, and a slender hand with a grip of steel closed over my arm. I jerked my head around to meet the enchanter's gaze, the flames in his eyes even more intense. I stared, fascinated for a moment, then drew my head back, shaking it. At that moment, Laurel's paw closed over my other arm, his claws pressing through my clothes into flesh. My staff was taken from me and given to a startled Jeff, and they lifted me up. I started to fight in earnest, reaching for the wind, water, anything to stop them. But all the aspects slid through my fingers like sand, even the fire and earth spheres drifting away, as if they were watching me from a distance. Desperate, I even tried for more mundane weapons, but I couldn't get to my sword or dagger.

Others could, though. I heard the sound of steel against leather as swords were drawn. "You will put him down, now," Jusson said, his voice soft as he held the edge of his sword against Wyln's neck.

Wyln ignored both king and sword as he and Laurel deposited me on the ragged edge of the dark; however, Laurel looked over at Jusson. "*Dauthiwaesp* was worked here, honored king, involving the killing of the unfortunate jailer."

"So you've told us all about it last night. What has it to do with our cousin?"

Keeping one paw clamped on me, Laurel shoved his staff into the crook of his arm. "The how was answered last night with the finding of the unfortunate's body, the where was answered this morning with the finding of this place. The questions now are what and why?"

"I don't care if you have the question to the answer of life," Jusson said. "You will release Rabbit—*Holy God and His saints!*"

There was a clatter of dropped swords falling on the stone floor as Laurel lifted his paw, the rune on his middle pad brighter than the noon sun, my own rune growing hot in response. Laurel *touched* the rune against my forehead and I was blinded by a white flash. Crying out, I closed my eyes against the excruciating light, hanging suspended between two breaths. Then the pain eased and I cracked open my eyes, blinking away tears.

The warehouse was gone. I stood in the middle of grassland, stretching out in every direction as far as I could see. It was spring, the grass not yet having the height and sturdiness of summer, nor the rich, rustling gold of fall. The sun shone overhead in a cloudless blue sky that went forever, the wind a soft movement over the plains that reminded me of waves over the sea. A hint of a memory arose of another sea, angry and dark, and I frowned trying to recall.

"It is a metaphor, Rabbit," Laurel said. "Not a true seeing."

I spun around, my hand going to my sword—or at least where my sword should've been. I glanced down and saw I wore a hodgepodge of clothing: soldier's boots and trousers, and a farmer's smock with the device of Chause on one sleeve cuff and Flavan's on the other. Over that was a mage's robe that bore the king's device, and a silver chain and medallion hung on my chest with the crescent moon and three stars of the Fyrst's line. The wind blew gently around me and I felt the feather flutter against my cheek.

"What is a metaphor?" I asked, looking back up at Laurel.

"This," Laurel said. "Here." He parted the grass with his staff to reveal the ground. He then shaded his eyes with his paw, and I could see his rune, still white, but in the sunshine its brightness was bearable. As I was barehanded, I could see that my rune was also white, but its heat had calmed down into a warmth that echoed the sun across my shoulders.

"And where is here?" I asked.

Laurel, with his eyes still shaded, slowly circled, looking in every direction. "Depending upon the school of thought, your soul, your spirit, your heart"—a brief smile swept back his whiskers—"or your liver."

"This is my soul?" I asked.

Laurel faced me once more and dropped his paw. "As I said, a metaphor. Next time, it could be perceived differently."

"Next time!" My brows snapped together. "What do you mean, next time?"

"Is it well, Laurel Faena?"

My head jerked around to see Wyln standing opposite Laurel. But while the mountain cat was solidly present, the elf enchanter was somewhat translucent. Beyond him, looking even less solid, was King Jusson with his sword drawn—apparently he hadn't dropped it when Laurel lifted the rune. Next to the king was Thadro, which was no surprise, but on the other side of Jusson was a dim outline of what looked like his majordomo, Cais. And beyond them all was a very pale shadow of Jeff, still holding my ash staff. Jeff stared at me, his eyes wide. Then again, Jusson and Thadro looked astonished too, Jusson's eyes round.

"It is well," Laurel said. "See for yourself."

Wyln stooped down and also prodded at the grass. He then stood and also did a slow circle, searching. Jusson watched the elf a moment before scanning the horizon himself. "What are you looking for?" Though the king's presence was weak, his voice was strong, resonating in me.

"Something was worked with the unfortunate jailer's death, honored king," Laurel said. "We just want to make sure that the working did not make its way here."

"Here?" I asked. "In me?" A gust of wind ripped across the grass.

"You've already been attacked once," Laurel said, watching the grass, his ears pressed forward.

"But that was before Menck's death."

"There is no law that says that you can't be attacked again."

That was true. Another memory arose and I frowned at

Laurel. "Is that why you had your paws all over me last night? You were looking for evidence of sorcery?"

"Wyln and I felt the working, and after your telling last night I was concerned that—something—might have attached itself to you in spite of your efforts."

The gusts became stronger. "Did you find this something?" I asked.

"No, but these workings can be extremely crafty," Laurel said. "We had to make sure that I didn't miss anything."

"And you did that by jumping me?" The gusts became steady, the wind whistling over the plains.

"By surprise, Rabbit, without giving whatever it may be a chance to hide, at the place where it had been worked, to see if you had any affinity to the remnants left behind."

I glanced at the tossing grass. "You thought that you'd find the same muck that's on the floor in here? In *me?*"

"We had to make sure," Laurel said again, his feathers blowing about his head, his beads swinging in the rising wind. "Whatever was done was big, Rabbit. More powerful than anything I'd ever known."

"I had once experienced something that strong," Wyln said, still searching. "A summoning of a Damned One. It took five adepts a week of preparation and they still lost control of it. It killed them, destroyed their temple and laid waste to their city."

"And where were you when you experienced this demon, Lord Wyln?" Jusson asked, his eyes narrowing.

"With the High King of Morendyll and his army, ready to lay waste to the city ourselves," Wyln replied. "It took ten enchanters working two days and nights to banish the Damned One again, Iver'son. By then it had expanded beyond what was left of the city. We called it Ujan's bane, Ujan being the prince we were warring against."

Jusson worked on that a moment. "You mean, the Jaban Waste?"

"Is that what it's called now?" Wyln asked. Finished examining my soul, he faced the king. "It was a vibrant place once, the middle of a very fertile valley."

"It's blighted land," Jusson said. "Nothing grows there but what's twisted and stunted. That's from a demon?"

"And from an idiot for a prince who had his equally idiotic adepts summon it in the first place," Wyln said. He turned to me, his hair whipping about his face in the wind. "I'd always intensely disliked it when my *cyhn* told me something painful or unpleasant was for my own good, Two Trees'son. But Laurel is right, we had to make sure. With both your strength and inexperience, you are very attractive to those who, like Magus Kareste, hunger after those who are—how did you once say? Young and seasoned with talent."

Any other time I would've been stunned by Wyln's near apology, but now I was more focused on other issues. "What would've you done if you'd found anything amiss?" I asked.

"Remedied the situation."

The flash of temper at my manhandling was slowly dissipating, but anger was building in its place at thought of my soul taken and used as a battleground. Dark clouds started to fill the sky. "But there's nothing here. Except me." I frowned. "And you, Laurel, Jusson, Thadro, Jeff and what looks like Cais." The massive thunderheads quickly reached the sun, boiling across it.

"They were caught in the backwash," Laurel said, tracking the storm.

"Oaths and vows," Wyln added obscurely. He again glanced at Jusson, with the Lord Commander and the outline of the majordomo. "But Two Trees'son is right. We should go. We've found out what we needed to—"

I didn't wait for Wyln to finish. A boom of thunder cut across the enchanter's words and everyone winked out, their footprints in the grass obliterated by the wind. Mine, and I'd be bloody damned if I'd share. Not with any sorcerer, not with my king and my teachers in the talent, not even with my best mate. I did my own circuit, though, just to make sure that I was alone.

"Rabbit," Laurel said.

Finished circling, I stooped down and parted the grass, touching the earth. And was surprised at the awareness that rushed back. But it was just me and nothing else. With a small sigh of relief, I straightened—and caught the flash of gray eyes. Startled, I met Peacekeeper Chadde's equally surprised gaze. Lightning forked, splitting the sky, and the wind howled, snatching my hair from its braid as my lips pulled back in a snarl. Then I realized that Chadde wasn't trespassing. She was in the street outside the warehouse, several of the town Watch with her.

"Rabbit," Laurel said, more insistent.

The sun had risen above the mountains and, though I was shrouded in storm clouds, I shaded my eyes against its brightness. Rising on the buffeting wind, I could see over the rooftops: residential red, blue for commerce, the yellow tiles of the playhouse, the gold of the town hall and other municipal buildings, all towered over by the crystal-and-silver spire of the church. And across town at the Westgate, I saw the faded purple of the garrison. Freston looked as it ought, with more of its people setting out to the just-opening shops and other businesses, traffic pouring through the town's gates to rumble through the streets—and no signs of *dauthiwaesp* anywhere. The church bells started to toll the hour, competing with a street vendor's song about his wares. Looking back at the peacekeeper, I saw that she had come closer, her eyes wide.

"Rabbit!" A paw slapped my face and my eyes flew opened to find myself back inside the warehouse, still held between Laurel and Wyln. I immediately got my feet under

me and pulled away. Taking my ash staff from Jeff, I
straightened my cloak and tabard, then lifted my head to
glare at all of them.

"We have company," I said.

Thirteen

"I received a report of suspicious-looking people lurking near the old Eastgate," Chadde said, "and when I came, I saw the gate here was open."

At my announcement, Thadro had sent several of the Own outside to retrieve the Keeper of the King's Peace. But they didn't have to go far as Chadde and her men were already crossing the yard. At Jusson's direction, the Watch were sent back to the street to guard the warehouse's gate. Chadde, however, was escorted in—and almost immediately had her gaze snagged by the pile of darkness on the floor.

Jusson gave a sharp smile at the peacekeeper's statement. "What a lively sense of humor the townspeople here have."

Chadde looked up, her gray eyes gleaming. "Yes, Your Majesty. I've often remarked on it." She continued her scan of the building's interior, her gaze now lighting on me. I stared back, stone-faced.

"I thought you were going out to the tavern this morning, honored peacekeeper," Laurel said. "To look for witnesses to the dumping of the unfortunate's body."

"I am, Master Laurel," Chadde said. "Later. The patrons of the Copper Pig are generally unconscious until almost midday. I have, however, been to Menck's house to speak with his wife." Her gaze moved to Wyln, and a line appeared between her brows. Wyln smiled back.

"What did she say?" Jusson asked.

"That she didn't know who killed him or why, Your Majesty," Chadde replied.

"Do you believe her?"

"Not usually," Chadde said, "but in this instance I do, given the way her husband died." Her eyes drifted once more to the dark. "If I may ask, Your Majesty, what *is* that?"

"According to Master Cat and Lord Wyln, it's where the head jailer was killed," Jusson said.

"It is?" Chadde walked over to the ragged edge and squatted down. "This was caused by Menck's death?"

"Remnants of the spell, honored peacekeeper," Laurel said, joining the peacekeeper.

"Death magic done in my town," Chadde said, frowning.

"In *my* town," Jusson said. He and Thadro also joined Chadde and Laurel to stare down at the mess on the floor. "In my kingdom. Against my people."

"Yes, Your Majesty," Chadde said. "Menck's wife did say that when he usually went out, he was careful to be with his friends."

"So as to not be caught alone?" Jusson asked. "This rogue was the head jailer?"

"The mayor's kinsman, Your Majesty," Thadro said.

"I remember," Jusson said. "Go on, Peacekeeper Chadde. You said usually. Did he meet with his fellow scoundrels this last time?"

"No, Your Majesty," Chadde said. "His wife said he went out by himself yesterday evening—after he changed into his best shirt. She said that he only did that when he was meeting Gawell or going to the Hart's Leap. And Gawell has already told me that he hadn't seen him last night."

Thinking on Chadde's misdirection at the charnel house last night, I wondered if she also believed his honor the mayor. Then I remembered what Jeff had told me about the lecherous jailer and the inn. I must've twitched for everyone turned to look at me.

"Yes, cousin?" Jusson asked.

"Do you think he was lured here, Peacekeeper Chadde?" I asked, my voice cool.

"It seems probable, my lord," Chadde said. "Why else leave behind his friends? Given Menck's interests, if it were anything else, he would've wanted a show of force *and* the extra protection." The peacekeeper shook her head as she stood. "It must've been a surprise when he discovered what was waiting for him."

"A surprise indeed," Jusson said. "What shall be done about this? We can't leave it here for the unwary to stumble upon." A thought occurred to him and his brows snapped together. "Can it be used to work more sorcery?"

"Not without the proper rituals, Iver'son," Wyln said. "And those can be performed anywhere." He had been standing a little apart, but he now joined the klatch at the darkness. "However, you are right, this should not be allowed to remain as it would become an attraction for other unwholesomeness."

I had a sudden image of dark wisps and threads slipping along the cracks and crevices of Freston to congregate here. A shiver coursed down my back.

"And so become a sinkhole full of corruption," Jusson said, echoing my thoughts. "Well, I've no desire for this to become known as Jusson's Bane. How do we get rid of it?"

Laurel had been examining the high windows and now, at the king's question, he beckoned to Arlie, standing next to Thadro—who stayed put. I frowned. "Arlis," I began.

"See to the Faena, Guardsman Arlis," Thadro said over me.

Saluting Thadro, Arlie went over to Laurel, who immediately sent him out of the warehouse. However, he quickly returned and handed Laurel a large chunk of the yard's wall. After moving everyone back, Laurel hefted it a couple of times, then threw it at one of the windows. The stone shattered the glass, the grimy pieces falling onto the floor with a tinkling crash, and sunlight flooded the interior. The patch of dark roiled before disappearing in a puff of oily smoke, leaving a round, shallow pan sitting on the floor. It was a plain, everyday one—my ma had several like it that she used to bake pies—filled to the brim with clear water that lay placid in the light.

"Water aspect," Wyln said.

"Yes," Laurel agreed. "The unfortunate's wounds were frozen."

There was nothing overtly wrong about either the pan or the water, but as Laurel and Wyln talked, I found myself backing up, stopping only as I bumped into Jeff standing behind me.

"It is the twisting of the aspect that you're feeling Two Trees'son," Wyln said. "Ujan's adepts used fire for their summoning. I'd been close enough to feel it and it was like a razor against my heart."

I looked away from the reflecting water, about to say that I hadn't felt anything—not the working, not even Menck's ritual murder—when I became aware of Chadde's interested gaze. I kept silent.

"Earth or fire?" Laurel asked Wyln.

"Fire," Wyln decided. "It will cleanse." He held out his hand and his fire sphere flew into it. "Like this, Two Trees'son."

Remembering how my sphere had stood off from me, I wondered if it would come at my call. However, when I pulled off my glove and held out my own hand, the sphere immediately flitted to my palm.

"On my mark, throw it on the pan," Wyln said. He lifted his hand, counting, and at three we both flung the spheres down on the water. It boiled and hissed before also disap-

pearing in a puff—this time of white steam. The flames followed the steam up in a column of fire until all was consumed. Then the flames flowed down upon the pan and the
surrounding floor, where they burned yellow with flickers
of white. After a few moments, the flames divided into two
spheres once more, leaving behind a melted puddle of
metal.

"That's it?" Jusson gave a short laugh. "I expected something a little more complicated, with elaborate words,
smells and sounds. Not breaking a window and saying 'one,
two, three.' "

"We're not quite done yet, honored king," Laurel said.
"I'd have your church elder perform a purification rite to rid
this place of lingering effects."

"Lingering effects," Jusson repeated.

"Have you ever been in places where great evil was done
and felt a coldness or oppression?" Laurel asked. "Even
though the evil happened years past?"

"Ah," Jusson said, nodding. "The palace at Iversly has a
few spots like that—" He broke off, realizing what he was
saying and who he was saying it to.

"Cold spots in the palace?" Wyln asked, interested.
"Where? In the throne room? Or perhaps in the seraglio and
its nursery?"

In the silence I could hear the clicking and popping of
the melted pan as it cooled. Jusson then smiled. "Let's deal
with what's before us, Lord Wyln, before we start on what's
past."

"As you wish, Iver'son," Wyln murmured, his flame-
filled eyes bright.

Jusson ignored the enchanter, turning to Thadro. "Send a
guard to see if Doyen Dyfrig can come immediately. I do
not want any effects lingering about any longer than necessary."

"Yes, sire," Thadro said, and sent a guardsman running.

Jusson glanced around as the guardsman's footsteps faded, his mouth pulled down as if he tasted something foul. He then started walking towards the door, his pace once more brisk. "I've had enough of this place. We will await his reverence outside."

There wasn't any mad scramble among the guards to follow Jusson outside. Thadro had them too well trained for that. But there was a certain tightness to their formation as they fell in behind the king, no one willing to be last. That was left to me and Jeff.

Jusson let loose a small sigh as he stepped out into the yard, lifting his face to the sun rising over the rooftop. After counting heads and making sure everyone was out, I closed the door and hurried to stake a claim on my own patch of sunshine, Jeff right behind me, the earth and fire spheres hovering over my shoulders. The guards shifted easily to make room for me, despite the spheres, despite Thadro's constant carping, despite my being held helpless as a baby as Laurel *touched* me with his rune. A knot or two in my spine loosened. It tightened again, though, when I caught Chadde's speculative stare. My face went stony again.

Jusson lowered his gaze to the building. "A rather ordinary place, even so." He turned to Wyln who, despite Thadro's vigilance, was standing next to him. "What shall we do about the sorcery? How do we find out the who of it, along with the what and why?"

Wyln moved his shoulders, more of an easing of tight muscles than a shrug, all hint of amusement gone. "You'd think that something of this magnitude would blaze like a city on a mountaintop, Iver'son. But whoever has done this has hidden it well."

"A master sorcerer, honored king," Laurel put in from where he'd joined me in my patch of sunshine. "One who has learned how to mask his actions."

"There must be a way to find out who," Jusson insisted. "How does your Fyrst do it?"

"Contrary to popular belief, the Border is not teeming with practitioners of the dark arts," Wyln said, his amusement returning. "Magus Kareste was the first in a long while. But when we do suspect sorcery, we hunt the practitioner just like we would any other criminal."

"It's very similar to finding a murderer," Laurel said. "Means and motive. What was done to whom and why? We have part of the puzzle with the attack on Rabbit and the unfortunate Menck's death, but we need to find the rest to flesh out the solution. A good place to start is the honored peacekeeper's investigation into the unfortunate's death."

"So we've circled right back to the questions first posed," Jusson said. He turned his gaze back on the building. "I suppose that we should find out who this belongs to, if only to let them know what has been done inside. Is that a question that can be answered without puzzle pieces, Peacekeeper Chadde?"

"Yes, Your Majesty," Chadde said. "It's owned by a family that, since the closure of Eastgate, has fallen on hard times. I doubt that they've had anything to do with this, but I will make inquiries."

"Oh, yes," Jusson said. "The bricked-up gate. Tell me, why was that done? Isn't Eastgate where the King's Road intersects Freston?"

"Yes, Your Majesty," Chadde said again. "At least, it was before the closure."

"Yet when we arrived here, we had to travel halfway around the town to Kingsgate," Jusson said. "That doesn't make sense."

"It's a rather involved story, Your Majesty," Chadde said.

"I have some free time," Jusson said. "Do you have to run off to this tavern right away?"

Chadde judged the position of the sun. "No, Your Majesty."

"Then you can come back and tell me all about it so I can pose questions of my own—" Jusson suddenly stopped, turning his head to the yard's gate, listening, Wyln and Laurel doing the same. After a moment, I could hear a commotion in the street, growing louder. At Thadro's signal, a couple of the King's Own hurried across the yard to the gate and pulled it open to reveal the town Watch still standing guard. However, instead of moving to block whatever was approaching, they were stepping out of the way and bowing. The next moment, Doyen Dyfrig appeared in the gateway, flanked by his two church clerks, Keeve and Tyle. Trailing behind all three was the royal guard Thadro had just sent running for the doyen.

"His reverence was already on his way here, sir," the guard said to the Lord Commander.

"Oh?" Jusson asked, not waiting for Thadro to tell him what the guard had said. "Any particular reason, your reverence?"

"Oh, yes, I have a reason," Dyfrig said. The doyen was wearing his everyday brown robe, and his white hair, free of his big hat, was disordered by his walk. But in his hand was his Staff of Office, complete with small silver bells, and there was nothing faded about his blue eyes as they blazed at Laurel. He gave a sharp rap of his staff against the cobblestones, causing the bells to ring like judgment.

"What have you done to Menck's body, Faena?"

Fourteen

Though the Watch had been left guarding the abandoned warehouse, it was still a large and varied group that flowed into the courtyard of the charnel house. The King's Own entered first, marching quick step, their boots thudding as they struck the paving stones in unison. Jusson came behind them, his long strides easily keeping pace. With Jusson were Thadro and Dyfrig. The doyen, despite his age, also kept up easily, his knuckles white as he thumped the Staff of Office against the ground with each step, the bells constantly ringing. Flanking Dyfrig were his two clerks, Keeve and Tyle. Next were Laurel with the beads clacking, feathers fluttering and knotted cloth swaying on his own staff, Wyln with a fire sphere over his shoulder, Chadde completely unencumbered, and me, with feather, braid, stick and my own spheres, and more royal guards brought up the rear.

The small courtyard filled up fast.

But in spite of everyone crammed into the courtyard, it looked as dreary in the morning light as it had the night before. Even the buildings that rose up over the house of the dead presented blank faces with no windows or other openings visible anywhere, as though they had turned their backs on the proof of our mortality. Or at least mortality for some of us. Wyln stopped next to me, his young face turned to the charnel house, his ancient eyes tracing the lines of warding.

"Thorough," he remarked quietly to Laurel, who stopped on my other side.

Laurel rumbled agreement. "They won't burn the body."

Wyln actually blinked twice before swiftly turning his head to the Faena. But before he could speak, folks clustered near the house's doorway moved to meet us—Mayor Gawell, Master Ednoth, several servants and a couple of guards I recognized from my stint in jail. My hand went to my sword while Jeff made a soft snarling noise behind me and Arlie, loitering in the vicinity of Thadro, stiffened.

"It is an outrage, Your Majesty," Gawell said as he reached Jusson. He bowed with a short bobbing motion as if he could only bend so far before his massive stomach bounced him upright again. "I've come to tend to my kinsman and I'm locked out!"

The servant behind the mayor did carry a large washbasin in which were a sponge, a cake of soap, a stoppered bottle of perfumed oil and a jar of unguent. (Menck was going to smell better dead than he ever had alive.) But, though Gawell was dressed more soberly than he had the night before, in a plain shirt, coat and trousers, I couldn't quite picture him washing and anointing Menck's body as he wore his chain of office, its starburst glittering in the sun. Unless it was to remind the corpse who was mayor.

"You're tending Menck?" Chadde asked. "Where's his wife?"

"At home, overcome with grief and worry," Gawell said, scowling at the peacekeeper.

"Odd," Chadde said. "When I saw her earlier this morning, she wasn't overcome at all—at least not with grief. something about Menck's death leaving her high and h a parcel of brats."

Gawell seemed to swell, his belly thrusting out his chain of office. "You forget yourself, peacekeeper—"

Master Ednoth touched Gawell's arm and the mayor stopped midswell. Ednoth smiled at the king. "Forgive us, Your Majesty, for airing our squabbles in front of you. It's just a little disconcerting for his honor to be denied access."

"Don't worry, Master Ednoth," Jusson said. "So far my stay here has been one revelation after another."

"A revelation? Is that what you call it?" Doyen Dyfrig asked. The doyen had moved in front of the door and he now indicated it with a wave of his hand. "I call it vile. I can feel it out here, radiating like a forge full of loathsomeness."

Dyfrig was right. Something was coming from the charnel house, right through the wards. It was like what had infected the coins and jewels we'd found sewn into Menck's clothes, but darker and heavier. I started to join the doyen, but stopped, the same reluctance I felt in the warehouse coming over me.

"It wasn't like this last night," Laurel said, his brows knit. "Something has changed."

"Something has changed all right," Dyfrig said. "You arrived. What have you done, Faena?"

"Nothing, Elder Dyfrig," Laurel replied. He lifted his head, scenting the air.

"Whatever is in there arrived without the Faena cat's help, as his whereabouts have been accounted for at the time of the murder and beyond," Jusson said, conveniently omitting Wyln and his disappearing act. "But talking out here won't uncover what's in there. Open the door, peacekeeper. Let's see what is going on with the jailer's body."

A thin line appeared between Thadro's brows at Jusson's order, but Chadde started towards the charnel house immediately. As she pulled at the key on her belt, Wyln looked across me to Laurel. "Think the warding is enough?"

"Fire and earth against water, drawn both inside the death house and out," Laurel said. "Let's hope so."

But Laurel spoke to Thadro, and the Lord Commander, the line deepening between his brows, had the King's Own clear the space in front of the door—leaving Chadde standing at the door all by her lonesome. The peacekeeper turned the key and the loud click echoed against the stone walls. All of us held our breaths as she pushed open the door— and let them out again in a whooshing sigh as nothing happened. Then the door seemed to stick.

"What's wrong?" Jusson asked.

"Something's in the way, Your Majesty," Chadde said. She shoved with both hands, but the door wouldn't go any further.

"Thadro," Jusson said, and the Lord Commander, now frowning deeply, sent Arlis to help the peacekeeper. I caught a hastily smothered grin on Jeff's face.

Both Arlis and Chadde managed to muscle open the door wide enough for someone to slip through—just barely. They moved back and Mayor Gawell tried to push his way past them.

"No, Gawell," Jusson said as royal guards blocked the mayor. "I go first." He looked at Dyfrig. "Your Reverence, would you care to join me?"

At first I thought I was going to be allowed to stay out in the courtyard, away from ritually slain bodies and cursed jewels, but Wyln and Laurel moved quickly to join Jusson and Dyfrig, taking me with them. We crowded behind the king and doyen, earning a side glance from Thadro and an indignant shout from the mayor. Gawell gave another shout as Jeff pushed the mayor out of the way to take his place at my back. But Jusson stopped at the earth and fire warding lines drawn across the door, all of us piling up behind him.

"A moment, honored king," Laurel said. Reaching past Jusson, he touched a shimmering earth line, and it grew brighter before forming into another sphere, slowly spinning with whorls of browns and greens, the scent of fall grasses and ripe fruit filling the air. I glanced at the earth sphere at my shoulder, suddenly remembering that it too was Laurel's. I also remembered how quickly the cat had found us at the abandoned warehouse.

"Rabbit," Laurel said, cutting into my suspicious speculations.

I touched one of the lines of fire and it grew hot before shooting out, a stream of flame merging with the fire sphere hovering at my shoulder. That one at least was mine.

All obstacles gone, Thadro slipped in front of Jusson and looked inside. Seeing nothing alarming, he went in and was immediately followed by the king, both angling their bodies to get through the door. Once inside, Jusson paused to look down. "Well, that explains why the door wouldn't open." He then moved further into the charnel house to allow the rest of us to enter.

The room was wrecked. The shroud that had been neatly draped over Menck's body was tossed on the floor. As were the privy-infested clothes. The bowl Laurel had used to wash up after his examination of the corpse had been shattered against the wall, and even the burnt torch shafts had been pulled from their brackets and lay about, broken in pieces. And mixed in with the havoc were the coins and jewels, all seeming to pulse with malignancy.

But there was no body. At least, there was no body on the slab where we'd left it. I looked down and saw a bare foot sticking out from behind the door. As I watched, someone brushed against the door and the foot moved. I backed away, barely avoiding treading on a dully gleaming coin.

Laurel and Wyln also stepped carefully as they went to the stone slab where Menck's body had lain the night before, the warding lines of fire and earth that Laurel and I had drawn around the slab gone. However, there were thin scorch lines on the edge of the stone, while the top glistened in the weak light coming through the windows' grilles as if it were wet. I peered at it. Not water. Ice.

"The wards failed," Wyln murmured, staring down at the scorch marks. "Strong lines of fire and earth and they failed. It is good that you warded outside too."

Laurel growled low in agreement and lifted his head, once more scenting. In the air were the pungent smells I recognized from last night, but overlaying them was a new one. I frowned, trying to place it. Then my frown cleared and the hair stood up on the back of my neck. It was the odor of burnt flesh.

"Laurel was right," Jeff whispered to me, his eyes wide as he stared around. "It wasn't like this last night." He started to shift, looked down to see a diamond sparkling by his foot, and drew back.

"Desecration," Dyfrig said, his mouth a flat line. "What have you brought here, Your Majesty? What have you unleashed on my people?"

"I have already had this discussion, Doyen," Jusson said. "My kingdom, my town, my people—the quick and the dead."

"I have two and eighty years," Dyfrig said, "sixty-seven of them in the church here in Freston. Your visit is the first hint of royal interest that I've seen. Never before. Not even five years ago when your close cousin arrived in that dumping place they call a garrison."

I'd been watching Laurel as he examined the slab, but at Dyfrig's words, I looked at the doyen. "But I didn't want any interest, Your Reverence," I said, "and I liked being at the garrison."

"You did?" Dyfrig's white brows were pulled together, forming a thick bar. "Even when that cancer Slevoic showed up?" He didn't wait for my answer. "Well, you're not at the garrison now, are you? And you're certainly not the plain soldier you once were." He flung a hand out at me. "Look at him, Your Majesty! He once was as normal as any boy his age. Look at what came back, returning with the same magical that took him. Flames, feathers, braids, trailing destruction in his wake! And look at this!" His hand encompassed the room. "A murder where there hasn't been any for years, dishonoring the dead, and a vileness that reeks—"

"Rabbit, why do you look like that?" Jusson asked, cutting across Dyfrig's diatribe.

I stared at the king a moment, then my mouth quirked in comprehension. "Because I'm mage-born, Your Majesty."

"I know that," Dyfrig snapped.

"Do you?" Jusson asked. "Do you know? And knowing, do you understand?" Reaching up, he pushed back his hair and suddenly his face was alien, with nothing human about it. Dyfrig's two clerks' eyes grew wide while, beside me, Wyln made a humming sound.

"We are changed, Your Reverence," the king said, his own eyes full of gold. "Not changing, not going to change, not perhaps will change. Changed. Right here, right now."

Dyfrig let out a breath. "So you say."

"I do say. As does His Holiness the Patriarch. As does the evidence right before your eyes. Rabbit is what he always has been, a powerful mage, no matter his looks and the damned feather. Just as I am who I've always been." Jusson let his hair fall again. "Not pay attention to Freston? It has been constantly on my mind my entire reign. I sent Prince Suiden here when he came to me for sanctuary from his tyrant of an uncle, the Amir of Tural. When Rabbit fled his corrupt master, I posted him here under the care of Suiden." The king saw my surprise. "You didn't think I knew, cousin? The Qarant spread word about Magus Kareste's missing apprentice long before the Magus sent me the message last spring asking for you back."

"Yes, sire," I said, my heart thumping at how far and wide Kareste had looked for me—and at how exposed my hiding place had been.

"I sent both Suiden and Rabbit here," Jusson said, "because it was the safest place I had. But as we have changed, so have others. Do not accuse me of bringing evil to Freston. It was here waiting for us."

"No, it wasn't," Dyfrig said. "It was not." He hit his staff end on the floor, the bells jangling. "We do *not* have this in us. Not this evilness, this defilement."

"Already waiting," Jusson said. "Beginning with the head jailer, Menck, and his larcenous, rapacious soul. Cancer? He was a man who made a habit of beating, robbing and despoiling with impunity. With impunity, Doyen. You tell me to look. *You* look." Jusson pointed at the floor. "Where do you think that came from? A fortune in coins and jewels, sewn into his clothes."

Dyfrig became still. "What?"

"You snort and rear up at Rabbit's natural talent," Jusson said. "Yet you winked at Master Menck's prolonged crime spree. And this is just what lies on the surface. It makes me wonder what I'd find if I dig a little."

Dyfrig looked down at the gold and jewels glittering among the debris on the floor. "Menck had this?" He suddenly swayed, the fight draining out of him. Concerned, I went to his side and, beating his two clerks, took his arm to steady him. His bones felt fragile under my hand.

"A fortune that made two very wealthy lords of the realm sit up and take notice, somehow in the possession of a lowly jailer in a back-mountain trade town," Jusson said. He took in Dyfrig's pallor. "Shocked, Doyen? Or worried?"

"I—" Dyfrig looked at Chadde. "Does Gawell know?"

"He didn't," Chadde began.

"Dyfrig!" Gawell shouted from outside.

"Until now," Chadde finished.

Surprised that the mayor hadn't pushed in behind us, I looked out the door. Or tried to. Thadro had filled both the doorway and the immediate area outside with royal guards, displacing Gawell, Ednoth and their servants to the far end of the courtyard. But the courtyard was small and neither Jusson nor Dyfrig had kept their voices down. Even if they'd missed the occasional word, Mayor Gawell, Master Ednoth and the rest had to have heard enough to understand that serious loot had been found on Menck's person—and Jusson's thoughts on how the head jailer had acquired it.

"Dyfrig!" Gawell shouted again, sounding frantic.

"You will have trouble if you don't let him in, Your Majesty," Chadde said, her voice soft. "However, you'll have trouble if you *do*."

Though still unsteady, Dyfrig pulled away from my supporting hand. "That's true, Your Majesty. But perhaps we can minimize it." The doyen turned to his clerks. "Go to the church and bring back the implements of blessing."

"Leave you, Your Reverence?" Tyle protested, casting suspicious glances at Laurel and Wyln. "Alone? With them?" Keeve, seeing me trying to retake Dyfrig's arm, stepped between us, pushing me away.

"Yes," Dyfrig said, moving Keeve back while at the same time placing a restraining hand on my shoulder. "Hurry."

The royal guard opened up to let the two clerks through, but closed again before Gawell could make his way to us. Once clear of the crowd, the slap of Keeve and Tyle's shoes echoed as they ran.

"Will someone let me in?" Gawell wailed as Ednoth began a measured speech about how magicals were allowed inside while Menck's near kinsman was made to wait outside like a beggar at the gate.

"Quick, Rabbit," Dyfrig said. "Get Menck back on a slab."

My skin crawled at the thought of touching the head jailer's corpse, but I obediently moved towards the body, motioning Jeff to help me. However, Wyln caught my arm.

"Do not," the enchanter said.

"No, Rabbit," Jusson said at the same time. "Leave it where it is."

"Your Majesty," Dyfrig began, glaring at Wyln.

"There is no hiding the disarray in here and I will not have it said that I tried," Jusson said. He turned to Thadro. "Let the mayor in."

Dyfrig watched with worried eyes as the guards in front of the door once more parted, and Gawell trotted quickly to the charnel house, his footsteps light for a man of his girth. Wedging his way inside, his eyes narrowed as he took in the wreckage, his gaze lingering on the coins and jewels on the floor. As Ednoth, the servants and jailhouse guards squeezed in around him, Gawell turned to Chadde, livid. "You said that Menck's purse was stolen."

I blinked at the fact that though Menck's body had been tossed on the floor, the first words out of his honor's mouth were about money.

Chadde, however, seemed neither worried nor surprised. "His purse *was* stolen," she said calmly. "These were hidden in his clothes."

Gawell's jowls took on a purple hue, his eyes bulging out a bit. "And you didn't think it necessary to tell me that?"

"No," Chadde said. "I didn't."

"That's it!" Gawell roared. "I've had enough of you! You're through! Get out! Get out of here and get out of Freston before I have you thrown out!"

"First our cousin is beaten and robbed in jail, and now our officer is dismissed and threatened before us," Jusson said.

Gawell's head snapped around to the king, the purple fading rapidly from his jowls, leaving red splotches behind.

"Your Majesty," he stammered. "You heard her; she lied to me."

"No, she didn't," Jusson said. "She withheld information, which is different. Just ask the Faena."

Gawell shot a wild glance at Laurel, but Laurel ignored the mayor. Done with the slab, the cat was examining the wall under one of the empty torch brackets where the gray stone had streaks of what looked like white rime. I stepped closer to Wyln, the enchanter's hand moving to my shoulder, while Jeff crowded in close behind, all three of us watching Laurel.

"The Keeper of the King's Peace doesn't report to the mayor anyway, sire," Thadro put in. "She reports to the province's governor."

"So she does," Jusson agreed.

"But we haven't a governor," Gawell said. "Not since Lord Ormec died."

"So you don't," Jusson once more agreed. "However, that only means that, until we appoint a new governor, those who were reporting to Ormec now report to us, including our peacekeeper. Surely you know that as you've been mayor for, what? Nineteen years?"

The red splotches also faded, leaving Gawell's face pale, but before he could reply, Ednoth spoke. "Forgive Gawell, Your Majesty. He's naturally upset about the death of his kinsman— Hey!"

"Pardon," Laurel said as he pushed past Ednoth and Gawell. He stopped at the door. "Please move, honored folks."

The purple bloomed back into Gawell's cheeks. "Insolent magical!" the mayor began, while Ednoth said, "Such disrespect, Your Majesty." Both sputtered to a halt when Laurel looked at them, his amber eyes molten.

"Move."

Ednoth and Gawell both backed away, their hands shaking as they blessed themselves. Doyen Dyfrig scowled, but his expression changed as he stared at the door. "What *is* that?" he asked as he started to join Laurel. I snagged him, though, pulling him back.

"No, Doyen," I said. "Don't go any closer." I could see rime on the door edge, leprous white against the dark wood and iron bands.

"Is that frost?" Jusson asked, his brows pulling together.

"So it seems." Extending a claw, Laurel pushed the door almost closed and revealed ice covering the back completely—thick, white and uneven, like melted wax. And Menck's body, shoved against the wall by the opening of the door, was now freed from its tight confines. It flopped onto its back, the head lolling to the side, aiming those leering eyes right at me.

"Heaven forefend and protect us!" Doyen Dyfrig whispered.

Fifteen

"**R**evenant," Wyln said as he moved me out of Menck's line of sight, his hand coming up to trace fire. He didn't have to pull very hard, though, as I was already moving. Bravado was all very well on a battlefield, but I had no need to prove my manhood by having staring contests with day-old corpses with fresh eyes. The rest of the body seemed pretty fresh too—there was no sign of stiffening, the stab wounds still glittery red. Overlying the wounds were thin lines that formed a mesh on the fish-belly-white skin. I eyed them, thinking that their spacing was about right for the warding lines Laurel and I drew last night. I blessed myself and willed the flames in front of me hotter. All of a sudden I was feeling very cold.

Doyen Dyfrig turned his scowl on the fire tracery, but everyone else's attention remained on the dead jailer. Laurel leaned over and, without touching, examined the dark lines. As he did, the body shifted again and the head moved so that its leering gaze was now aimed up at the Faena. Laurel's whiskers swept back to show his fangs, his ruff standing straight up.

"Everyone out," he said, his voice a low, rumbling growl. "Now."

"Do it," Jusson said, already moving, and the Own pushed everybody out of the charnel house. Reaching the courtyard, I turned to see the mayor's party hustled out, Gawell protesting, Ednoth full of outraged dignity.

"What was that?" Dyfrig asked as he stopped by me, distressed. "What has happened to Menck?" He stiffened, his voice going sharp. "And what are you doing, Faena?"

Chadde and Laurel had been the last to leave, Chadde once more locking the door behind them. Now Laurel was carving a rune into the door's wood and iron bars with an extended claw, filling the space between lintel and threshold, from post to post. "Warding, Elder Dyfrig," he said. "Sealing."

I had seen that particular rune only once before—carved into a stone placed on a burial mound near Magus Kareste's tower during my brief stint as the Magus' apprentice. I'd been told that the rune was there to ensure the barrow's occupant stayed put and didn't go wandering. I'd been also told, despite the protections in place, to never go near the mound on certain nights at certain times of the year.

Another shiver shook me.

Done with the door, Laurel moved to the windowsills, scratching the same rune under all the windows, quickly circling around the building until he came to the front again. "Wyln," he said.

Wyln held out his hand to me. "Your sword, Two Trees'son."

Wondering what the fire enchanter wanted with my sword, I drew and handed it to him. I started to follow as Wyln walked towards Laurel; however, I was stopped by both.

"No, Rabbit," Wyln said.

"Stay with Elder Dyfrig, Rabbit," Laurel said at the same time. "Too much interest has been shown in you by the dead."

Staying with the doyen was also good. I quickly stepped back to where Dyfrig stood.

"Too much interest by the dead?" Recovering from his fright, Gawell tried to push through the royal guards in front of him. "You're the one with too much, magical! This is a ruse, keeping me from my kinsman, whose body has been desecrated—"

"*Now* you mention it," Thadro said.

"Silence, Mayor," Jusson said over Gawell's furious gasps. "Master Laurel and Lord Wyln have as much interest in the jailer as you do, and none at all in the coins and jewels. However, I have a great interest in both, and so the morgue and everything in it is placed under my edict."

"As does the throne, so does the Church," Dyfrig said, still distressed. He tapped his staff against the ground, the tiny bells ringing. "So be it."

"No!" Gawell wailed.

"So sealed by king and priest," Laurel said over Gawell. "So sealed by She Who Is the Earth. Fiat." The Faena touched the rune on the door and light filled it, exploding around both sides of the house, to each rune under each window, and a hum filled my bones from the power of them, the ground under me trembling as they rooted themselves in the earth.

"Oh, my," Dyfrig said, his voice soft, his face full of reluctant wonder. He turned half-angry, half-expectant eyes to Wyln. But instead of touching the rune as Laurel had, the enchanter held my sword up, the blade becoming brighter and brighter, flickers of fire appearing on its edge. He then flung the sword up in the air.

"Guard," Wyln said.

The blade burst into flames as it came down, blade first, to hang in front of the door.

"And so magic returns to Iversterre," Jusson murmured over gasps and cries.

"It returned five years ago with Rabbit, sire," Thadro said, his voice equally soft.

"Perhaps," Jusson said. "Or perhaps it was here all along, biding its time." He turned his head to the courtyard entrance and a moment later I heard the slap of running feet. Keeve and Tyle hurried in, carrying a chest between them. They came to an abrupt halt, however, as they took in the runes and the flaming sword. They quickly put the chest down, their eyes wide, their mouths hanging open.

"You should bless this with everything you can, Elder Dyfrig," Laurel said as he and Wyln returned to where I was standing. "As much as you can."

"I know what to do, Faena," Dyfrig said. "But when I'm done, we will talk about what has happened. What *is* happening. And your part in it." He flung the chest lid open, revealing a large glass flask of blessed water, a porcelain bowl, censer and incense, a bell, a container of salt and sprigs of hyssop, all bedded down in a lining of green velvet. I frowned at the velvet, its smooth nap teasing the back of my mind.

"It will be a morning of needful discussions, Your Reverence," Jusson said, watching Dyfrig pull a stole from the chest and drape it around his neck. "Beginning with why Master Menck, with all his extracurricular activities, was allowed to remain the head jailer, then continuing on to the closing of the Eastgate and the rerouting of the King's Road, and most likely ending with the office of Keeper of the King's Peace."

Gawell, who'd begun making noises of discontent again, froze. "Your Majesty?"

"Oh, you will be joining us, Mayor," Jusson said. "You too, Master Ednoth."

"Probably for the good," Dyfrig said, sighing. He handed the bell to one clerk, while giving the censer to the other. "Things *have* changed."

At the doyen's signal, Keeve rang the bell as Tyle lit the censer, and rang it again as the blessed water was poured into the bowl. Then the doyen walked around the charnel house, describing a line against whatever lurked inside, even as Laurel and I had drawn lines of warding the night before. The two clerks kept pace with him, one continuing to ring the bell while the other swung the censer, causing fragrant smoke to pour out as Dyfrig dipped the hyssop into the bowl of blessed water and splashed the charnel house walls, all the while chanting about the goodness of God and His light. Finished, he turned to face us, and even Laurel— even Wyln—was quiescent when Dyfrig dipped the hyssop into the remaining blessed water and sprinkled us as he prayed for our protection and covering.

My surprise must have shown on my face for Wyln murmured to me when it was all over, "Sixty-seven years as a priest. He carries the authority and power of that as a mantle about his shoulders. I'd be stupid to turn away his blessing."

"Even if you don't have the same beliefs?" I asked. While I hadn't expected bloodshed—not exactly—between Wyln and Dyfrig, I also hadn't expected the dark elf to join His Reverence's congregation either. I'd heard tales, both in the Border and in Iversterre, of Church-sanctioned slayings of the People in the not-so-distant days of the kingdom, and even now some doyens preached against the Border as if it were an outpost of hell.

Wyln gave a graceful shrug. "Who said we don't?" he asked as he maneuvered us so that we stood in the middle of the King's Own—and next to Jusson. "Whatever the beliefs, there is no denying that there is power in your Church, and Elder Dyfrig wields it with a deft hand."

That was true. I could feel the weight of the blessing settling into place, like a massive bulwark raised against whatever was in the charnel house. However, I could also feel pressure from what the blessing, sword and runes held back, and once, in between the ringing of the bell, I'd

thought I heard another noise—the clink of coins as if
something had slithered on top of them.

Blessing and warding done, Jusson once again showed
no inclination to loiter, waiting only for Dyfrig to repack
the implements of blessing before he had Thadro give the
order to move out. I kept pace with the Lord Commander as
we left the courtyard, very glad that I had not only Jeff, but
the whole contingent of royal guards behind me.

Sixteen

Everything was so wonderfully ordinary in the town square after the gray horrors of the charnel house. The sun shone brightly, the fountain tinkled and the Harvestide decorations fluttered in the breeze. People bustled about, some intent on errands, others standing in groups gossiping. They shifted out of the way as we came barreling out of the side street, staring at us in speculative surprise, and Jusson slowed to a more sedate pace. He did, however, glance over his shoulder a couple of times, maybe making sure that he hadn't left anyone behind—or maybe checking that nothing had followed us from the courtyard of the dead. But it was just us, and I let out the breath I didn't know I was holding while all around me there was an easing, with shoulders relaxing and hands falling away from swords.

Taking advantage of the more relaxed atmosphere, Chadde moved through the Own to speak with Jusson. "Majesty," she said, reaching the king, "if I may, I'd like to post watchmen at the charnel house."

Jusson nodded, his face preoccupied. "Yes, of course."

"I'd also like to be excused from your meeting this morning."

That caught the king's attention and his gaze sharpened. "Oh?"

"As I'd said, I had planned to be at the Copper Pig

around midday, as that's when its patrons start to arrive. If I go later, they'll be rather incoherent."

"I suppose there is an art to interrogating the drunken," Jusson said. He stopped at the church steps, his Own bunching about him. "Well, we can speak this afternoon when you return." His gaze rested on Laurel. "Take the Faena with you. Perhaps the two of you can find some of those puzzle pieces."

"Honored king," Laurel began, his brows pulling together. Apparently he'd forgotten that he had already agreed to accompany Chadde to the Pig.

"Don't worry, Master Cat," Jusson said. "Rabbit will go with you."

Then maybe Laurel was frowning for a different reason. Expecting to hear the opposite from Jusson, I was suddenly leery. I'd enough of interesting events and was very willing to be bored by the three-way political maneuvering between the king, the mayor and the doyen. Besides, I was hungry. Very hungry. As if I'd not eaten this morning, last night or even last week. Realizing that it had my attention, my stomach growled.

A faint smile crossed Jusson's face. "What are you? A bottomless pit?"

"Seems so, sire," I said. My stomach gave another rumble. "With your permission, maybe I can join them after lunch."

Jusson shook his head, his amusement fading. "Something is going on here, cousin. Something beyond whatever malfeasance the mayor is sunk in up to his double chins. Something that seems to want to involve you. Until we discover all the pieces of Master Laurel's puzzle, I want you safe. And there are only two safe places I can think of— with Doyen Dyfrig or with Laurel Faena and Lord Wyln. However, I don't know the good doyen's involvement with

Gawell and company, and so that leaves the cat and my lord elf."

"So happy to be of service, Iver'son," Wyln murmured.

"You think Doyen Dyfrig's involved with whatever the head jailer had going, sire?" I quickly asked as Jusson frowned.

Jusson turned away from Wyln to look up at the church's facade, still frowning. "As he's pointed out, Dyfrig has lived in Freston for over eight decades, and has been part of the church here for almost seven of them. He has known Gawell and Ednoth all their lives. He saw them born, catechized and baptized them, performed their marriages, catechized and baptized *their* children, and perhaps their children's children. He may even be related to them. If he's not involved, he was still aware—if only of Menck's activities—and has done nothing."

I looked over at Mayor Gawell and Master Ednoth, separated from us by the royal guards. The two clerks had been sent on to the church with the chest of blessings, but the doyen had joined the mayor and head merchant. Dyfrig's face was stern as he listened to Gawell and Ednoth, the mayor gesturing as he spoke.

"I don't know if that's arrogance or ignorance," Jusson said, also watching. "To talk with them before I can, *after* I'd announced that I would. And to do so right in front of me."

"A little of both," Jeff said as he stood next to me. "Dyfrig *is* the Church here." His eyes then widened and darted to the king. "Your Majesty."

The faint smile reappeared on Jusson's face. "So he is. Another discussion we'll be having: what is the Church's and what is mine." He turned to Chadde, who was also watching Dyfrig, Gawell and Ednoth. "Go to your duty, Peacekeeper. Take my cousin and his guardians. Also take my Lord Commander."

A light flush appeared on Thadro's face. "Sire—"

"Is that wise, Jusson Iver'son?" Wyln asked, speaking over Thadro. "To strip yourself of your protections? Rabbit is a target, but perhaps you are one too. Why settle for the journeyman mage when the king is also vulnerable? Keep your eorl commander with you, even as you deal with the treachery of the town elders."

Jusson's eyes swiftly turned gold. "You forget yourself, Lord Elf."

"No, *you* forget, King of Iversterre," Wyln said, moving closer so that he and Jusson stood nose to nose with eyes blazing—one set afire, the other solid gold, neither one blinking. "You are not immortal, no matter what your mirror tells you. Do not take stupid chances."

Figuring the last time the king had been publicly repri-manded he was still in leading strings, I started to step between them again, hoping to maybe draw some of the royal ire on me before it boiled over Wyln—and Wyln boiled back. As I started to move, though, something passed over Jusson's face, his expression changing as it had in the derelict warehouse. . . .

"I know you. . . ." Jusson shook his head as if to clear it.

"Elfin families," Laurel muttered, his ears shifting back in exasperation. "The king is not vulnerable, Wyln. There is honored Cais. You saw him when I *touched* Rabbit."

Wyln eased back a bit. "Cais?"

"The king's majordomo," Laurel said. "He was standing next to Iver'son."

"Ah, yes." The enchanter was once more his gently amused self. "I did see him."

"I—" Jusson began. Then stopped and glanced around the square, ending at Peacekeeper Chadde, who made no pretense of not listening. "We will discuss this later." With that, Jusson gathered his Own and, sweeping up the Freston contingent, strode out of the square, leaving us blinking after him.

"That was quick," Jeff said, watching the last of the royal guards exit the square.

Thadro ignored Jeff for more legitimate prey. "First in the warehouse and now here," he said to Wyln. "Who the pox-rotted hell do you think you are?"

"Sir," I said, keeping my voice low. "He's the king's great-uncle."

Thadro jerked his head to me, his blue-gray eyes wide and full of anger. Chadde made a smothered sound of shock.

"He's also an elder of his lineage," I said, "and brother-in-law to His Grace, Loran the Fyrst, the Line's Eldest—and Jusson's many times great-grandda."

"I don't care if he's freaking Firewalker come in the flesh," Thadro began.

"But I am," Wyln said. "At least, that's what Iver Bloody-Hand called me."

Thadro's mouth stayed open but the words had dried up. He closed it with a snap and tried again. "*Iver?* The founder of Jusson's *House?* The first king of *Iversterre?*"

"After we finally checked his army at the battle of Sorota." The enchanter smiled. "I've always preferred Wyln, though."

Thadro's chest heaved as he sucked air into his lungs. He then looked around the square. With the insulation of Jusson and his guards gone, some people were trying to hear what had the Lord Commander so worked up. Others were staring at Wyln, pointing and whispering behind their hands, while a third contingent divided glowers between Laurel and me. I supposed it had something to do with my braid and the fact that Laurel was a cat. Or maybe it was our staves, feathers and spheres. Then again, it could be that they just remembered what happened last time I'd been in a square. One of the double church doors opened and the clerk Keeve stepped out to add his disapproving stare to the mix.

"This might be a good time to go to the Pig, sir," I said to Thadro as one shopper dropped a package he'd been carrying and, in picking it up, managed to edge closer to where we stood. At the same time, a burly teamster put his hand on the whip hanging from his belt, his mates around him scowling and muttering about magicals.

"Yes," Jeff seconded, watching the teamster. "A very good time."

"I don't know about King Iver and the battle at Sorota, Lord Wyln," Chadde said as we walked quickly out of the square, "but I do recall my grandfather telling tales his father told him of a wizard called Firewalker who fought in the last war between the Borderlands and Iversterre."

"Enchanter, Peacekeeper Chadde," Wyln corrected. "Wizard is a Turalian term."

"I see," Chadde murmured. "And you, Lord Rabbit? What are you?"

"What I've always been, Peacekeeper Chadde," I said. "A farm boy turned horse soldier."

"Not a mage?" Chadde asked.

"No," I said. "Not for several years yet."

As we were riding to the Copper Pig, we went to the royal stables. And there, in the middle of the groomers and horses, we found Arlis waiting. "His Majesty sent me to get the horses ready for you, sir," he said to Thadro, giving the Lord Commander a crisp salute.

It was more likely that Jusson realized that Arlis was with him and sent my personal guard back to where he should've been—guarding me. I said nothing, thinking to have a long talk with him when we were alone. However, Jeff had no inhibitions.

"Toe licker," he muttered.

Arlis pretended he didn't hear.

Mounted, we exited Freston by the Kingsgate, working our way through the heavy traffic of folks afoot and a-horse, in carriages and carts. Their reactions to us were the same as in the square: some muttering and making warding gestures, others bright with curiosity as they watched us go by. One man caught Wyln's eye and offered a smile and a nod.

"Interesting," Wyln murmured, nodding back.

"We're not all ravening Border-haters," Chadde said. "Though we do have our share—which all seem to congregate at the Copper Pig. Please do not take offense at what may be said there, Lord Wyln, Master Laurel."

"Do not worry, honored Chadde," Laurel said as he paced before my horse. "We will consider the source of any insult."

Leaving the crowded gate behind, we rode out onto the King's Road. It was close to midday, with the sun casting foreshortened shadows on the packed dirt of the road, but that changed as the cleared space around the town walls gave way to stands of wood that grew denser as we went on. The light turned dappled, the leaves on the branches the same brilliant colors as those on the mountains. Behind the screen of trunks, I could see the beginnings of the farmland and orchards that took up the greater part of the valley. Workers moved through fields and fruit trees as they hurried to gather the harvest before Harvestide and the coming fall rains—and my back twinged in sympathy as I remembered my own days of reaping and picking. The wind swooped down around me, bobbing my earth and fire spheres, telling me of discovered lairs and winter burrows. I held out my hand and it swirled into a sphere, laughing as it joined the others.

"This is good," Jeff said from where he rode beside me. "I always think that I miss the town, until I actually get into town. Then I can't wait to leave."

I too could only tolerate a short time in Freston before the walls started to close in. But then I *was* a farm boy from the back provinces, and to me the small town was full of rumpus and riotous living. Jeff, though, had a more metropolitan upbringing. "I thought you grew up in Gresh," I said.

"A town to the northwest," Jeff said. "But close enough to go to Gresh every year at Festival. My family's still there. They'd laugh themselves silly if they could see me, pining for the mountains."

I started to grin but was distracted by my stomach once more growling. Laurel, still at the head of my horse, flicked an ear back towards me. "Didn't you eat this morning, Rabbit?"

"At dawn," I said. "And it's now pushing noon, so its natural that I'm hungry."

"I ate at the same time, Rabbit," Jeff said, "and I'm still full. And you ate three times more than me."

"He did?" Wyln asked. Riding on the other side of me, the dark elf reached over and grabbed my chin, turning my face to him. "Even so, you've lost weight, Two Trees'son."

"He has food on him, Lord Wyln," Jeff said, worried.

"Thanks, Ma," I said, even as my hand went towards the fruit and rolls I'd snagged from Jusson's table.

"Eat," Wyln said. "If necessary, I will speak to the eorl commander."

With that threat dangling over me, I dug out the fruit and rolls, a little the worse for being in my pocket. I inhaled them.

"It's good to take a breath now and again, Two Trees'-son," Wyln remarked.

I ignored him, busy polishing off the fruit. The echoing emptiness in my belly dissipated somewhat—as did the headache I hadn't been aware of until it eased. Frowning, I tossed away the remains of an apple. "This is not normal, is it?" I asked. "This gnawing hunger all the time."

"When was the last time you felt like this, Rabbit?" Laurel asked back.

Bards prophesied through song, dragons sought the Pearl of Wisdom, elves held their lineages and swords sacred. And Faena practiced enlightenment through illumined questioning that drove the one questioned to find the answers in frantic self-defense. I heard a snicker from Jeff as I sighed, my head dropping down.

"I don't know—" I stopped as the air sphere unraveled to once again whirl about me, reminding me of another time when I'd been encircled by the wind. And why. I sighed again, enlightened despite myself. "When I fought the djinn storm," I said. "But I haven't done anything like that here. Have I?"

"No," Laurel said. "Even your battle yesterday against the invisible hand shouldn't have made this kind of demand on your body. Something is engaging your talent."

"He has his aspects present," Wyln said to Laurel. "Except water."

"The spheres are not all mine, honored *Cyhn*," I said. I indicated the earth sphere. "That one's Laurel's."

"Yet it is here with you and not with the Faena," Wyln said. "As are fire and wind. But no water. Why not?"

Apparently Faena weren't the only ones who used questions as a blunt instrument. "Happenstance, honored *Cyhn*," I said. Pulling off my glove, I started to hold out my hand to summon water, but felt the same tightening that I had felt at the warehouse gripping my chest and throat again, hard. "Blast," I said, letting my hand fall.

Wyln's brow rose. " 'Happenstance'? When water is used not only in the service of the dark, but also to desecrate the dead?"

I remembered the ice throughout the charnel house and Menck's frozen stare, and was enlightened some more.

"Jusson Iver'son is right, Rabbit," Laurel said. "Someone is trying to involve you in their sorceries, either as a means or as an end. As Wyln said, you're full of talent and inexperience. A very attractive combination."

"Like Kareste?" I asked, worry creeping into my voice and down my spine. "But you said he's still bound. Isn't he?"

"There are others," Wyln said before Laurel could. "There always are."

"Then why aren't we out looking for them instead of playing adjutant peacekeepers?" I asked, my worry turning to anger.

Laurel shook his head, his beads rattling. "Elfin families," he muttered.

Wyln, though, met my angry gaze calmly. "You weren't listening earlier, Rabbit. Who killed the jailer?"

I opened my mouth to say I didn't know and didn't give a good damn when, this time, the image of Menck's frozen stab wounds flashed through my mind. I hissed out a breath through my teeth. "Whoever worked sorcery."

"So by helping the peacekeeper find the killers, we will most likely find those who not only worked death magic, but would use you for ill. And if they're not one and the same, at least it'll be a good starting point. Correct?"

I scowled at my horse's ears. "Correct, honored *Cyhn*."

"But until we do find them, you will not stray from Laurel and me. Understand? No wandering off as your fancy takes you." Wyln glanced across me at Jeff. "You will make sure of that, Jeffen—"

"Corbin, my lord," Jeff said. "My father's name is Corbin."

A smile crossed Wyln's face. "Jeffen Corbin'son."

Thinking that Arlie wasn't the only suck-up, I glared at Jeff. However, he was looking ahead, his brows creased as he glared at my other personal guard. To be fair to Arlis, he did try to ride with me. However, Jeff refused to give him room, forcing him to ride behind us where he ate our dust. So Arlis shifted positions so that he rode in front of me. But now, instead of being my vanguard, Arlis was right behind the Lord Commander and peacekeeper, leaning forward in his saddle, his attention fixed on the conversing Thadro and Chadde. I frowned again, opening my mouth to call Arlis back to me.

Before I could, though, Chadde turned off the King's Road, leading us down a small lane. Immediately we were forced into a tighter formation, as the badly rutted lane was barely wide enough to allow two skinny horses to ride side by side without scraping the riders off on the tree branches that jutted out—and Jusson's mounts were well-fed, hefty steeds. Even going single file the underbrush slapped at our legs and I thought that it was a perfect place to be picked off in ambush. But we continued unmolested until we rounded a bend and the trees and brush dropped away, revealing a sprawl of ramshackle buildings surrounded by a rickety fence. The buildings were weather-beaten, their stone walls crooked, the roofs black with soot, though I could just make out in spots the green tiles sported by taverns and inns. On the foremost building a sign was hung, creaking slightly as it swung in a light breeze. The animal painted on the sign was vaguely porcine, its color a faded red-brown. It stood upright, holding a cup of foaming ale in one cloven hoof and a pair of dice in the other. One eye was closed in a sly wink while its mouth smirked under its snout.

The Copper Pig.

Seventeen

I'd been in the Copper Pig a few times when I first came to Freston, but I'd quickly decided that my ma and da had brought me up better. It wasn't the gambling and prostitution that had me looking for more wholesome venues. It wasn't even the rotgut spirits it served, though that hadn't helped. It was that the Pig caused me more disgust than any desire to sin. It was dark, it was dank and it stank to high heaven.

Walking in with Chadde and company, I saw that nothing had changed in my years'-long absence. The air was stale with the smells of sour ale, unwashed bodies and the strong presence of the jakes out back. And, even at midday, it was dim and smeary, the shutters closed over the dirty windows, a film of grease lying over everything—including the patrons.

Chadde, though, had timed it just right. Despite the relative earliness of the day, the taproom had a good number of folk in it—all with filled cups, true, but also all seeming to be on the right side of sober. For now. They looked up at us, taking in our state of armed vigilance before returning to their drinks, seeming disinterested. However, there was more than one bloodshot glance in the surprisingly clean mirror over the bar. Over the muttered conversations, I could hear the rattle of dice in an adjoining room. Down the entry hall the private parlor was apparently in use as its door was closed, and there were footsteps on the stairs leading up to the second floor. The bawdy trade had started.

One of the bawds standing at the taproom bar smiled, pushing away from the bar and headed towards us, her eyes sliding over Laurel and Wyln before moving on to me. "Well, you're a handsome one, even with the feather and braid," she said as she sidled up.

As Jeff gave a muffled snicker I stared down into her face. "What did you say?" For a brief moment I saw another woman laughing up at me in challenge, but her hair was bright red, not oily brown.

"Flirt later, Lieutenant," Thadro said, his gaze sweeping the taproom. Wyln and Laurel did the same, their attention lighting on the mirror. They moved to a corner, watching the room's reflection—and more than a few in the room watched them back, including the tapster behind the bar.

"You too, sweet chuck," the bawd said to the Lord Commander as her arm snaked around my waist. "A fine, strapping man you are." Her gaze encompassed Arlis and Jeff, who stopped snickering. "Always did like the army. So soldier-like with their swords and standing at attention and everything."

"Right," I said, catching her hand before she could reach my purse. Removing her arm from my waist, I stepped aside, but she just shrugged and strolled towards Thadro.

"Give over, Isa," Chadde said. "They're helping me investigate Menck's killing." She walked to a window and flung back the shutters. Though the light coming through the panes was a dingy gray, the patrons cried out, cursing the peacekeeper.

Isa stopped stalking Thadro to turn to Chadde. "Investigate? Here? You can't. You don't have jurisdiction," she said, sounding the word out as if she had learned it by rote.

"Yes, I do," Chadde said calmly. "Over the entire valley

and the mountain villages." She opened another window, and there were more groans and abuse.

"No you don't," Isa said. "Not since Ormec died. You're just Freston now. And from what I heard, you're not much there, either." Flouncing back to the bar, she picked up a cup of ale someone had left unguarded, lifting it high. As she did, the tapster put aside the noxious-looking rag he'd been wiping the counter with and slipped out a door by the bar. Isa drained her cup in one swallow and then smiled at the peacekeeper, showing a surprisingly whole set of teeth. "You have no business here, Chaddie Laddie."

I blinked at the slur while Thadro frowned; though plainly dressed in her usual tabard and breeks, there was nothing masculine about the peacekeeper. However, Chadde was unfazed by the muffled snorts and guffaws from the listening patrons. "Yes, I do," she said again. "King Jusson affirmed today, not only my office, but said as there's no governor I report directly to the throne. To His Majesty himself."

Isa blinked. "Gawell—" she said, starting to look worried as the muted merriment died.

"Who do you think His Majesty said it to?" Chadde indicated us. "The King's Own, Isa. The one with the feather and braid? His cousin and heir. And 'sweet chuck' is his Lord Commander."

"Why would the king care about Menck's death, Chadde?" a smooth voice asked behind us. "As intriguing as the jailer was, I didn't think that he had the prominence or, ah, provenance to catch royalty's attention, dead or alive."

I turned to find Jeff and Arlie already facing a man standing in the entryway. While I wasn't familiar with everyone in Freston's valley, I had made the acquaintance of a good number and could usually guess the identity of the rest. The man before me, however, was a stranger. He was on the plump side, and his head barely cleared Jeff's and Arlie's shoulders as he walked past them into the taproom. He was neatly dressed, his face clean-shaven, his fingernails clean and he fit the tavern like four shoes on a three-legged horse.

"Know him?" I murmured to Jeff.

Jeff shook his head, but Arlis answered. "That's Helto. He bought the Pig from Elaf a couple of years ago." He saw our looks and shrugged. "Seen him around town on occasion."

Wondering why someone so sleek would want a rat hole like the Pig, I watched the taverner make his way to a spot against the back wall.

"His Majesty's just that way, Helto," Chadde said as she crossed the taproom to the windows by the hearth. "Caring about a murder done right under his nose."

As the peacekeeper spoke, the tapster reentered by the same door and slid behind the bar again. He picked up Isa's cup and refilled it, handing it to her with a nod. But instead of looking at the bawd, he was once more staring at Laurel and Wyln. He picked up another cup—and dropped it with a muffled thump on the floor. He ducked down behind the bar to retrieve it.

"The king sent you out here in search of Menck's killers?" Helto asked, watching Chadde struggle with a window shutter.

"Yes." Using her truncheon, Chadde knocked the latch a couple of times, and a large chunk of soot fell out. "But I was coming anyway, seeing as this is where Menck's body was found." Opening the shutter, she moved to the last window.

"An insult," Helto said, his mouth tightening, his eyes staying watchful. "It perturbs me that someone used my tavern as a dumping place, and so I did my own questioning. Unfortunately, no one saw anything—"

Opening the final pair of shutters, Chadde threw them back, illuminating the last dark corner in the taproom. She also illuminated Wyln and Laurel—and the room exploded.

Isa screamed, throwing her cup and splashing ale over the men sitting at the tables in front of her. They and the others throughout the room shouted, some because of their dousing, but most pointing at the large mountain cat and elf suddenly standing in the light. Chairs and tables were knocked over as they jumped up, reaching for their weapons.

"Pox rot it," Jeff said, shoving me behind him and pulling his sword just in time to knock away another airborne cup. A chair followed and then a lunk dressed as a farmhand rushed at us. "Bloody bones and ashes!" Jeff hit the farmhand with the flat of his blade, shoving him aside.

But more came at us—and each other. Apparently several took the opportunity to settle old scores and fistfights broke out. Two grappling with each other landed on a table and it crashed down under their weight, its legs giving way. There was a piercing shriek as another bawd grabbed a chair and slammed it over a man's head, who sank down, his eyes crossing. Arlie danced by, his sword flashing against a short staff, and more tables and chairs crashed as folks fought to get out of their way. Thadro and Chadde were back-to-back, Thadro holding his sword while Chadde had her truncheon in one hand and a long dagger in the other. I reached for my own sword, only to remember that it was now guarding the charnel house. Grabbing my knife, I looked up again to see the tapster stand up from behind the bar with a cocked and loaded crossbow that he aimed at Wyln.

"*Cyhn!*" I shouted and pushed past Jeff to get to Wyln. As I did, the crossbow wavered, then shifted to me, and I froze, staring at the quarrel, its metal tip gleaming in the dim light. I then raised my gaze to the tapster's. Expressionless, he pulled the release.

"Rabbit, get down!"

I needed no urging. With a yell, I dropped to the floor, my staff falling beside me with a clatter. My yell changed to a grunt, though, as someone landed on top of me. Then Laurel gave a bellowing roar and all noise cut off. I cautiously raised my head and looked around, but could only see legs, broken furniture and my fire and earth spheres floating in front of me. My head was pushed down again.

"Damn it, stay put," Thadro said.

"Yes, sir," I muttered, staring at the floor. It was as appealing as the rest of the tavern.

"The disturbance is over, honored commander," Laurel said. "Isn't that right, House Master?"

"Yes," Helto said, his smooth voice sounding strangled.

Thadro hesitated, then slowly rose. After looking about, he held out a hand and helped me to my feet. (It took a little tugging as my tabard had stuck to the floor.) Picking up my staff from the floor, I then did my own scan.

The room was in a shambles—tables and chairs broken, dented cups on the floor along with puddles of ale and strong spirits. The people also were a wreck, with bloodied faces and rising lumps and bruises. But none of that was surprising—it was the aftermath of a tavern brawl, after all. Nor was I surprised that Laurel had Helto pinned to the wall, the mountain cat's claws to the plump man's throat. Or that Wyln stood in front of the bar, the crossbow in one slender hand, the other raised as dancing flames formed a cage around the tapster. The tapster stared back at the dark elf, his own hands raised in the air, his face still blank.

What riveted my attention was the quarrel frozen in midflight at eye level. My right eye, to be exact.

I'd faced death before—both on the battlefield and off— and violence aimed at me was nothing new. However, when

I looked back at the tapster, it was like staring down a tunnel. Without conscious thought, I shoved past Thadro, something building in my chest rumbling low and deep as I pushed through the former brawlers. Wyln looked over his shoulder at me, and there was nothing amused about his smile as he stepped aside. Expression did come over the tapster's face, his eyes growing wide, his mouth opening as he began to flinch away. But I was already reaching into the fiery cage, my hand grabbing his jerkin to drag him through the flames.

"I said, stop!" Thadro spun me around, and everything became normal-paced again. I faced the Lord Commander, ready to snarl back if he started in on me. However, Thadro had other fish to fillet. He looked at Helto, still held against the wall by Laurel's claws at his throat.

"I could set fire to this place right now for the attempt on the king's heir's life. Burn it down with all that you have in it, and leave you nothing but the clothes on your back. And if I choose, I could burn those too." Thadro gave a nasty smile. "Or I could just let Lieutenant Lord Rabbit loose."

Helto's eyes were bulging out, either in fear or because of pressure from Laurel's claws. "My lords, sirs, in the confusion— He didn't mean— The cat and elf— It was an accident!"

"Who is he?" Chadde asked, looking at the tapster. "And where's Jeb?"

"Jeb went back to his village last night as he received word that his father took sick. Bram happened to be looking for work and I hired him."

"A stranger to the valley wanders by looking for work? And you just happened to have a position available? How convenient," Chadde marveled. "Though I suppose that shouldn't be surprising as *you* happened to come to the valley just as Elaf decided to sell the Pig."

"Coincidence," Helto choked. "But surely we can discuss it, Chadde, like civilized people—"

"I'm always willing to be civil," Chadde said. She looked around the room and jerked a thumb at the door. "Everyone out."

The patrons and bawds looked at Wyln and his cage of fire. They looked at Laurel, the cat's claws pressing into Helto's skin. Then they looked at me. They left quickly, the last one out shutting the door behind him without being asked. Jeff started to go to the door to stand guard, but Thadro stopped him.

"You and Arlis take Bram and lock him in a stable stall to await our escort back to Freston."

Giving me a worried look, Jeff joined Arlis at the bar and, securing the tapster's hands with his own belt, they led him from the room. While Chadde and Thadro righted a table and some chairs, I went to where the quarrel still hung midair. It dropped into my outstretched hand, the air around it once more swirling into a sphere. It moved to hover at my shoulder, the other spheres shifting to make room.

"Neat trick," Chadde said, watching me. "I heard that you'd once stopped a flight of arrows, Lord Rabbit?"

"During the rebellion," Thadro said before I could answer. "A whole lot of people would've been killed otherwise, including His Majesty. Including me."

"A very neat trick, then."

"It's the wind," I said, thrusting the quarrel through my belt. "It does as it wills."

The peacekeeper's eyes narrowed in speculation. "I remember you saying that last night—"

"Chadde," choked Helto.

"Maybe we can talk later, my lord," Chadde said. "Master Laurel, if you please."

Laurel released Helto and the taverner stumbled away from the wall and bent over, his hands on his knees as he coughed and wheezed breath back into his lungs. Taking him by the arm, Chadde led Helto to the table and gently pushed him into a chair. "I would get you something to drink," the peacekeeper said as she also sat, "but I'm afraid anything here will make you gag worse."

"If my customers wanted fine wines and smooth ales, they would go to the Hart's Leap," Helto rasped, massaging his throat. I could see the indentations Laurel's claws made in his skin, and thought the taverner was going to have an interesting pattern of bruising.

"And you always do that, don't you?" Chadde said as Thadro sat next to her. "Providing your patrons what they ask for: bad ale and worse brandy, weighted dice and light-fingered bawds. And, that all-time favorite, a loaded cross-bow."

Standing at the Lord Commander's back, I looked over at Laurel, but neither he nor Wyln appeared interested in joining us at the table. Still holding the crossbow, the enchanter had moved behind the bar, while Laurel shifted to where the taverner had stood, the cat's eyes raised to the mirror.

"As I said, I know my customers." Helto's hand fell from his throat and he took a shuddering breath. "There are times when strong measures are needed to keep order."

"You must not get much repeat business using a quarrel's flight to quell brawls," Thadro said.

"The crossbow's for show," Helto said. "This is the first time it's been shot."

"It looks pretty well maintained for something that's just a prop," Thadro said, glancing at the weapon in Wyln's grip.

"Soldiers visit my establishment, and a weapon in disrepair wouldn't be very convincing to them," Helto said. "Jeb would wave it about, and most times everybody would calm down. Unfortunately, Bram *is* new and was most likely spooked by both the magicals and the fight. I'm sure it was just a mistake. An almost fatal one, certainly, but still, a mistake."

"'Would wave it about'?" Chadde's smile didn't reach her eyes. "The hell he did. Jeb would've shot himself in the ballocks before he got the crossbow above the bar top. However, Bram handled it like he was once in the army himself—or was a mercenary. Maybe both." The peace-keeper leaned forward. "Bram did not shoot out of confusion and fear, Helto. I myself have marked how much Lord Wyln resembles His Majesty. Bram had that crossbow aimed at his lordship until Lord Rabbit shouted kin—"

"Close," I murmured.

"—and Bram realized Lord Wyln wasn't the king. So he shot at Lord Rabbit instead."

"So you're saying that Bram and Jeb conspired to assassinate either the king or his heir?" Helto asked. He didn't wait for Chadde's answer. "I assure you, that's not the case. Not only do they not know each other, but they didn't know that Lord Rabbit or the elf were coming."

"But you knew I was," Chadde pointed out, "and that I was bringing Laurel Faena with me."

"So I did," Helto admitted. "However, why would I want you dead? You're harmless enough. No, Chadde, it definitely was a mistake, and so I shall say to Magistrate Ordgar—"

"Not a mistake, House Master," Laurel said. "The crossbow was shot on purpose."

Helto did not look at the Faena. "A civilized discussion, Chadde, does not include magicals."

"But we are very civil," Wyln said from behind the bar. "At least I am. Laurel is a little rough with claws and fangs and hunting his dinner down. You, however, are an ill-mannered dog who has violated the most basic tenets of Hospitality." He waved a hand up at the mirror. "From where you stood against the wall, you could see the entire room, including your tapster. You saw him duck down to pick up the crossbow, you saw him aim it and you saw him shoot it. And you said nothing."

A derisive look came over Helto's face as he kept his gaze on Chadde. "Why do I have to listen to the blatherings of dolts? I wasn't looking anywhere except right in front of me. It was a barroom brawl, for Heaven's sake! I was more concerned about chairs flying my way than what my tapster was doing on the other side of the room."

"I watched you," Laurel said. "You didn't take your eyes off the mirror at all, which makes me wonder about the genuineness of the fight."

Helto, brave now that he was away from Laurel's claws, suavely sneered, "And who's going to believe you, pussycat?"

"I find him very believable," Chadde said.

"As do I," Thadro said.

"I also believe him, sir, Peacekeeper Chadde," I said. "Especially about the fight. Bram signaled Isa just before she started it by screaming and throwing her ale."

"He did, Lieutenant?" Thadro said, not taking his eyes off Helto. "Perhaps we should ask Mistress Isa about that."

"Oh, we're going to question everyone in the entire inn," Chadde said. "See what they all have to say."

The sneer disappeared off Helto's face, leaving it as blank as the tapster's had been. Then he exploded up from his chair with a flash of steel as his hand came up with a knife. Shoving the table against Chadde and Thadro, he threw the knife at Laurel in one smooth motion. Laurel twisted out of the way and the knife embedded itself in the wall. Thadro's chair knocked into me, causing me to stumble, but I recovered fast, pulling my own dagger as Chadde and Thadro pushed the table out of their way. Another knife appeared in Helto's hand and he jabbed it at Chadde, the peacekeeper jerking back. Freed, Thadro drew his sword as he headed around the table and I started the other way, seeking to trap Helto in between. But before either Thadro or I reach could reach him, I heard a muted twang and a sharp thunk, and a quarrel bloomed out of the table, pinning the taverner's sleeve to the wood.

"Such an ingenious engine," Wyln said. Apparently he had found Bram's stash of quarrels for he reached under the bar and brought up another one. Cocking the crossbow with one hand in a casual display of strength, he loaded the quarrel and aimed it at the taverner. "Shall we discover where else I can put one of these?"

The "magical" must've rankled.

Helto stared at the enchanter, then let the second knife drop from his hand to clatter on the table.

"Wise choice," Laurel rumbled. Plucking the first knife out of the wall, he walked over to Helto and placed a paw on the taverner's shoulder. Laurel's claws dug in as he shoved Helto back into the chair.

"Pussycat" probably touched a sore spot too.

Chadde picked up the second knife from the table, examining it. "Very nice. Turalian steel, isn't it? From one of Ednoth's caravans." Holding the knife in one hand, she went to Helto and moved Laurel a little to the side. Grabbing a handful of hair, the peacekeeper yanked the taverner's head back, her gray eyes cold as they stared down into Helto's pale blue ones. "No more shoveling muck at me," Chadde said. "Or I will help Lord Commander Thadro burn this place down. With you in it."

"No need for more violence, honored peacekeeper," Laurel said, also staring down at Helto, his paw still on the taverner's shoulder. "I can *touch* him for you."

"Touch, Master Laurel?" Chadde asked.

Laurel lifted his paw from Helto's shoulder, the rune bright in the dingy room. "Use this to, hrmm, dig for the truth." He held it where Helto could just see the glowing rune out of the corner of his eye. "It's wondrously effective."

" 'Dig for the truth'?" Chadde asked, her face growing intent. "You can do that?"

"Yes," Laurel said. He gave a rumbling purr. "It's amazing how much I can unearth."

Helto's face also grew intent—with fear—and he strained away. Chadde, however, took a firmer grip on Helto's hair, keeping him in place, and the taverner looked back up into the peacekeeper's face.

"What do you want?" Helto asked.

"Talk to me, Helto," Chadde said. "Tell me about Menck. And Slevoic ibn Dru."

Eighteen

Thadro was the only one who did not react. Helto grew still while Laurel and I stared at the Keeper of the King's Peace in astonishment. Even Wyln looked surprised.

"Well, now," the enchanter murmured. "The Vicious One, not so gone and forgotten after all."

"Slevoic spent three years in Freston, my lord," Chadde said. "More than long enough to keep his memory here green for quite some time."

After fouling up enough so that even his noble connections couldn't save him, the late, unlamented Lieutenant Slevoic ibn Dru was transferred from the Royal Garrison in Iversly to the one in Freston, the last place for those whose families were too powerful to kick them out of the army completely. But while the Vicious spread his particular kind of charm in the garrison with a liberal hand, he was much more circumspect when he was in town. Due to the House of Dru's royal connection, the garrison commander winked at Slevoic's antics towards his fellow soldiers; however, Commander Ebner had very strict notions about our behavior towards those we were supposed to protect.

"Ebner would've carved Slevoic like a Festival goose if he'd acted badly towards the townsfolk," I said, frowning.

"Oh, when ibn Dru came into Freston he was all goodness and light," Chadde said. "But he had interests outside of town. Interests that seemed to be centered on this tavern." Chadde gave a tug on Helto's hair. "Interests that seemed to involve smuggling."

The room once more grew still. Then Wyln came from behind the bar as I yanked the table away, ripping Helto's sleeve as the table went skidding on spilled ale. Looking down, I saw that the taverner had managed to pull a third, smaller boot knife. Laurel, growling, batted it out of Helto's grasp, the blade hitting the floor with a thump. We crowded in very close, Wyln pointing the crossbow at Helto's chest. The taverner shrank back in his chair.

"Some just never learn," Thadro remarked. Picking up the knife, he joined the circle we made around the taverner. "They had friends murdered, Helto, friends whose ghosts followed Rabbit around for weeks, waiting for justice."

"So I've heard," Chadde said, still firmly grasping Helto's hair.

"Ghosts and smuggling?" Helto tried a smile, but it went crooked. "That's a little far-fetched. I do admit that some of my customers may be involved in things that aren't quite legal, but it's all local and very petty—"

Sighing, Chadde tugged on Helto's hair again, shaking the taverner's head slowly from side to side. "Helto, Helto, Helto. News flows up the Banson, just as goods float down it. News that pelts, skins, ivory and other body parts from the Border were found not only in the patriarch's See but also throughout the kingdom—an entire warehouse just in Iversly alone. News of how Dru used the smuggling to finance Teram ibn Flavan's rebellion against the House of Iver. Of how the peace treaty had been violated and the kingdom was teetering on the brink of another war with the Border."

Helto's throat worked as he swallowed. "I heard that too. However, none of it had anything to do with me or the Pig—"

Chadde gave another series of slow tugs. "But it did, Helto. Slevoic ibn Dru used to sit with Menck in this room, and suddenly Menck was swanking around town with a pair of fancy boots made of a kind of leather I'd never seen before. And after Elaf left the valley and you took over the tavern, both Slevoic and Menck would join you in your private rooms, smoking cheroots and drinking brandywine from your private stock—and suddenly you were sporting a knife with a fancy bone handle."

Helto licked his lips, his eyes on Chadde's.

"And just as suddenly there were folks slipping in and out of Freston after the gates were shut for the night, bandits with new swords and horses, a village elder's wife with a new gold necklet, and packages and people traveling the back-mountain paths, just when the Mountain Patrol happened to be busy elsewhere."

I jerked my head up to look at Chadde, wondering if maybe my old troop had been under suspicion too, but the peacekeeper was focused on Helto.

"Then the news flows up here that the smuggling has been uncovered, a rebellion put down, the House of Dru outlawed, and both Slevoic and his kinsman, Lord Gherat of Dru, on the run. Just as suddenly, Menck's boots and your fancy knife disappear. And when the twin news arrives of Slevoic's death and the king's progression, Menck—who rode like a sack of potatoes—borrows a horse to hurry out here and is once more shepherded into your private snug."

A distant shout sounded outside, but we all remained intent on Helto. All except for Laurel. His brows knit, he started for the window. The second shout, though, did have me and the others looking up. That had sounded like Jeff. There was a third shout, cut short, and then the thuds of hoofs against packed dirt—and as we were distracted, Helto once more exploded out of his chair, leaving a lot of his hair behind in Chadde's grasp. He pushed past me and Thadro, heading for the door, and I snatched at him, catching his torn sleeve. However, the sleeve ripped completely, coming off in my hand, and he wiggled free. Wyln swung around, aiming the crossbow at Helto's fleeing back, but the taverner slid on a patch of ale, going down on one knee, and the quarrel passed over his head to thunk into the doorframe. Helto scrambled to his feet and flung the door open, dashing out.

Wyln grabbed the quarrel from my belt and, loading it in the crossbow, took aim again, but Thadro shoved the crossbow up and the quarrel went into the ceiling. "Shoot him out there where everybody can see, and there'll be riots," the Lord Commander said.

"And what would've happened if that tailless dog of an assassin had shot *me?*" Wyln asked, yanking the bow away from Thadro's grip.

"We can debate that later," Thadro said as he started after Helto. "You and the Faena cat stay here. With me, Lieutenant."

I hadn't waited for Thadro and was already out the door to see Helto running down the hall to the back of the tavern—the taverner pounding on doors and shouting at the top of his lungs about magicals and murderers. I ran after him and, with my much longer stride, was easily gaining. However, just before I reached the private parlor, the door opened and a crowd of people poured out, blocking the hallway. Slamming into them, I bounced back and tried to go around, but one of them caught me in a vise masquerading as a bear hug. Unable to break free, I brought the heel of my hand up, hitting his nose, and brought the heel of my boot down on his instep. There was a bellow of pain, but instead of releasing me, I was once more slammed—this time into the wall—and saw stars as my head cracked against the wood.

"Well, look at the murdering magical I just caught," said a familiar voice.

I blinked to clear my vision and saw the evilly grinning face of Lord Ranulf. Next to him, his silver eyes gleaming in the dim hallway, was Lord Beollan.

Nineteen

"How the hell could I have known he was chasing some-one you wanted to catch?" Ranulf asked, all good humor at manhandling me gone. "I hear somebody crying 'murder' and I come out and see Magic Boy with his float-ing balls pelting down the hall, so I stop him."

Both Helto and Bram had escaped. Apparently some of the brawlers were more than midday tipplers and a group of them had descended on the stables, where they demon-strated the effectiveness of many armed with quarterstaffs and other large sticks against two unmounted men with swords. Overwhelming Jeff and Arlie, they freed Bram, who immediately took off on Thadro's horse. They then locked the two guardsmen into a stall before disappearing into the surrounding woods.

And Helto had ridden off on my horse a few moments later.

I now paused from nursing my sore head to look at the Lord of Bainswyr. "Sod you and your mother," I said, care-fully enunciating.

The scowl disappeared from Ranulf's face to be replaced by a snarl, his dark brown eyes seeming to glow red as he started towards me. Showing my own teeth, I shoved my-self up from my chair, ignoring the fact that my head felt like it was about to split open and fall off.

"That's enough," Thadro said, pushing me back down, while Beollan caught Ranulf's arm.

"I would think that we've plenty of folk trying to do us harm without us doing it ourselves," Laurel said as he was tending Jeff and Arlie's hurts. Seeing our faces, he shrugged. "Just an observation."

I gave my own shrug and, wincing, returned to the important task of holding my head on my shoulders.

After freeing Jeff and Arlis, and securing the rest of the horses, we had returned to the tavern to lick our wounds. Instead of going back to the taproom, though, Chadde led us upstairs past discreetly closed doors to Helto's private quarters in the back of the tavern. To our surprise—and disappointment—the door was unlocked. It seemed unlikely that Helto would've kept secrets in unsecured rooms.

Another surprise was the taverner's quarters themselves. There were two rooms, the outer a tidy snug with a massive desk, a thick rug and a cabinet that contained crystal decanters of spirits. The room's windows were clean, giving us a view into the fall woods surrounding the tavern, and in the fireplace a fire filled the room with warmth—without soot or smoke. Beyond, in the interior room, there were more large pieces of furniture, including a huge, curtained bed with a stepstool by its side.

The taverner had made up for his short stature by surrounded himself with the monumental. But while there was plenty of big furniture, there was nothing about Slevoic, Menck or smuggling. Or anything else illicit.

"Helto has been very careful," Chadde said, closing a drawer. She sat at the desk, receipts and papers scattered in front of her, all related to the running of the Pig. The tavern's strongbox was also in front of her. But it held nothing of interest, just a mound of copper coins with the glint of a few lonely silver ones mixed in. Apparently running a tavern wasn't nearly as lucrative as Menck's strong-arming.

The peacekeeper picked up a receipt, frowning at it. "He also paid good money for his bad ale."

"That's surprising," Thadro said. After putting me in my place, he had returned to searching the cabinet. "Judging by the smell, I would've thought he brewed his own—from old hosen."

"No," Chadde said, her frown deepening. "According to this, he bought it from the town brewer, and at these prices the ale should've been premium." She picked up more receipts, flipping through them. "As should've been the flour from the miller, the meat from the butcher, the brandywine he purchased from Ednoth—" Falling silent, she went through the rest of the receipts.

"Brandy and Turalian steel?" Thadro asked. "Your head merchant has his fingers in a lot of pies." He shut the cabinet doors with a quiet click. "Nothing. Probably got rid of anything incriminating months ago, along with his bone-handled knife."

"Or it was never here to begin with," Chadde said. She set down the receipts and looked through the door into the bedroom. "I'll check in there, but I don't think I'll find anything under the mattress."

Thadro nodded, a line appearing between his brows as his gaze fell on Wyln sitting next to me. The enchanter had kept the crossbow like some battle prize, having even retrieved the rest of the quarrels and the crossbow's goat's foot from behind the bar. The weapon now sat unloaded across the elf's knees, but apparently that was no comfort to the Lord Commander. He'd seen how fast Wyln could load and shoot.

However, Thadro's irritation wasn't fazing Wyln— mostly because he *was* Wyln, but also because the dark elf's attention was on our guests. Or, to be more accurate, on Ranulf and Beollan's guests. They had been with the two Marcher lords in the private parlor, and despite the throbbing pain in my head, I'd recognized them as the street players Jeff, Arlie and I had seen perform a lifetime ago yesterday. Chadde and Thadro had herded them into Helto's study with us, and the troupe now stood near the door to the hallway—as far away as they could get without leaving the room—watching us as they would something wild and probably rabid.

"They're street players, elf," Beollan drawled. After stopping Ranulf, he'd remained standing and now his lip curled up in a very impressive sneer. "Don't worry, they won't bite."

I lifted my head to look at Beollan, surprised. After seeing his interaction with Laurel last night, I had thought that the Lord of Fellmark was remarkably free of the prejudice that infected most of his fellow northerners—Ranulf very much included. But apparently Beollan had just hidden it better. The Lord of Fellmark's expression was tight, his silver eyes alive with some emotion that made them blaze as he stared down his nose at Wyln.

Wyln, however, merely leaned forward. "Street players?" he asked. "They're actors?"

"Yeah," Ranulf said, having gone back to his normal scowl. "They've been abandoned by their master and were talking to Beollan and me about patronage."

Squinting through my pain, I examined the players. The man with the motley cape *was* missing from their numbers. As was another. "Did Master Rodolfo take Rosea with him?" I asked.

Both Arlie and Jeff stirred at the mention of the Fair Rose, but Laurel rumbled at them and they subsided. Ranulf once more aimed his scowl at me; however, before he could speak, one of the players took a tiny step forward.

"You know us, my lord?" she asked, as she dropped an equally tiny curtsey.

Upon further examination, I saw that the player was

Lady Alys' nurse, minus the wig and padding that had made her look matronly while onstage. Without them, her form was slender and supple, her face full of interesting planes and lines. The sunlight coming in through the windows slid along her high cheekbones and gleamed in her black hair, while humor lurked in her brown eyes and wide mouth. "Yes, Mistress," I said, sitting up a little straighter. "We saw you yesterday in Theater Square."

"I am Gwynedd, my lord." Dropping another, deeper curtsey, the actress' generous mouth curved up into a hint of a grin. "I remember you. Your appearance in the audience caused quite a panic in the wings." She considered the spheres hovering about my aching head. "But weren't there butterflies?"

Ranulf's evil grin reappeared. "What? Floating balls *and* butterflies?"

I made a very rude gesture.

"They're faeries, honored folk," Laurel said as he spread ointment on a bruise on Arlis' face. "From Queen Mab's own court." He frowned slightly. "I'd forgotten about them, Rabbit. Where are they?"

"They flew off when we got out of jail," I said.

"Those butterflies were fairies?" Thadro asked, also frowning. "You've been allowing courtiers from a foreign queen to hang about you, Lieutenant?"

"Sir," I said, holding in a sigh. Commander Carp was back.

"Their presence was a condition of the High Council in allowing Rabbit's return, honored commander," Laurel said. Finished with Arlis, the cat lifted Jeff's face and gently began to dab something from a vial on his cut lip. "The Faery Queen demanded parity, as Rabbit was already being accompanied by the head of the Faena and a *deorc oelf* who's of Loran the Fyrst's lineage."

"A what?" Chadde asked.

"Dark elf," I said.

"Queen Mab was very persuasive and the Council agreed to her terms." Laurel recapped his vial and, tucking it into his pouch, came over to the fireplace. At first idly tracking him, I stiffened as I saw the teakettle hanging on the hob. Laurel reopened his pouch and took out a small sack. I whimpered.

"We were doing very well to limit it to just us," Wyln added. "There were others who wanted to accompany Rabbit back here. Including a dragon."

That was true. Dragoness Moraina had debated about coming with us as we returned to Iversterre. Fortunately for everyone involved, she decided not to. For now.

Beollan's face lightened a bit. "My word. All that for you?"

"Yes," Wyln said before I could answer. "Great things are expected from Rabbit, son of Lark and Two Trees."

"Great for whom?" Ranulf asked, his expression turning appraising.

"Everyone," Wyln said.

While they all chewed on that, Laurel, carrying his kettle of vile tea and a cup, came over to examine my injuries. Wyln stood, moving to give the cat room and, still holding the crossbow, leaned against my chair, his gaze returning to the players. The troupe cowered against the door, all trying to find someone to hide behind.

Wyln gently smiled at them. "Your master has abandoned you?" he asked.

Gwynedd, braver than the rest, spoke up. "It seems so, my lord. Rodolfo and Rosea have disappeared"—her mouth pulled down—"along with our purse."

"Yeah," muttered one of the women. "The trollop stole it."

"No, she didn't," another one said. "She bared her ankles and Master Rolly tripped over his tongue to give it to her."

"He wasn't the only one," the first player said, giving one of the male troupe members a glare—and the man's face flushed with embarrassment.

My own face heated a little as I remembered my own re-action to those same ankles. Then I realized what the player had said. "What do you mean, 'tripped over his tongue'?" I asked, pulling away from Laurel's ministrations. "Isn't she Rodolfo's sister?"

The troupe forgot Wyln enough to break into noises of derision while Gwynedd shook her head, her mouth going flat and thin. "No. She is not. Rolly is *my* brother. Rosea is his wife."

Jeff, Arlie and I all went very still. "His wife?" I asked. Laurel pushed a cup of the vile tea into my hand and I blindly accepted it, drinking it down without tasting any-thing.

Chadde had been sorting through the rest of the papers on the desk, but at Gwynedd's revelation, looked up. "His wife?" the peacekeeper echoed. "Then why was he passing her off as his sister—" She broke off, her eyes sliding to me. My face heated more.

"Because it's easier to catch gulls when they can't see the hook in the bait," Gwynedd said, her voice tart. Then she sighed. "I beg pardon, messirs, ma'am. It's just that when Rolly and I founded our troupe, we spent years of traveling the road, playing where the devil himself wouldn't go, to audiences who'd just as soon pelt you with garbage as look at you. If you were lucky."

"An actor's lot is a hard one," Wyln murmured.

"Yes, my lord. But we finally began to do well, playing better places to better audiences. Then Rolly met Rosea."

"Where?" Ranulf asked unexpectedly.

"One of the villages north of here," Gwynedd said, wav-ing a hand. "We were only there a day or two, but it was long enough for her to latch onto him. Next thing I knew, what was ours had become hers, and I had no say in the running of it." She looked at me, Laurel and Wyln, her eyes hard. "Don't you think I'd know better than to stage that benighted play in the middle of a town overflowing with magicals? But she wanted it so she could shine in the lead. So she thought."

Recalling the messenger's dropped pouch full of tinkly things and the nurse's hard stomps as she crossed the stage, Rosea had been having a hard time working up a dim glimmer. By the smirks on the faces of the other troupe members, it seemed that they also did their best to sabotage her scenes.

"Hardly overflowing," Wyln said, still propped against my chair. "Just Laurel, Rabbit, myself and a few fugitive faeries. But you said your money is gone. Is anything else missing?"

"We have all our sets, costumes and our book of plays," Gwynedd assured Wyln. "Unfortunately, our creditors won't take Lady Alys' wig as payment." Her mouth crooked. "*You* wouldn't happen to be interested in sponsoring an acting troupe, my lord?"

"Perhaps," Wyln said.

The room became absolutely silent, even the fire forgetting to crackle. Laurel looked up from pouring me more tea to meet my gaze. We both turned to look at the enchanter, me shifting in my chair.

Wyln ignored our stares. "But I would need to see your book first."

"Now wait just a damn moment," Ranulf said, finding his voice, while Beollan's fair brows snapped together, his thin lips now lifting in a very impressive snarl.

Wyln, however, ignored them too—as did Gwynedd. The player took a step closer to the dark elf, her eyes assessing the quality and cut of his clothes, and her mouth curved up again. "Yes, my lord. Of course. I can fetch it right away, if you'd like."

"No," Wyln said. "Bring it to me later. You'll find me at King Jusson's residence."

"Lord Wyln," Thadro began, his own mouth twisting with annoyance.

"You're staying with the king?" Gwynedd breathed, her dark eyes bright and gleaming. Behind her, the rest of the troupe stirred, visions of "His Majesty's Players" filling their heads.

"Yes," Wyln said. "But whatever is decided, you should pack. You won't be staying here."

Gwynedd's mouth went anxious. "But our bill—"

"It'll be taken care of," Wyln said.

That marvelous mouth curved upwards once more. "Yes, my lord. Thank you!" Gwynedd gave another curtsey and, turning, she opened the door, hustling the troupe out before her. In the hallway, their voices rose in excited chatter. As the door snicked closed behind them, Ranulf and Beollan sucked in breath to speak. However, Thadro beat them both.

"You presume, Lord Wyln," the Lord Commander said, directing his mud-puddle stare at the enchanter. "Inviting street players to the king's residence."

"Oh?" Wyln asked, amused. "I'm going back to the garrison?"

"No, but—"

"I won't be allowed visitors, then?"

"Of course you'll be allowed—" Thadro stopped and let out a breath, glaring. "You're enjoying yourself, aren't you?"

"Yes," Wyln said.

"You have a yen for an acting troupe, Lord Wyln?" Chadde asked before Thadro could explode.

Wyln's amusement faded. "Perhaps," he said again. "But I'm more interested in how quickly two of their members had fastened onto Two Trees'son."

"But our meeting was just happenstance," I said. "They didn't know I was going to be in the audience yesterday. *I* didn't know until Jeff, Arlie and I went by Theater Square and saw them performing."

"So?" Wyln looked down at me. "If you hadn't appeared, they would've just had to wait until you did. It *is* a small town, after all."

Thadro's anger eased back a bit. "You think they were trying to snare Rabbit?"

"Ha, ha. Sir," I muttered.

"You heard the troupe mistress," Wyln said. "Her brother's wife was set out as bait. Why else if it wasn't a trap?"

"It's possible that they knew he was the king's cousin and sought to gain royal favor through him," Beollan said. His silver eyes were once more narrowed on the elf. "It wouldn't be the first time someone tried to get to His Majesty through a side door."

I blinked at Beollan describing me as a secondary entrance, but Wyln just shrugged. "You may be right," he said. "But like the peacekeeper, I have a deep distrust of coincidence. Of events happening—or folks appearing—at just the right moment."

Beollan's face darkened in anger, but Jeffen, with perfect timing, spoke up. "Rodolfo called Rabbit 'my lord' before Rabbit told them who he was, Lord Wyln," he offered.

So the master of the motley had.

"That's true, sir," Arlis confirmed to Thadro. "In fact, the whole conversation was aimed at Rabbit. Jeff and I were pretty much irrelevant."

So much for my sparkling wit and scintillating personality. I stared down into my cup, wondering if my life was now going to consist of folks doing their damnedest to get next to me because of my relationship with Jusson.

"Is that so?" Wyln asked. "Then we should definitely

keep the troupe close until we discover *why* Master Rodolfo was dangling his wife in front of Rabbit."

"And the possibility of 'Wyln's Players' does not enter into it," Laurel rumbled softly.

A very faint flush appeared on Wyln's cheekbones.

"Something to take back to the king," Thadro said, his frown remaining. "Along with attempted assassinations and old associations with smugglers."

"Yes." Sighing, Chadde stood, gathering the receipts and papers together in neat stacks. "I don't look forward to telling His Majesty not only how Bram and Helto escaped on two of his horses, but that we've found no evidence linking Helto to any illegal doings. Even if we catch him, if he proclaims his innocence loud and long enough to the right people, he'll go free."

"But there is evidence, honored peacekeeper," Laurel said.

Chadde looked up. "What?"

Laurel pointed at the rug. "This is Border-made; however, there isn't trade between the Border and Iversterre. Not yet. Where did the House Master get it?"

Everyone looked down. "Border-made?" Thadro asked. "This isn't a Perdan?" He bent closer. "No, you're right. It's not. The Turals don't make rugs like this."

So they didn't. Perdans tended towards intricate, sharp-edged designs in bright colors. This one was made up of soft greens and gentle browns all flowing into and out of each other, evoking the floor of a forest during summer.

"It is a Border pattern," Laurel said. He flexed his feet, his toe claws digging into the rug. "The dye and the fiber itself come from one of our provinces."

"But you do trade with the Qarant," Beollan said. He'd given up glaring at Wyln to peer down at the rug. "It could've come through them to a merchant here."

Laurel shook his head, his beads clacking. "No. Border

goods do not go to the human kingdom. As there are plenty of other places to sell, the Qarant agree to our stipulations."

"That's true," I said, gently running my booted foot over the thick pile. "My da headed up the Weald's trade council, and they refused to have any dealings with Iversterre." My mouth crooked. "It was a matter of principle."

Principle, and deep-seated dislike and distrust. Many of the long-lived fae remembered when Iversterre was theirs. Like the elves. They also remembered being driven out. Also like the elves. I glanced at Wyln, who was also staring at the rug. He stooped, running his hand over the pile. Then, straightening, he walked to the edge and flipped a corner over to examine the back. "This is from Belde Forest," he said, frowning. "The folk there don't sell to the Qarant. They won't even sell to Border provinces where there are humans."

"I thought you said that you people considered Lord Rabbit the hope of the ages?" Beollan asked.

"Some wounds go very deep, Marcher Lord," Wyln said, looking at all the human feet on the rug. Then his eyes widened slightly and he stood quickly, staring about at the wood furniture.

"It's not spritewood," Laurel said. "I checked while you were involved with the troupe."

Wyln slid Laurel a side glance.

"So you're saying that this rug was smuggled in from the Border?" Thadro asked.

Laurel shrugged. "While there is a slight possibility of a rug from Belde arriving in one of your large port cities by some circuitously legitimate means, I doubt very much that one would end up on the floor of a place like this."

"Two rugs," I said, looking into the bedroom.

"Then there's no possibility whatsoever," Laurel said.

Chadde stared at Laurel before scrambling through her

neat stacks of receipts. She snatched one and held it up, reading. "Two rugs from Master Ednoth." She lowered it, her eyes brilliant. "Who also sells Helto his god-awful brandy *and* Turalian-made knives. Such a coincidence."

Twenty

There wasn't anything under Helto's mattress—nor in the rest of the bedchamber. Besides the rug, the inner room yielded nothing but some well-made clothes hanging in the clothespress and an impressive array of grooming aids. A locked trunk that at first had seemed promising only contained fine sheets and blankets for the massive bed. Deciding that we'd found all that there was to find, Chadde returned to the desk to gather the receipts and papers together once more, placing them in the tavern's strongbox. Then she helped shift the heavy furniture so that the rugs could be rolled and taken with us. After a brief but intense discussion, we left the taverner's rooms with Laurel and Wyln carrying a rug apiece. The rest of us followed behind them, Thadro, Ranulf and even Chadde miffed at how the Faena and enchanter had declined their help.

"As if they're some bloody holy relics," Ranulf muttered.

"Yeah," I muttered back, then blinked at finding myself in agreement with the Lord of Bainswyr. He hadn't seemed to notice our moment of accord, though. He stared straight ahead, his mouth held tight, lines of strain showing around his eyes and disappearing into his beard. And as we moved in the dimness of the hallway I caught a flash around the

Marcher Lord, like the one I'd seen the night before. I frowned, moving closer. "Are you all right—?"

"Lord Commander, these rooms are empty."

Turning from Ranulf, I looked to see Jeff standing at an open door. He crossed the hallway and opened another door, revealing a cubbyhole that contained nothing but a narrow bed stripped of whatever covering it once had. "This one too," he said.

Beollan came up behind Jeff to see for himself. "How unappealing," he said as he stared at the bare, stained mattress. He transferred his distaste to Jeff. "And you discovered this how?"

There was enough light coming from the room's sliver of a window for me to see the flush on Jeff's face. But he manfully faced Beollan's silver stare. "A couple of the doors were cracked open, my lord. I was making sure that there wasn't anyone waiting for us to go by."

"Really," Beollan said, and Jeff's face flushed more.

"One of the first things Captain Suiden pounded into us, my lord," I said as I opened a door onto another empty room. "And he would've pounded on me for not checking, especially after what happened earlier."

"Yes," Thadro said, though he cast a glance at me. "Well done, Guardsman Jeffen."

The downstairs was empty too. Apparently figuring that, with Helto on the run, the Copper Pig would be permanently closed for business, the patrons, bawds and remaining servants had quietly stolen away while we were in the snug, taking as much as they could with them. There were lighter spots against the grime on the walls and floors of the various rooms where chairs and tables once stood, and all the ale kegs and bottles of spirits had been taken from the taproom. Exiting through the kitchen, we went past the ransacked larder and cabinets, holding our breaths against the scorching stew pots. Even the outbuildings were looted—

the pigsty was relieved of its occupants and feathers on the ground were all that remained of the tavern's chickens. Fortunately, our remaining horses were still there and we quickly saddled them, Chadde and Thadro hurrying us along, both anxious to get back to Jusson. But I needed no urging. Dismal while occupied, vacant the Pig had an air of desolation that made me think of tales of deserted villages where terrifying things happened to unwary travelers who stumbled upon them. As I helped tie the rugs to Wyln's saddle, the wind swept through the yard, swirling up the feathers in a whirlwind. A chill covered me.

"Stop that," I murmured to the air sphere at my shoulder.

The sphere moved to hover in front of me, its familiar hum full of overtones like the peal of a bell. However, there was no echoing hum from the whirlwind. I stared past the sphere at the feathers swirling all by their lonesome. My chill deepened, raising goose bumps.

Just then a puff of black smoke came out the kitchen door, and Thadro, helping Chadde secure the tavern's strongbox on her horse, turned his head to glare at Wyln, who looked back, impatient. "What now?"

"It's the stew pots, sir," Arlis said to Thadro as the smell of burning food swept over us.

"Oh, that," Wyln said. "That isn't my doing, Eorl Commander."

Flames suddenly exploded out of the taproom window, shattering glass and causing the horses to shy and rear.

"Now that; *that* was me," Wyln said. More flames shot out the windows on both the first and second floors, and sprouted out the chimneys. Calming his horse enough to swing up into the saddle, he smiled down at us. "We should leave before the stables go too."

Still frowning, Thadro also mounted and led us out of the yard at a fast trot, Laurel loping beside us. The Lord Commander rode Arlis' horse while I was on Jeff's (privileges of rank). Jeff doubled with Chadde, and Arlis was on Ranulf's massive beast of a horse. I drew up my feet a little as we went through the feathers, but they now lay unmoving on the ground. Just a stray breeze, I told myself as we reached the rutted lane. I glanced back over my shoulder to see the tavern fully engulfed in flames, its sign swinging violently in the fire's draft.

"A little presumptuous to burn it down, don't you think, elf?" Beollan asked. The tavern had disappeared as we rounded the bend, but we could still hear the roaring of the flames.

"No," Wyln said.

"It's all right, Lord Beollan," Thadro said, surprisingly. "The tavern was forfeit. I would've had to come out here with several of the Own to fire it and this just saves me a trip." He glanced at Wyln. "Though it will make things difficult if the flames spread to the woods and the farms beyond."

Wyln looked vaguely insulted. "Please."

Thadro smiled, suddenly looking like the easygoing commander of last spring. "I beg pardon, Lord Wyln," he said, settling back into his saddle.

The shadows were growing long as we approached Freston. Conscious of the nipping coolness of the afternoon, I tucked my cloak more firmly about me. I was looking forward to getting back to the king's residence where, hopefully, warm hearths and hot food waited. What I'd eaten earlier was long gone and my stomach was making pitiful noises, though I supposed we were all more than a little tired and hungry. While Thadro sat straight and easy on his horse, I could see lines of fatigue carved into his face, reminding me that the Lord Commander had been up all night. As had Laurel and Arlis. And those of us who had managed some sleep didn't look any better. Even the eternally young Wyln had creases between his brows, though that may have been because he was staring ahead at the large amount of traffic crowding around the gate into the town—rather unusual this late into the day. At least it looked like traffic. As we drew closer, it began to look more like a swarm and an angry buzz filled the air. Then they caught sight of us and the buzz changed to a howl.

"There he is! The murdering witch!"

"I think that they mean you, Lord Rabbit," Beollan said.

I gave a tired sigh. "No, really?"

Twenty-one

"Mayor Gawell and Master Ednoth's audience with us did not go well," Jusson said, his gold eyes catching the fading sun's rays through the study windows. "Not only did they refuse to answer our questions, but they accused Rabbit of murdering the felonious Menck and planting the jewels and coins on his body. We had them escorted to the garrison stockade where they could contemplate the folly of intemperate behavior before their king, and they managed to spread their accusations while en route."

Several of Jusson's Own had appeared before we reached Kingsgate, and by dint of the royal guards clearing a path for us, we managed to get through without any blood spilled. The mob fell away as we neared the king's residence, but the air was sullen and heavy as we rode through the empty and silent streets. It was only when we were bowed in by Cais, his face familiarly and wonderfully impassive, that my spine eased with relief. Murmuring that His Majesty was waiting, Cais ushered us all into the king's study—where my relief fled when I saw the assortment of town elders, local gentry and Great Lords from last night's salon waiting for us, all wearing sour faces. While the others of our group made their way to Jusson's desk to place our spoils before the king, I stumped over to the fireplace and stood in front of the fire with my arms folded across my chest, glowering at everyone who was glowering at me.

"He was jailed for witchcraft before Gawell accused him, Your Majesty," Almaric, a town alderman, now said, shooting me a vicious glance. "And lo, the head jailer is now dead."

A rumble of agreement went through the miniature mob.

"It's because of him that we've had rebellions and mayhem, sire," a southern lord said. "Ranulf is right, he is too dangerous to have next to you and much too dangerous to have as your heir. At the very least, he'll rend the kingdom apart."

Cais had swept Ranulf and Beollan into the study with us, and Ranulf blinked at hearing his words echoed. He then gave a faint smile, his eyes gleaming with satisfaction as the other lords muttered agreement. However, Beollan frowned.

"Send him back to the Border," a Marcher Lord said. "For we'll not have him here!"

The rumble of agreement grew louder and the minimob shifted, as if they would push me out a window, if not out of Iversterre. Jeff and a couple of the royal guards who'd remained close moved in front of me, but the show of force did not calm the crowd down. Shouts of "murderer" and "filthy magical" and "burn him" filled the room as they reached for their weapons. Snarling, I reached for my own, but again realized that I didn't have my sword. I lifted my hand instead, my rune turning painfully hot while the rest of me felt as cold as the ice lakes in the Upper Reaches.

"Have you all lost your pox-rotted minds?"

Jusson didn't raise his voice, but it cut across the noise of the tumult, everyone freezing where they were. As one, they looked at each other, then down at the knives and swords in their hands, before sliding a look at Jusson. Still seated at his desk, the king looked back, his face mildly disgusted.

"To draw in the king's presence is a capital offense," Thadro remarked. The Lord Commander had moved to the side of Jusson's desk so he could move without being hindered by pesky things like furniture and kings. "Those who do so are subject to execution. Immediately."

At once, all twinkly metallic things with sharp edges disappeared.

"I would ask for mercy, Your Majesty. Obviously their wits have been stolen by a very cunning thief."

My head snapped around to see Doyen Dyfrig standing between Laurel and Wyln, all three of them having moved out of the way of the violence. Laurel's gaze lifted, his ears flicking back, and I realized that I still had my hand raised. I lowered it quickly and shoved it into my pocket, ignoring the burning on my palm.

"I don't think they had any wits to begin with, Your Reverence," Chadde said, and several of the town elders turned dull red.

"What I find marvelous is that everyone has focused on ibn Chause when we have two excellent examples of, ah, Borderdom in front of us," Beollan said. "Especially one who probably knows how to inflict all kind of nasty magical things on mankind." He turned his silver eyes on Wyln. "What did *you* do during the war, elf?"

Wyln smiled. "Which one?"

There was silence as the glances now slid to the enchanter.

"We are sure that Lord Wyln has seen plenty of battles, Fellmark," Jusson said. "Including the one that almost happened here in our presence."

"But the witch," some anonymous soul murmured from behind his fellows.

Jusson sighed. "We've *had* this conversation. Is Rabbit a witch, your reverence?"

Dyfrig shook his head, his face troubled—but whether at me or the crowd I couldn't tell. "No, Your Majesty. Rabbit is a good son of the Church. I've reread the Patriarch's missives and His Holiness clearly states that he has examined him and found nothing of hell—"

"So you say," one of the southern lords broke in, sneering.

There was a moment of stunned silence from the Freston folk, then Dyfrig strode over to where I stood, the townspeople leaping out of his way, pushing before them any who hadn't moved. Stopping in front of me, he reached past the royal guards and Jeff to snatch my staff and replace it with the Church Staff of Office. There was a collective gasp of shock and several people ducked from the lightning bolt that was sure to descend from the ceiling to strike me dead. Flinching myself, I closed my eyes and started praying, telling God this was *not* my idea.

Instead of the cracking thunder of my doom, though, all I heard was the hiss and pop of the fire in the fireplace. I slowly opened my eyes to stare at the staff, surprised at how warm it was, as if it were alive. "Uhm," I said.

Dyfrig gave a grim smile at my continued existence. "So I do say—"

The air sphere that had been hovering over my shoulder suddenly unraveled and swirled around the Staff of Office, laughing. The staff's tiny silver bells began to ring, softly at first, then faster and louder, as if they were joining in the wind's joy. I looked away from the bells to meet Doyen Dyfrig's gaze, his eyes no longer faded but the deep blue of a summer's sky.

Heigh-*ho*, I thought.

Jusson, though, was focused on more immediate matters. "We trust that the question of the condition of Rabbit's soul has been settled?" he asked.

Wearing his habitual scowl, Ranulf drew breath to speak. Beollan elbowed his side—hard—and Ranulf let it out again in an explosive rush. The rest muttered something that might have been agreement.

"So enthusiastic," Jusson said. "And so blind. Don't you understand what Rabbit is?"

No one said anything.

The king sank down into his chair and leaned his head against the back, looking very tired. "Have I been talking to myself these past days? These past months?"

There was more silence. "Sire?" the anonymous voice asked.

"The Turals have recently suffered a series of setbacks to their expansion efforts to the south and east," Beollan said, leaving off abusing Ranulf's ribs. "Some say that the Empire has gone as far as it can in those directions, between natural barriers and ferocious opposition. Which leaves north and west."

"You restore my faith, Fellmark," Jusson murmured.

"But we're to the north and west," anonymous said.

"So you are," Laurel said, entering the lists. "As is the Border."

"Exactly," Beollan said.

"But just a moment ago you were against an alliance with the Border," the brave southern lord said. "You accused the elf of doing nasty things to humans."

A faint flush dusted Beollan's angular cheekbones. "That's different—"

"The threat isn't from the Turals," Ranulf said, interrupting. "It's from the Border. The spring rebellion was a plot hatched right in their High Council, no matter that Lord Teram carried it out."

"Not the entire Council, honored lord," Laurel said. "Just a few overly ambitious members."

"With the Turalian ambassador, Sro Kenalt, speaking tenderly into the ears of both the Border Council and our rebel Houses, like a man wooing two maidens at once," Jusson said. "What do you think would've happened if Teram ibn Flavan had succeeded?"

"Banquets, sire," the southern lord said. "Lots and lots of banquets."

Laughter broke out. My plump cousin *had* prided himself on his table and wine cellar. The laughter died quickly, though, as the king remained unsmiling.

"Teram wouldn't have sat long enough on the throne to make it through the coronation feast," Jusson said. "Before the first dish was served, he would've been deposed and Iversterre annexed as the twenty-third principality of the Turalian Empire. Remember who made up the rebels' triumvirate?" He held up a finger for each one. "Lord Gherat, Lord Teram, *and* Ambassador Sro Kenalt of Tural."

"But, the Border," Ranulf began.

"It wouldn't have been able to move fast enough, Bainswyr," Jusson said. "Before the Border Milita could've finished mustering—"

"If the cabal had been able to convince the High Council to war, which was by no means a given, honored folk," Laurel interjected.

"—the Imperial fleet would've been in our ports debouching the Army of the Sun into our cities, their war wizards leading the way to ensure our obedience. Wizards that we didn't have a defense against, messirs, until Rabbit and his oh-so-close ties to the Border—including Lord Wyln and Master Laurel Faena." The king stretched his legs out under his desk, folding his hands over his stomach. "You would've all been sporting clan markings and tattoos before the year was out."

"Or dead," Beollan said, the flush fading, leaving his face pale.

"Or dead," Jusson agreed. "We need Rabbit *and* the Border if we are to survive as a kingdom."

"But he's a *mage*," Ranulf said.

"That's the idea," Jusson said. "A mage sworn both to the throne and to his king. He'll not break his oaths. Will you, Lord Rabbit ibn Chause e Flavan?"

What was I going to say, with the truth rune drawn on one hand and the Church Staff of Office held in the other? "No, sire," I said. "I am yours."

"Are you?" Ranulf said. "From what I've heard, you're a lot of other peoples' too. Sort of like the trollops at that tavern, shared among many and true to none."

Our brief moment of accord was long gone. I smiled at Ranulf, showing all my teeth. "Where did you say we met, my lord?"

Puzzled expressions passed over most everyone's face at my inconsequent question, though a couple of the southern lords looked uneasy, including the vocal one.

Beollan gave a slight smile, his silver eyes glinting. "Caught in your own trap, Ranulf."

"Rabbit has more than proven himself true, Bainswyr," Jusson said, rescuing Ranulf. "Both at my side in battle and across the seas in foreign lands. Let us hear no more about his soul or his loyalty." His gaze dropped to the spoils we'd placed in front of him. "What we do want to hear is what's all this and why you've returned from this infamous tavern with a crossbow, a pair of Turalian throwing knives and the rest."

"Yes, sire," Thadro said. Motioning for Chadde to join him, he launched into a recounting of our afternoon's adventures. At first there were the normal rustlings of an audience politely listening, but the room grew very still as the Lord Commander and the peacekeeper told of the staged tavern brawl, the attempt on my life, the conversation with Helto, ending with the discoveries in the taverner's quarters.

"So Slevoic ibn Dru, this taverner-turned-assassin Helto, and the felonious jailer Menck had formed an unholy trinity in Dru's smuggling schemes." Though Jusson's voice was mild, his eyes had turned gold again.

"Yes, Your Majesty," Chadde said. "However, I could never get proof. My authority was sharply curtailed during Lord Ormec's illness and subsequent death."

"Curtailed by the jailer's kinsman, the mayor," Jusson said, his gaze on the town elders standing together in a defensive clump. "It makes us wonder who else is involved besides those three."

"I assure you we knew nothing of this, Your Majesty!" Magistrate Ordgar said. Alderman Almaric and his fellow aldermen chimed in with vehement agreements and furious nods.

Ignoring the outburst, Chadde softly thumped the strongbox holding the receipts. "I would dearly love to question Master Ednoth about these rugs, Your Majesty."

"So would we, Peacekeeper Chadde," Jusson said. "Along with his honor the mayor. Send a guard to the garrison, Thadro, requesting their return to our presence—"

The king stopped, turning to stare at the door, as did Laurel and Wyln. A moment later it opened, revealing Cais and a royal guard, supporting between them a town watchman.

"Peacekeeper Chadde," the watchman gasped, his chest heaving. "The charnel house."

Twenty-two

I huddled in my cloak as the last of the daylight slipped away. Just a row of buildings over, I could hear people in the main square, the tenor of their voices more confused than angry, calling questions to each other and to Thadro and the royal guards who were searching the surrounding area. Inside the courtyard of the dead, though, it was muted, as if it were muffled in wool—or a winding sheet—everyone speaking in hushed tones, heads lowered, stepping softly. The chill that had been hovering all day seized me and I shivered hard.

At the watchman's words, Jusson didn't waste any time with questions but strode out of the study, everyone else in the room rushing to keep up, the King's Own flowing around us as we poured down the front steps. Refusing to wait for horses, Jusson set out on foot and we moved fast through the streets, those we came across hurrying out of our way to avoid being mowed down. In the mad rush Dyfrig and I had kept each other's staves, and the townsfolk's hostility disappeared in astonishment as they saw me walking beside the doyen, the Staff of Office in my hand, its bells ringing loud and clear. They too looked up at the fading sky, expecting God's displeasure to descend with a flash and a bang—and were even more astonished that it did not.

The sun was descending behind the rooftops as we rushed into the courtyard, the walls casting long shadows. We'd checked first at the entrance, where two watchmen lay on the ground, and Laurel and Chadde dropped down beside them as the rest of us continued on. However, our momentum slowed more as we neared the charnel house itself, coming to a complete halt a short distance away, with no one—not even Jusson—showing any inclination to go closer. The door was open, hanging drunkenly off one hinge. Long fingers of ice curled around its edge and filled the rune carved into its wood. Ice also filled the runes under the windows and dripped in great globs from the grilles. Through the gaping doorway I could see the glint of more ice, thick and white. It coated everything inside— floors, walls, ceilings, the stone slabs. However, the bright lines of earth that warded the house of the dead were gone. As was my burning sword.

As was Menck's body.

The shiver tightened its grip and, wrapping my cloak more firmly about me, I left Jusson, Wyln and the rest of the mob that had accompanied us, and started back to where Laurel and Chadde tended the two watchmen. Behind me trailed Jeff and some of the Own, the quickness of their steps suggesting that they were more than happy to put a little distance between them and the charnel- turned icehouse.

"Rabbit."

I turned to see Dyfrig coming towards me, carrying my ashwood staff. Even before the staff was within reach, my hand was stretching out for it. I wanted my own back, but even more I wanted to give the doyen his. Maybe God didn't mind that I had it, but I did not want to presume. I figured that we'd need all the help Heaven could give.

Dyfrig, however, shook his head, his grim smile reappearing. "No, let everyone see that you can carry that without shriveling up into a dried husk."

One of the more attractive fates said to be visited upon those aligned with hell who come in contact with holy objects. I held in a sigh even as my body hunched in—faithful son of the Church or not, there were some things that I'd just as soon leave to the clergy. "Yes, Your Reverence," I said, dropping my hand.

Dyfrig's smile faded, his worn face falling into lines of worry as he turned his head to the charnel house. "I've seen strange and sometimes frightening things, Rabbit. There's a house near the northern wall that took three blessings before anyone could sleep in it without having screaming nightmares. And a farm on the way to Cosdale has a pasture where shadows move though there's nothing blocking the sun."

Great. Just what I wanted to hear. Ghost stories. I hunched in more, an icy chill coursing down my spine, while Jeff and the Own edged in closer, their eyes darting around the courtyard, making sure all the shadows were legitimate.

"But this," Dyfrig said, his voice soft. "This is the most frightening thing I've ever seen. I could feel the power of what the elf and the Faena did. *Feel* it, Rabbit. It hummed inside me, resonating like the ringing of a bell—"

That sounded very familiar. I looked at Dyfrig, but he was intent on the house of the dead.

"—but it was all for nothing. Nothing! What could brush aside all that we did?"

I was about to deny any knowledge of the dark when I realized that I'd be lying, not only with the truth rune etched on my palm, but also while holding the Staff of Office. Deciding that wasn't wise, I looked around at my guards, making sure that they had been with us in the abandoned warehouse and so wouldn't be hearing anything new. "I don't know who's behind it, Your Reverence," I said, keeping my voice low so the town elders and aristos couldn't hear. "But Menck was killed as part of someone working *dauthiwaesp*. Death magic."

Dyfrig's eyes went incandescent as the wind swirled around both of us, causing the bells on the Staff of Office to chime. "Death magic!" he said, his voice just as soft as he made a sign to ward off evil. "Here, in my town?" His gaze went to Laurel, still tending to the watchmen. "Has His Majesty questioned everyone?"

I frowned at the doyen's not-so-subtle accusation. "Both honored Laurel and the Enchanter Wyln have just as much tolerance for the dark arts as you do, Your Reverence," I said.

"Who else could it be?" Dyfrig asked. "We have malefactors; what place doesn't? But we do *not* have sorcerers. How could we? No one knows how."

"No one that will admit it, Your Reverence," I began.

Dyfrig hit my staff against the paving stones. "I know everyone in the valley, and in the mountain villages too. There aren't any! His Majesty should look to the north."

"When the penalty for practicing sorcery is hanging and burning, your land and property forfeit, and your family cast out and branded, most become very good at hiding, Your Reverence," I said. "But it doesn't have to be someone local. Laurel and Wyln aren't the only strangers in town. Freston is full to bursting with outlanders." I gave a small shrug that turned into another shiver. "Even so, Menck was lured to his death by someone he either knew or didn't consider a threat. There is no way he would've gone off with Laurel or Wyln. No way at all."

As Dyfrig's white brows drew together in a frown, the sound of many echoed in the side street and we both looked to see Thadro and the Own—Arlis with them—entering the courtyard. Jusson swept by us to meet his Lord Commander, the aristos and town elders trailing in the royal wake.

"We'll talk more on this later," Dyfrig said, and walked away to join Jusson.

"That went well," Jeff remarked as we attached ourselves to the end of the king's train.

"Yeah," I said. Another shudder shook me.

"Are you all right?" Jeff asked. "You've been shivering all afternoon like you have the ague."

"Just tired, hungry and cold," I said.

"I'm scared spitless myself," Jeff said. A couple of the royal guards made sounds of assent, their eyes still on the deepening shadows.

"That too," I said.

Thadro and Jusson converged where Chadde and Laurel tended the injured watchmen. Both remained kneeling on the ground, intent on their ministrations to the fallen.

"Did you find anything?" Jusson asked Thadro.

"No, sire," Thadro said. "There's no sign of Menck's body anywhere. And if anyone saw a naked corpse being carried off, they're not saying."

"We can't tell if whoever took the head jailer also took his hidden treasure," Jusson said. "The ice must be a span or more thick in places."

Thadro glanced at the charnel house but showed no desire to go look for himself. "And you didn't see anything?" he asked the watchman who'd come to the king's house.

"No, sir," the watchman said. "Kenelm and I'd thought at first that they'd left their post as we didn't see them when we came to relieve them. Then, all of a sudden, there they were, right in front of us, lying on the ground like they'd been thrown about."

The two watchmen had looked like rag dolls, their limbs bent in unnatural positions before Laurel and Chadde had carefully straightened them out. However, I didn't think it was any better with them on their backs looking ready for burial.

"Illusion," Wyln said from where he stood next to Jusson. "An ability of the water aspect."

"Explain," Jusson said.

"It is the reflecting and bending of light, sire," I said before Wyln could. Under the cover of my cloak, I absently ran a hand over my tight chest. "Like a lake, where you can't see what's under the surface. But why did the illusion fail at that moment?"

"That is the question," Wyln murmured, watching me— or rather my hand.

"And where is Kenelm?" I asked. "Why isn't he here?" Someone I'd hoisted a few cups with at the Hart's Leap, he was conspicuous by his absence.

"Well, Mauger?" Chadde asked when the watchman remained silent.

"He went back to the Watch House, ma'am," Mauger said, glaring at me. "To get help."

I stared back. "Then he should've returned by now."

Suddenly realizing how long Kenelm had been gone, Mauger blinked and turned, looking out the courtyard entrance as if he expected the other watchman to appear at any moment.

"Broken arms and legs, bruised heads, sprains, bruises," Laurel said from where he knelt. "I need splints, bandages, blankets, hot bricks and litters."

"See to it," Chadde said to Mauger. "And bring Kenelm when you return."

With one last hostile glare at me, Mauger left the courtyard, sliding past Arlis on his way out. Jeff muttered an exclamation when Arlis stepped aside for the watchman and then returned to his spot on the other side of the circle that enclosed both the king and the injured men. Seeing the glances the Own were giving him, I realized that I was going to have to very soon deal with his reluctance to fill his duty as my personal guard.

Unaware of the minidrama happening behind him, Thadro rubbed his neck, his face tired. "With your permission, Your Majesty, I'd like to get troop units from the garrison to search both for Menck's body and for Helto and Bram."

"Do it," Jusson said, and Thadro sent two guards off, running.

"Do you think we'll find anything, sire?" I asked. Another shiver shook me and I clenched my teeth to keep them from chattering. I gave up trying to ease the tightness in my chest and huddled deeper in my cloak.

"No," Jusson said. "But then, I didn't expect this."

"None of us did," Dyfrig said. Apparently my assurances didn't take, for he glared at Laurel. "A year ago this was unimaginable. Now it's a nightmare come to life."

"Your Reverence," Jusson said, beginning his own frown.

"That's all right, Iver'son," Wyln said, his voice surprisingly gentle. "It is always a shock when one is confronted with the dark. Especially when it arises out of what is familiar and comfortable."

"And what do *you* know of the dark, elf?" Beollan asked over the mutters of the town elders and aristos.

The flames in the center of Wyln's eyes were bright in the twilight. "I've been His Grace Loran's enchanter since he ruled as High King in Morendyll, Jewel of the Sea. I know plenty, Beollan of Fellmark, including the day when Iver and his human army boiled out of that same sea, slaughtering everyone in their path."

"Morendyll—" Beollan began.

"You call it Iversly." Wyln's eyes became brighter. "The palace there has cold spots in its seraglio and nursery. Have you ever asked why?"

"I've not said that," Jusson said before Beollan could

reply, his voice sharp. "And even if there are, that's not at issue here."

"Truth," Laurel said. He shifted on his haunches, looking back at the charnel house, the white of the ice stark in the surrounding darkness. "What we should be concerned about is how the protections Elder Dyfrig, Wyln and I put in place were crushed like old eggshells."

Giving over baiting Beollan for the moment, Wyln also looked at the charnel house. "And Rabbit's sword taken," he said, a crease between his brows.

Laurel's ears went back against his skull. "Taken, and none of us aware."

I wasn't very superstitious—well, no more than most of the other lads at the garrison. However, the thought of my sword in the hands of whatever had broken through the wardings and turned the charnel house into an icehouse caused my shivers to increase. Then the memory popped up of the flurry of feathers in the tavern's yard and I opened my mouth to tell Wyln and Laurel, but a particularly hard shivering tremor hit me, shaking my voice silent.

"My town, my people, my heir, all threatened by something I've yet to see," Jusson said. He looked down at the injured watchmen. "Will they recover, Laurel?"

"I believe so, honored king," Laurel said. "Though it'll be a long convalescence. As soon as the litters arrive, we'll move them to a warmer—and safer—place."

"I hope they come soon then," Beollan said, giving over baiting Wyln for the moment. "I'm not a fanciful man, Your Majesty, but I do not want to be here when true night falls."

There were murmurs of agreement as folks drew in tighter, those on the outer edge turning so that they could see anything that might decide to creep up on them, townspeople and aristos both moving their cloaks to free swords and dagger hilts.

I tried to speak again, but another bout of shivering hit

me, the cold locking my muscles so tight that I couldn't move. It began to dawn on me that maybe my chill had nothing to do with being tired and hungry.

"Rabbit, you're shaking like a blancmange," Jeff said.

Everyone turned from staring at the shadows to stare at me.

"Cold," I managed to stammer out, my breath misting before me. My face went numb, as did my toes and the tips of my fingers.

"It's not that cold," Jusson said. "Your lips are blue."

All of a sudden, my fire sphere dimmed, then winked out. Wyln said something in elvish, pushing aside a couple of the town elders to get to me, while Laurel gave a low, rumbling growl as he leapt up and hurried around the prone watchmen. "Under our very noses!"

The enchanter reached me first and grabbed my face, but I couldn't feel his hands. "He's near frozen," Wyln said.

No, not frozen, I thought. The charnel house was frozen. But I was so very cold. The numbness spread to my feet and hands.

"Your cloaks," Laurel said, taking off his coat and throwing it around my shoulders. "Quick!"

The king pulled off his cloak, also flinging it about me. "Do as he says."

I could feel the weight of the cloaks as they were piled on top of mine; Ranulf's thick fur all but swallowing me. But even warm from everyone's body heat, they did nothing. The cold seemed to be in the marrow of my bones.

"—fire," Wyln said.

"What?" I asked, my voice slurring. The shivers were easing off, but I was vaguely aware that wasn't necessarily good. My eyelids started to droop as lassitude slid over me.

"By the Lady, Rabbit!" A hand struck my face. "Call fire!"

I forced my eyes open, meeting Wyln's blazing gaze.

"Call it!"

Dyfrig caught the Staff of Office as I dropped it and forced my hands up to grip Wyln's, the dark elf enchanter surrounding me in flame. But I didn't feel that either. It was as though there was a layer of ice right under my skin. I pushed against it, a groan rising from my gut and up through my chest, locking my teeth together. For a terrifying moment nothing happened, then something gave with a soft creak. I pushed harder and there was a sharp, splintering crack.

"My God!"

I staggered, slipping out of Wyln's grasp as my knees gave way, but Jeff and Jusson both caught me before I fell. I took a deep breath, my heart stuttering, the false warmth chased away by hard, racking shivers, feeling rushing back into my arms and legs with sharp, agonizing stabs. In the distance I thought I heard a cry of pain, but there was a sound much closer—the roar of flames. I took another breath, heat filling my lungs.

"That's it, Rabbit," Laurel said. "Breathe."

Something trickled down my face and, fearing it was tears, I managed to get a hand up to wipe it away. But water continued to drip down my face and neck. My hair was sopping wet, as was the rest of me. I glanced down to see that I was standing in a puddle. But not all the water had come from me. Wearily lifting my head, I traced a small stream flowing from the charnel house. It seemed that the ice was melting, which wasn't surprising as the house was on fire.

But that didn't make sense for, except for the door, the building was made of stone. And the door was the one thing not burning. As I watched, the ice filling the rune carved into the wood slid off and fell to the ground with a slushy splash.

"Ma'am!"

Carrying supplies and litters, Mauger and several others

of the Watch ran into the courtyard, only to pile up at the entryway, their eyes wide as they took in the burning building. Chadde frowned and pointed, and the watchmen unpiled themselves, going to where the injured men lay on the ground. The peacekeeper looked over the group of men. "Where's Kenelm?" she asked.

"He hasn't returned to the Watch House, ma'am," Mauger said, he and the others giving their bundles to Laurel. A couple of the watchmen knelt down and began to competently help the Faena splint and bandage. The rest divided their stares between me and the burning building. "We sent out a couple of the lads to look for him."

"Good," Chadde said. "I also want men sent to the warehouse to make sure that those there are all right—"

The flames from the charnel house shot up into the sky with a whoosh, the smoke white from the steam. The wind began to rise, causing the flames to leap even higher and, at the same time, little flickers of flame appeared on my hands and arms. Both Jeff and Jusson started to snatch their own hands away, then paused, the king's eyes rounding a bit as the flames played over his skin without burning.

"Sa-sa," Beollan said, reaching out to cup a flame in his palm and allowing it to run over his fingers. Ranulf pressed closed to Beollan's side, the lines of discontent on his face disappearing as he stared, fascinated.

"That's it, Rabbit," Wyln said. Fire flickered over him also, the wind pushing back his hair. He once more gripped my face. "Yield. Let it fill you."

Yield? Yield to what? I already had the aspect. But that thought faded as I stared into Wyln's fire-filled eyes, flames filling my vision—

"Haven't you done enough without encouraging him in his magicks?" a town alderman shouted at Wyln.

I jerked my head back, blinking as everything snapped back into focus. Again there was the sound of running footsteps, and more people appeared, many carrying buckets of water, hooks and axes. They too corked up at the courtyard entrance, eyes wide and mouths gaping open as they took in the burning building.

"Don't stop him, Geram," Dyfrig said unexpectedly. Holding both staves in one hand, he lent an arm to keep me steady. Or to show support. "Let it burn. Let the unwholesomeness be cleansed with fire."

Hearing the doyen's voice, the crowd figured it was safe and poured into the courtyard. Some went to help Laurel with the injured guards, but more went to stare at the wonder of a stone building burning. A few intrepid souls stood at the doorway, peering in.

"Fiat," Laurel said, the flames catching in his amber eyes. "By the Lady and Her goodness, let all sorceries be consumed."

Dyfrig's grip on me tightened. "Is that your rapprochement, Your Majesty?" he asked Jusson. "I'm supposed to agree to that?" He then frowned. "By the holy God and *His* goodness, you're soaked through, Rabbit."

"My cloak," Beollan said, sighing, both he and Ranulf glancing away from the dancing flame in his hand to look at the puddle at my feet.

"I admit that there are some rough edges, Your Reverence," Jusson said. "Places that we're bound to clash." He also frowned. "Damn it, Rabbit, you're shaking again."

"Just very tired, sire," I said. I stiffened my knees to keep from sagging.

"Poor child," Wyln said. "You're almost done in." He then smiled at Jusson and Dyfrig, the flames in his eyes dancing. "Don't worry. We've no desire to convert you to the worship of Gaia—"

"Oy!" called out someone standing at the charnel house doorway. "Someone's in there."

"Well, of course, you looby," one of his fellows said, peering over the man's shoulder. "It's Menck."

"Menck was never that skinny," the first one said.

There was a moment of stillness, then Jusson walked swiftly back to the house, Laurel snatching up his staff to join him, Dyfrig and Wyln dragging me with them as they followed. Reaching the doorway first, Jusson entered before Thadro and the royal guard could stop him, the fire parting before him. The Lord Commander and the Own plunged in after their king, as did Dyfrig, Laurel, Wyln, Jeff and I; Beollan and Chadde following right after.

It was like walking into a blasting furnace, but without the killing heat—it was as warm as a mild summer's day. And while the flames didn't touch any of us, they covered everything else, burning most fiercely on the slab where Menck's body had lain. The ice was gone and even the meltwater evaporated, leaving nothing but stone and what looked like a long bundle of colorful rags on the floor by one of the other slabs. Jusson stopped at the bundle, staring down.

"So," Wyln murmured. His gaze was thoughtful as it rested on Jusson for a moment before shifting down to the object on the floor. "And so again."

The rag bundle was actually a cape of motley wrapped around a stick-thin body. It seemed that the charnel house contained a corpse after all—one that had died very happy. Then I realized that what I was seeing wasn't teeth bared in a grin, but the bone of his spine as his neck had been sliced from ear to ear.

"Poor sod," Jeff said softly from behind me.

Poor sod indeed. Master Rodolfo would never mount another play.

Twenty-three

The charnel house was still afire when we quit the courtyard, the flames bright against the dark sky. A few of the townsfolk threw their buckets of water on the fire just to see what would happen but, except for some hissing and steam, it burned just a strongly as it had when it first started. I figured that probably had a lot to do with me—I started it, therefore I would have to stop it. Fortunately, no one asked that I do so as I didn't think I had the strength. My legs reminded me of a noodle dish I once had in Iversly, loose and wobbly, and just as capable of holding me up.

Many, both outlanders and townsfolk, were of the very vocal opinion that the entrance to the courtyard should be bricked up, flames and all. Not disagreeing, Doyen Dyfrig convinced them to remove Master Rodolfo's body to the church first. Another litter was retrieved and the dead player placed on it; he was stiff as a board when they lifted him, though that could've been because he had been under a thick layer of ice rather than from rigor mortis. Through my weariness I felt a stab for Gwynedd at the murder of her brother; I also was concerned about Rosea, no matter that she was the bait in the hook to catch gullible me. Something moved in the back of my mind about the redheaded player—an image of pearls and a green velvet gown—but I was too tired to nudge it to the forefront.

However, surprise did penetrate my fog of exhaustion when Ranulf volunteered to help carry the dead player's litter. The Marcher Lord had remained outside when we first entered the charnel house, but he stepped in when the litter arrived, his head instinctively ducking from the flames blazing on the ceiling. He and the other litter bearer carried the dead player with unexpected dignity through the town square into the church, led by Dyfrig, who had both my and his staves. The clerks, Keeve and Tyle, hurriedly put up a makeshift bier behind the altar and everyone who could crowded around—Jusson, his Own and his nobles, Chadde and a few of her watchmen, the town elders and leading citizens. After seeing off the injured watchmen to their respective homes for tending by their families, Laurel pushed through the mob and began his examination. Figuring that this was a better show than any the town's theater ever offered, they all pressed closer, Jusson taking the best vantage because he was king.

Thadro had paused outside to speak with Albe, the blacksmith, and the town's mason about constructing a barrier across the courtyard entrance, but Wyln and Jeff, still supporting me, also pushed inside the church. Immediately upon my entrance all the lamps brightened, flickers of flame appearing at the tops of the lamps.

"Lord Wyln?" Jeff asked.

"Do not worry, Jeff Corbin'son," Wyln said. "He won't set your church on fire." Making way through the church interior, he and Jeff deposited me on a bench shoved against the wall.

"What's going on?" I asked as the lamp above me exploded with light.

"You have opened more to your fire aspect—stretched if you will—so it takes up more room within you. And the more space something occupies, the more it affects its surroundings." He adjusted the multitude of cloaks I still had about me. "But we will work on your control, Two Trees'-son, as we don't want you creating firestorms wherever you go."

"Yes, honored *Cyhn*," I said, my voice rough with weariness. Sinking back to allow the wall to take the weight of my shoulders, I felt the touch of Wyln's hand on my head. He then held a murmured conversation with Jeff about letting me rest before he went to join the mob around the bier. I didn't mind being left behind; I'd enough of mutilated dead bodies to last me a while. I made myself more comfortable on the bench, the cloaks forming a nice cocoon around me. I was warm for the first time in what seemed like forever. It didn't matter that I was also damp in uncomfortable places—I'd done enough patrolling in bad weather to learn to ignore a little wet. Besides, though I had stopped sprouting flames, it felt as if a hearth had been lit inside me, and in the increased lamplight I could see steam rising off the cloaks.

More folks pushed into the church, spilling out to either side of the altar and into the main part of the church, all eager to see Rodolfo's final performance. I ignored the forest of legs and backsides, though I did glance up briefly when Thadro entered the church. But he paused only for a moment to also have a murmured conversation with Jeff before going to Jusson, standing at the bier. Leaning my head against the wall, I allowed my eyes to drift shut.

"The Lord Commander is going to get tired of that pretty soon," Jeff said.

Cracking my eyes open, I saw the earth sphere hovering in front of my face. Figuring Jeff wasn't talking about it, I shifted a bit and saw, between the press of bodies, Arlis, who'd worked himself very close to Thadro and Jusson. Both the Lord Commander and the king seemed oblivious to Arlis' proximity, but the Own were very much aware and

I saw that sideways glances had changed to frowning looks. Sighing, I struggled to sit up. "Bring him here," I said.

Jeff turned to me, opening his mouth.

"Jeff," I said.

Jeff shut his mouth and, breathing hard through his nose, rose and worked his way to Arlis. After a moment's muttered talk, they both returned, neither one wearing a happy face.

"What do you want?" Arlis asked. Gone was the easy companion of yesterday morning. In his place was someone who looked down at me with remote eyes, impatience in his voice and stance. The royal guards around me grew very still and the heat inside me cranked up a notch.

"I don't know what you're bucking for," I said, my voice soft, "but you've managed to annoy just about everyone here. Including me." I pointed at the bench. "Sit."

Arlis didn't move. "I'm on duty," he said, remaining standing. "Besides, you don't need me, as you already have your own lackey."

"A pot claiming everything else is black," Jeff said, crowding into Arlis. The guards fell back, giving them room.

"Not black, but brown, like your nose," Arlis said, crowding back.

"Go suck a bull's teat. Your mouth is already puckered—"

"Are you two stupid?" I asked, cutting across a guard's muffled snort of laughter. "You're going to brawl in *here?* In front of His Majesty, Thadro *and* Dyfrig?"

Jeff and Arlis sprang apart, both casting worried glances at the crowd around the bier. Fortunately, all there seemed to be engrossed with Laurel's examination.

"I'm too tired for this rotting nonsense," I said, reclaiming their attention. "I gave you an order, Guardsman Arlis. Sit. Now."

Arlis' eyes went to my lieutenant's insignia—just visible

among my multitude of cloaks—before flinging himself down on the bench. Jeff followed, sitting more sedately on the other side of me, each with their faces turned away from the other. Weariness washed over me again as I pondered Arlie's insubordination. Not only did it not make sense on the surface, it also didn't fit the man I thought I knew. While none of the troopers at the Freston garrison were shining examples of soldierly rectitude, there were those who showed a sort of battered competence in performing their duties. And there were even more who were clever enough to figure out on which side their bread was buttered—and how to keep both bread and butter coming. Up until today, I would've included Arlie in both groups, which made his present behavior baffling. The only reason why he was in the Royal Guard was because of me; it seemed the height of idiocy to drop his trousers and wave his bare backside in my direction.

Another wave of weariness crashed over me and, setting aside Arlis' behavior, I leaned my head once more against the wall, my eyes once more drifting shut.

"There you are!" Rosea exclaimed. "I've been looking for you, my lord."

We were back in the lord's council chamber, though it had changed. It was still candlelit, but the map table had been pushed to the side and the smaller table with the alabaster half globe in its center was placed in the middle of the room. Chairs were around the table, as if the occupants had all just risen. However, as I watched, one of the chairs seemed to shift and something flickered in the cloudy glass of the mirror on the wall. Frowning, I started to go closer, but Rosea moved towards me with a rustle of her green velvet gown. The pearls around her throat and ankle echoed the luminescence of her skin and her hair shone, but instead of the sunlit brilliance of before, it was now a dark red. The color of blood, I thought.

Stepping back, I gave a small bow, my hand over my heart. "Mistress Rosea." I caught a flash of a brighter red and, glancing down, saw that I held my feather pressed against the blue and white of my King's Own tabard. I still didn't have my sword, though; my other hand drifted to my scabbard and found it empty.

"Oh, so polite," Rosea said, pouting. "Surely we've moved beyond that?"

"Beyond what?" I asked, angry. "There's nothing to move beyond. Rodolfo is your husband, not your brother." And Rodolfo was dead. I hesitated, my anger fading, but Rosea gave a full-throated laugh.

"It's a *dream*, silly," she said, waving a small hand. And I saw a flash, like light upon a metal. "What does it matter what I am out there? Here I am whatever you want me to be. Whatever you dare me to be." Her eyes dropped down. "But only if you get rid of that feather. It's a wicked thing, my lord, and I cannot come near it."

Holding the feather like a shield before me, I began to refuse, not wanting any part of the tangle that seemed to lie about Rosea, dream or not. However, her eyes raised to mine again, and I found myself looking into a sea of ice. Which was odd as I could hear the crash of waves in the distance, as if they were driven by a storm against a great seawall. My thoughts stumbled, then slowed.

"I've been so lonely, waiting for you," Rosea said, once more moving close. She smiled, her teeth so very white against her pink lips. "Will you let a feather keep us apart?"

"Apart?" I repeated, frowning over the word as if I had never heard it before.

"Yes, my lord," Rosea said, her voice becoming smoother, melodic. "Let it go and we'll be together." Her tongue darted out, licking her lips. "Always."

I stared into the frozen depths of her gaze and my hand started to open to let the feather fall.

Not winter—

"Rabbit!"

With a jolt, I sat up, my heart pounding. But seeing nothing more alarming than Jeff's face, I slumped down again. "Hell," I muttered.

"You wouldn't wake," Jeff said, his hand on my shoulder, "and you were doing something weird with your feather."

I blinked at him before looking down to see I was holding my feather in my hand. "Weird like how?" I asked, my voice blurry.

"You'd taken it from your braid and were going to drop it on the floor," Jeff said.

I rubbed my face. "Must've been dreaming," I said.

Jeff's hand fell from my shoulder. "Yeah? Well, that's not surprising. You were sawing a whole forest of logs."

I sat up a little straighter. "I don't snore. Now you, you've been known to make dogs howl and people's ears bleed."

"Har," Jeff said. "I was thinking that as Laurel has finished, I'd awaken you anyway before the Lord Commander returns and starts chewing on your arse for sleeping while on duty. But why don't you go on back to sleep and when he comes in you can tell him you were just doing your handsaw imitation."

"Thadro's gone?" I asked. I started to put my feather back into my braid, then tucked it into my shirt instead— where it would be harder to remove, no matter my dreams.

"He went to check on the barrier across the charnel house courtyard," Jeff said.

Nodding, I sat up completely and stared around the church. Laurel stood at a small table, washing his paws in a bowl, Rodolfo's corpse on the bier behind him covered by the cape of motley. Ranulf and Beollan were on either side of the Faena, the Marcher Lords listening intently as he talked. The rest of the crowd were moving away, softly discussing what they'd just seen, Jusson, Chadde, Dyfrig and several town elders forming their own discussion group in front of the altar. Wyln was with them, though he seemed more interested in his surroundings than the conversation. He was surveying the plain white plaster walls, the clerestory windows encircling the high dome ceiling, the alabaster lamp hanging from the center, the smaller lamps attached to the walls. He then turned his attention to the simple altar made of polished wood, with the runes of truth, judgment and mercy carved into its sides. Stepping closer, he stared down at the bundle of wheat stalks left on the altar from that morning's prayers for a bountiful harvest before nudging them aside to examine the rune of charity carved into the altar's top. He looked up again, his face thoughtful and, noticing I was awake, headed in our direction. As he did, Dyfrig shifted to watch him, the doyen's face blank. Beollan too moved to watch the enchanter. His expression, though, was dark and brooding. Then Laurel said something and the Lord of Fellmark once more became his usual urbane self.

Seeing Wyln coming towards us, Jeff rose and gave a discreet stretch before lending me a helping hand. As I was entangled in the cloaks, it took some unwrapping to get me on my feet. More than warm enough, I left the unneeded coverings on the bench and, taking a chance on staying upright, stood. As I did, I became aware of a certain lack.

"Where's Arlis?" I asked.

Jeff shrugged, his mouth pulling down. "He left with Thadro—"

"I don't care if Lord High and Mighty of the world is in there! Let me in!"

All conversation stopped as everyone turned towards the front door, except Jusson, who looked over at me—but as I was Thadro's second and Thadro wasn't there, I was al-

ready moving. I made my way to the entrance, Jeff and several of the royal guards with me. I wasn't worried,
though—at least not about the king's safety—for I recognized the voice. Wyln recognized it too, his winged brows
drawing together as he changed direction to meet us at the
double doors. We stepped out together onto the church
steps to see Gwynedd standing in front of a barrier of both
Watch and King's Own, her players arrayed behind her. She
looked up at me, the streetlamps catching the sheen of tears
in her eyes, her marvelous mouth held like a wound.

"I want to see Rolly."

"Let her in," I said. "Let them all in."

Twenty-four

Doyen Dyfrig's study was like King Jusson's in its simpleness: it had plain wooden furniture and the same white plaster walls that were in the church. But Dyfrig's scarred pieces would not have made it through the royal back door, and Cais probably would've suffered the torments of the damned before allowing Jusson's study to reach the level of chaos that the doyen's had achieved. Scrolls, books, parchments and papers were jumbled together with dried herbs and flowers, small smooth stones, ceremonial bowls and a mouse skull, all of which was crammed onto shelves, scattered on a couple of tables and formed into shaggy piles on Dyfrig's desk. On one wall hung a detailed map of the valley and surrounding mountains. Another wall had a row of windows that overlooked rooftops, catching at the edge of one window frame the rising moon, while on the opposite end were the flames from the charnel house, blazing against the night sky.

Gwynedd sat on one of the wood guest chairs that had been hastily cleared off, a cup of Laurel's tea in her hand. Wyln and I had escorted her and the members of her troupe to the bier where Rodolfo lay, her expression calm as Laurel lifted the motley cape. After staring down for a long moment at her brother's face, she'd turned away, her dark eyes blindly drifting over the crowd in the church while several of the players started weeping, their arms going around each other seeking comfort. Wyln and I had hung back to give Gwynedd as much privacy as possible in a room full of people, but before either of us could respond to her silent grief, Dyfrig was by her side. With a few softly spoken words, he led her away from the bier, the noisy sobs of the troupe and the eyes of the avidly curious, taking her to a side door that connected to the rectory. Jusson, Chadde, Wyln, Laurel, I, Jeff and the royal guards formed a wedge behind them as they went upstairs to the study. As did Ranulf and Beollan. The two Marcher Lords had moved swiftly to accompany us, walking into the study with us as a matter of course. To my surprise, Jusson said nothing, merely lifting a brow as they arranged themselves against the windowsills. The rest of us sat in borrowed chairs wrestled into the room by the Own. I ended up next to Gwynedd, holding my own cup of tea, Jeff standing at my back. Wondering if Laurel had a never-ending supply of the stuff, I took a sip, not bothering to shudder at the bitterness. It filled my very empty stomach and calmed the reawakened tremors in my arms and legs.

"When was the last time you saw your brother, Mistress Gwynedd?" Chadde asked, her voice gentle. She'd moved her chair next to Dyfrig's desk and sat facing the player.

I could see the liquid in Gwynedd's cup tremble as her hand shook. "Yesterday," she said, "when he and Rosea had come back from chasing after Lord Rabbit. I was disgusted with him, with her, with the play, with everything. We argued and he flung off again, the little sow right behind him, smirking at me as they left."

"And you didn't see which direction they went?" Chadde asked.

Gwynedd shook her head. "Was Rolly killed in the dead house?"

"No," Laurel said, placing a battered kettle on an equally

battered brazier. "All indications are that he was killed elsewhere, some time before we found him." The Faena laid a
gentle paw on Gwynedd's shoulder. "I'm sure you've heard
rumors. He was murdered, true, but that's all."

Gwynedd nodded. "What's going to happen to him?"

"We'll see him buried, Mistress Gwynedd," Dyfrig said.
The doyen sat on the other side of her, while Jusson sat in
the chair at the desk. It wasn't so much of the lesser yielding to the greater as it was easier for Dyfrig to comfort the
bereaved player while at her side than from behind the
paper mounds on the battered monolith. He'd returned my
ashwood staff to me, but kept his oak Staff of Office with
him, a reminder to everyone in the room that he was the
Church and a vicar of God. Jusson had picked up the mouse
skull, and his long fingers turned it as he gazed at the Staff,
then Laurel, sliding over to Chadde, before coming to rest
on Gwynedd.

Gwynedd was unaware or uncaring of the king's
scrutiny. "I've no money to pay for the offerings or the burial," she said.

"Do not worry," Wyln said before anyone else could
speak. "It'll be taken care of. As will the rest of your ex-
penses." With Thadro absent, the dark elf had moved to
stand next to Jusson, and Gwynedd lifted her gaze from her
tea to look at the enchanter and the king, taking in their
racial and familial likeness. She then nodded again, dropping her eyes back to her cup. Jusson, though, continued to
stare at the player, a slight crease between his brows.

"Were there any threats made against your brother?"
Chadde asked. "Someone who was offended by a play or
took exception to a particular persona?"

Gwynedd shook her head again. "No. No one threatened us."

"There is robbery," I offered, beating back a yawn.
"Master Rodolfo had taken the troupe's funds with him."

"That's true," Chadde said. "But the fact that he was found in the charnel house and not in an alleyway would argue against that. He was deliberately placed there. Why?"

"Find out that and you'll find the killer, honored peace-keeper," Laurel said.

"The killer!" Dyfrig's face turned angry. "For years we've lived peaceably in our valley and now there are two murders in the space of two days."

"Not so peaceably, your reverence," Jusson said, returning his gaze to the doyen. "Or I wouldn't have a garrison here."

"Depredations by bandits aren't quite the same, Your Majesty," Dyfrig said.

"Tell that to those who've been depredated," Jusson said back. His restless fingers turned the mouse skull again. "Still, there is something gleefully intimate about both Master Menck's and Rodolfo's killing—though I cannot see the connection between the larcenous jailer and an itinerant street player."

"There is one, Your Majesty," Beollan said, crashing our conversation just as he had crashed the study. He waved his hand at me. "Rabbit."

Jusson's frown looked more tired than angry. "You too, Fellmark?"

"I'm not accusing him, Your Majesty," Beollan said. "Despite all the furor and name-calling, his guileless innocence shouts to the stars. But it does seem that he's at the center, having enjoyed both Rodolfo's and Menck's attentions yesterday."

Guileless? I had plenty of guile. Five years in the Freston garrison—three of them dodging Slev Vicious—saw to that. However, figuring that now wasn't the time to argue about my worldly wiles, I scowled at the floor, ignoring the very faint snicker Jeff gave as he stood behind me.

Jusson turned the mouse skull once more. "So it does.

But being jailed and being propositioned aren't quite the same thing—"

"Rolly had dealings with the dead man," Gwynedd said, also uncaring that she interrupted the king. "The jailer, Menck."

Seeing that my cup was empty, Laurel had lifted the kettle to pour me another but, at Gwynedd's words, he jerked up abruptly, the hot tea just missing my lap to spill on the floor. That went unnoticed, though, as we were riveted on the player.

"Dealings with Menck," Jusson said, his fingers stilling.

"He came to our rooms at the Copper Pig several nights running, Your Majesty," Gwynedd said. "At first I thought him one of the johnnies come to try his luck with the women of our troupe. But though he leered plenty, he spent all his time with Rolly and Rosea. Him and that smooth runt of a taverner."

"Helto," Chadde said.

"Yes," Gwynedd said. "Then, all of a sudden, Rolly's flushed with the ready, buying the sow trinkets, taking her to eat at the swank inn here in town, and getting her this ridiculous velvet dress that made her look even more of a tart—"

I'd just become aware of the near catastrophe with the tea and was making sure no damage was done; however, at the mention of Rosea's dress I lifted my head. "Velvet dress?" I asked, my voice sounding rusty.

"Yes, my lord," Gwynedd said. "Green, with a bodice that was cut down to her ankles."

"Control yourself, Rabbit," Jusson said, misreading my face.

Gwynedd shrugged. "Young boys and foolish men were always Rosea's prey, Your Majesty."

This time I did open my mouth to protest, but I met Wyln's narrowed stare—and I thought that maybe it wasn't just Thadro being irritable. Maybe there was something about standing next to Jusson that caused people to snarl and snap. I shut my mouth, sinking back into my chair.

"So your brother suddenly had a lot of money?" Chadde prodded.

Gwynedd nodded. "But when I asked Rolly about it, he told me that as it didn't come out of the troupe's purse, it was my never mind. He said he and Rosea had other enterprises—other enterprises! Like he knew anything outside of playacting. I told him that if he struck a bargain with yon leering villain, then he'd better count his fingers *and* his toes. He said that it was with someone else, someone with substance, and the man was just a messenger. He wouldn't tell me more, but I figured the sow had convinced him to pander her to one of the fancy lords who had been pouring into town." She shrugged again, her mouth trembling. "Now he's dead."

"Did your brother take anything besides the troupe's purse with him when he left?" Ranulf asked unexpectedly.

"No, my lord," Gwynedd said. "At least, I don't think he did. His and Rosea's trunks are still there—with us, I mean."

"Perhaps if the peacekeeper were to look through them, she'll find something that'll tell her who your brother's silent partner was," Ranulf suggested. "It would've had to have been someone local to use the jailer as a go-between."

That actually made sense. Snapping out of my brooding, I looked behind me and met Jeff's wondering gaze before moving on to the Marcher Lord. Ranulf, though, was focused on Gwynedd, his forehead wrinkled in concentration. Or in pain, I thought, noticing the lines radiating out from his eyes.

Gwynedd waved her hand in consent. "I've been through both trunks and haven't seen anything out of the ordinary, but you can look if you wish. Heaven knows that Rolly no longer has any use for his things, and I'm ready to give the sow's to the first beggar I meet."

"That would be interesting," Jusson said. "Especially with that green gown."

For a moment Gwynedd's dark eyes came alive as her mouth lifted in a grin. "It does boggle the mind, Your Majesty. I looked for the dress to sell when I realized that we'd been left high and dry, but that and her trinkets she took with her." Her grin faded. "Took everything of value with her."

Dyfrig began comforting Gwynedd again, with Chadde as a counterpoint in making arrangements to get at the trunks and question the other troupe members. I, though, was distracted by Laurel once more trying to pour me tea, and this time succeeding. I took a sip, then, cradling the cup with one hand, propped my elbow on the arm of my chair and rested my head on my other hand, the sound of their voices washing over me. My eyes began to close.

"Cousin."

I jumped, my elbow sliding off the chair arm to knock over my staff, which just missed the brazier as it thudded on the floor. I grabbed the chair arm to keep from falling after it, my legs flailing, sending my cup flying across Gwynedd to land at Dyfrig's feet, the tea splashing the front of the desk. At the same time, flames whooshed up from the brazier, causing Laurel to leap away with something that sounded perilously close to a yowl.

"I'm awake, sire," I said, my eyes opened wide.

"I think we all are after that," Jusson remarked.

"That flame came up rather high, Laurel," Wyln said, solicitous. "Your whiskers weren't singed, were they?"

Laurel stalked back to the brazier, dropping the kettle on it with a clang. "Instead of pulling my tail, Enchanter, you should be concerned about your *cyhn*. Rabbit needs to rest."

"You're right, Master Cat," Jusson said before Wyln

could respond. He set down the mouse skull and stood, forcing the rest of us seated to rise also. "It's been a very long day after a short night and we're all due some respite. We will pick this up tomorrow morning."

"Yes, Your Majesty," Gwynedd said. "But where will I and my people stay? Despite Lord Wyln's generosity, the Hart's Leap is too posh to let us rooms and it's rather cold to camp out in the fields."

"If you please, Your Majesty," Chadde said and, at Jusson's nod, continued. "There is another place, Mistress Gwynedd. Freston's old posting inn. It's not in the best part of town, but the inn itself is clean and respectable, the prices reasonable and the food excellent."

"Was it that inn we saw this morning, Peacekeeper?" Jusson asked, interested. "Over by Eastgate?"

"Yes, Your Majesty," Chadde said, standing aside to let the king step out from behind the desk. "It fell on hard times, as did the rest of the neighborhood when the gate was closed and traffic rerouted. But the new owners are making a go of it."

My face hot, I picked up my staff and my cup, placing the latter on Dyfrig's desk. I then fell in behind Jusson, and we clattered back down the stairs, reentering the church to find it empty, the clerks Keeve and Tyle having ejected everyone in order to prepare for Eveningsong. They were now laying out the benches in neat rows, having already placed the censers and candles on the altar. Rodolfo's body remained behind the altar, but someone had found a more sober shroud than the cape of motley and extinguished the lamps around the bier, so that he was now a suggestion of an outline under a dark cloth surrounded by shadow. Still, I figured that the dead player would be the main attraction. Except on holy eves, Eveningsong was usually sparsely attended, but I now could hear the muted rumble of the crowd waiting outside to be let in. Church was going to be standing room only tonight.

"I will come by tomorrow to speak with you regarding your brother's rites, Mistress Gwynedd," Dyfrig said, walking with us to where I'd left the cloaks draped on the bench. Most of them were gone, those who hadn't accompanied us up to Dyfrig's study having already taken theirs.

Looking resigned, Beollan picked up his, but it was completely dry. The Lord of Fellmark lifted his brows as he donned it, shooting me one of his speculative glances.

"Yes, Your Reverence," Gwynedd said. She'd kept her rather worn cloak with her and now settled it firmly on her shoulders, tying the strings. "I'll be there—we're not going anywhere. At least for the time being."

"I don't think any of us are going anywhere anytime soon," Beollan said, watching Ranulf struggle with his own fur cloak. The brawny lord was uncharacteristically clumsy, dropping the cloak on the floor. He creakily bent down to pick it up again.

"True, Fellmark," Jusson said, fastening his cloak's gold chain across his chest. "I'd planned to leave Freston a couple of days after Rabbit's troop returned. That's obviously not going to happen."

"But despite the horror of all this, Your Majesty, it has has been good for us," Chadde said. Her gray eyes were bright in the soft, alabaster lamplight. "Things have been out of kilter for a long time and now it's as if our balance is being restored. Violently, yes, but then the greater something is out of true, the more force is needed to make it plumb again."

Laurel and Wyln had also handily donned their outer wear, Laurel putting on his coat before moving to my side and discreetly tucking a paw under my elbow. But at Chadde's words, Laurel looked at the peacekeeper as if she were a plump deer slowly waddling by and someone had just rung a dinner bell.

"Laurel," I whispered, and the cat's face immediately went bland, his tail twitching.

Wyln gave a soft laugh anyway. "Caught," he murmured.

"Perhaps you're right, Chadde," Dyfrig said, not hearing Wyln. He cast a glance at Gwynedd, but she had moved closer to the altar, her eyes once more blind as she stared behind it at her brother's form. Still, the doyen lowered his voice, his blue eyes fierce under his shaggy white brows. "But there are other things—much more recent things that have nothing to do with past misdeeds—that we very much need to speak about. As soon as possible."

"I disagree, Your Reverence," Jusson said. "I believe the past has everything to do with the present. In any case, we will have the discussion that we missed this afternoon. See me first thing tomorrow morning."

"Immediately after Morningsong, Your Majesty," Dyfrig promised, herding us to the door. He then stopped, blinking. The benches weren't the only things that had been rearranged: Keeve and Tyle, taking advantage of a full house, had moved the offering box in front of the doorway. Dyfrig frowned even as his mouth twitched into a smile. "Goodness. My lads *have* been busy."

"Lads?" Jusson asked. He glanced over his shoulder at us before turning back to the doyen. "Are they kin?"

Kings don't carry money on their persons, but the rest of us certainly did. Taking the royal hint, we all reached for our purses.

"More connections, Your Majesty, than blood relatives," Dyfrig said. His expression turned benign as we dropped coins into the box—though Ranulf's clumsiness remained and he missed, dropping his on the floor. With a grunt, he stooped down to pick them up. "My sister married Keeve's grandfather's brother's wife's second cousin twice removed," Dyfrig continued. "While Tyle is related to my great aunt's husband's mother's—"

Rising, Ranulf staggered and grabbed at the offering box, trying to stay upright, but it couldn't hold his weight and both he and the box went down with a crash. I had been sleepily amusing myself with the thought of demanding a share of the door for Gwynedd, but all amusement fled as I stared down at the jewels and gold coins spilling across the floor, twinkling in the light.

"Someone is having a good laugh at our expense," Jusson said into the sudden silence, his eyes as gold as the coins. "But we are not amused."

Twenty-five

Diligent questioning of Keeve and Tyle elicited nothing—they hadn't seen anyone with a double fistful of gems and gold coins hovering near the offering box. That wasn't surprising as, besides Laurel's very distracting examination of Rodolfo's body, the church had been full of people, all of whom mixed, mingled and moved about.

Producing a large key, Dyfrig unlocked the offering box to reveal more treasure inside. While it wasn't as large a fortune as had been hidden in Menck's clothing, there was enough for a junior officer in His Majesty's Royal Guard to purchase two or three really decent horses—plus a stable and paddocks to put them in—with enough left over for spurs. Silver ones.

"I could buy into a theater in Gresh with that," Gwynedd said, echoing my thoughts. "One right in the middle of the theater district, with a marble front, red velvet curtains and a grand staircase sweeping up to the balconies." The player stared at the gold and jewels that were piled on the altar, her face dreamy. "Or, better yet, I could build one in Cosdale with the troupe's name carved on the cornerstone."

"It's enough to more than ease anyone's way," Chadde said. She wore a frown as she prodded a diamond. "I don't think this is part of what's missing from the charnel house."

Jusson, Wyln, Laurel and I all drew breath to speak.

"You're right," Beollan said, beating us. "It's different." He picked up a sapphire, nestling it in his palm. "It's not cursed."

Gwynedd blinked, her dreamy expression vanishing. "Cursed, my lord?"

Apparently that was the one thing from Menck's death that we'd managed to keep secret. Until now. Beollan looked up from the sapphire at the silence that had fallen, then realized what he'd let slip. Color dusted his cheekbones. "I mean—"

"Something else we need to discuss, Your Majesty?" Dyfrig asked, his eyes fierce once more.

"It's all of the same fabric, Your Reverence," Jusson said, his voice mild. "Whether sewn up in seams and hidden pockets or ditched in your offering box."

Dyfrig thumped his staff on the floor, the bells jingling. "Do not treat this lightly, Your Majesty. I *saw* the malignancy of the coins and jewels in the charnel house, and now they're who knows where—"

"I'm fully aware of the seriousness, Your Reverence," Jusson said, interrupting. "But while curses and malign forces are your and the Faena cat's province, I'm more concerned about what was sold for so high a price—and who bought it with a purse so deep." His eyes hadn't lost their gold sheen and they now glittered at Dyfrig, at odds with his quiet voice. "*Think*, man. If this isn't part of the jailer's cache, then what does that tell you?"

Some of Laurel's puzzle pieces abruptly shifted into place and I lifted my head to stare at the king, my eyes wide. "Conspiracy, sire," I said.

"Yeah," Ranulf said. He looked none the worse for his spill. However, he didn't look any better either, and his voice was creaky as the rest of him as he once more fell into accord with me. "Or at least two or more people who've been bribed to work towards the same ends." He too prodded a gemstone, a bloodred ruby. "One of whom is now getting cold feet."

"Very good, cousin, Bainswyr," Jusson said. "Very, very good."

Gwynedd was standing very still next to me, her mouth folded in to prevent anything else slipping out. But despite her best efforts at invisibility, Jusson found her anyway and gave her a smile that was just as gentle as any of Wyln's. "However, it *has* been a long day and we should all retire to rest," the king said. "Peacekeeper Chadde and a couple of my Own will escort your troupe to this posting inn, Mistress Gwynedd, but it would please me if you'd be my guest. I assure you that my house is just as clean and respectable."

For a moment, alarm flashed over Gwynedd's face, then it disappeared as her mouth went wry, and she dropped a curtsey. "Thank you, Your Majesty. I would be honored."

Dyfrig refused to keep the coins and jewels, which was just as well as Jusson had no intention of allowing them to remain. The king directed Chadde to count the coins and jewels, then he had me present my purse and the peacekeeper swept them in, Beollan sighing as he dropped the sapphire in last.

Keeve and Tyle also sighed, standing by the altar, watching. "The alms work we could've done with that, Your Reverence," Keeve said, while Tyle murmured about how it would be more than enough to repair the roofs of both the church and rectory.

Dyfrig's expression was fierce once more. "Cursed or not, it is anathema if only because of its origins, and would corrupt any good work, no matter how holy." The doyen caught Jusson's gold stare at the two clerks and moved, shielding them. "They know very well when to keep quiet, Your Majesty." He turned his own incandescent blue gaze on them. "Right?"

Keeve and Tyle nearly strained their necks with their furious nods. "Yes, Your Reverence," they said.

"Look to your own, Your Majesty," Dyfrig said, walking to the arched double doors of the church, "and do not concern yourself about mine." He opened a door himself, revealing the large crowd clamoring to get in. The crowd looked back at the doyen, suddenly pious, with all eagerness to see murdered bodies disappearing without a trace. Dyfrig gave them a grim look before stepping aside to let us out. "After Morningsong, Your Majesty," he said as we went past him.

"As has been said, I'll be there—I'm not going anywhere," Jusson replied.

We got through the throng of churchgoers. Upon reaching the clear, Chadde gave a bow and, with a promise of joining the morning meeting, started out for the rest of Gwynedd's acting troupe standing on the far side of the fountain. Jusson headed in the opposite direction and we were soon home—where Cais greeted us at the door, his familiar face once again wonderfully impassive even when confronted with Gwynedd's feminine presence invading the king's bachelor establishment. Finn appeared at my elbow even before we shed our cloaks and he hustled me upstairs to hot food and a hot bath, after which he tenderly tucked me into bed. Pausing only long enough to put my feather under my pillow, I sank down into the warmed bedclothes and was immediately asleep.

Twenty-six

"I think not."

My eyes flew open to see Wyln standing over me, his slender hand holding mine closed like a vise. The room was dark, the candles extinguished and the fire in the fireplace a few glowing embers. In the darkness I could just make out the curve of the enchanter's face and form; however I had no problem seeing how his eyes flamed in the night and my spine tightened.

There weren't any elves in the Weald where I grew up; the fair northern clans were ranged in the lower mountains, forests and steppes of the Upper Reaches, while the dark elves were concentrated in the city-states along the Border's coast. Every once in a while, though, one or more would come through, traveling from one point to another or part of a merchant's caravan, and our parents would confine my brothers and sisters and me to the farmhouse until they were gone. There were stories of the games elves played with humans—and what was left when they were done.

And despite the adventures of the past months, I'd never truly been alone with the Enchanter Wyln. Keeping my gaze on him, my free hand crept under my pillow, reaching for my knife.

There was a soft, snuffling snort and, turning over in his trundle bed, Jeff started snoring in earnest. I froze. Then, letting out a long breath, I rolled onto my back, my heart pounding at how close I had come to knifing my *cyhn*.

"Your knife is in your trunk," Wyln said. Though his light voice sounded easy, he kept my hand in a viselike grip. "Finn worried when you didn't place it under your pillow as apparently is your habit, but I assured him that you'd have no need for it."

All right, so I hadn't been that close. Somehow, though, that made it worse. "I beg pardon, honored *Cyhn*," I whispered. "I was startled."

Wyln gave a soft, singing sigh. "I think you've been since we've met."

That was very true. "I find it all rather—strange."

"No more bizarre than it is for me to not only have a human as *cyhn*, but one of Iver Bloody-Hand's line. Still, I thought we were past wanting to kill each other over it."

"I've never wanted to kill you, honored *Cyhn*," I said. "It's just that—" I exhaled my own sigh. "Humans did not fare well at elfin hands where I grew up."

"Nor did elves when humans invaded the land where I was born and raised," Wyln said. "There are several centuries of history between the two races, Two Trees'son, none of it very edifying. Some say that we've let you in once and look what happened. The same ones say that the only way to keep it from happening again is to cleanse our remaining land of humans. Others, like His Grace, the Fyrst, argue that if we do that, then we're no different from Iver and his ilk. But then the argument comes back that at least we'd have our homes and our families."

Something else that I remember from my childhood. While Dragoness Moraina's favor kept us safe from even the most rabidly antihuman, there were continual debates throughout the Weald about our presence—and the fact that we had the farm meant that someone fae did not. "I've heard it said, honored *Cyhn*," I murmured.

The mattress dipped as Wyln sat on the bed. "Look at me."

I turned my head to the enchanter and the candle on the nightstand flared into life. I winced in the sudden light.

"You are my *cyhn*," Wyln said, his face intent. "I have sworn to the Oldest One of my lineage to see to your up-bringing until you are ready to stand before the *Gaderian á Deorc Oelfs* and declare your adulthood."

I blinked at him. "Me? Stand before the Council of Dark Elves?"

Wyln's amused smile appeared. "Where else would a son of Loran the Fyrst declare it? Some village green swarming with goats and geese in the hinterlands?" His smile faded. "I have sworn it, Rabbit. Fiat, I have sworn it. And nothing—either here or in the Border, either fae or human, above or below, on all the earths past, present or future, will cause me to forsake my oath."

I stared up into Wyln's face, realizing maybe for the first time that there were two sides to this *cyhnship*. I'd known of my obligations to the lineage. I was even aware, as much as someone not born into it could be, of the lineage's obligation to me. I hadn't thought, though, of what it personally meant to Wyln that he had taken on me as a fosterling, considering the fact that my oh-so-distant ancestor Iver not only drove Wyln and his people from their land, but also killed the enchanter's wife and children in the process.

"Why?" I asked.

Wyln's brows drew together. "Why what? Why I won't forsake myself?"

"No," I said. "Why did you swear in the first place?"

"Ah. Many reasons, Two Trees'son." Wyln's grip suddenly shifted, easing. "Including this one. Open your hand."

Obeying, I looked down to see the feather resting on my palm, the truth rune like a scar underneath it.

"While you were sleeping, you took it from under your

pillow and were about to drop it on the floor when I stopped you. Jeff Corbin'son said you did the same when you fell asleep in the church. What were you dreaming?"

Staring at the feather, I sat up, a maneuver made awkward by the fact that, though Wyln's grip had eased, he hadn't relinquished my hand. I vaguely recalled soft whispers of my name, the flash of a knife and the sound of crashing surf, but like all my dreams of late, it was a jumble of fading images.

"I don't remember," I said, my voice very quiet. "The sea, I think."

"The sea," Wyln repeated. He let go of my hand and I brought it in front of me, studying the feather in the candlelight. It seemed the same—bent and somewhat mangled. There was a rumble that didn't sound like Jeff and I looked up to see Laurel sprawled in the second trundle bed, also fast asleep, his earth sphere hovering over him. Being up the previous night must've finally caught up with the cat. Unlike Wyln. But then, being ageless had some side benefits and I'd heard of elder elves who didn't sleep at all.

"Laurel didn't wake," Wyln said, following my gaze. "Despite your very strong bond, he didn't even stir. *I* wouldn't have known anything about it if I hadn't been watching."

I set aside the thought of the enchanter watching over me. "Our strong what?"

Wyln once more looked amused. "You didn't know what you'd struck when you ate with the Faena, did you? And he didn't tell you either, did he? Haven't you ever wondered why His Grace Loran gave you into Laurel's care when the Faena was the one who delivered you to Kareste?"

"His Grace said that he couldn't have me running around masterless . . ." My voice trailed off as I realized that the Fyrst probably had scores of talent-workers who could've taken over my training. Including Wyln.

"Others could've just as easily overseen your burgeoning talent," Wyln said, echoing my thoughts. "Better, in fact, than someone with a cat's knowledge of the working. But the covenant is very strong in and of itself, and it is augmented by the rune Laurel has drawn on your hand. His Grace was concerned what would happen if you two were separated."

"Laurel and I have been apart many times," I protested. As Beollan had said, we hadn't been joined at the hip and there were times when Captain Suiden had kept the Faena away from me or I went places he couldn't go. Then I remembered how Laurel seemed aware of events when he wasn't with me—like him knowing what was said during the king's salon. Or how he easily found us—and me—in the warehouse yesterday morning. Thought-scrying, I suddenly wondered, or something else? My gaze went to the second earth sphere, also Laurel's, hanging in midair by my bed.

"Were you truly apart, Rabbit?" Wyln asked. When I remained silent, he smiled once more. "Even so, it's not necessarily a bad thing. The covenant gives protection from the Lady Gaia Herself through her shaman. If this were spring or summer, I'd have no worries. However, the Lady is coming to Her time of sleep during the dark of the year. A time of dreams, a time where water holds sway—water that was used to work *dauthiwaesp*. And not only did you try to remove from you the symbol of her covering, but you've been dreaming of the sea."

"An angry sea," I said, my voice distant. "Full of storms and pounding waves."

"So you do remember something: an aspect turning elemental." Wyln tilted his head, considering. "But how does that fit in with everything else—the attempted binding, the ritual sorcery and the attack at the house of the dead?"

"I don't know," I replied, supremely uninterested in

dreams and the dark arts. "Is my covenant with Laurel stronger than our *cyhn*?"

"Stronger? No. However, the covenant does rival it. As the covenant also rivals your fealty to your king. As strong a binding as any you ever had, even the one during your apprenticeship with Magus Kareste. It is very good that Iver'son, Laurel and I are all pulling in the same direction where you're concerned. More or less."

I was also supremely uninterested in Jusson. "Laurel told His Grace Loran that the covenant hadn't blocked Kareste from binding me anew when I was brought back to the Border."

"If Laurel said so, then it must be true," Wyln said. "He is head of the Faena, after all. I'm sure his own rune glowed as he said it."

So it had. But then, as Jusson said, Laurel was very nimble with the truth. I laid the feather on my knee. "I've had no choice in this, have I, honored *Cyhn*?"

"There are always choices, Two Trees'son," Wyln said.

"Are there?" I asked, looking up. "Since the day my talent manifested, it seems that everyone has been busy making them for me. My parents, Kareste, Jusson, Laurel, the Fyrst and now hidden sorcerers with invisible hands dripping with death magic, all deciding the shape of my life. No matter what I want."

I expected a lecture on how I should quit whining. On how I ought to be grateful that Jusson and His Grace Loran had even deigned to notice the provincial in their midst. On how I was given much and therefore so much more was expected, and that the universe didn't revolve around me or my wishes and wants. I started to scowl as I marshaled my counterarguments.

"Is that so?" Wyln asked, the flames in his eyes brighter. "What are you going to do about it, then?"

Twenty-seven

I stared at Wyln. Realizing that my mouth was hanging open, I used it to suck in air, only to let it out again in an explosive rush. "Do?" I asked, my voice rising enough that Jeff stopped snoring and Laurel shifted on his trundle bed.

Wyln gave that damned amused smile again, keeping his own voice soft and low. "As you pointed out, Two Trees'-son, this *is* your life. Shouldn't you take charge of it?"

"How am I supposed to do that?" I demanded, my voice rising so much it squeaked. "March into Jusson's study and pound on his desk—?"

Wyln suddenly held up his hand, turning his head to the window. A moment later I heard the ringing of the church bells. Jeff sat up, wide awake, while Laurel tumbled out of bed with a grumbling growl. I flung back the covers and stood, the low tone of the hour bell reverberating through me.

"What is it?" Wyln asked, also rising.

I quickly moved to the window, but there was no vantage and all I saw were the facing houses, lights appearing in their windows as their occupants also came abruptly awake. I turned and hurried to the clothespress. "I don't know," I said. Removing my nightshirt, I moved aside to let Jeff pass to his locker. "But that's the signal for an attack against the town."

Which was odd. While the mountain villages and merchant caravans did suffer bandit depredations, Freston, with its fully staffed garrison, did not. Our outlaws weren't the best and the brightest, but they were still able to work out the consequences of attempting a walled town that was more than willing to retaliate with well-trained troopers riding warhorses and wielding heavy cutlery. This was the first time that I knew of that anyone had even tried.

Dressed, I hurried to the bedroom door, buckling on my sword belt as I went. I still didn't have a sword, but I figured that one of the Own had to have a spare one or two lying about that I could appropriate. My feather I pushed into my pocket—old habits die very hard. I flung open the door, expecting to see Thadro bustling about organizing. Instead I saw the night rota royal guards milling in confusion. I stopped, surprised, Jeff, Wyln, Laurel and both earth spheres piling up behind me.

"Sir!" One of my guards turned, coming to attention. The rest did the same, relief on their faces. "I'm sorry, sir, but Cais had been very insistent on not letting anything disturb you and we didn't know if this is important—"

"Where's the king?" I asked, cutting off the explanations. I stepped out into the hallway, allowing the others behind me to exit.

"In his chambers—"

At that moment, the door to the royal suite opened and Jusson emerged fully dressed, also buckling on his sword belt.

"Sire," I said, hurrying to him. "Where's Thadro?"

"Out chasing fugitive taverners and mobile dead men, I suppose, as he hasn't returned," Jusson said. One of his brows rose as he saw both Jeff and my hauberks. Jeff's hood was up, but my braid was too thick for my hood to cover my head, so it lay about my shoulders, its mesh dully gleaming in the light of the wall sconces lining the hallway. Turning, Jusson called into the room for Cais to bring his armor. He then pulled off his coat and shirt, dropping them on the floor as the majordomo hurried out carrying the king's battledress. "What's the alarm?" Jusson asked.

"I don't know, sire," I said again. "But that is the signal for an attack against the town." All along the hallway doors were opening, the rooms' occupants popping out in various stages of undress, while pounding feet coming up the back stairs signaled the arrival of the rest of the royal guards.

"My flag flies over the garrison and they attack anyway?" Jusson said over the questions, demands and exclamations filling the hallway. "Are the bandits that bold here?" He removed his sword belt and Finn appeared to take it.

"It has never happened before as far as I know," I said, scanning the guards. I didn't see Arlis—most likely he was still with the Lord Commander. "We need horses, sire."

"See to it," Jusson said as Cais and Finn began to quickly assist him into his armor.

I snared a couple of long-legged guards and sent them to the stables. They left running, dodging past a few of the king's guests who had remained in the hallway demanding answers. Most, however, saw the king's armor and, able to put two and two together, had ducked back into their rooms. As Cais flung Jusson's tabard over the king's head, they emerged again, this time more or less dressed. After buckling on his sword belt and putting on his helm with the battle crown, Jusson took his shield from Cais and strode through the mob to the stairs. Everyone fell in behind him, jostling each other and the royal guards for position at the king's back. Apparently Jusson's nobles noticed that the king's Lord Commander was missing and thought that they were just the ones to take Thadro's place. I started to follow, but felt a tug on my sleeve.

"My lord," Finn said, holding another sword.

With a murmured thanks, I took it, thrusting it into my

scabbard as I hurried after Jusson, catching up as the king reached the front door. Behind him was a snarl of people and, as they pushed outside and down the front steps, the jostling turned into shoving with contradictory orders flying. I managed to get in front of them all, planting myself against the tumult.

"Those of the Own on guard rota will remain," I shouted over the noise in the street. "The rest, formation!"

Despite the royal griffin we all sported on our tabards they weren't my men—nor was I their lieutenant. Not yet. Still, at my shout, those on guard duty separated out, while the others fell into line, creating a wall between the aristos and the king.

"Very good, cousin," Jusson said. "Here." He shoved his shield into my hands. "Stay to the left, out of the way of my sword arm."

"Yes, sire," I said, my voice going faint. I stared down at the shield's device. It was the same that was on the king's tabard and that flew on the king's banner: a plain sword, crowned—to lead, to rule, to defend.

"Something from the past that I'd once seen again and again, always for ill," Wyln murmured, "the last time leading behind it many thousands, bright and mighty with blade and buckler as they came to war against us."

I turned, surprised to see the enchanter at my shoulder, also looking down at the shield. Next to him were Laurel and Jeff. Somehow all three managed to be on Jusson's side of the wall of guards, to the anger of Jusson's nobles left bereft on the other side.

"I heard it was a sight, with the human forces arrayed to the horizon," Laurel said. He raised his head, scenting.

"Like locusts upon a field and just as ravening," Wyln said. "How very odd that I should now be following it into battle." His eyes drifted to the nobles behind us to light on Beollan and Ranulf. "With certain folk as shield brothers."

Jusson turned to stare at the enchanter.

"Not battle, honored *Cyhn*," I said, frowning. "If anything, a skirmish. This attack is *stupid*."

"Probably a false alarm sounded by someone made nervous by everything that has happened in the last two days," Jeff suggested.

"A possibility, Guardsman Jeffen," Jusson said. Facing forward again, he stepped out into the street as the two guards rode up at the head of a string of horses, the royal groomers with them. "But we won't know until we get there." With a groomer holding the bridle of his horse, he swung up into his saddle. "And while I would welcome either of you at my side, Lord Wyln and Master Laurel, I cannot let you, as emissaries from another country, fight against my own people—even if they are outlawed and broken men."

It was Wyln's turn to frown. "Your eorl commander is not here—"

"We understand," Laurel said, interrupting. Laying a paw on on Wyln's arm, he turned his head in another direction, still scenting.

Jusson gave his sharp-edged smile. "Don't worry, I will bring Rabbit back safe."

"And yourself, Iver'son?" Wyln asked. "Will you bring yourself back safe?"

Jusson stared down at Wyln before giving a brief shake of his head. "I will do what is necessary," he said, turning to me. "Have Bainswyr and Fellmark ride with us, cousin. That will calm everyone down. Somewhat."

Jusson was wrong—his nobles didn't calm down, but the mutters did change from pushy magicals to opportunistic Marcher Lords. I paid no attention, having other things on my mind as I also swung up into my saddle, the king's shield on my arm, one of the earth spheres at my shoulder.

Jeff took his place at my back along with the other royal guards.

"Where to?" Jusson asked me.

I assessed the street to see if there was any movement, but the residents were either dashing from house to house or wandering about looking as confused as we were. I lifted my head to scan what I could see of the mountains over the rooftops, but they were dark shapes against the starry sky—with not one signal fire visible.

"The Kingsgate, sire," I decided.

"Why there?" Ranulf asked, scowling. The groomers had managed to bring his horse-beast and he'd slowly mounted, the lines of pain carved deep into his face making him look twice his age in the moonlight.

"If there is a threat to the town, it most likely would be at the Kingsgate and not at the Westgate, where the garrison is," I said. "And if it's one of the outlying farms that's under attack, then the gate will allow us easy access via the King's Road."

Jusson nodded. "Give the order, Rabbit."

At my shout we began to move. One of the guards had the king's banner and he rode ahead of us. Jusson was just behind his bannerman and I was next to the king as his shield-bearer. Behind us were Beollan and Ranulf, then came the royal guards, including Jeff, with their own banner—the griffin rampant—and behind them were the rest of the aristos. At first we had to ease through the townspeople crowding the street, but when they saw the king's banner they parted to let us through, many joining us to run alongside as we picked up speed to a trot, their coats and cloaks flapping open to show their nightdress underneath, cudgels, short swords and other weaponry in their hands. We were a sizable crowd, and growing larger as we made our way to the Kingsgate with not only more townsfolk joining us, but those armsmen quartered in town appearing out of the night to join their masters, also carrying banners with their lords' devices. The cries and calls of confusion changed as the townspeople began to shout "King Jusson!" and "Majesty!" and "Golden Eye! Golden Eye sees!" and over it all was the ringing of the bells. They hadn't stopped tolling, the deep tone of the hour bell shaking through me. I turned my head as I rode, scanning the streets, but I saw nothing unusual. I stood up in my stirrups in an attempt to see over the rooftops to the garrison, but gave it up and dropped down again.

"What is it, Rabbit?" Jusson asked.

"We're blind, sire," I said. "There's nothing indicating what's happening or why. No signal fires, no panicked people fleeing, no messengers with news from the fight. Nothing." I now scanned the street ahead of me. The regular citizens keeping pace with us on foot had been joined by members of the Watch, but that was all. "And where are the garrison troopers?"

"Perhaps they're already where we're going, ibn Chause," Beollan said, urging his horse next to mine.

"Maybe," I said. "But Commander Ebner would've also sent a detachment to the king. And aren't your armsmen quartered at the garrison? Where are they?"

"Again, perhaps they are all on their way," Beollan said, though his fair brows pulled together in a frown. "You're reasoning ahead of all your facts. You made a good case for going to the gate. Let's get there, then decide what to do based on what we find."

Though that made sense, my uneasiness wouldn't go away, and I motioned to the same two guards that had gone to the stables, sending them to scout ahead to the Kingsgate with instructions to return immediately with whatever news they could gather.

Ranulf grunted in what sounded like approval, though the scowl hadn't left his face. Then, reminiscent of Laurel, he lifted his head as if he were scenting. I too lifted my head, trying to see the twin watchtowers of the Kingsgate, but the buildings also blocked them. However, there was one thing—well, two now—that did rise high above the roofs. I looked over my shoulder and saw, past the hovering earth sphere, the church spire and, opposite it, the column of fire at the charnel house. Both speared into the night sky, bracketing the moon between them, Lady Gaia's consort beaming down on us with a maniacal grin. I looked forward again as we swept around the corner and into the main street, and looming ahead of us was the solid mass of the Kingsgate. A solid and rather quiet-looking mass, with its attendant watchmen at the gate proper and in the watch-towers seeming more intent on our approach than anything happening outside the town walls.

"There's Chadde!" Jeff shouted from behind me.

I quickly dropped my gaze to see the peacekeeper riding between the two guards-turned-scouts, all three heading towards us. I held up my own hand and the cavalcade behind us slowed, then stopped.

"Your Majesty," Chadde said as she reached us. "What's happening?"

My frown spread to Jusson's face. "You tell me, Peacekeeper," the king said. "Didn't you come from the gate?"

Beollan and Ranulf jostled my horse as they pressed forward and Chadde's gray eyes flashed to them before returning to the king. "Yes, Your Majesty. But there's nothing there."

"Nothing there?" Jusson repeated. He looked towards the Westgate. "Then is the garrison itself under attack?"

"No, Your Majesty," Chadde said. "I looked out from the Kingsgate watchtower and didn't see anyone attacking anywhere against the town. Of course, the church has a different vantage and maybe they're seeing something I couldn't—"

The bells suddenly stopped ringing and Chadde's last word echoed in the hard-falling silence. King and towns-folk, noble and guard, all turned, those a-foot lifting their heads and standing tiptoe to look at the church, its crystal-and-silver spire bright in the reflected moon- and firelight.

That is, all except Lord Beollan.

The Marcher Lord leaned forward, his gaze fixed on a building a little ways up the street, his silver eyes glowing in the night. "There's something there—"

There was a swift thud and the king's bannerman screamed and went down on his horse's neck, a crossbow bolt sticking out of his shoulder. Beollan flung up his shield over his head. "Ambush! Cover the king!"

I was already moving, lifting the shield over Jusson. I was just in time as I felt a couple of thumps against my shield arm. Then I felt another in my side. Glancing down, I saw a bolt just above my sword belt.

"Rabbit!" Jeff pushed next to my horse, using his shield to cover me. The crowd roared in panic as people shoved to get out of the way of the hail of quarrels, our horses and each other. Another one went down with a cry, this time an aristo. Ranulf's horse bellowed, maddened by the smell of blood, and the Marcher Lord fought to keep it from lashing out with hooves and teeth. The Own pulled in around the king and me, their shields raised in a turtle, just as another flight of quarrels struck, this time coming from the opposite direction.

"Hauberk stopped it," I told Jeff as I felt more thumps against my shield arm. I held my horse steady with my knees against another surge of the crowd.

"We are caught in crossfire," Jusson said, also control-ling his shying mount. "We need to move."

"Yes, sire," Beollan said, his face fierce, his eyes wide and blazing. "We should split our forces and surround the ambushers. Ibn Chause and Guardsman Jeffen know this town. You and he can lead one while Jeffen and I take the other—"

"This way, sire," I said before Jusson could agree. Keeping the shield over the king, I forced our way through to a dark side street. As soon as we were free of people, I urged my horse into a gallop—but not towards any possible sniper hideouts. Instead I headed in the opposite direction. I didn't bother to look back, but a clatter of hooves told me that at least Jusson was still with me and we swiftly rode through narrow back streets and alleyways, ducking under jutting upper stories, twice cutting through courtyards and once trampling someone's back garden, the king matching me hoofbeat for hoofbeat as we twisted and turned our way towards the center of Freston, me crying "ha-ha-ha!" as I urged my horse faster, not caring that I risked a broken neck on the slick cobblestones, not caring about anything except that I had led everyone in the wrong direction—not only into an ambush, but also away from where the alarm was ringing. Away from the church. Away from Doyen Dyfrig.

We rounded a final corner in a small, cramped passage, my horse's back hoof slipping before he found purchase, and a moment later we burst into the town's main square. In spite of all the ruckus, the square was empty and I didn't stop until I reached the church steps. Flinging myself off my horse, I grabbed my staff from my saddle and raced up the steps to the double doors—and was snatched back by a grip on my sleeve.

"No, cousin," Jusson said, pulling me back down the steps. "We don't know what's in there. Wait for the guards."

"It took you long enough, Iver'son."

Pulling from Jusson's grip, I turned to see Wyln standing with Laurel. Behind them was a horse that Wyln had appropriated from the groomers, its sides heaving and steam rising from its flanks. Apparently the enchanter had done his own wild ride with Laurel loping by his side. As had the

King's Own. They were pouring out from the same alley-way Jusson and I had, Jeff leading the wounded banner-man's horse, followed by Jusson's nobles with their armsmen hard on their heels, all of them thundering to where we stood.

"We were unavoidably detained," Jusson said over the noise of the arrivals, but he'd lost his audience. Wyln's gaze became fixed on the crossbow bolts bristling in the king's shield before dropping to my side. The enchanter's brows snapped together.

"You are injured."

Laurel, already helping with the wounded bannerman, turned around, but I shook my head. "My hauberk stopped it," I said, impatient. My hand went to remove the bolt but I was distracted by both Beollan and Ranulf shoving through the dismounting men to where I stood. Chadde also hurried to us.

"Why are we here and not rooting out the snipers?" Beollan demanded.

"Maybe Magic Boy got lost," Ranulf said. "Or maybe he needed to pray—"

"Shut the sodding hell up," I said.

"Rabbit has brought us to the right place, my lords," Jusson said, his mild voice contrasting violently with the gold of his eyes. "Despite the ambush, there wasn't anything at the town's gates, so it follows that since here the alarm sounded, here the battle is—"

I interrupted Jusson, worry causing me to gasp, making it hard to catch my breath. "Sire, please, Doyen Dyfrig's in there."

"I know," Jusson said. He motioned and several of his Own gathered about him, as did his nobles, as did Chadde and Wyln. I started to join the king, but my legs wouldn't work. Surprised, I looked down. And swayed as my eyes went blurry. My staff dropped from my suddenly nerveless fingers.

"Rabbit, you *are* injured." Jeff hurried to me as I collapsed to my knees. I put my gloved hand to my side, but when I pulled it away I couldn't see any blood. Even so, I swayed again, and the earth sphere bobbed down in front of my face, spinning slowly.

"The fire!" one of the aristos called out, and with an effort I turned my head from the sphere to look at the charnel house fire. The flames had been yellow-white, but now there were flickers of orange. As I watched, more orange appeared, with flashes of red, and the flames began to shrink.

"The Lady and Her mercies!"

Turning my head again, I blinked to see Laurel and Wyln, both kneeling along with Jeff, Jusson standing behind them, all of their faces strained with worry. Wyln put his arm around my shoulder and eased me down to the paving stones, Laurel already ripping at my tabard, his paw on the bolt, holding it steady.

"Why didn't his air aspect stop this?" Wyln asked Laurel. "It has done so before, even yesterday at that forsaken tavern."

"I don't know," Laurel said. He made a pad of what was left of my tabard and held it to my side. "His shortness of breath must be blood loss. The quarrel isn't in near deep enough to have reached anything vital." His whiskers lifted as he scented, and he pulled the pad away again, staring down at it. "He's not bleeding."

"Maybe it hasn't seeped through his hauberk yet," Jeff said. "Or maybe it hasn't gotten past the quarrel."

"I don't feel it," I gasped. "I don't feel it at all—" I faltered, staring past Jusson as one of the double church doors creaked open. Thin streaks appeared on the wood, gleaming leprous white in the light from the lamps on either side of the doorway arch. The streaks thickened, spreading over the door before jumping over to its mate.

Wyln rose and moved swiftly to stand in front of us. "Behind me!"

No one argued, not Ranulf or Beollan, not Jusson. Laurel also rose to stand with the enchanter, the rune on his middle pad glowing brightly. While I didn't feel the wound on my side, I could feel my own rune heat up in response. But it was weak, so very weak. The streaks on the second door also became thick and white, spreading up and out to the stone archway. The first door creaked open more and a tall, sticklike figure moved into view, a dark cloth over its shoulders like a cape. The lamplight caught its eyes, shining on their flat surface as it stepped out of the church.

"Holy Father defend us," Jeff whispered, making a warding sign against evil. "It's Rodolfo."

So it was. The dead man walked further out into the portico, its head swiveling to look down at us. Its flat eyes fixed on me, its mouth flashing in a rictus of a smile and, with a flourish of its shroud, it started down the stairs. Laurel raised his staff as Wyln lifted his hand and was outlined in flame. Fire, white-hot, exploded from the enchanter and Laurel bellowed, the Faena's words heavy with power, and for a moment, Rodolfo staggered back. Then the corpse's head swiveled again to stare at me, its face shiny as if encased in ice, its death smile still in place, the wound in its neck gaping open in a second grin. It raised its own hand and ice-cold air blasted down on us, hitting Laurel and Wyln hard and rocking them both back. But I didn't see any more. As the cold rolled over me, I felt it in my injured side first as a kiss, then as a bite, growing in pain as it spread out. Screaming, I arched up, shutting my eyes against the agony. As I did, I saw glittering green eyes set under delicate russet brows gazing at me, pink lips gently parting in a smile that showed even, white teeth.

"Rabbit!"

My own eyes flew open again to see Jeff's worried face as he held my shoulders down. He looked about for help but Jusson was standing with his Own, his nobles, their armsmen and his peacekeeper, swords drawn, shields up as they stood behind Laurel and Wyln, their faces painted with terror. Wyln disappeared in a column of flame, tongues of fire sprouting from the lamplights and up from the cracks between the paving stones. Another stream of white fire shot out at the descending corpse and Laurel drew brilliant runes in the air. The corpse once more faltered, its limbs flopping loosely as the shaman of the Goddess of life and death fought with whatever had usurped what was Hers. However, Rodolfo raised its hand, this time holding what looked like a javelin of ice. The dead man flung it, and it went right through Laurel's runes, the Faena twisting aside, just barely avoiding being hit. The javelin shattered against a paving stone, the stone turning white with frost, tentacles of ice spreading out. The ice reached the flames coming up from between the stones and there was a hiss as the ice melted and turned to steam, the vapors drifting along the ground.

Another wave of agony swept over me and I screamed again, twisting in my extremity. I reached for fire, but the hearth warmth that I had within me just moments ago was swiftly dying, along with the fire in the charnel house. I strained for wind, water, but they slipped through my fingers. Gasping, I looked up to see the earth sphere still hovering in my face. Not mine, but I didn't care. I reached up and grabbed hold.

And found myself standing in a forest. The afternoon sun streamed through the colorful autumn trees, and the nippy air held the fragrance of leaf mold, earth, with a hint of the coming fall rains. I recognized the tree stump of some ancient patriarch, and realized that behind me was my parents' farm and ahead was the way to Dragoness

Moraina's lair. There was crackling in the underbrush and out the corner of my eye I caught someone mottled brown and furry hurrying off about the business of preparing for the coming winter. I frowned up at the multihued canopy above me. "This," I said, "is *not* a good time to be having visions."

Foolish boy.

I quickly looked about to see who spoke, but saw no one.

Foolish boy, take it out.

"Take what out?" I asked.

There was a sighing sound and the trees' leaves rustled, even though there was no breeze. **The quarrel, foolish boy. Take it out.**

Abruptly I was back in the racking agony of my body. Rodolfo had made it to the bottom step and was now advancing on Laurel and Wyln. The Faena's ears were flat against his skull, his fangs bared, while Wyln, still a column of flame, had thrown up a short wall of fire, behind which the Own and the aristos and their armsmen crouched, shooting their own crossbows. But the quarrels bounced off the same shield of ice that had met Wyln's efforts. The line wavered as the corpse neared, the guards and armsmen crying out.

"So we discover who we are," Jusson said as he stepped out from the wall of fire, his sword drawn and holding his shield, the House of Iver's device shining in the light of Wyln's flames. "Shall we flee and let evil pass? Or shall we swear by all that is holy that here it will stop?"

There was a moment of hesitation, then Beollan joined Jusson, followed by Ranulf and another aristo, then three more, then the rest of the men, crossbows going down as the men also drew their swords, their faces grim.

The corpse, though, ignored them. It scuttled sideways towards me and its hand rose again, holding another javelin

of ice. Snarling, I reached down and yanked the quarrel out
of my side, and immediately the pain stopped.

"Damn it!" Jeff snatched up the pad Laurel had dropped
and now tried to press it against my side. "What are you
doing? You'll bleed to death!"

I pushed Jeff's hand away and, rolling, I came up in a
crouch. With its dead man's smile, the corpse drew back the
javelin and let it fly. I tensed, ready to spring to either side,
but a flame shot out from Wyln, hitting the javelin midflight, knocking it back to shatter against the church steps.
Ice sprawled across the stone as I stood and reached for fire,
and the aspect flooded into me with a roar as the fire in the
charnel house shot up again. At the same time, flames flickered over the church steeple, spreading down from the roof.
Rodolfo paused, swiveling its head up to look and a ragged
cheer went up from the men at the flames overrunning the
ice-covered doors. My gaze fixed on the dead man, I
walked towards it, picking up my dropped staff and drawing my sword. Behind me, Jeff scrambled up, taking his
place at my back.

Seeing me up and moving, Ranulf and Beollan left the
line to also approach the dead master player, Ranulf circling around to one side hefting his battleaxe, while Beollan flanked the corpse on the other side holding his own
sword. At the same time, Wyln moved, stepping out of the
flaming column, holding a sword of fire. His long mane of
hair whipped about him as he lifted his arm, a fiery shield
on it.

"Art thou well, *Cyhn* Rabbit?" Wyln's voice was a song.

"Yeah," I said, meeting up with Jusson. "I'm just fine."

"So," the enchanter sang. "Fire against water, kindred of
the earth. Master against master, little brothers. This one's
mine."

I'd once seen Loran the Fyrst in a sword fight, and His
Grace had an economy of movement, being where he

needed to be and doing what he needed to do at exactly the right moment, no more and definitely no less. I'd expected the same with Wyln, his centuries of experience paring his style to just the essentials. But while there was no wasted motion, the enchanter moved as if he were dancing. He swept towards the dead man, his fire sword coming up in a stroke that would've removed the corpse's head if it had connected. Rodolfo dodged it by skittering sideways again, then, jerking around to face the enchanter, produced a sword of ice and parried. Fire and ice met with a long hiss, steam again rising as Wyln and the dead man tested each other's strength before springing apart, and then coming together once more. More steam rose from each sword strike against sword, against shield, from where their footsteps mingled—one set fire, the other ice—the vapor cloaking them in billowing clouds that now showed them in firelit silhouette, parting to give a glimpse, now closing again. Wyln was grace as he flowed from stance to stance—some I recognized from my own sword training, some I'd never seen before. Rodolfo, though, moved with the same abrupt, jerky flashes that reminded me of a spider and I shifted uneasily. As I did, the steam clouds parted and the corpse turned its head to stare at me—and for a brief moment its flat eyes shone blue in the firelight of Wyln's sword and shield.

A blue as innocent and mild as the spring sky.

"Slevoic," Jeff gasped behind me.

My first impulse was to step back, way back. My second, stronger impulse was to smash the corpse's face. I raised my staff over my shoulder like a club, wanting to destroy all signs of what I thought was dead and several months gone.

But before I could move, Wyln, taking advantage of the corpse's distraction, lunged forward, thrusting his sword through its belly. Rodolfo's head swiveled back to the enchanter, its death grin stretched tight as the corpse grasped the flaming sword, holding it—and Wyln—in place while its other hand swung its sword of ice. The blade, though, whistled over Wyln's head as the enchanter dropped to one knee, the other foot extended as he gripped his sword hilt with both hands and pulled sideways, cutting the corpse nearly in two.

Flames curled up from the bisecting wound as Rodolfo faltered, its lower body not quite in sync with its upper, its movements once more loose and floppy. The corpse again raised its sword but Wyln, already on his feet, again spun into the same stroke he had used in the beginning of the fight. His sword of fire trailed flames as it arced around, slicing through Rodolfo's neck. The dead man's head toppled off and the headless body seemed to hang in midair before it collapsed in a heap, like a puppet with its strings cut.

There was silence, then a long, collective sigh. Looking around, I saw that the square was packed with townsfolk. Realizing I still had my staff raised like a club, I quickly lowered it—which was good as I needed something to prop me and my suddenly weak knees up. Returning my gaze to the church, I could see that the fire had melted the ice on the church doors. However, steam shrouded the entryway and was drifting down the steps in wispy tendrils, like fingers reaching for the ground. We were going to have to go up those steps and through those doors in order to find Doyen Dyfrig and his clerks, Keeve and Tyle. Or what remained of them.

Jusson walked over to Rodolfo's body parts and prodded the headless torso with his sword. Getting no response, he turned and also looked up at the church. For a moment I could see the king's shoulders slump. Then he straightened, his chin lifting. "We need to go in—not you, Rabbit," he added as I started to gather the royal guards together.

"I'm fine, Your Majesty," I protested.

"That's good, but you're still not going inside. As has been said, too much interest is being shown you by the dead."

Jusson himself organized a search party of his Own, his nobles, Wyln, Chadde and some of the braver town elders who pushed their way to the fore of the crowd. A small part of me was relieved that I didn't have to go with them; a larger part was full of dread. It was extremely doubtful that Dyfrig, Keeve or Tyle were still alive and even now their bodies could be under the control of whatever had animated Rodolfo's corpse.

"Maybe we should check on the injured," Jeff said, touching my shoulder.

That was as good a distraction as any. Nodding, I started walking to where Laurel and several citizens were tending to the wounded bannerman and aristo. Wyln and the cat must've drawn straws and Laurel won—or lost—and had to remain behind with me. Or maybe it had nothing to do with me and everything to do with those wounded. Laurel raised his head as Jeff and I approached, his eyes appraising, while behind me I could hear Jusson leading the search party up the steps, the king's boots crunching the ice that had formed on the stone.

"Did you see?" Jeff asked me. "How Rodolfo looked like Slevoic?"

"I saw," I said, my voice tired.

"But the Vicious is dead."

I thought back to Slevoic's drawn-out scream in the enchanted forest and Trooper Ryson riding back from the trees carrying the Vicious' hauberk streaked with blood. "Yeah, but so was Rodolfo—" I stopped midstride, suddenly wondering why, after the master player's second death, there was still ice anywhere. Frowning, I met Laurel's gaze and we both turned to the church to see Wyln, just behind Jusson, staring down, also frowning. The enchanter then lifted his head to look past the king, studying the church doors. A fire sphere formed by the enchanter's shoulder and in its reflected light, I could see a faint sheen on the wood—

"It's moving!" someone screamed.

I swiftly looked back to see Rodolfo's severed head lying on the ground, its flat eyes fixed on mine. The torso suddenly rose up, holding in one hand another javelin of ice. I cast a wild glance about for some sort of cover; however, neither Jeff nor I had a shield—Jeff's was on his saddle and Jusson had taken his back. We were totally out in the open. Hurriedly calling up fire, I flung it at the corpse, but at the same time Jeff tried to pull me behind him and the fireball splashed harmlessly beyond it.

"Rabbit!"

Both Jusson and Wyln tried to go back down the steps, but were blocked by those below them who were frozen in shock. The king shoved—and knocked a royal guard into Wyln, who slid on the slick steps, scrambling to find purchase. Laurel roared, and I could hear over the shrieks of the crowd the screech of his claws against the paving stones as he scrambled to his feet and began racing towards me.

Rodolfo's torso came together with its bottom half and stood, still holding its javelin of ice, and I desperately formed a shield of fire as I let loose another fireball. The reconstructed corpse, though, sidestepped and the fireball again missed. It raised the javelin as its head, still on the ground, grinned at me, its eyes once more shining like frozen puddles.

At that moment the double church doors blew open the wrong way, with a splintering crash, the force of it causing most of the search party to stumble down the steps. Jusson managed to stay upright by latching onto a column, Wyln also somehow stayed on his feet, and both of them turned to see Doyen Dyfrig stepping out from the church carrying his Staff of Office. The wind swirled around him in a mad storm, his white hair waving wildly about his head, as his gaze lit on what had once been Rodolfo.

"By all that's holy!"

Dyfrig raised the Staff and slammed it down hard against the stone porch, and the wind ascended to the sky in a howling whirlwind. There was a sizzling crack and boom that shook the ground under my feet, and lightning zigzagged down, hitting the headless corpse. White and black reversed on the back of my eyelids as I shut my eyes against the blinding light, and when I opened them again Master Rodolfo's body was again collapsed on the ground with smoke rising from all three parts.

The wind's howling dropped to a soft moan as Dyfrig gripped the Staff of Office with both hands, his body drooping, his face white in the streetlamps' light—which could've been the result of battling the revenant, or it could've been just the nighttime leeching him of color.

Or it could've been the fact that Dyfrig had just come into his full mage power—some sixty years later than normal, true, but with all the attendant signs, wonders and trauma. Just as I had experienced when I'd done the same some months earlier, triggered by the terrifying crises of Magus Kareste finding me after five years of hiding. Then too there were thunderclaps without a cloud in the sky.

Jusson hurried down the stone steps and, striding to the smoking corpse, once more prodded it with his sword. And again the dead man stayed inert. This time, though, the king raised his head, his eyes brilliant gold.

"Burn it. Now."

Twenty-eight

We found Keeve and Tyle in the spire. Patches of melted ice showed how they were chased up the ladder to the wooden platform just under the bells. Their bodies were also wet with melted ice, their faces wearing the same look of horror that had been on the dead jailer Menck's.

Jusson had changed his mind and decided that the best place for me was with him, but he still wouldn't let me help with removing the two clerks from the tower. Instead, some rope was found that was then tied around them, and they were gently lowered down to the ground floor, where town officials just as gently placed them on wooden benches. A low moan filled the square from the waiting townspeople as the bodies were carried outside, while up in the spire the wind whistled through the arched openings. It caused the giant iron bells to hum, the tones mingling with the sounds of grief.

We went through the rest of the church, but other than additional puddles of melted ice marking the movements of Rodolfo's corpse, there was no sign of upset—certainly none of the destruction we saw in the charnel house. Still, as I looked at the altar streaked with water, I found myself backing away, the tightness in my chest creeping up to my throat and causing each breath to ache. It could've been as

Wyln had said while we were at the abandoned ware-house—I was feeling the aftermath of one of my aspects being used to raise a revenant. But riding the crest of the pain was the guilty knowledge that if I hadn't led everyone the wrong way, Keeve and Tyle would still be alive.

Finished searching, Jusson herded us outside again and had the guards prop the blown-apart doors closed. He then had melted wax dripped on the two doors and sealed them by pressing his signet ring into the wax. Such a small thing and in no way physically capable of barring anyone—or anything—determined to pass, but I felt its binding as strongly as I had felt the wardings on the charnel house.

To our surprise, one place Rodolfo hadn't gone near was the sacristy. Even so, Jusson and the town elders decided to remove its contents, and the king now led us down the church steps, himself carrying Dyfrig's big hat and vest-ments. Jeff and I followed, toting between us the chest filled with the implements of blessing, and behind us the Own, nobles and town elders carried the rest of the para-phernalia. Even Wyln had brought something from the church—the bundle of wheat that had been part of the prayer for an abundant harvest. It was all put on a table one of the aldermen had produced from the town hall and, at Jusson's softly spoken command, I had two of the Own stand guard over the rescued church accoutrements. Chadde was there also, but she and her watchmen were by the bod-ies of Keeve and Tyle. At first I thought they were holding vigil, but as I watched, people ran up with kindling, wood and rags soaked in oil, and immediately began building two pyres.

Despite the northern view on burning and burials, it seemed that no one was taking any chances with the two clerks. Then the thought crossed my mind that Menck was still missing, and I turned to look at the charnel house fire, but it burned just as brightly as before, with no sign of dimming.

Doyen Dyfrig and Laurel Faena had both opted to stay outside to oversee Rodolfo's burning while we searched the church. They now left the master player's dying fire to join us at the clerks' bodies, the doyen's face pale and drawn. Laurel leaned over first Keeve, then Tyle, but stood straight again without touching either. He gave a soft, rumbling sigh and shook his head, his own face troubled.

"They rang the bells as I tried to draw the abomination off," Dyfrig said, his voice breaking. "I didn't succeed very well."

"The fact that the dead man isn't rampaging through the town is proof of your success, Your Reverence," Jusson said. "Do not make yourself impotent with guilt."

I didn't bother to see if Jusson was also aiming that barb at me, but kept my gaze on the mounting piles of wood. He touched my arm.

"You too, Rabbit. You are no good to me if you allow yourself to wallow in what-ifs and if-only's. As Beollan said, you made a reasoned decision based on the facts you had."

"Truth," Beollan said wearily. "And left up to me, we would've been still chasing snipers by the Kingsgate."

"Yes, sire," I said. "My lord."

Jusson sighed. "We will talk about this later, cousin. Though I would've supposed that after almost six years in the army, you would know how to handle good choices that turn sour."

At that I did turn to look at Jusson, but the king was also watching the preparations. The clerks were placed on the stacks of wood, with more kindling and rags placed on top. Someone shook a jug of oil over them and then a tinderbox was struck, sending sparks flying down on the oil-soaked pyre. Tiny flames sprouted—and as they did, the wind swooped down, blowing about Dyfrig and causing his Staff of Office bells to chime.

"Rabbit," everyone said.

"It's not me," I said back.

The wind now swept over the pyres and the flames exploded as if fanned with bellows, steam rising up in a white cloud. However, Dyfrig ignored the aspect even as it pulled on his robes. Moving as if his bones ached, he went to stand before the burning pyres. The townspeople pressed around, forming a solid wall of mourners that displaced all the outlanders—including me and Jeff. Including the king. None of us argued, though. At Jusson's nod, we fell back to the outer edges to give them more room as Dyfrig immediately plunged into the ceremony for the dead.

"As we came into this world, so we go out—"

Despite his frail appearance, the doyen's voice filled the square, even as he competed with the wind.

"What?" I asked, my voice very soft.

But the aspect didn't answer. Instead it blew harder, echoing in the spaces between the buildings with a mournful wail.

"Now's not the time for signs and wonders, Rabbit," Jusson said, his voice also very soft. "Control it."

I had already come to the same conclusion and was holding out my hand. The wind whirled around me, the force of it causing the hair that had escaped my braid to beat about my face. But instead of swirling into its normal sphere, it flew back to Dyfrig and formed at his shoulder. Wyln turned to stare at me, his brows pulling together in a frown. As did Laurel.

"What happened?" Jeff whispered, his eyes wide.

"I don't know," I said. Feeling stupid—and oddly bereft—I dropped my hand. Off in the distance, just at the edge of my hearing, was a heavy sound, like storm-driven waves crashing against the shore. I edged closer to Wyln and Laurel, worried. "Maybe Dyfrig's need is greater, or something."

"Fire and earth weak against water, their wards failing," Wyln said to Laurel, his voice low. "And then air also fails. The quarrel *hit* Rabbit, Laurel."

Running a claw through the fur on his chin, Laurel remained silent a moment. He then shook his head. "Cub stories told in the night," he said, his rumbling voice also soft and low. "Fantastic tales from the Age of Legends—"

"Do you think a water sorcerer could have done this?" Wyln asked, interrupting. "The master player was not slain in *dauthiwaesp*. Yet this sorcerer controlled the player's body like an earth master turned necromancer, defying you who *are* both earth master and the head of the Faena. Defying the Lady through you, her favored shaman. Defying and prevailing."

Chadde had fallen back with us, and now her brows crooked. "What difference does it make whether it's fire, water, earth or air?" she asked. "Sorcery is sorcery. Isn't it?"

"There are certain abilities that are tied into the aspects, honored peacekeeper," Laurel said. "If someone in the talent becomes unbalanced, then his or her aspect becomes unbalanced too. But—"

"But still, someone with one aspect will not suddenly have abilities of another," Wyln said, again interrupting. "Water is the storm-bringer, the merry trickster, the master builder, the judge, the keeper of time and measurements, the lord of illusions, mirror images and dreams. It has nothing to do with earth's cycle of life: fertility, birth, healing, dying and the dead. The dead, Faena, who are the Lady's—"

"I don't know about pagan goddesses and water witches," Ranulf said, his voice more of a croak than a whisper, "but it seemed to me that Master Rodolfo was after Magic Boy, here."

"I rest my case," Wyln said, his eyes fire-bright as he looked at Laurel.

"Case?" Beollan asked. "What case? What are you arguing?"

"I don't know," Jusson said before Wyln could answer. "But I do know that I don't want to find out in the middle of the town's square during a funeral. Let's finish here and then get back to my house, where you can tell me all about what you've just declared proven, Lord Elf."

At Jusson's words we fell silent, speaking only to join in the remaining responses, the townspeople in front of us stirring only a little as Laurel and Wyln added their voices to ours as we wound towards the conclusion. At the end, Dyfrig also fell silent and bowed his head, the only sounds in the square the crackling of flames. Jusson moved through the crowd to the doyen.

"You need to rest, Your Reverence."

"After I see to disposing of the ashes, Your Majesty," Dyfrig said, his voice once more breaking.

"Do not scatter them, honored elder," Laurel said, joining them.

"We don't scatter the ashes of those burned for witchcraft, Master Laurel," Chadde said as she came to the other side of Dyfrig. "They are dumped in the town's midden."

"No dumping, either," Laurel said. "Gather them up into earthen jars that have not been fired and bury them as you normally would, i.e. with a tombstone, flowers and anything else that you'd put on a grave."

"But you scattered Trooper Basel's ashes in the sea," I said. I'd tagged along with Jusson and now took Dyfrig's arm as he swayed on his feet. As I did, the air sphere moved to the doyen's other shoulder, away from me. I fought against a scowl.

"If you'd look around, ibn Chause, you'd see that we don't happen to have a sea handy," Beollan said. He too had joined the knot of people around Dyfrig. As did Wyln, Ran-ulf and Jeff.

I decided to keep the pounding surf I'd heard to myself. "Of course not. But there are streams or brooks that do flow down to the sea, eventually—" I broke off, as I remembered exactly what had animated Rodolfo's corpse.

"We do not want to add any of these ashes to water, Two Trees'son," Wyln said. "Nor do we want to have them open to the air, to be carried on the wind."

"Truly no, we don't," Laurel said. "The White Stag's bones and ashes were given to the sea to keep them from those who would use them in ill-considered ways. We have no danger of that here. Let these unfortunate ones return to the earth. They will be more than safe there."

Some of the tension went out of Dyfrig's shoulders and he swayed once more, tremors beginning to wrack him. I took a firmer grip, steadying him even as I ignored the sphere ignoring me.

"We shall inter them all at daylight, then," the doyen said, taking a shuddering breath. "Even the player Rodolfo."

It was still dark, the moon hanging just over the rooftops, when the last of the pyres burned out. Several townspeople began shoveling the bones and hot ashes into three large earthen jars someone had produced. When they were done, Dyfrig opened up the chest of blessings and, taking out the container of salt, poured a handful into each jar. Then Jusson had wax dripped onto the jar lids into which he again pressed his signet ring, sealing them. After-wards, though, there was a brief but intense discussion of where to keep the jars until their burial the next morning. There were those who wanted to leave them at the bottom of the church steps, available to mourners, while others wanted them up the steps by the church doors, out of sight and hopefully out of mind.

"I will not have them hidden away," Dyfrig told one of the leading shopowners. "Let them be visible to all." The doyen's mouth twisted even as his hands shook. "And who knows? Perhaps those who come to pay their respects will also visit your chandlery, Serlo."

"I think that Harvestide commerce will be affected regardless of where you put the jars," Jusson said over Serlo's indignant exclamations. "Whether for good or ill remains to be seen. However, I don't think that they should stay here unguarded, either in the shadow of the church portico, or out in the openness of the square."

Both the King's Own and the Watch gave the king very unhappy looks.

A faint smile passed across Jusson's face. "We will take them with us to my residence, where an eye can be kept on them more readily."

Now all the king's guests gave him unhappy looks.

Jusson's smile widened for a moment, then was gone. "In the meantime, there is nothing we can do until the morrow. Let's go home."

"I have no home, Your Majesty," Dyfrig said. Though the rectory had been untouched, there had been another brief but intense discussion on the doyen continuing to occupy it. That one Dyfrig lost.

"But I do," Jusson said. Moving me aside and taking Dyfrig's arm himself, he steered the doyen away from the jars. "And there is a room with a bed for you. You will not stay alone this night, Your Reverence."

I fell in behind the king, eyeing the air sphere still at Dyfrig's shoulder. A stab of jealousy churned through me, but recalling how Jusson and Laurel seemed to wander at will through my mind, I clamped down on that hard. Instead, I turned my thoughts to how we were going to get the doyen to the king's house. I doubted if Dyfrig could ride and though we could've walked while leading the horses, all of us were moving as though our boots had lead soles. However, Chadde showed that she was a forward thinker for at that moment watchmen drove up with a couple of carriages. The doyen and the injured men were gently loaded into one, while the jars of ashes and the contents of the sacristy were placed in the other. The rest of us mounted our horses, forming a guard around the two carriages.

"Let's go home," Jusson said again.

Rising up in my stirrups to make sure I had everyone's attention, I lifted my hand. But before I could give the signal, I heard the footsteps of several people running down one of the streets leading into the square. I gave a sigh and dropped back down into my saddle.

"Pox rot it," Jusson said, tired. "What now?"

"Hell if I know, sire," I said. I reached for my sword, everyone else around me doing the same, while the townsfolk shifted to face this new threat with obvious reluctance, their own weapons being readied—only to relax with obvious relief as Thadro and several of the King's Own, including Arlis, stumbled into the square.

"Thadro!" Jusson swung down from his horse and hurried to his Lord Commander. "What happened to you?"

"Your Majesty," Thadro said. He came to a weary halt in front of the king. "We were lost."

"That sounds familiar," Jeff murmured.

So it did. Very familiar, with loud echoes of when another group of men was lost while on a routine patrol. However, while the Mountain Patrol's stumbling about last spring was caused by my burgeoning talent, this time whatever had happened to the Lord Commander had nothing to do with me. I hoped.

Twenty-nine

"It was like we were caught a maze, sire," Thadro said as he received a cup of tea from Cais. "Even though we'd just gone across the square to the morgue, we couldn't find our way back to the church. So we tried for the house, and became even more lost."

We were once more in Jusson's study—the king sitting at his desk, the Lord Commander seated in one of the trio of guest chairs still in front. I'd tried to take Thadro's place at the king's back, but Jusson waved me to the one of the other guest chairs, with Jeff taking his place at *my* back. The rest sat wherever they could, with Cais overseeing the shifting of additional chairs from other rooms. The study was packed with aristos, guards, town officials and leading citizens. Moving among them were servants, dispensing tea and whatever food they were able to liberate from the king's kitchen. Arlis sat with the other lost royal guards at the end of the room, a half-eaten plate of food on his knee. Though his last meal had to have been dinner the night before last, he showed no desire to finish his food. His face was drawn and tired, his eyes fixed on some distant point.

And though the sun hadn't yet risen—or maybe because it *hadn't* risen—nobody showed any desire to seek their beds. Apparently no one wanted to be alone in the dark. Or lost wandering the streets of Freston.

Or both.

"That sounds familiar," Ranulf said from where he sat to the side of me, unknowingly echoing Jeff. "Getting lost right in plain sight of where you want to go."

As my stomach had become empty again, I was making what food came my way disappear as quickly and politely as possible. At the Marcher Lord's words, though, I swallowed and turned to scowl at him. However, my scowl became a frown of concern when I saw Ranulf's face. There were the usual lines of strain, but what snagged my attention was how his dark eyes glowed red in the candlelight, as if something feral was looking out from them.

And next to him Beollan was shining bright, like the glaciers of the Upper Reaches at noon on a clear day, with hints of purple, a tinge of green, a delicate flash of pink.

"So it does," Jusson said, his voice mild. "Very familiar."

Hearing Jusson's words, I set aside glowing red eyes and shades of ice. "It's not me, Your Majesty," I began.

Jusson's voice remained mild. "I'm aware of that, cousin—" He broke off, leaning forward in his chair as Laurel Faena returned from tending to the injured. "How are they?"

"They are resting, honored king," Laurel said, coming to where I sat. "Both should recover, though it'll probably take a while with Lord Gerold. He started to bleed again, but we managed to stop it." He sighed and ran a paw over his head, rattling his beads as he looked at me. "However, I suppose it could've been worse. Much worse."

So it could've been. My hand crept to where the quarrel had struck me. As soon as we returned to the king's residence, Laurel had me lift what remained of my tabard and hauberk to examine my side. But even with the light from a branch of candles, only a scratch could be seen where the quarrel tip had poked through the chainmail links. Certainly nothing to induce the screaming agony I'd felt.

Laurel dropped his paw and turned to Doyen Dyfrig, sitting silently on the other side of me, staring off into space. Dyfrig had refused to go to the promised bed, even though the tremors wracking his body had grown worse. The doyen's knuckles were white as he gripped his Staff of Office, the bells trembling in a faint jangle while the air sphere hovered anxiously by his head. The Faena dug into his carrypouch and drew out leaves, and the scent of mint filled the air.

"These will ease your symptoms, honored elder."

Having also missed several meals, Thadro had taken advantage of the king's distraction by shoveling more mouthfuls in. However, he stopped midchew to stare at the leaves lying across the truth rune on Laurel's middle pad. Recognition flashed across his face, and his eyes narrowed as he considered the doyen.

Dyfrig roused himself. "What are they?" he asked, his voice weak with pain and exhaustion.

"Mentha," Laurel said.

"Mentha?" Chadde asked, frowning. "I remember hearing something about Lord Rabbit having to take that when he became a full mage."

So I had.

"I heard the same," Beollan said. "How Rabbit refused to take it and almost died."

That was true too. Not knowing then of the king's intention of welcoming me into the royal fold, I was terrified of being banished back to the Border and to my old master Kareste's tender mercies by those intolerant of all things fae. I hid what I was, denying anything to do with my talent—including the mentha when my crisis was upon me. All I accomplished, though, was to make myself very sick.

And I was much younger and a whole lot less frail than the doyen.

"I did nearly die, Your Reverence," I said. "The mentha kept me alive."

"A magical plant grown by magicals for magicals," Ranulf said, looking at me as if my dying would've been no great loss.

"It's not so magical, Bainswyr," I said, my scowl returning. "It grows wild in and around Iversly."

Wyln had been sitting quietly, wearing an expression that on anyone else I would've called brooding. Now, however, he gave his gentle smile. "So it did when I lived there, Leofric'son. As it did in other places."

"It's medicine," Laurel said, "and is given to those talent-born who've entered into their full power. You chew it, honored elder. It'll take away your aches, fever and nausea."

"What do you mean 'full power'?" Alderman Almaric asked. "He's a doyen. He defeated the revenant by the power of God, not by magic."

There was a murmur of agreement, not quite hostile, but only because no one had the energy to work up much antagonism. I rubbed my forehead, thinking that Laurel could've chosen a better time and place to confront the doyen about being talent-born. Jusson, though, remained silent, his gaze on Dyfrig.

Who continued staring down at the leaves in Laurel's paw, the truth rune softly shimmering underneath them in the candlelight. Then, lowering his head, Dyfrig reached out, taking a leaf and putting it in his mouth.

A gasp filled the room, some of the town leaders crying out, "No!"

"We are changed, messirs," Jusson said, watching Dyfrig chew and swallow. "Not will change, not in the middle of changing. But fully and completely changed. The question isn't how to return to what we were, because we can't. Rather, it is where do we go from here?"

Without looking up, Dyfrig took more leaves to chew.

Laurel rumbled encouragement. "Finish them all, honored elder."

"But we can't have magicals in the Church, let alone let them lead it," a southern lord said, watching the doyen. "Can we?"

Jusson shrugged. "You'll have to talk to His Holiness the Patriarch about that. Though I suspect His Reverence here is not the only doyen with magic. I myself know of a couple who probably are—at least from the reports I've read." He saw my wondering expression. "You know them too, cousin."

"I do?"

Wyln spoke before Jusson could. "Neither of the church elders translated with the others during the battle in His Grace Loran's throne room, Rabbit."

They were right. While fighting Magus Kareste and the High Council cabal, I had again caused those from Iversterre to translate into fae and fantastic beasts. Except for Doyen Allwyn of Gresh—and Archdoyen Obruesk, who was second only to Patriarch Pietr.

"Heigh-*ho*," I whispered.

The king gave a razor-edged smile. "Oh, it's a pretty tangle, cousin, no mistake. But then, why should those in the Church be any different from those without?" He shrugged again. "In any case, who is what appears to be moot. The Patriarch and his scholars have diligently searched and researched this past summer, and they can find nothing in holy writ or canon against mages, elves, talking cats or anything else that calls the Borderlands home. The only proscription they've found is against the dark arts. And that, gracious sirs, is a matter of intent, not being."

There was another collective gasp, this one of astonishment, while Dyfrig's eyes closed, lines bracketing his mouth. "But the holy pogroms—" someone began.

"Puts a different complexion on them, doesn't it?" Wyln murmured.

"We will debate church doctrine versus actual practice later," Jusson said firmly. "For now, my Lord Commander was telling me how he lost his way going the very short distance from the morgue to the town square."

"It wasn't me, sire," I said again.

"Illusion, Iver'son," Wyln said. "Any competent talent-worker with the water aspect could do the same."

"As you've said, Lord Wyln." Jusson's eyes traveled over the royal guards who had returned with the Lord Commander. "If I remember correctly, Thadro, you only took Guardsman Arlis with you to check the morgue's barrier. Where did these others come from?"

"They are the ones I'd earlier sent to the garrison, Your Majesty," Thadro said, setting his empty teacup down. Cais, hovering with a teapot, filled it again. "For troops to search for the fugitives from the tavern and look for Master Menck's body. We happened upon each other while wandering, they too unable to find their way."

"But you did, finally," Jusson said. "Find your way back."

"We heard a thunderclap and then, suddenly, there was the church spire and the flame, and we could truly see where we were." Thadro rubbed his neck, giving a rueful smile. "Sire, we were *outside* the town, standing in the middle of someone's damned orchard."

Muffled snorts of laughter sounded as color bloomed on some of the Own's cheekbones. However, Arlis' face stayed pale. He still was staring at a distant point, this one on the rug.

"Though I suppose it could've been worse," Thadro continued. "We could've been knee-deep in cow pats in some pox-rotted pasture."

"Or on the ledge of a cliff ready to go over," Wyln said.

All sounds of suppressed hilarity ended.

"Yes," Jusson agreed. "I am also concerned about the guards I had escort Mayor Gawell and Master Ednoth to the garrison stockade. You didn't see them in your wanderings, Thadro?"

"No, sire," Thadro said. He looked at me; however, I didn't even know who the guards were, let alone whether or not they'd made it back from the garrison. I shook my head and Thadro frowned.

"Rabbit wouldn't have known," Jusson said. "I sent them before you all had returned from the tavern. However, he did point out just before the ambush—"

Thadro's frown abruptly disappeared. "You were *ambushed*, sire?"

Jusson waved that aside impatiently. "Yes," he said again. "But Rabbit pointed out that no one from the garrison was where they should've been. And even now, after all the alarms, fights and frights, there hasn't been a hint of a trooper. Which, as Rabbit also pointed out, is unlike the garrison commander."

And very unlike Captains Suiden and Javes. The events at the church had put the garrison's no-show out of my mind, but now the image arose of Keeve and Tyle huddled in the church spire and my spine tightened.

"Cousin."

I turned and found myself standing, looking down at Jusson. Jeff was next to me, his body pointed towards the study door, and even Arlis had risen and taken several steps away from the clump of King's Own.

Jusson pointed at my chair. "Sit."

"But, sire—"

"You three running off helter-skelter will not help," Jusson said. "Sit. Now."

At the royal command I sat, though every muscle I had was twitching in anxiety.

"Very good." Jusson watched Jeff and Arlis return to their spaces, then leaned back in his chair and, thrusting out his feet, folded his hands over his stomach. "Now, the distressing lack of Royal Army soldiers."

"None of the troopers showed, Your Majesty?" Thadro asked.

"Not one," Jusson said. "Obviously, there is something very much amiss. But we—*we*, cousin, meaning all of us—allowed ourselves to be herded not only into an ambush, but also away from where we needed to be. So this time we will gather as much information as possible, consider our options, and then act."

"I saw nothing that would indicate anything was wrong at the garrison when I looked out the Kingsgate watchtowers earlier, Your Majesty," Chadde said. "Though I suppose with the spell of illusion that doesn't mean anything."

"I suppose also, Peacekeeper," Jusson said. "And I further suppose that the only way to find out what's going on is to actually go there."

"Uhm," began one of the town officials, his own brows crooking.

A faint smile crossed Jusson's face. "Yes, I know. A circular argument. However, before we rush off to the rescue, I reckon we need to know at least two things. We've just been told the first—what happened to my Lord Commander. The second we've yet to find out: What was going on with Master Rodolfo's body?"

"Demons," Ranulf began.

I closed my eyes, exasperated, while Jusson gave a deep sigh.

"You were there during Laurel's examination, Bainswyr," the king said. "You heard the Faena. Rodolfo had the misfortune to get his throat cut. He was not killed in any ritual using dark magic—"

"Ranulf Leofric'son is right," Wyln said. "It is a demon."

A bird trilled and I looked out the study windows to see the eastern sky begin to lighten. Sunrise was finally coming. Beside me, Dyfrig stirred. After the revelation of church doctrine on the fae and fantastic, he, like Arlis, had been communing with the floor. Now, though, he lifted his head to stare at Wyln, a faint crease appearing between his brows as he brought his Staff of Office closer. And I could see that not only had the tremors stopped, but there was actually a little color in the doyen's face.

"A demon?" Thadro asked, his voice careful. "You mean like the one you said caused the Jaban Waste?"

"The Waste was caused by a demon?" an aristo put in, his eyes wide as a murmur ran through the room, several blessing themselves. The crease between Dyfrig's brows deepened.

"According to Lord Wyln," Jusson said as he stared at the enchanter. "Is that what you and Master Laurel were arguing about earlier? That a demon is—involved?"

Laurel had moved to confer with Cais at a tea cart, and he now poured familiar tea leaves from a small sack into a pot full of steaming water. "That's just it, honored king," he said. "You heard Wyln's tale. Five experienced adepts working in sync still lost control of it. And it took twice that number to contain and banish it again. Regardless of the changes your people have gone through, you don't have anybody in the talent experienced enough to even get a whiff of a Damned One, let alone summon it."

"There are ways other than coercion, Faena," Wyln said.

"Old stories," Laurel said, his beads clicking together as he shook his head. "Muddled by time. They could not be really true . . ." He faltered, staring at the rune on his middle pad, his cat pupils rapidly expanding until his amber irises were just thin rings as he stretched his paw out.

"No?" Wyln asked, his face somber.

Jusson thumped his desk. "What?"

"There *is* a demon, Your Majesty," I whispered. "Laurel's truth rune just confirmed it."

"Not confirmed, Two Trees'son," Wyln said. "It just let him know that what he'd declared impossible is not. And to be fair to the honored Faena, he *is* right in that there aren't any talent workers here strong enough to summon and then contain a demon—"

"Including yourself, elf?" Beollan asked.

"Baiting me will not change the outcome and consequences of your war, Beollan Wulfgar'son," Wyln said. He looked back at Jusson. "There are other ways to catch a demon. It can be—invited."

Jusson was silent a moment. "You mean like possession?"

Another murmur, this one of distress, swept the room, and Dyfrig's blue eyes started to burn.

"In a way," Wyln said. "But in a true possession the demon is limited to the person it has taken residence in. No matter how powerful, it cannot give someone the ability to go beyond his or her own strength. Or, it can but it's like a load on a wall. Too much and eventually the wall will crumble."

"But if the—the inviter is powerful in and of themselves," Thadro began.

"Oh, we don't want someone like Two Trees'son to succumb to hell's seduction," Wyln said.

"Or yourself, Lord Elf," Jusson said.

"Or myself, or Laurel, or Elder Dyfrig, or even you, Jusson Iver'son. Any would be a catastrophe. That is not the case here."

"And it never will be," I muttered, also blessing myself.

"Whoever invited this Damned One is not strong," Wyln continued. "He had to kill the head jailer in *dauthiwaesp*, using water. But the fact that the dead *was* animated indicates the skill of an earth master, while at the same time

Two Trees'son's air aspect is blocked, also indicating someone with a mastery over air."

"Blocked?" Jusson asked.

"Rabbit was hit by a quarrel," Wyln said. "And now air avoids him."

Jusson's gaze went to the sphere hanging over Dyfrig's shoulder.

"Perhaps this person has all the aspects too," Thadro said. "Or at least those three."

"If he were that powerful, he wouldn't have needed the ritual of the *dauthiwaesp* to get the Damned One's attention in the first place, Eorl Commander."

"But, according to you, the demon would then be limited in what it can do," Jusson said.

"Yes, normally," Wyln said. The flames were bright in his eyes. "But there are stories from the Age of Legends. Of how the dread lords of old would kill, taking each death into themselves and thereby having two, or ten, or a hundred souls for the demon to feed on. Suddenly the limitations don't apply, as you are legion, with all their strengths and abilities—and as soon as one soul crumbles, you replace it with another. Or several others. Whole cities were said to have been consumed."

"Dear God," Dyfrig whispered.

"Myths," Laurel softly yowled, then stretched out his paw again, his face wrinkling in pain.

"But the master player wasn't killed in death magic," Ranulf said.

"It wasn't necessary," Wyln said. "The Damned One was already here. All the vessel needed to do was be present as the player's soul fled his murdered body."

"So how are these 'dread lords' defeated?" an aristo asked.

"I don't know," Wyln said. "The stories don't say."

In the silence that followed I could hear the birds ratchet

up to full chorus as dawn arrived. Then Jusson began to laugh.

When I was a new recruit in His Majesty's Royal Army, my troop unit rounded a mountain path during a patrol and unexpectedly met an exceptionally large group of well-armed and mounted bandits, all facing us with intent expressions. Some of the older soldiers in the troop had laughed then just as Jusson was laughing now, even as they lowered their helm visors and reached for their weapons. I, though, had felt very little amusement, instead understanding for the first time how someone could be scared spitless and still ride towards potential death and dismemberment.

Jusson caught his breath, his laughter devolving into his sharp-edged smile. "And I was certain that my stay here would be uneventful, and perhaps even a little dull."

Thirty

The threat of demons and sorceries notwithstanding, Jusson would not be swayed from going to the garrison. The king had Cais produce a map of Freston and spread it out over the king's desk while we crowded around—including Dyfrig. He stared down at the detailed map as Thadro questioned everyone about the attack, the doyen's fingers tracing the route we took from Jusson's residence and pausing at the ambush site. With the long night my mind had begun to drift and I'd been idly thinking that Dyfrig's brows didn't seem as bushy as before. Then I blinked as Dyfrig suddenly looked up, his eyes fierce as they fastened on the town elders standing across the desk. Most of them either looked away, or if they did manage to meet the doyen's stare, it was with a very troubled expression. The only one who returned Dyfrig's gaze easily was Peacekeeper Chadde, and it was the doyen's eyes that dropped.

Lord Beollan did his best, yet Wyln had still been able to squeeze in next to Jusson—though the enchanter was more interested in the crossbow bolts that we'd carried back in shields, saddles and bodies, than in the king. The bolts were stacked next to the map and Wyln picked up one to examine it. Laurel joined him and they both bent their heads over it, muttering to each other. As far as I could tell, it looked like an ordinary crossbow bolt, but I shifted to the far end of the desk, wanting as much space as possible between me and them.

"You stopped too soon, sire," Thadro said. Also picking up a quarrel, he pointed at the map. "They were waiting for you there and there."

"But wouldn't they have also shot each other?" Magistrate Ordgar asked. Recovering from his staring contest with Dyfrig, his gray brows were knit as he stared at the facing buildings.

Thadro shook his head. "You heard Lord Beollan and the rest. They were on the balconies, shooting down." He traced a path on the street with the quarrel tip, stopping at a point between the buildings. "If you had continued thus, sire, your casualties would've been worse."

"Much worse," Jusson said. "Fortune truly smiled on us."

"Yes, Your Majesty," I agreed, staring at the map. "But why an ambush in the first place?"

A southern lord gave me a patronizing smile. "Politics—"

"Here?" I interrupted. "In Freston?"

"Remember the tavern, Lord Rabbit," Chadde said. "The tapster was aiming at Lord Wyln, thinking he was the king. When Bram realized his error, he aimed at you."

"All right," I said. "Kingdom politics here in Freston. But if there's a sorcerer with a pet demon running about, then why ambush us with regular weapons? Were the snipers working with whoever raised Rodolfo? Or were they just taking advantage of the confusion of the moment? And if so, does that mean there are two separate factions? Or is it just one working at cross-purposes?"

Jusson smiled. "Those are very good questions, cousin." He too picked up a crossbow bolt, tapping it against his palm. "But let's start with the simplest and easiest to answer: Who owns these buildings? Magistrate Ordgar, do you know?"

"Owns?" Magistrate Ordgar gave Jusson an owlish look. "Uhm, I—"

"Ednoth owns them, Your Majesty," Chadde said. "In fact, he and Gawell own most of the property along here." She traced a section near the Kingsgate. "All acquired before Eastgate closed."

Jeff, peering over my shoulder, gave a near-silent whistle while I blinked. "*Before* it closed?" I asked, eyeing the prime real estate. "They must've made a killing with the rerouting of all the trade traffic."

"So they did," Chadde said, her face calm, her eyes gleaming. "Others did too."

"Now just a moment, Chaddie Laddie," Alderman Almaric snapped.

"Again our peacekeeper is abused before us," Jusson said.

"I apologize, Your Majesty," Almaric said. "But Chadde's insinuations—"

"Are also very interesting," Jusson interrupted, "and we will talk about them later. In depth. At present, getting to our missing soldiers is more important than shady dealings." He tapped the map with the bolt. "So we figure Gawell and Ednoth are behind this—"

The town elders shifted as if they would protest the mayor and head merchant's innocence. Jusson's gold gaze stabbed at them.

"Would you argue otherwise? After what has been revealed, could you?"

Magistrate Ordgar ran his hand over his face. "No, Your Majesty," he said, tired. "I suppose not."

"I am absolutely, positively sure not," Jusson said. "Think on it," Jusson held up a finger for each point. "Gawell's kinsman is killed to raise this demon. As assassination is attempted by a taverner who has ties to rebellious Houses and smuggling rings, and who also has ties to Ednoth through contraband goods. And now an ambush from property Gawell and Ednoth own. Plus, there's the absence of the soldiers from the garrison—the same garrison both were sent to earlier." The king closed his hand into a fist before lowering it. "The stench of corruption hangs heavy around both the mayor and head merchant. Can you argue otherwise?" Jusson looked around, but no one seemed inclined to take him up on his offer. "No?" he asked. "Then tactics, messirs. Let us discuss ways and means to confound them."

Finally settling on a big sodding mob with lots of weapons, Jusson put the bolt down and stepped away from the table, his gaze traveling over the drooping townspeople, continuing past the bleary-eyed aristos, guards, armsmen and watchmen, and coming to rest on me. "Those who wish to accompany us, be welcomed. Those who do not, no shame to you." He headed for the door. "We left in a rush earlier. Anyone who needs to retrieve anything, do so now. Cais, I wish to speak with you regarding the defense of the house—" He exited the room with the majordomo at his side, Thadro and the Own at their heels, the rest of us following them. In the hallway, some of the guards split off and hurried to the back stairs—those who'd been lost with the Lord Commander going to get their armor.

Since my presence hadn't been commanded, I did my own hurrying, thinking to change my torn tabard before we left. Going up the stairs as fast as my wobbly legs would take me, I walked into my bedchamber. It never looked more welcoming. There was a cheerful fire in the fireplace and my bed was made, with the covers turned down. Resisting the call of fine linen, I started for the clothespress, but stopped as I caught sight of myself in the washstand mirror. No wonder Jusson had been staring. In addition to my torn and dangling tabard, my shirt and trousers were stained, my face dirty and beard-stubbled, and my feather forlorn as it drooped in my unraveling braid. Wincing, I turned away from the mirror just as the bedroom door opened and Laurel, Wyln, Jeffen and—to my mild surprise—Dyfrig and Arlis trooped in. Laurel was still carrying that same damn crossbow bolt as he, the doyen and the enchanter went to the window, where they continued their muttered conversation, while Jeff went to his footlocker, flinging it open to rummage inside. Arlis, however, sat on one of the trundle beds, his head down as he now stared at his hands dangling between his knees, his face drawn. I supposed that was not surprising as, by my reckoning, he had just one night of sleep since we arrived in Freston three days ago.

But then we were all operating on short rations.

Idly thinking that Dyfrig's robe must've gotten wet and shrunk during his fight with Rodolfo, I started for my trunk to do some rummaging of my own. At that moment, the door opened again, this time revealing Finn with a clean uniform on one arm. "I thought you might want to change, my lord," he said, stepping inside.

Smiling, I finished undoing my sword belt and placed it on my footlocker lid. "You thought correctly, Finn. Thank you."

"You're welcome, my lord," Finn said, carefully laying out the uniform on my bed. Then, without seeming to hurry, he was at my side, helping me remove the torn tabard. "I understand there was an arrow strike? Perhaps we should remove the chainmail too so as to dress your wound."

"No, we won't," I said. "We don't have time—"

"Do so, Rabbit," Laurel said, without raising his gaze from the bolt. "I want to look at the wound more closely."

Sighing, I allowed Finn to remove the hauberk and the padding I wore underneath. As soon they were off, though,

I took them back to inspect. There was a slight deformation in the hauberk's metal links where the quarrel had struck, which corresponded to a small tear in my padding where the tip had poked through. While there wasn't any blood on the hauberk, there was a bit on the padding, but no more than when I nicked myself shaving. Looking down at my side, I could see more clearly where the quarrel had hit me; the skin was slightly broken and red, the area around it bruised from the force of the strike. But there was nothing that would have caused me to fall out in pain.

Finn must've thought the same thing, for he frowned and stretched out a hand to the bruised scratch. And frowning back, I shifted out of reach. Helping with shirts and armor was one thing; gratuitous touching was another. Besides, I had enough of people taking liberties with my person. The diminutive servant blinked, then flushed red. "I—I have some salve, my lord," he offered.

I shook my head. "Not now." I looked over at the trio at the window, but they were all still engrossed. Figuring that I'd waited long enough for the Faena, I started to don the padding again, but Finn pulled it from my grasp and, before I could stop him, went to the fireplace, where he examined it and the chainmail in the light of the flames. Scowling, I started to go after him but was stopped by Jeff. "Don't be stupid," he said, standing and tucking various sharp instruments away. "The king will wait while you tend to your hurts." He gave a small shrug. "Anyhow, I don't know that we need all this rushing about. Just because no one from the garrison has been seen doesn't mean that anything's happened to them."

I looked at him.

Jeff's mouth crooked in a half smile. "All right, *I'm* being stupid. It's that I can't imagine anything happening to Suiden."

I couldn't either. "He's not invincible," I said anyway.

"No, he's not." Jeff sighed. "Even if he seems like it."

"I know," I said. "I was just thinking about the time we were patrolling by the village Omeagh and found all those bandits waiting for us. Suiden didn't even blink."

There was a creak as Arlis raised his head, his red-rimmed eyes staring at us—and a suspicion flashed through my mind. "I wonder, though, how they knew we were coming," I added.

Arlis flinched.

"They must've heard it from the villagers," Jeff said, not noticing. "I've always wanted to know where all the bandits were coming from in the first place. You wouldn't think that there'd be that many broken men in all the northern marches, let alone in the mountains above Freston—"

A whole series of creaks sounded as Arlis tried to stand. He fell back on the bed, his legs giving out.

I sat aside my suspicions on how the Mountain Patrol's schedule became known to smugglers. Sort of. "Maybe you should stay here, Arlis," I said.

"No," Arlis said.

"You haven't slept for two nights running," I said. "It's not good to be exhausted going into battle."

Arlis put his hands against the mattress and pushed, this time successfully levering himself off the bed. "You and Jeff haven't slept either."

"Like you care," Jeff said.

I shook my head and Jeff fell silent. "We've had more than you," I said to Arlis. "You look bloody awful."

"Do I?" The side of Arlis' mouth kicked up. "Well, you're not looking so sweet yourself."

"It's not just lack of sleep, Arlie," I said.

Arlis' mouth went flat. "Are you ordering me to remain here? Sir?"

"Perhaps all three of you should stay," Laurel said, finally looking up from the bolt.

"What?" Jeff, Arlis and I asked at the same time.

"Separate Rabbit from Iver'son?" Wyln asked. "That may not be wise, Laurel."

"I will also remain with them," Laurel said.

"You've had just as much sleep as they have," Wyln said.

"I have gone without before and managed not to hurt myself," Laurel said. "Besides, there are other protections. Like Cais."

Finn, still at the fireplace with the padding and chain-mail, gave Laurel a narrowed stare.

"True," Wyln said. "Still, do we want Two Trees'son here while all the others are elsewhere?"

"*Cyhn?*" I asked.

"You'd have to fight the king to keep Rabbit here when he leaves, Faena," Dyfrig said, entering the lists.

At least, I think it was Dyfrig, as I knew everyone else's voice and whoever had spoken wasn't any of them. Standing in the halo of light from the window was a young man—well, younger than Dyfrig had been in a long while. He looked the same age as my eldest brother, all lines and wrinkles gone, his body straight and tall, and his blue eyes piercing bright, his hair the color of ripened wheat. Though he wore church robes, he looked as though he should've been wielding a doubled-edged broadsword.

Or a flourishing a cutlass while sailing the ocean blue.

"Bones and bloody ashes," Jeff whispered.

"He has come into his full power," Laurel began.

"I didn't change like that, Laurel," I said.

"No, lad," Arlis said, his eyes wide. "You surely didn't."

"That's because you're not him, Rabbit," Laurel said. "Nor is he you."

"Profound," Dyfrig said in a light baritone. "But while it would be interesting to discuss the mysteries of individuality and the singularity of the person, we do have more pressing concerns." Plucking the quarrel from Laurel's paw, he hefted it in his hand and my shoulders twitched. "I've heard how you were laid low by one of these, Rabbit, yet there's hardly a wound."

"Maybe the bolt was magicked," Jeff suggested. "I've seen Rabbit hurt before and he's never screamed. At least, not like that."

Arlis looked at the scratch on my side and his brows flew up in astonishment. "*That* made you scream?"

"It hurt," I said, my gaze fixed on the quarrel. "A lot."

Wyln took the quarrel from Dyfrig's grasp. "There are no marks on any of the quarrels. Nothing about them that would make them any different from any other crossbow bolt. We asked Elder Dyfrig if he could find aught amiss, but he could not. Even Iver'son, who has an acknowledged 'feel' for the talent, handled one like it was a stick found in the woods." He started towards me and I found myself backing up. "However, you made sure that you had the length of Iver'son's desk between you and them. And even now you retreat as if I held a fanged asp—or a Pale Death."

"Pale Death?" Dyfrig asked.

"An extremely venomous weaver," Laurel said. His ear flicked back. "One moment you were on the ground writhing in agony and the next you were on your feet, ready to fight the revenant. What happened?"

Just a vision of the Lady Gaia—however, I wasn't about to say that in front of the doyen, even if he looked as if he could be the scourge of the southern seas all by himself. Or maybe it was because he *did* look as though he should be sailing under a pirate's flag.

"I took it out," I said.

"That was obvious. Why?"

"Why?" Damn. I tried to come up with something that my rune would accept, but my thoughts felt as though they were moving through treacle. "It just occurred to me—" Pain exploded across my palm. Hell. I'd bent the truth too far.

Laurel looked down at his own truth rune and then his other ear went back, both flattening against his skull at the confirmation of my lie.

"I see," Wyln murmured.

They both moved towards me and I backed up, my mouth twisting in a snarl.

"Keep away from me."

"Rabbit!" Jeff said. "What are you doing?"

I turned my snarl on him. "Shut the effing hell up—"

"You saw a goddess?" Dyfrig asked.

I blinked, my mouth open midcurse. Aware of a weight, I looked down and saw that I held my sword, the naked blade gleaming in the light from the bedroom window. I did not even remember picking it up, let alone drawing it from its scabbard. It blew like a cold breath of air across my hind parts that not only had I been ready to skewer Laurel and Wyln, but also Jeff and anybody else who got in my way.

"You saw a *goddess?*" Dyfrig asked again, apparently seeing nothing wrong with me pulling my sword on my teachers in the talent. Not because he wanted to see me attack them—probably—but because other things were occupying his mind. Like a baptized and catechized son of the Church being tapped by some pagan deity.

My heart thumping triple-time, I lowered my sword and gently slid it back into the scabbard, then I opened my footlocker and carefully placed the sword belt inside. I shut the trunk lid, nodding as I did so. "Yes, Your Reverence."

"What goddess?" Dyfrig asked.

I looked up at the doyen and saw the air sphere hovering over his shoulder. Though not speaking to me, apparently the aspect had no problem spilling secrets to him. Including the fact that a goddess had dropped by for a chat.

"*What goddess?*"

"The Lady Gaia, Your Reverence," I said. "She who governs earth. I didn't actually see Her—"

"What then did you *see?*" Laurel whispered, his eyes wide, his ears now pushed forward.

I stared at my rune. The pain had receded just as fast as it had flared up, leaving behind a deep itch. "A forest. The one that surrounds my parents' farm."

"And?" Laurel prodded.

"She spoke to me—"

"And you *listened?*" Dyfrig asked.

"They all speak to me, Your Reverence. At least air and water did. Fire hasn't, but the way it's been acting I figure it's only a matter of time—" I stopped as the flames in the fireplace leapt up the chimney with a whoosh. "Though maybe it has been speaking and I've just not been listening," I finished.

"Perhaps," Wyln said, his face unreadable.

I hunched my shoulder. "Yeah, well, I suppose it's not surprising that earth would speak too."

"It's not the first time She has come to you, Rabbit," Laurel pointed out.

I stifled a sigh, thinking that was the last thing Dyfrig needed to hear, even though it was true. I had received my ashwood staff in a vision, also about my parents' farm. I now glanced at the staff propped against the wall, wondering why I had gone for my sword in a fight against two talent-masters.

"Not the first time?" Dyfrig began, his voice tight with anger, but Laurel held up his paw, the truth rune still shining, and the doyen shut his mouth with a snap, his face turning wary.

"What did the Lady say, Rabbit?" Laurel asked.

"She called me foolish and told me to take the quarrel out. And when I did, the pain stopped."

"Told you to take it out," Wyln repeated.

"Yes, honored *Cyhn*," I said.

Wyln considered the bolt for a moment. Then he moved

swiftly towards me and I yelled, doing my best to climb the clothespress. I reached for the dagger I wore in the small of my back, but before I could draw it, the enchanter was on me. He laid the quarrel against my bare shoulder and I damn near shrieked, everything whiting out. And in the middle of the blinding whiteness green eyes glittered like emeralds. Bloodred lips smiled.

There you are.

"—are you doing to our cousin!" Jusson shouted.

Gasping, I blinked and Wyln's face swam back into focus. Beyond him I could see the king, Thadro, Chadde, several aristos, town elders, royal guardsmen and Finn. I struggled and Wyln let me go, only to catch me again to keep me from falling down. I held on for dear life while I practiced breathing, shivers coursing through me, my skin covered in goose bumps.

"Answer His Majesty, elf!" Beollan snarled.

"For a moment there he was freezing cold," Wyln said, ignoring Beollan. He must've handed the quarrel off to Laurel for I could see the Faena place it on the table. Then Wyln lifted my face and flames filled my vision. I leaned into their warmth.

"I also saw something looking back at me," the enchanter said. His brows pulled together. "It's gone now."

There was the sound of swords being drawn.

"Stop!" Jusson ordered.

There was the sound of swords being resheathed.

"You saw this something in Rabbit?" Jusson asked. I heard footsteps and the king's face joined Wyln's, one gaze gold, the other bright fire. They were both hard to sustain and I dropped my forehead to Wyln's shoulder as the last of the shivering eased.

"No," Wyln said. "Not *in* him. But close. Very close."

At that moment my stomach decided to give a loud growl.

There were more footsteps and Thadro's face joined Wyln's on the other side, Chadde standing behind the Lord Commander. "He ate enough for three men downstairs, and he's hungry again?" Thadro asked.

"Something is engaging his talent," Laurel said, "and it's draining him."

"Is this the same something that is lurking about him?" Jusson asked.

The image of a huge beast arose in my mind, prowling around the boundaries of my self as it sought a way in, and I once again felt a touch of cold in the quarrel scratch, as if someone reached an icy finger towards it. I clamped my hand to my side, pressing the heat of my rune against the wound. The cold retreated.

"There," Wyln said, his voice soft. "Did you feel that?"

"Pox rot it, yes," Jusson said.

"So subtle," Wyln murmured. "Like the brush of a snowflake."

"Lord Wyln?" Jeff asked. "This something you saw. Did it look like Slevoic?"

There was a creaking thump and I lifted my head to see that Arlis had dropped back onto the trundle bed.

"No," Wyln said, interested. "It did not, Corbin'son. Why do you ask?"

"Because for a moment, just before you gutted him, Rodolfo looked just like Slevoic," Jeff said. "Blue eyes and all."

The silence roared—and, at the window, Dyfrig turned to stare down into the street.

"You weren't going to tell us, cousin?" Jusson asked, as many blessed themselves against the Vicious returned from the dead.

"Other events drove it out of my mind, sire," I said, trying to move away from Wyln. I staggered, though, and the enchanter again took hold of me.

"It has been a rather crowded couple of days," Jusson agreed. He went over to the table and picked up the quarrel, examining it. "Is there anything else that you'd like to mention? Other sightings? Visions, perhaps? Dreams?"

Figuring that my vision of the Lady Gaia would go over just as well with my new audience as it had with Dyfrig, I started to shake my head, but stopped. There *were* dreams. Dreams that had me waking covered in sweat. Dreams that had me divesting myself of whatever protections I had. Dreams that were seeping into my waking hours.

Nightmares that even now hovered only a blink away.

There you are.

"I have been dreaming, Your Majesty," I admitted.

"Oh?" Jusson asked. "What kind of dreams?"

"I think—" I took a deep breath, the sound of it rasping in my throat. "I think I'm being stalked, Your Majesty."

Jusson stared at me, then looked down at the bolt he held in his hand. He dropped it back on the table, wiping his hands on his trousers. "Stalked by what?" Jusson asked.

I moved away from Wyln, and this time managed to stay upright. "I don't know," I said, rubbing my forehead, a throbbing ache beginning. "I can't remember."

"Perhaps, Your Majesty, we should wait until we figure out all the angles of this new attack against Rabbit before we go haring off to the garrison," Ranulf said.

"Ha, ha, " I muttered, but was drowned out as a murmur of agreement arose from not only the other aristos and the town elders, but also royal guards, nobles' armsmen, watchmen and even servants, all crammed into my room. Those who couldn't fit inside spilled out the door, filling the hallway. Cais, however, had managed to work his way in and now stood with Finn at the fireplace, Finn softly talking as he showed his uncle the hauberk and padding. They both turned to stare at the bolt lying on the table.

"No," Jusson said. "I do not want to find out later that if I hadn't tarried, they would still be alive."

Laurel ran a paw over his head, rattling his beads. "There's that," he admitted.

"In any case, all I have is one complement of royal guards," Jusson added. "We need the extra men."

"There are our armsmen, sire," an aristo offered.

"Only those who were lodged in town," Jusson said. "The rest are also penned up at the garrison, remember?"

"There is the Watch, Your Majesty," Chadde said. She'd been eyeing Dyfrig at the window, but now turned to join in the conversation.

"So there is," Jusson agreed. "But considering what we've already faced, if we have to fight our way out of here, does anyone think what we have is enough?"

No one said anything.

Jusson gave his sharp-edged smile, which faded as he looked back at me. "We have to go, but I don't know what to do with you, cousin. I daren't leave you here with you so obviously a target. Yet with everything that's happening to and around you, it may be best for you to remain, out of the way of sorcery and stray arrows."

"We have Cais, honored king," Laurel said.

"Yes," Jusson agreed absently. He then frowned at Laurel. "But that's neither here nor there."

My spine abruptly tightened at the thought of being left behind with none but Laurel and servants, no matter how capable. "I want to go, Your Majesty," I said.

"You can barely stand," Ranulf protested.

I opened my mouth, but Jusson waved me silent. "Except possibly for my lord elf, none of us are at our best, and I have my doubts about him. In any case, Rabbit staying here makes me just a little more nervous than Rabbit going with us—"

My sigh of relief was drowned out as my stomach gave another plaintive growl.

"—as soon as he's eaten," Jusson said, also sighing.

"Yes, sire," I said. "Thank you."

"There's the old saying about not thanking me until you know what you've got yourself into," Jusson said. "However, what *I* want to know—" He turned his head. "Who the bloody hell are *you?*"

There was another moment of dense silence as everyone followed the king's gaze to Dyfrig standing at the window, the doyen's back still turned to us. Then Dyfrig looked over his shoulder and a gasp rose up.

Jusson didn't gasp but he did blink. Twice. "Your *Reverence?*"

"He has come into his full power," Laurel began.

"I want to be a mage," Magistrate Ordgar said in a loud whisper.

"Truly a miracle," Dyfrig said. "But before we lift up praise and holy offerings . . ." He turned back to the window. "Has anyone noticed how quiet it is?"

Thirty-one

There was a pause, then a mad dash for the window with Jusson in the lead. But before the king could pull the curtains further aside, Thadro caught up with him.

"Sire, please. Remember the snipers."

Casting a glance at the bolt, Jusson shifted so that he stood behind the wall and peered out the window at an oblique angle. "From what I can see, it looks normal," the king said. "Quiet, but normal."

"The hum is missing, Your Majesty," Dyfrig said, still standing in front of the window. The thought of folks wielding crossbows apparently didn't faze him. "We should hear traffic, people, the sound of a town in the morning."

"Perhaps everyone's staying home," an aristo said. "As His Majesty pointed out, the last few days have been eventful."

"We'd still hear something," Dyfrig said. "Birds, a dog barking, someone going on an unavoidable errand."

"Farmers heading for market," Chadde said, standing with her head cocked, listening. "Delivery carts and street vendors. Even the rustling from the wind is missing."

"You're right," Alderman Geram said. "It's like we'd just had a heavy snowfall."

So it did. Not only was there no sound, but the silence itself was flat—as if any noise would be swallowed without a trace. Frowning, both Arlis and Jeff met my gaze before all three of us turned to the window, Arlis rising from his bed.

Jusson let the curtain fall. "Who's guarding the front door?" he asked.

Thadro looked at me. However, while duty rotas were technically my responsibility, I hadn't had the time or the opportunity to go over the lists. Before Thadro could give me his mud-puddle stare, one of the Own inside the room spoke up.

"It's Berand and Joscelin, sire."

"Do they know enough to report anything out of the ordinary?" Jusson asked as he started walking towards the door, Dyfrig with him. "*Would* they know what is not ordinary?"

With Jusson and Dyfrig out of the way, more mobbed the window. Ranulf and Beollan gave the street below a quick glance before withdrawing to follow the king, Beollan's gaze unusually troubled. Others filled their places, pressing in close to the glass panes, forgetting about potential assassins. The crowd shifted again and Jeff and Arlis took their turn to see.

"Yes, sire," Thadro said, walking with Jusson and Dyfrig. Their pace quickened. "They each have enough sense to separate shadows from substance—"

There was a tinkling crash of breaking glass and everyone whipped around to look at Arlis, who was staring at the blood blooming on his shirt. He then lifted his wide-eyed gaze to the still-quivering quarrel that had grazed him before it struck the wall.

I shoved through people. "Damn it, Arlie! Move!"

Jeff was already in motion. He grabbed Arlis' arm, yanking him out of the window, and pulling the curtains closed at the same time. Most everyone hurried to them, exclaiming. Jusson and Thadro, though, took off running out of the room. A moment later, the rest of us caught on and we scrambled after them. We thundered pell-mell down the main stairs, skidding onto the black-and-white tiles of the foyer floor, and catching up with Jusson and Thadro at the front door. Motioning for quiet, Thadro unlocked and unlatched it and, standing to one side, used his dagger to open it and peer through.

"Blast," he whispered. "They're gone." He opened the door wider, trying to see more without sticking his head out. "So are the horses, carriages and watchmen, all gone without us hearing a bloody thing—"

"Hello the house!"

I and several others jumped at the sudden shout in the leaden quiet, but Thadro merely paused, frowning. "I know that voice."

It was familiar to me too and I tried to place it. All around me, though, the town elders' mouths dropped open, and the lines of pain and discontent on Ranulf's face disappeared as he and Beollan looked at each other in astonishment.

"Of course you know it, my lord," Chadde said, her gray eyes molten. "It belongs to Helto. The owner of the pile of ashes that once was the Copper Pig."

"Hello the house!" Helto called again.

Magistrate Ordgar tried a couple of times before he found his voice. "What the hell is he doing here?" he rasped.

"Right now, hailing us," Beollan said softly, recovering from his astonishment. "Sire, if Thadro keeps him occupied, we can slip out the back—"

"We have your guards," Helto shouted. "We also have all your exits covered."

"It seems that Master Helto has anticipated us, Fellmark," Jusson said. "But just in case he's exaggerating,

Thadro, if you would please have someone verify his claims."

"Yes, Your Majesty," Thadro said, signaling a couple of Own. The remaining guards surrounded Jusson, gently pushing back all who stood around the king—except me. I was herded next to Jusson. Finn appeared outside the circle of royal guards to pass through new padding and hauberk— I supposed he considered the slight deformation in the links grounds for disqualification—and I began to dress quickly.

"Do we have any crossbows ourselves, sire?" I asked, my voice also soft as I lifted the chainmail over my head.

"Yes, and longbows too," Jusson said.

"If there's extra, some of my watchmen are competent bowmen," Chadde said quietly. The aristos also began offering their armsmen.

"Is there roof access, sire?" I asked, pulling on a clean tabard Finn had found for me.

"Yes," Jusson said again. "See to it."

"Take the bowmen and go up," I said to Jeff. "Defense only. For now." Jeff nodded and hurried off, a mixture of guards, armsmen and Watch tagging after him. Arlis started to follow but, thinking of coincidental crossbow bolts, I stopped him. "No, you're with me."

Finn produced my sword and I buckled it on. As soon as I was done, Jusson nodded at Thadro, who looked back out the narrow opening of the door. "All right, you have us surrounded," Thadro called out. "Now what?"

Helto laughed, sounding nearer. "I like a person who cuts to the essentials, Lord Commander."

"I live to please," Thadro said, his voice affable. "I'd stop there, taverner. Any closer and who knows what may come winging on the wind."

"No violence is necessary, Lord Thadro," Helto said. "All I want to do is come in and talk, like civilized folks. See, I am removing my sword."

"That's good," Thadro said. "And your knives? Will you remove those too?"

Helto must have acquired more after leaving his at the Pig, for he fell quiet. "There," the taverner called out finally. "I'm completely unarmed. May I have safe conduct?"

Thadro looked over his shoulder at Jusson, who nodded again. "Yes," Thadro said out the door. "Safe conduct."

A moment later, Helto stepped inside and gave a sleek smile. "How cozy."

"Yeah," Thadro said. "Nice and snug." He shut the door, locking and bolting it. "Where are my men?"

"They're safe," Helto said. He swept a bow at Jusson. "Your Majesty."

Jusson said nothing, his gold eyes glinting in the dimness of the foyer, but the taverner's smile only brightened.

"You wanted to talk," Thadro said. "So talk."

"Here?" Helto asked, waving a hand about, indicating the crowded entranceway. No one said anything, and he shrugged. "As you wish. The town is ours—"

"Who is 'ours'?" Thadro interrupted.

"That's not important—"

"Is it Gawell and Ednoth?" Chadde asked. "Are they with you? Or are they in the garrison stockade?"

Helto sneered. "Ah, Chaddie Laddie. Once again you have less effectiveness than a tinker's damn." He turned his back on the peacekeeper. "As I said, 'who' is not important, Lord Thadro. What *is* important is that you are completely cut off with no hope of rescue and, well, there are demands."

"Of course," Thadro said. "Tell us these demands."

"Freston is ours—"

"Yes, we got that part," Thadro said.

"—and we demand that you withdraw from both the town and the valley."

Thadro waited a moment. "That's it?" he asked.

"Yes," Helto said. "We are a peaceable folk and for years we managed to bump along fairly well. I'm not saying we've hadn't had friction. What community doesn't? But it was *our* friction, both familiar and familial, and easily dealt with."

Surprised at the town elders' silence at Helto claiming kinship with Freston, I glanced over to see them staring at the taverner as a cornered mouse would a snake.

"Then the royal entourage arrives, complete with magicals," Helto continued, "and all of a sudden we have a witch boldly attacking people in Theater Square, murders, defiled corpses, walking dead men and dark magic that has been able to reach into the very church."

"You forgot the ambush of the king last night," Thadro said, "and the crossbow quarrel that was able to reach through a window here moments ago."

"I firmly believe that more can be accomplished by talking than by violence," Helto said earnestly. "However, people who are frightened will do desperate things, and there are many who are terrified of what you've brought to our town. I tell you, my lord, they were ready to burn you out, but fortunately saner heads prevailed."

"Thank goodness for sanity," Thadro said. "What about this unnatural silence? Are they also terrified of that?"

Helto once again gave his sleek smile. "Silence? What silence? *I* hear fine, Lord Commander."

"I see," Thadro said. "Let's get back to your demands. What about the king's guests and his garrison? Will they be allowed to leave?"

"Anyone who wants to can." Helto glanced at the peacekeeper. "Even you, Chadde my lad. In fact, I strongly recommend that you do, for your health's sake."

"And the deadline for this mass exodus?" Thadro asked.

"You have until sunset to be out of the valley, which is

more than enough time for a civilized withdrawal. Until you're ready to go, though, do not leave here—"

Alderman Almaric wetted his lips. "Are we also banished?"

Helto flashed Almaric a contemptuous look. "Those of the town may stay, if they wish. Or they can go. However, know that if you do leave with the witch and the magicals, you will not be allowed to return. Ever." He turned back to Thadro. "When you're ready to go, Lord Commander, hang a flag—"

"White?" Thadro asked. "Or perhaps yellow?"

"Color doesn't matter. Hang it on the front door and we will come to escort you, so as to avoid misunderstandings."

"And what about my men?" Thadro asked.

"As soon as you're out the town gates, you'll get your guards back," Helto assured him. "Right now they're hostages to your good behavior. Behave well and they'll be returned to you."

"All of them?" Thadro asked. "You never did answer Peacekeeper Chadde's question about Gawell and Ednoth. Where are they and the guards who escorted them?"

"They are all safe, my lord," Helto said. "Do not fret, everyone will be returned to their proper places at the appointed hour." He gave his sleek smile once more and he bowed. "Until later, Your Majesty, my lords, gracious sirs."

At Jusson's nod, Thadro opened the door to let the taverner out, and shut it again with a heavy thud, snapping the locks and bolts in place and dropping a stout wood bar into the slots on either side of the door frame.

Beollan looked at Jusson, his eyes heavy-lidded. "Are we leaving town, Your Majesty?"

"No," Jusson said. He turned on his heel and headed down the hall towards his study.

"Oh," Beollan said, his face clearing. He quickly followed, as did everyone else. "It's just that you didn't say anything."

"You think I should've lifted my sword and cried defiance?" Jusson asked.

"A simple 'go to hell' would've been nice," Ranulf said wistfully.

"I wouldn't have dignified yon serpent tongue's demands by breaking wind, let alone by engaging in dialogue, no matter how invective." Jusson went past his study and continued towards the rear of the house. "Let him think we're cowering behind locked doors, frantically packing."

"I don't think the House Master believes that," Wyln said. Somehow he managed to get past Beollan and was walking with Thadro, right behind the king. "Not with you staring holes through him, Iver'son."

"No?" Jusson said. He reached the back stairs and ran lightly down them. "Well, let him believe what he wants, Lord Elf."

"What are we going to do then?" Magistrate Ordgar asked, anxious.

"What I've planned to do from the beginning—get to the garrison. One way or another," Jusson said as he disappeared from view. I had stood aside to let everyone go before us—especially the town elders. I had seen their shock and worry, and wanted to make sure that no one decided that the odds of survival were better if they joined Helto. But none showed any inclination to amble out a side door and I started down the stairs, along with a few of the Own that had stopped with me, Arlis, Finn and Laurel—who was frowning.

"What's wrong?" I asked.

"The House Master," Laurel rumbled. "He didn't smell right."

"What do you mean?" I asked. To me Helto seemed just

as he had at the last time I'd seen him—well fed and smug with it.

"Not like he did at the tavern," Laurel said. "His scent was different."

"Perhaps he, like the rest of us, hasn't had a chance to bathe recently, Master Laurel," Arlis said from behind us, overtones of his old self in his voice.

"He has bathed," Laurel said. "With the same soap he had in his private rooms at his tavern. But if he hadn't he would still smell the same, only more so." The Faena shook his head, causing his beads to clack together. "His fundamental scent has changed. If I were a dog, I would've howled."

"What did he smell like, then?" I asked.

Laurel's tail lashed. "The remnants of the *dauthiwaesp* we found in the warehouse."

On that cheerful note we reached the bottom, following the others to where Jusson had led us—the kitchen. Despite Freston's trend towards the tiny, it was large and filled with light. It was also filled with tantalizing smells that caused my stomach to knot with hunger. Hooking my hands on my belt to keep from snatching something, anything, I hurried past Cook and his minions as they bustled about, creating meals fit for a king.

"The guards' quarters," Arlis murmured, nodding at a door in the kitchen's far wall. "Armory's in there. Perhaps the king is going to make a surprise attack."

Dragging my mind off food, I nodded back. That made sense. Given the number of seasoned fighting men we had with us, we could easily defeat Helto, despite his boasts. And despite the attacks on me, we still had two talent-masters, plus a doyen with decades' experience in the defenses of the Church who also had come into his mage-power. We were a match for any sorcerer, regardless of any adjunct demons.

What didn't make sense, though, was Helto challenging us in the first place. He hadn't seemed idiotic enough to think that Jusson would meekly allow himself to be banished from any part of his realm. And even if the taverner were smiled on by the winds of war and fortune, and somehow defeated us, he also had to know the rest of Iversterre would rise up against him. Which meant that he also had to think that he could withstand the force of both the king and the kingdom.

It was a laughable thought, but with all that had happened in the past two days, I didn't feel like chuckling much. Rubbing my aching head, I headed for the guards' quarters and the armory therein. However, I didn't get that far for Jusson had stopped at a hearth set in the same far wall. It was a large one—while not quite big enough to roast whole oxen, a couple of haunches could've been accommodated with room to spare. For now the roasting spit was empty, though the hearth itself was full of fire. And stoking the flames was the king's majordomo, Cais.

"I still say we should've sent Master Helto off with something to think about," Ranulf was saying, his voice still wistful. "Maybe cause him to reconsider his actions."

"No, His Majesty's action was beyond wise," Beollan said. "Let them think we're acquiescent until we strike." He turned a blazing gaze on the king, his silver eyes almost too big for his narrow face. "How are we going to get to the garrison, sire? Fight our way out?"

Arlis and I weren't the only ones expecting the formation of a battle plan. As Beollan spoke, several aristos nodded in agreement and even some of the Own put their hands on their sword hilts. Jusson, though, kept staring into the flames.

"No," he said. "We will use magic to get there."

Thirty-two

"**M**agic," an aristo repeated carefully. "You mean like waving a wand and clicking our heels together and suddenly we're at the garrison, Your Majesty?"

"This isn't a children's pantomime," another said. "He means that Lord Rabbit will do some sort of translocation spell. Right, Your Majesty?"

"No," Jusson said again. "Lord Wyln, you spoke with Rabbit through the fire yesterday morning."

Wyln smiled, the flames in his eyes brighter than the morning sun pouring through the windows. "So I did, Iver'son."

"Can you do the same with the garrison?" Jusson asked. "Speak to them from here?"

"I would be able speak to anyone in your kingdom from here, Iver'son—if they have the fire talent."

"*Anyone* in Iversterre?" questioned Thadro, intrigued.

"It *is* the king's hearth, Eorl Commander," Wyln said, walking to the fireplace. "And this is his land, bound to him by oath, covenant and law. Be aware, though, that anyone else with the talent would be able to listen in."

"So I discovered yesterday," Jusson said.

"Eavesdropping, Iver'son?" Wyln asked. Though his expression remained amused, his eyes were intent on the king. I too stared at Jusson, surprised at the explanation of how he knew of Wyln summoning me to the abandoned warehouse yesterday morning. Then I realized what the king had just admitted and my mouth fell open. As did others.

"Just being aware of what is going on in my house," Jusson said, ignoring the astonishment rippling around him. "And with Helto threatening and my Own missing, discovering what's happening at my garrison far outweighs any evil sorcerer also becoming aware."

"So it does," Wyln agreed, turning his gaze to the flames. "Anyone in particular you wish to speak to?"

"I don't know who's able to hear you and who isn't." Jusson shifted so that he stood side by side with the dark enchanter, both of them so similar in looks, their faces painted by the fire in the hearth. "An officer would be better, but whoever you get, tell him about the events of the past three days and especially of the taverner's demands this morning."

"Are you with me while I'm saying this?" Wyln asked.

Jusson considered. "Yes," he said, "but I'm arguing with the town officials who want to go home and my nobles who want to leave the valley."

"That's right, Your Majesty," one of the southern lords said, his voice faint. "Slander us with cowardice."

"We're not exactly shining here either, my lord," Alderman Almaric said, his eyes wide as he gazed at our fire mage king.

"Everyone will have their moment in the sun all too soon," Jusson said. "Find out, Lord Wyln, what their status is. Ask especially if they are able to ride to the rescue."

"And if whoever the elf, ah, raises says yes, sire?" Beollan asked.

"Then we know he's lying and the garrison has fallen as they would've been here by now," Jusson said. "At your pleasure, Lord Wyln."

Wyln made no elaborate gestures, no muttered chants,

no runes drawn in the air in flames. He simply stared into the burning hearth for a couple of heartbeats. Then he smiled. "Well, you discover all sorts of things through the fire. Though I really shouldn't be surprised, Dragon Prince—"

"Sro Wyln," Captain Suiden said from the hearth. "Where the hell are you?"

Hearing Suiden's voice, my spine snapped to attention. Next to me, Arlis started. "What?" he whispered. "What happened?"

"It's Suiden," I whispered back.

Arlis' red-rimmed eyes wheeled as he too jumped to attention, and there was a stir among not only Jusson's nobles, but the townspeople too. Apparently Freston's leading citizens knew the Mountain Patrol captain very well. Or maybe it was that the events of the past few days had made them realize that Wyln's "Dragon Prince" was probably more than a nickname. Beollan transferred his attention to the fire.

"I am here with Jusson Iver'son at his residence, Your Highness," Wyln said. "Rabbit Two Trees'son is with us, as is Laurel Faena, Jeffen Corbin'son, and the soldier Arlis from Captain Javes Wolf Merchant'son's troop. We are all safe—"

"Lieutenant," Suiden said.

I stood straighter. "Sir! Present, sir!"

Thadro gave me a considering look.

"You can fight with Iver'son's Eorl Commander later about who gets to reprimand Two Trees'son for playing truant, Prince Suiden," Wyln said. "Though it's good that he had, as he's safer here with Iver'son than he would've been with you at the garrison."

"So you say," Suiden said.

"So I do," Wyln replied. "Do you doubt me?"

"No," Suiden said slowly. "Not about this. And not with all that's happened. *What* is happening, Sro Wyln?"

"Rebellion and sorcery, Your Highness," Wyln said, and launched into the agreed-upon explanations.

"A ritual murder and an assassination attempt," Suiden said after the enchanter had finished. "An afrit, walking dead men, a desecrated church, all circling around the remnants of Gherat and Slevoic's smuggling ring. And a publican issuing ultimatums to the king." The captain's voice was neutral. "Sounds as though His Majesty has his hands full."

"Doesn't it?" Wyln asked, his tone amused. "What about other sounds? A most unnatural silence has fallen here, where even the birdsong is ceased."

"No," Suiden said. "We have all the requisite noises, though what's happening with you has to be connected with our situation. How Helto fits in is the puzzler— Excuse me." I could hear murmuring in the background, then the captain spoke again. "The senior staff and I are with Commander Ebner in his office, and while no one here knows much about Helto, some of the officers from the south of the kingdom say there was a Bram who served at the Royal Garrison before he left to join Gherat's House as an armsman."

"What is it?" Ranulf asked, watching Wyln's eyes narrow.

"The tapster at the Copper Pig belonged to the House of Dru," Beollan said before Wyln could, and the side looks were now aimed at him—though Jusson's look was a frown as he made shushing motions. Beollan blinked, then a faint flush dusted his cheekbones.

"Who's that?" Suiden asked.

"One of Iver'son's eorls is with me," Wyln said lightly. "Beollan of Fellmark."

"Lord Beollan is there?" Suiden asked. "With *you?*" Apparently my former captain wasn't the only one with a reputation.

"Ranulf of Bainswyr is here too, Your Highness," Wyln said, even more amused. "With Laurel Faena's illuminating presence, both sides of the last war are well represented."

The flush deepened on Beollan's face as his eyes narrowed on Wyln, and I spoke quickly before the Marcher Lord could. "But going back to Bram, sir. Dru has been disbanded for several months, and the Vicious dead almost as long. Why would an armsman from a disgraced southern House all of a sudden show up here in the northern marches?"

"From what Wyln has just said, Peacekeeper Chadde's proven that Helto had ties to Slevoic," Suiden said. "It seems the taverner also has access to what is left of Dru's House. Again, the question is, how does it all fit?"

Chadde nodded as Wyln relayed Suiden's answer. "True," the peacekeeper agreed. "And what do Mayor Gawell and Master Ednoth have to do with it? Could you ask Suiden if they ever made it to the garrison, Lord Wyln?"

"No, they didn't," Suiden said after the question was repeated. "But then, no one's been able to come or go here since yesterday afternoon. Every time we try to leave, we end up back at the same place, no matter which direction we take. When we heard the alarm last night, we thought that perhaps, with a large enough group leaving at once, we might be able to break through. However, even with all the garrison companies riding great big horses, the same thing happened and we damned near met ourselves coming out as we were going back in."

"Water aspect," Wyln said. "Keeper of time and of measurements, the master builder, lord of illusion and the mirror image. It seems that someone has built you a merry maze of time, space and illusion, Dragon Prince."

"Very merry," Suiden said dryly. "Many of the troopers

had to have a lie down after that last effort, they were so exhausted from merrymaking."

"But you're all right?" Wyln asked.

"Other than having ridden through our own shadows, we're fine," Suiden said. "Commander Ebner asks what are the king's plans?"

"I don't know," Wyln said. "Iver'son is still arguing with those who think that we'd be better off doing as this Helto says."

"I see," Suiden said again, his voice once more neutral.

"Though the ones with me think the House Master has less integrity than pond scum," Wyln continued. "I was hoping that you at the garrison would be able to help, but it seems that you are just as bound as we are. I don't know that I will tell Iver'son of our conversation—though the news about Bram's ties to Slevoic ibn Dru might make a difference with Iver'son's eorls and the town elders."

"If you don't, then Lieutenant Rabbit will," Suiden said blandly. "Or at least he'll tell the Lord Commander. There *is* such a thing as chain of command—"

Captain Suiden's voice abruptly cut off as the flames shrank down to the red flickers. Frost appeared at the back of the fireplace with an icy blast, causing both Wyln and Cais to stagger back, Wyln with a look of astonished pain on his face. And I found myself snared by ice green eyes as a bloodred mouth smiled.

Found you, little rabbit.

Arms, white as a cadaver long drowned, reached out from the hearth. But before they could grasp me, there was a bellowing roar and I was yanked back. Moving in front of me, Laurel planted his carved staff against the stone floor, his claws and fangs bared.

"Our House? This dares to come into our *House?*"

Regaining my balance, I saw Jusson drawing his sword. The frozen green eyes turned to the king and the smile broadened, showing even white teeth. "Majesty!" I shouted. At least I meant to shout. My voice came out as a wheeze. "No!"

I wasn't the only one to see the creature's interest shift from me to Jusson. The rest of the room rushed to the hearth, those with swords also drawing them, even Cook and his scullions running over with knives and cleavers. Wyln, elfin quick, recovered enough to get a hold of Jusson's tabard to pull the king from the hearth; however, Thadro grabbed Jusson's arm at the same time and pulled the other way, while the press of bodies behind the king kept him front and center.

Those dead white arms reached for Jusson, curved as if to enfold him in an embrace.

"No!" I panted again and barreled into Jusson, knocking him, Wyln and Thadro back. However, because of the crowd behind us, we didn't go down. There was a soft laugh behind me and I felt the cold as a spear thrust in the wound in my side. My mouth opened on a silent scream even as I heard the sea pound as if it were trying to match the frantic beating of my heart.

Then there was another soft laugh that abruptly cut off, and the heat of the flames returned with a familiar whoosh. I turned my head to see Laurel with his paw raised, the rune shining. Next to him was Cais, holding what looked like a sprig from a rowan tree, and on the other side was Dyfrig, his Staff of Office held like a quarterstaff. And standing at my back was Arlis, his sword drawn and his eyes bugging out.

"Did you see?" Arlis stuttered into the stunned silence, his teeth chattering with cold and fright. "Did you see it?"

"I saw." Jusson shifted in the press of bodies. "Get off me."

Thadro, Wyln and I untangled ourselves, and I stepped back. Or tried to. My strength sapped, my legs gave out and I collapsed to the floor. Shivering hard, I managed to roll over and sit up, resting my face on my knees as I dragged air into my lungs—out of the way of those stepping around me. They tried to help Jusson up, but the king knocked away their hands. Standing by himself, he yanked his tabard down, straightened his crown and snatched his sword from Thadro, who'd picked it up from where it had fallen, all the while glaring at Wyln. "What the pox-rotted hell did you let in our House—?" The king's voice faltered. "Lord Wyln?"

I lifted my head to see Wyln swaying, his hand pressed against his chest. All color had drained from the enchanter's face and his eyes looked wrong. It took me a moment to figure out why, then I realized that the flames in their center had gone out, leaving them black and empty.

"And so when Ujan's demon rose, it was like a razor against my heart," Wyln said, his normally lilting voice harsh and strained. He held out his other hand and a flame appeared in his cupped palm. But instead of the normal yellow-orange, or even a sullen red, the flame burned blue. "Blocked," he rasped. "As easily as a youngling in the talent."

A murmur rose, increasing in anxiety as folks pressed away from the hearth. However, Arlis didn't move, his eyes bugging out as he stared into the renewed fire. "Demon? That wasn't a poxy demon. That was Rosea. The player Rosea. But what happened to her? What the bloody hell happened?" He started to sheathe his sword, then stopped, now staring at how the blade glistened weirdly. "Damn it, look. Look! It's frozen!" He dropped it and the steel shattered on the kitchen's stone floor. Everyone watched the pieces skitter, too numb to move out of the way.

Jusson had hurried to Wyln's side as the dark elf swayed, sliding a supporting arm around him. However, at Arlis' words, the king gaped. "Mistress Gwynedd's Rosea? The one Rabbit tried to chat up in Theater Square? *That* Rosea?"

"Down to the green gown, sire," Beollan said unexpectedly. He stood with Ranulf, the Lord of Fellmark holding his sword in one hand, the other tucked under Ranulf's arm. Ranulf was also swaying, his eyes closed, lines scored deep in his face—and superimposed on the Marcher Lord was another shape, its muzzle raised to the sky in a roar of anguish.

My shivering increasing, I tried for the aspect but also got the sickly blue flame. Letting it extinguish, I hugged my knees. "She's been in my dreams," I whispered.

There was a flash of amber as Laurel glanced over his shoulder at me. He and Cais were busy warding the hearth. At least I knew Laurel was; I guessed about Cais as he was speaking a language I'd never heard before. He waved his rowan twig at the flames while Laurel, having obtained salt from Cook, poured a line on the hearth and then threw some into the flames. The fire burned green and blue, changing the cast of Cais' features, before returning to its normal yellow-orange, but the merry crackle was gone. Finn appeared with an armful of rowan branches that he carefully arranged along Laurel's salt line. Dyfrig, though, had moved apart, his once-again broad shoulders bowed, the air sphere bobbing by his head. The sphere was wrapped tight on itself and I couldn't even hear a hum.

"Dreams," Thadro repeated. He walked over to where I sat and helped me to my feet. "That is what's been stalking you?"

"Yes, sir," I said. I gripped Thadro's arm tightly to keep from falling again.

"But what does an itinerant player have to do with the plague of sorcery that has descended on us?" Jusson asked, still supporting Wyln.

"She has become a vessel," Wyln said harshly. He closed his hand on the sickly blue flame, his empty eyes wide and oddly vulnerable. "The Damned One, invited through *dauthiwaesp*, now resides in her."

"That's a long leap, elf," Beollan began, but Arlis cut him off.

"The demon's in *her?*" he gasped. "Oh, God! What have they done? What have they given place to?"

Chadde stooped down and, using her handkerchief, picked up one of the frozen sword pieces to examine it. She now looked up from where she crouched, her face intent. " 'They,' Guardsman Arlis?"

Thirty-three

I heard the sound of someone hurrying and looked up to see Finn come in from the guards' mess carrying a couple of chairs. He tried to set one down next to me, but I waved him off, pointing to Ranulf and Wyln. They both must've looked worse than I did as Finn didn't argue, but quickly placed the chairs by the elf and the Marcher Lord. The diminutive servant took off again—but before he got to the mess door, his uncle said something to him in liquid tones. Finn nodded and, without breaking stride, changed direction for the door to the back stairs. Thadro watched Finn leave, the Lord Commander's face thoughtful as if he understood what Cais had said. Then, after sending a couple of guards to fetch more chairs, Thadro turned back to Arlis.

"The peacekeeper asked you a question, Guardsman," he said, his voice mild.

"Yes, sir," Arlis stammered. "I don't know who. I just meant generally—"

I dragged in a breath and let it out again at Arlis' waffling denial as his actions of the last two days coalesced in my mind: Arlis standing next to Thadro, listening. Arlis standing behind Thadro and Jusson, listening. Arlis riding behind Thadro and Chadde, listening. Always close to the king or the Lord Commander, always listening.

And Arlis in my bedroom, standing in the window in clear view of Helto and friends lurking in the street below.

"That crossbow quarrel was on purpose, wasn't it?" I said, interrupting Arlis midwaffle. "You were the target."

Arlis' mouth hung open but nothing came out. One the guards appeared with a chair for me and I plopped down into it, not caring that I sat in the standing presence of my king and my commanding officer.

"You weren't trying to suck up," I said. "You were trying to find out how much everyone knew about Helto, Menck, Slevoic—and you. Because you were involved in the smuggling too. One of the Vicious' lads at the garrison."

"Guardsman," Thadro said when Arlis remained silent.

Arlis hunched his shoulders in, his head going down. "It was just something to do," he said, his voice low. "Make life tolerable in this arse-backwards town."

"Something to do," I repeated, thinking of friends killed, the attempts against my own life. "A diversion to keep from getting bored."

Still warding the hearth, Laurel gave a low, rumbling growl, while Wyln stared at Arlis with wide, blind eyes.

"They," Chadde prodded. "Who are 'they'?"

"Involved in the smuggling?" Arlis asked, his hand creeping up to his wound. "Helto, Menck, Gawell and Ednoth were the main ones. There were others, not as prominent, both in the valley and the mountain villages."

There was a jangling of bells and I looked over to see Dyfrig face the window, his knuckles white as he gripped his Staff of Office. My heart sank.

Arlis sought the Lord Commander's face. "I admit my fault, sir, but I didn't know about the rebellion. I didn't! I'm no turncoat. It was only a little free trading—"

"Perhaps more than a little," Wyln said, still hoarse. "Was that your treasure in the church offering box, human?"

"Yes, my lord," Arlis admitted. "But that wasn't from free trading. My share was never that much. Helto was waiting for me when I was sent for you at the garrison."

"By himself?" Chadde didn't wait for an answer as he frowned over the timing. "Menck must've already been killed, then."

"Perhaps," Arlis said. "Wherever he was, he wasn't with Helto. Jeff and Laurel Faena had already left the garrison and I was returning to report that Lord Wyln was missing. Helto caught me by the Hart's Leap and gave me a purse full of jewels and coins. Said there was more, if I did what I was told. I told him that I wasn't interested—"

"That was an extreme about-face," Thadro said.

"Yes, sir," Arlis said. He managed a smile, though it trembled at the edges. "I translated in the Border embassy along with everyone else. I was a hawk." His smile collapsed. "And then there was that damned death ship."

When we sailed to the Border last spring, our ship's holds were full of pelts, skins, ivory, choice hardwood and other body parts of murdered Border citizens found stored in a harbor warehouse in the Royal City. During our journey, the wards and bindings Laurel and I put in place failed and the ship became full of haunts.

"Didn't like it, did you?" I asked.

"No," Arlis said. "I didn't. Especially with Basel's ghost flitting about."

"Given the fact that your partner in crime had killed him?" I asked. "And had tried to kill me several times?"

"What was it that Helto wanted you to do?" Chadde asked into Arlis' silence.

"Intelligence," Arlis said. "He wanted me to keep him informed about Rabbit and the king's movements."

"And did you, Guardsman Arlis?" Thadro asked, his blue-gray eyes as cold as anything that tried to come out of the fireplace.

"Sir, no, sir," Arlis said, tired. "The couple of times I wasn't with you, I was with Rabbit."

That was true—except for yesterday morning, when Jusson had to send him back to accompany us to the Copper Pig. Then, Helto's tavern was probably the last place Arlis had wanted to be.

Thadro's expression didn't thaw. "Covering your backside, Guardsman?"

"Blocking access, sir," Arlis said. "After last spring, I'd enough of—of diversions and adventures. I didn't want any more."

"An admirable sentiment," Thadro said. "You said that there were others involved in the town and valley. Who are they?"

Some of the townsfolk shifted, looking as though they had just heard one shoe drop and were expecting the other to come crashing down at any moment. And I remembered Chadde finding the receipts from Freston's business and shop owners in Helto's snug. The brewer, the miller, among others—including Master Ednoth—all had sold the Copper Pig inferior products at vastly superior prices. More of the puzzle pieces slotted in.

"They're here, sir," I said, watching the town elders. "Sacks of flour, barrels of beer, kegs of brandywine and spirits. Who would question such innocuous cargo as it wends its way to other villages and towns? And if anyone were to wonder about the sudden increase in wealth, why, there's Helto's receipts showing how they were making a killing in selling the gullible outlander shoddy goods at wildly inflated prices."

"Very good, cousin," Jusson said, entering the interrogation. Though a guard had brought a chair for him, he ignored it to stand at Wyln's shoulder—reversing, as far as everyone else was concerned, the natural order of things. "And as my Keeper of the Peace has probably figured out,"

the king continued, "the receipts aren't only a cover for illicit gains, but also record who was paid what, and if we are
able to decipher them, why. Correct, Peacekeeper Chadde?"

"Yes, Your Majesty," Chadde said. Something flashed
out from the edges of her calmness and I found myself glad
it wasn't aimed at me. "I was aware of Slevoic, Helto and
Menck, and I strongly suspected Gawell and Ednoth's involvement. But it wasn't until yesterday at the tavern that I
realized how widespread it had become."

"As Arlis said, Your Majesty," Alderman Almaric said,
his own face tired, "it was a diversion that also rounded out
coffers that can grow distressingly empty at times. One bad
winter—" He shrugged.

"They were *people*," I said. "Not entertainment."

"Yes, Lord Rabbit," Almaric said, his eyes sliding to
Wyln and Jusson before moving to Laurel and Cais at the
fireplace. "However, remember, this is the north and, unlike
what I've heard of the south, we have very clear memories
of the last war with the Border."

"Including the fact that you started it?" Wyln whispered.

"Almost all the men in the Valley and surrounding
mountains who could went to fight, Lord Wyln," Almaric
said. "But only a handful returned, and most of them broken in some way. An entire generation gone with their children mourning their loss." Now his gaze went to Dyfrig
staring out the window. "Some still are."

"So you figured that you were doing a good deed in ridding the world of magicals?" I asked. "If you hate us so
much, then, why are you here and not with Helto?"

"Because of what happened last night at the church,"
Magistrate Ordgar said, "and the fact that those who defeated the revenant are in here and not out there."

"How ironic, then, that your vicar who delivered the
deathblow is as magical as any of us from the Border,"
Wyln whispered hoarsely. "But then, as Jusson Iver'son has

pointed out, you have all changed—into the very thing you hate and despise."

"So it seems," the magistrate said, running a hand over his face. "But whatever we may have done, Your Majesty, like Arlis we never had any intention of rebellion. You are—and have always been—our king."

"Such loyal subjects," Jusson said. "But did you think that because you didn't want to play anymore that your fellows would say all right and go home?" He held up his hand as Ordgar and several others all started to speak. "No, do not answer. It is obvious that you did not think. You did not consider that it is a smuggling *ring*, which not only circles to you but also circles away too, to other people and other lands with their own agendas. And now this ring has circled back once more, bearing diamonds and gold tainted with darkness and death. All of it landing here, where you had given place to it once before, again demanding that you play."

There was another sound of bells and Dyfrig turned to face us, his face grim—or maybe, like Ranulf's, it was lined with pain. I opened my mouth, then closed it again, not knowing what to say.

Jusson, however, did. "Were you involved in this round-robin of corruption, your reverence?"

"My sin is one of omission, Your Majesty," Dyfrig said. "I wasn't involved, but I knew. Not the particulars, not that. I knew my people, though, and did nothing."

"You knew," Chadde said, aiming that brilliant gaze at the doyen. "Hell, yes, you knew. And you let them hobble me anyway. Now we've sorcery and murder flourishing like a green tree, with Keeve and Tyle slain right before you. What will you tell their parents? That you omitted to do what's right?"

"Chadde," murmured Jusson, not very hard.

The peacekeeper didn't hear the king. Maybe. Those

gray eyes flashed around at the town elders. "Who else? Give me names." She waved a hand at the hearth. "Including those who are pursuing Lord Rabbit to the gates of hell—"

Normally, we wouldn't have heard the small gasp. But the preternatural quiet made each noise stand out, even in its muffled flatness, and the intake of breath filled the room. We all turned to the kitchen door. There were sounds of a short scuffle, then Finn walked into the kitchen, a bundle of crossbow bolts in one hand, and dragging Gwynedd with the other.

"Ah, Mistress Gwynedd," Jusson said. "We were just talking about you. Please. Come in and join us."

Thirty-four

At Gwynedd's entrance, Jusson once more retook his rightful place by leading us out of the kitchen. Refusing a guard's arm, Wyln was able to walk on his own with only a little unsteadiness in his normally graceful gait. But both Ranulf and I needed all the help we could get, Ranulf leaning heavily on Beollan while Thadro kept me from falling over my own feet as we followed the king into the guards' quarters.

The quarters looked exactly like what they were: a barracks. There were long tables with wooden chairs, a stone floor and braziers for warmth. A second set of doors opened onto a small armory and along one plain, white wall were stacked cots, indicating that when the Own were finished eating, their mess became their sleeping room. At Jusson's direction, Thadro opened the armory and set guards sorting through the surplus weapons. As swords, maces, axes and other instruments of mayhem were laid on one of the tables, Jusson pulled out a rather battered chair from the head of another table and sat, indicating that we were to join him. His nobles did so promptly, their faces shining with the knowledge that the misdoings in Freston couldn't be laid at their feet. The town elders, though, seated themselves at the far end of Jusson's table—and did that only when prodded by the guards standing behind them. Dyfrig, however, remained in the kitchen.

"A moment, Elder Dyfrig," Laurel said, stopping the doyen, and Dyfrig joined the Faena and majordomo at the fire—not reluctant, but not showing any great enthusiasm either.

Not knowing what else to do, Arlis followed me into the mess and now stood behind my chair. And I, also not knowing, didn't prevent him. After seeing me seated, Thadro took his accustomed place at the king's back and now considered Arlis over my head. He then let his gaze drift over the Freston folk before coming to rest on Gwynedd, placed at the king's left. Finn too had remained in the kitchen, leaving the player in the stewardship of a King's Own. Though it had been three days since I'd been co-opted into the Royal Guards, I had yet to learn any of the Own's names, let alone who they were as people, and the guard was a face in the ranks of many. He too stared over my head with just a hint of a sneer on his face and I wondered whether he were making his opinion known of me or Gwynedd. Then I realized that he was staring at Arlis.

"Guardsman Hugh," Thadro said, and Hugh's expression went properly blank.

Instead of choosing a place near the king, Wyln sat next to me. Glancing down, I could see a fine tremor in his slender hands, and I started to ask him something really intelligent, like if he were all right, but was distracted by a commotion at the door. It was servants bearing food, and I set aside all thoughts of my wounded *cyhn*, betraying friends and corrupt towns. In moments a full plate was placed before me and I fell on it with knife and fork, ignoring the stares from those who'd seen me eat enough for a company of grown men a short time ago. Beollan's attention, however, was on the growing arsenal on the adjacent table.

"We're still going to the garrison, Your Majesty?" he asked.

"After Rabbit finishes eating," Jusson said.

"Oh," Beollan said. "I thought that we were in a hurry to get there."

"We were," Jusson said. "Part of the earlier urgency was because I didn't know what had befallen my soldiers. The other part because I was concerned about what would happen after Master Rodolfo's rising at the church— Ah," he said to Gwynedd. "Knew that, did you? Was it from eavesdropping or do you have direct knowledge?"

In all the times I had encountered Gwynedd, she always retained her self-possession, even when she'd viewed her brother's murdered body. However, now the street player's eyes went wide. "Rolly risen, Your Majesty?" she gasped. "He's not dead—?"

"We've already had someone try to play the part of ignorance," Jusson said, nodding at Arlis. "He didn't do well, either. Choose another persona."

Wyln, seated beside me, lifted his head to stare blindly at Jusson. Beollan and Ranulf seated across from me went motionless, as did Peacekeeper Chadde standing with Thadro. My chewing slowed, my gaze going between the king and the player.

Gwynedd stopped in midgasp. "Your Majesty?"

"I watched you yesterday eve in the doyen's office, Mistress Player," Jusson said. "So skillful you were in your role of grieving sister that most everyone believed it—believed you—and were falling over in their eagerness to offer comfort and aid."

"Surely, sire, you're being harsh?" Beollan's voice rose, questioning.

Jusson didn't bother to answer him. "See?" he said to Gwynedd. "A Great Lord experienced in kingdom politics setting aside common sense in your defense. Even my peacekeeper bought into your act."

A faint smile crossed Chadde's face. "Despite the slurs and innuendo, Your Majesty, not only do I like being a woman, but I enjoy men." She very obviously did not look at Thadro. "A lot."

"Oh?" Jusson asked. "Still, you and the others were fooled." His brows crooked for a moment. "I don't see it myself—she's not that pretty."

Wyln gave a soft, whispery laugh. "Jusson Iver'son *is* young," he murmured in my ear.

I supposed in a race that typically married after they entered their third century, Jusson was a babe in arms. But I also figured that now wasn't a good time to discuss certain aspects of the king's maturity and I kept my face politically blank.

"I'm not, Your Majesty," Gwynedd agreed. "And I assure you—"

"No, don't," Jusson said. "Don't assure me. Tell me what you know. Start with these gentlemen here. It must've been a shock for them to look up and see you sweeping into the church. But then, it probably was a shock for them to see Rodolfo's body in the morgue."

It was the town elders' turn to become still, and in the hush I could hear another whoosh, as if the fire in the kitchen hearth had flared up. I turned my head to the wall where the back of the hearth was delineated in brick, my eyes wide as I pressed my hand against my side.

"What is it, Rabbit?" Jusson asked.

"I think they've just burned the crossbow bolts, sire," I said.

Jusson's eyes flicked up to Arlis standing unaffected behind me before returning to the player. "You hear, Mistress Gwynedd?" he asked. "Or did you already know that too? Ambushments that wounded several of mine, including my cousin. My cousin who, from the very beginning, has been a target of attacks—like the one that is even now draining him so that he's starving as he gorges. And from the very beginning there have been you and your players."

"Please, sire," Gwynedd whispered. "Whatever Rolly and Rosea were involved in—"

"Yes, the mysterious meetings between your brother, Helto and Menck, with Rosea seducing everyone in sight. And you excluded, the scorned sister kept in the dark. Another role you've played to perfection." Jusson leaned back in his chair and, stretching his long legs out, folded his hands over his flat stomach. "How long have you had your troupe?"

Gwynedd frowned at the king's non sequitur. "Your Majesty?"

"Eleven years, sire," Ranulf said, unexpectedly.

"Eleven years," Jusson repeated. "Versus what? How long had your brother and Rosea been married?"

"A little under a year," Ranulf spoke up again when the player remained silent. He saw the looks aimed at him. "Gwynedd told Beollan and me when we met with her and her players at the Copper Pig."

"There's the rub, Mistress Gwynedd," Jusson said. "Eleven years of running the troupe versus your brother's year-old marriage to an outsider. An outsider who wasn't even of your profession until she joined you."

Gwynedd's perplexed frown shifted into a look of faint disgust. "You never saw Rosea, Your Majesty. She wielded her beauty like a weapon—"

"I did," Jusson said. "Just a bit ago I saw her—or what was left of her. But even if she were the most beautiful woman in the realm, what I saw at the church yesterday eve would've routed an entire army of Roseas."

Gwynedd's perplexed frown returned. "What you saw, sire?"

"A woman with a spine of steel, Mistress," Jusson said. "I cannot imagine you allowing anyone, let alone a villager from the back of the northern marches—no matter how beautiful—oust you from your headship of a troupe you have founded. In fact, Rodolfo may have had the title of troupe master for dealing with the authorities and other inconveniences, but I'd wager the royal treasury against a daisy chain that you were the one who actually ran things." The king gave his razor smile. "Even choosing to mount that benighted play about magicals in a town overflowing with them. What better excuse to shut it down when you saw that Rabbit, so obviously from the Border, was in the audience? Which then freed Rodolfo and Rosea to pursue their quarry."

Obeying the demands of my stomach, I'd gone back to shoveling food into my mouth. "But the attack in Theater Square wasn't done by either Rodolfo or Rosea, sire," I said, my voice thick. "They both were standing next to me and were as surprised as I was when it happened. And it couldn't have been Gwynedd because it was a man's hand, not a woman's."

Arlis gave a soft grunt of surprise and the town elders stirred in their seats. "The disturbance in Theater Square was because someone had attacked you with magic, Lord Rabbit?" Magistrate Ordgar asked carefully.

I blinked as I realized that this time I'd spilled a fact that hadn't been disseminated to the general public. "Uhm—"

Jusson, though, didn't miss a beat. "A sorcerer tried to bind Rabbit, but he was able to fight him off. Who was it, Mistress Gwynedd?"

"Ibn Chause just said it wasn't any of the players, sire," an aristo pointed out.

"No," Jusson said. "Rabbit said that it wasn't Rodolfo, Rosea or Gwynedd. But who said that the attacker had to be any of those three?"

"If that's true, Your Majesty," Beollan said, "then it could've been anyone in the square. And, from all accounts, it was very crowded at the time."

"It couldn't have been just anybody," Jusson said. "Laurel said there has to be line of sight. The sorcerer had to see Rabbit clearly. However, he also had to be inconspicuous. What better place than a raised stage? No one would look twice at a player on the boards, no matter what his actions are."

I swallowed, pausing between bites. "The curtain was closed, sire. It was brought down when the play stopped."

"Even better," Jusson said. "An unremarkable screen even if it were gaping open just enough for someone to see through. The play is halted mid-act and Rodolfo and Rosea stop you before you can leave, keeping you in view of the stage." The king smiled again. "I would say that Rodolfo and Rosea's subsequent surprise wasn't at the fact that you were being attacked, Rabbit, but that you were aware and countering it."

What little color Gwynedd's face had drained away. "Your Majesty, we're just simple players—"

"There is nothing simple about you," Jusson said. "Tell me, how well do you know Gawell and Ednoth?"

Gwynedd squeezed her eyes shut, her mouth once more trembling as tears leaked out. "Your Majesty," she began.

"They're acquainted," Magistrate Ordgar said. He probably figured it was better to tell than to be told on. "It was Gawell who paid for their license to perform."

"He did," Jusson said. "Why?"

Ordgar looked down, apparently fascinated with the table's wood grain. "As a gift for Lord Rabbit, Your Majesty. Everyone knows of Rabbit's fondness for theater and Gawell said that it would show Freston's appreciation for having the king's heir with us for the last five years."

"He said *what?*" I asked, incredulous. All around me the aristos and even some of the Own gawked in disbelief.

"You couldn't have actually believed that," Beollan said. "Did you?"

"No," Jusson said. "They're neither idiots nor naive."

I stared at the people I'd lived among for over five years, never realizing how much of an outlander they considered me—and how easily sacrificed. Wyln's hand came up on my shoulder even as he pushed a large bowl of porridge in front of me. I glared at it, ready to pick it up and throw it against the wall. Then my stomach rumbled and, holding in a sigh, I reached for the honey. As I did, I caught sight of Arlis' shadow cast on the table by the light from the windows. And sharp as a knife cut the memory rose up of how he stood next to me as Rosea curtseyed and bared her ankles.

My hand tightened around the honey pot. "Were you in on this, Arlie?" I asked.

Arlis' shadow shook his head. "No, of course not—"

"But you knew," I said.

The shadow Arlis raised his hands to his face. "Not when we first met Rosea, no," he said, his voice muffled. "I didn't. But later—Helto mentioned it when we met later that night."

"And to protect yourself, you said nothing." I heard Arlis take a breath. "No," I said before he could speak. "Don't justify it."

"We'd no thought of causing harm to you, my lord," Alderman Geram said. "You'd have a few pleasant days, then leave with the king and everyone's happy."

"And if in the seduction of my cousin you managed to get eyes and ears into my chambers, so much the better, right Master Geram?" Jusson asked.

Geram didn't reply and Jusson returned his gold gaze to Gwynedd. "You heard my peacekeeper's question. This master sorcerer who so greatly desires Rabbit. Who is he? And where?"

"Probably at the old posting inn with the rest of the players, sire," Ranulf said as Gwynedd remained stubbornly silent. He was as pale as the player, his freckles standing out in stark relief above his beard. But his dark eyes burned once more with a red light. "That's where Peacekeeper Chadde took them."

"If he is, then he came afterwards," I said. "Whoever it was wasn't with them either at the tavern or at the church. At least not when I'd seen him."

"And how do you know, ibn Chause?" one of the aristos asked. "From what all's been said, you've not actually come face-to-face with this sorcerer."

I swallowed porridge to bare my teeth. "I broke the effing pervert's hand—and none of the players had splints or bandages."

"Broken bones can be hidden, cousin," Jusson said. "I asked you a question, Mistress Gwynedd. I suggest you answer it—"

The king broke off in mild astonishment as Gwynedd sprung up out of her chair. She didn't make it very far, though, as Guardsman Hugh stopped her with a heavy hand to the shoulder. She was shoved back down, hitting the hard wooden seat with a spine-jarring thump.

"That was surprisingly stupid," Jusson remarked, "for stupid is one thing you're not."

Tears sparkled once more in Gwynedd's eyes. "I'm sorry, Your Majesty, I am so afraid."

Jusson's brow rose. "You weren't before. Why start now?"

"I didn't know what he'd intended, Your Majesty. None of us did. He came to us, making all kinds of promises—" Gwynedd swallowed. "But we were tricked—" She swallowed again as a tremor shook her. "Fooled—" Another tremor shook her, harder than the first. Her dark eyes turned sky blue, then rolled up into her head.

At first everyone just stared, wondering if it were another ploy. Then Jusson shoved back from the table, jumping to his feet as Gwynedd toppled from her chair, her body violently shaking.

"Cais!" Jusson shouted and the majordomo came running in from the kitchen, Laurel with him. They headed my way at first, but changed direction midstep as the king pointing to where Gwynedd lay convulsing. Beollan was already there, holding the player's head to keep it from banging against the stone floor while he thrust a rolled-up napkin into her mouth to prevent her from chewing on her tongue. Or chewing further. Blood-specked foam bubbled on her lips as she thrashed about. I started to rise to help, but Wyln grabbed hold of my arm with surprising strength, pulling me down.

"No," Wyln whispered. "I don't think you—or any of us—can do anything."

Cais knelt next to Beollan on the floor, and in the strong light from the mess windows the majordomo's features were sharper, his irises taking on a purple hue. "She is having a seizure, Your Majesty," he said.

"I can bloody well see that," Jusson said. "What caused it?"

"Some are prone to fits," Cais said, restraining her legs. "She may be one of them."

"If so, it was mighty convenient," Thadro said. He moved Jusson away from Gwynedd's thrashing limbs. "She was going to name the sorcerer behind all this."

Laurel had veered off to one of the braziers, picking up a teacup from the table on his way. At the Lord Commander's words, he turned, his amber eyes meeting Wyln's somber ones. The Faena then walked to where the player lay, smoke rising from the teacup, filling the room with the aromatic smell of burning leaves. Laurel handed the cup to Beollan, who held it under Gwynedd's nose. However, the player's convulsions didn't lessen.

"I don't think that will help, Faena," Wyln whispered.

"I agree," Laurel said.

"What do you mean?" Jusson demanded. "What won't work?"

"The leaves are a remedy for moon madness," Laurel said. "But I don't think she is moon struck." He crouched down, laying his paw, its rune shining, on Gwynedd's forehead. Immediately she stopped convulsing, though her eyes remained rolled-up white, her breathing harsh.

Jusson thumped the table. Hard. "What is it then? What's wrong with her?"

Laurel looked up at the king. "She has been bound—"

"Bound?" Ranulf asked. He too had risen and now stood staring down at Gwynedd. "Like what the sorcerer tried to do to ibn Chause?"

"Exactly like," Laurel said. "And through that tie, her master has taken her mind." He stood, wiping his paw on his fur. "I cannot find her; she is not there."

Jusson's face was full of rage. "This sorcerer would've done that to Rabbit?"

"Could have, certainly," Laurel said. "If the binding had been completed."

Everyone began talking at once, the town elders wringing their hands and exclaiming their ignorance, the aristos shouting at each other and at Laurel. Jusson, not bothering to go through Thadro, did his own shouting and immediately I was surrounded by royal guards, as if the Own could ward off an attack of the talent. I, though, didn't cavil at the invasion of my personal space.

"Did you see?" I asked, my voice shaking.

"Yes," Arlis said, his teeth chattering once more.

"What?" Jusson demanded. "See what?"

"For a moment the player looked like Slevoic—"

All of a sudden the wind gave a hollow moan that rose into a wail then died away again, the unnatural hush once more returning.

"God save us!" Again I started to rise, this time making it to my feet. "Where's Dyfrig?" I asked.

Laurel swiftly headed for the door. "He went upstairs with Finn to check on the wounded and make sure that the funeral urns had not been disturbed by the manifestation—" He stumbled, his eyes wide as his paw went to his chest. Ranulf caught him as his knees buckled.

"Laurel!" I tried to push through my wall of guards, but they held me fast.

Dyfrig and Finn hurried through the doorway, followed by a royal guard who had been sent to the roof. Finn went to his uncle, while the guard stopped next to Thadro and Jusson. The doyen headed towards me, the air sphere that had hovered over his shoulder gone.

"What has happened?" Dyfrig asked.

"Where's the sphere, Your Reverence?" I countered.

"It disappeared just before that unearthly wailing started," Dyfrig said, the skin stretched tight over his young-again face. His hand went to his chest. "It feels as though the weight of the world rests here and I can't catch my breath."

"The demon has just taken someone with air," Wyln said hoarsely. "As it has taken someone with fire. Can you summon earth, Laurel?"

Laurel shook his head, his beads rattling. "The Lady is far from me," he softly yowled.

Water, air and fire already gone, without me feeling anything other than cold and hunger. Now earth, without me feeling anything at all. My hand went to my wounded side.

"At the time of turning, when She is entering her time of sleep and is at her weakest," Wyln began, but he lost part of his audience. Dyfrig's gaze landed on Cais and Finn lifting Gwynedd onto a cot, and his brows snapped together.

"What did you do to her?" the doyen demanded.

"Even the aged doyen is not immune—though I suppose

you're not so aged anymore, are you?" Jusson asked impatiently. "The player was in league not only with this hellborn sorcerer who has been plaguing us, but also with whoever murdered the jailer Menck, her brother, your clerks, and who would kill us too. But never mind the treacherous player." He indicated the guard from the rooftop. "He has brought news."

The royal guard blinked at becoming the focus of everyone's attention. "Yes, Your Majesty. There is a crowd forming on the street but we can't tell if they're with Helto or not. They're armed."

"Every person who could've countered the sorcerer's attacks hobbled, and now people with weapons appearing in the street." Jusson drew in a breath and released it. "Well, we've two choices. Stay here and wait for Helto's challenge, or go out and meet it."

"There is a third, sire," Thadro said. "If the taverner is to be believed."

"We are not running away like whipped curs, our tails between our legs," Jusson said. "Two choices, messirs. Fight now at our choosing or fight later when it's forced upon us?"

"Surely it's better to spring the trap than to wait for its springing, Your Majesty," I said.

"Hah!" Beollan's silver eyes were molten. "Well said, ibn Chause. No more delays, sire. Let us engage the enemy."

"So we will." Jusson gestured at the arsenal laid out on the table. "Whoever doesn't have a weapon can choose from those. I suggest that you choose wisely."

Thirty-five

Though the king had earlier given folks the choice to stay behind, there weren't any takers. The fact that the sorcerer and his demon had been able to reach into the king's house with ease didn't make it seem the safe haven it once was, and those who were unarmed mobbed the table. It was only by Thadro's intervention that some weren't weighted down with as many weapons as they could carry.

It was decided to leave Gwynedd in the guards' mess. She lay unmoving on the cot, her eyes still showing white, her breathing still harsh. Even so, Cais wasn't taking any chances, locking and sealing the door and windows with sprigs of rowan, and then posting two servants as guards outside the door. There was some discussion of also leaving Laurel, Wyln, Dyfrig and me. However, we all forcibly refused to remain behind. Laurel, Wyln and I decided that though we might be blocked in the talent, swords and claws worked just fine, while Dyfrig again clutched his Staff of Office as if it were a quarterstaff. "Besides, Rabbit and I still have the truth rune, honored folk," Laurel pointed out. "That is a potent weapon in and of itself."

Jusson sent for those on the roof and they met us in the entryway, the watchmen quickly finding Chadde, the armsmen their masters, the Own joining the rest of the royal guards. Jeff pushed his way to me.

"Did you hear that unearthly wailing?" Jeff asked. "What happened?"

"We're going to fight," I said as I counted heads of the guard. While I didn't know their names, their faces had become familiar—and I knew that even if we survived there would be gaps in their ranks. Already some were missing, and I wondered if I would be the one to write letters telling of sons and brothers who would never come home.

Jeff scowled at me. "That's bloody obvious—" He broke off as Jusson climbed a couple of steps on the main staircase. Everyone quieted quickly and the king turned to Dyfrig, motioning for the doyen to join him on the steps.

"We don't have time for long prayers, Your Reverence," he said, "but if you would, please bless us. Something short, but potent."

Still clutching his Church staff, Dyfrig drew in a deep breath, his face troubled. "Your Majesty—"

"Is there a problem, Your Reverence?" Jusson asked.

Dyfrig looked around at all the faces turned to him and he let his breath out in a sigh. "No, Your Majesty," he said. "There's nothing wrong." Not moving from where he stood, the doyen lowered his head and recited something straight out of the Church's book of prayers. When he finished, there was silence, with everyone looking more perplexed than blessed.

Jusson tapped his hand on the banister, reclaiming our attention. The king looked over everyone, his gaze alighting on a face for a moment, before moving on, and I wondered if he were also thinking on the gaps that would be there after today. We stared somberly back.

"I suppose that if this were a heroic tale," Jusson said, "this is where I would make a speech about how we're fighting on the side of good against the forces of evil. But why state the obvious? This is also where I'd go over the plan of attack. It is very simple—keep your eyes open and stay close to me. We are going to try for the stables and our horses. If that doesn't work, we will go to the garrison afoot. If we're unable to do that, we will rally at the Kingsgate."

No one said anything, and Jusson's mouth crooked. "Here we go, then. For God and kingdom. May He have mercy on our souls."

Jusson stepped down off the stairs and moved to the door, his quick steps muted on the black-and-white tiles. Cais slid through the quiet mob to join him, his hand on the knob as he waited for the king's signal. The king nodded at the majordomo, who lifted the bar across the door and began undoing the locks. After a moment, the door swung open and the sun spilled into the foyer and the king became a dark shadow outlined in light. Instead of sending the Own out ahead of him, Jusson had walked out first. While the foyer was a defender's dream, it was an offensive nightmare and it only would take a few armed with crossbows to pick us off one by one, beginning with the king. With muffled cries, everyone surged at the same time and it took a few terrifying moments for me to reach the doorway. Then I was out the door and hurrying down the front steps—only to come to a halt, blocking those behind me. The street was filled. There was Albe the blacksmith, Kresyl the baker, Danel the postilion, the Hart's innkeeper, his son and several of his serving maids. There were folks who were in Theater Square two days ago during the aborted play, who rioted when I'd been released from jail that same day, who angrily mobbed us as we returned from the Copper Pig yesterday afternoon, who ran to the charnel house fire yesterday eve, who witnessed the fight with the revenant last night and who grieved at the funeral pyres of the church clerks, Keeve and Tyle, in the small hours of this morning.

All bowing to the king.

"We've all heard how we've been beset, Your Majesty," Albe said as he straightened.

"Aye," Kresyl said. "Captain Suiden and Lord Elf speaking in my oven as I was baking. Damn near dropped my loaves."

"In my candles as I stitched," a woman said.

"The fireplace in my common room," the innkeeper said.

All around the street, people called out about hearing Wyln's talk with Suiden in cookfires, braziers and, in one case, a man's pipe.

Albe gestured to his two apprentices standing behind him. "We heard it in our forge." The blacksmith smiled, his teeth flashing white in his dark beard, and he hefted his hammer. "And we figured that we could stay inside and hope that it'd all go away, or come outside and make sure that it does."

Wyln and I looked at each other, the enchanter's tilted eyes rounding a little, before we turned to survey the number of townspeople who had the fire aspect.

"So many," Laurel breathed, also surveying the newly discovered talent-born. "How many, I wonder, have earth?"

Or water and air, I thought.

Jusson, however, was uninterested in untrained talent. Instead, his smile mirrored the blacksmith's.

"An excellent sentiment, Master Albe," the king said. "Tell me, does anyone know where Helto is?"

There was a rippling wave as a sea of arms pointed to the center of town.

"The main square, Your Majesty," the innkeeper said. "Saw him heading there myself with all the town rowdies and skull-crushers. Little rodent."

"Yeah," Danny put in. "Master Rat took your horses and

carriages too." The innkeeper thumped him in the side and the postilion jumped, turning red. "Um, Your Majesty," he added.

"I see," Jusson said. He turned his smile on those of us crowding behind him. "My lords and gracious sirs. There's been a change in plans."

Thirty-six

It was a perfect fall morning. The sky was deep blue, the air crisp, the light soft and golden as the sun rose above the autumn-splashed mountains. Yesterday, the streets had been full of bustle and cheer as the people of Freston prepared for the end of the harvest and the coming feast day. Now the streets were empty and the cheerful commotion gone, with the unnatural silence wrapping around us like wet wool, muffling the jingle of our chainmail and the thud of our boots against the cobblestones. The familiar scents of the town were gone too. Instead it smelled damp and a little stale, like a room long closed—or another place where nothing stirred and the air hung still and musty: the grave.

Laurel paced beside beside me, the weakness caused by being blocked in his aspect seemingly gone, his tail lashing back and forth as he strode. But it wasn't all a picture of strength and vigor—the cat's claws dug into his carved oak staff with each step, and he was chewing a constant stream of mentha leaves. Wyln too had recovered, or maybe he was just better at hiding pain. He was with Jusson at the head of the mob and from behind he looked as he always did, his movements just as graceful, the sword he'd taken from the weapons table now in a sheath he wore on his back. Then the fire enchanter turned his head and I could see his eyes dark and blind, the light within them gone.

Chadde was walking with Albe the blacksmith and his apprentices, the peacekeeper and blacksmith's heads close together as they spoke. Suddenly Albe and the apprentices broke away to run up the front steps of three different houses and pound on the doors. Chadde shifted to another part of the crowd and more folks splintered off to pound on more doors. House after house it was the same as people darted off to roust their neighbors. Some answered the pounding looking annoyed, some wary, but most frightened. Even so, they joined us carrying what weapons they had: swords, dirks, cudgels, short and quarterstaffs, even meat cleavers and carving knives. And it wasn't just men; women joined us too, carrying bows and with full quivers slung across their backs. The royal guards and aristos' armsmen looked askance at the women archers; the Watch, however, greeted them with shouts, whistles and clapping hands.

"The women here fight?" a southern aristo asked, conveniently overlooking Chadde leading her watchmen.

"Not all men find wives in the valley or the towns to the south, my lord," I said. "Many marry women from the mountain villages, where bandit attacks and long winters give folks a different view on who should fight and hunt."

"Our garrison commander has said that he could make the entire northern marches safe if he had just one company of them," Jeff said.

Laurel gave a soft chuff of laughter, his tail stilling for a moment. "You should see the females of my clan in full battle mode, honored folk. *That's* a frightening sight."

"Huh," Ranulf grunted. "The women of Bainswyr do not fight—unless their homes are attacked. Then Heaven help the attackers." He and Beollan were walking with us—though it looked more like Beollan was walking while supporting Ranulf. Still, the Lord of Bainswyr's eyes were bright, though they glowed dull red in the sunlight. "You know, I've been thinking."

I swallowed the obvious comment, pressing my lips together so nothing could slip out.

"Thinking about what, honored Ranulf?" Laurel asked obligingly. He tucked his paw into the crook of my arm and squeezed warningly. I folded my lips tighter.

"How this all doesn't make sense," Ranulf said. He tried an encompassing wave of his hand and, when he didn't topple over, he continued, emboldened. "It would've been better for Helto to take off and disappear. It would've been easy enough, even after the fracas at the Copper Pig. A name change, a new location, and he's back in business. What he's doing now, though, will focus the attention of the entire kingdom directly on him, no matter the outcome."

"The outlaws here aren't exactly the brightest, my lord," Jeff began.

"They've been bright enough to run their smuggling ring under the unsuspecting nose of your garrison commander for the last five years," Ranulf said, "even suborning your fellow troopers without his knowledge."

Jeff started to look at Ranulf, but was snagged by the expression on Arlis' face. "Bones and bloody ashes," Jeff whispered. "What have you gotten yourself into, lad?"

Arlis scowled, hunching his shoulder.

"And then there was the conspiracy to topple the House of Iver," Ranulf continued. "They kept that well hidden too. If it hadn't been for the arrival of ibn Chause and Master Cat in Iversly last spring, Teram ibn Flavan would have taken the throne."

"Maybe," I said, my gaze on Jusson at the head of our ad hoc army. "And maybe not."

Ranulf grunted again. "Come much closer to it, in any case."

"So Teram and Gherat were intelligent while Helto and friends are idiots," the aristo said.

"Are they truly idiots?" Ranulf asked. "Think on this: the realm has already had several shocks—the first Border ambassador ever suddenly appearing last spring, followed by the rebellion with more ties to the Border, then rumors of the kingdom being overun by magicals—"

Everyone around Ranulf gave a weary sigh. "Ranulf," Beollan began, pinching the bridge of his nose.

"Wait, hear me out," Ranulf said. "What did you say, Rabbit? About other countries?"

I blinked at the Marcher Lord. "Huh?"

"They all have magic workers—Svlet, Caepisma, Tural, even the Qarant. Right?"

"Oh. Yeah. Iversterre is the only kingdom that does not have royal mages or their equivalent." Until now—and if I survived.

"A world full of magicals," Ranulf said. "However, we are aware of only one place that has them. What would happen if the king were killed by magic here, so close to the Border? Or at least killed while magic was being flung about every which way so that a blind man couldn't miss it? Nor miss the magicals right in the king's house, one of whom is the heir to the throne?"

There was a ripple in front of us, then Jusson appeared, moving against the flow, Thadro and Wyln with him. Thadro looked puzzled at Jusson's backward progress, but both Jusson and Wyln's gazes were fixed on Ranulf, proving that there was nothing wrong with their elfin hearing. Beside me, Laurel rumbled a low growl.

"Go on, Bainswyr," Jusson said as Ranulf paused, surprised at the king's sudden presence. "What would happen if magic figured in my demise?"

"Nobody would think about those other kingdoms, sire," Ranulf said. "I mean, if we were near the coast, or down in the southern part of the country, then all right, maybe there are outside influences and even some foreign bugger of an assassin running about. But up here, so close to the Border, it would *have* to be the magicals, right? No one would believe otherwise."

"No," Beollan said, his silver eyes once more too large for his face. "No one would. And what would happen is that we would war, both with ourselves and with the Border. With ourselves because we'd fight over who'd get the throne, and against the Border as the cries for vengeance go up and our doyens preach a holy war. Pox rot and damn it all to hell."

Doyen Dyfrig had been walking a little ahead of us, keeping himself apart not only from those from the king's residence, but from everyone else too. Or at least he tried. There was a constant flow of townsfolk around him as they discovered just who was carrying the Staff of Office. Eyes wide, they'd touch Dyfrig wonderingly, some of the older folks looking as though they hoped whatever happened to him would rub off onto them. He now showed that he too had nothing wrong with his hearing by frowning at us over his shoulder.

"No matter how holy, we'd still get slaughtered, Fellmark," a northern lord said. "The magicals would roll over us like they did before, perhaps not stopping this time until they reach Iversly. Damn it to hell is right."

Dyfrig stopped walking, allowing our knot of people to catch up with him.

"And then all the other countries would come against *us*, honored folk," Laurel said, his grip tightening until his claws pressed into my arm. "If not for the crime of regicide, then for using sorcery to achieve it."

"But all the magic seems to be aimed at Rabbit," Dyfrig said, "and not the king. Surely people would realize that the Border wouldn't attack one of its own."

I blinked—partly at the doyen assuming that there was such a thing as fae solidarity and partly at the thought that any of the nonhuman Border races would consider me one of theirs. But mostly my startlement was at Dyfrig's casual repudiation of my belonging to Iversterre. Apparently five years of sitting through his sermons hadn't made me one of his flock.

"I don't know about that, Your Reverence," Beollan said. "But even if we did, his loss would still be disastrous. As His Majesty said earlier, without ibn Chause we don't have anybody to counter other kingdoms' wizards—"

"Yes, you do," Wyln said. "His Grace Loran the Fyrst has declared Jusson Iver'son to be of his lineage. Your king has all the resources of His Grace at his disposal."

"Even you, elf?" Beollan asked.

"Especially me, Beollan of Fellmark," Wyln said. "But there would be those who, if Iver's throne suddenly became empty, would demand that it return to the lineage—and to His Grace to whom it originally belonged. Just as there would be others who'd claim the parts of the human kingdom that originally belonged to *them*."

Listening to Wyln, my vision abruptly shifted. I was standing on one of the mountaintops surrounding Freston, staring down into the valley. Flames appeared, little flickers at first, but then they suddenly exploded into a conflagration that swiftly raced down the length of Iversterre, jumping off from the ports to other lands until all the world was engulfed.

"Rabbit!"

I shook my head, stumbling a bit on the cobblestone street. Great. Another vision. "I'm all right," I said, my voice hoarse.

"What is it, cousin?" Jusson said. "Is it your wound?"

"He had a vision," Laurel said, his paw tight on my arm. "What did you *see*, Rabbit?"

I rubbed my brow, my head aching. "The world dying," I said before I thought.

Though—or possibly because—of the unnatural hush, the noise we made had swelled as our numbers increased. But at my words, those around us fell silent, and the silence spread out in ripples with folks repeating what I'd said over and over, with disturbing accuracy. Not moving all that fast to begin with, the crowd slowed down, then came to a rambling halt.

"That's just wonderful, Rabbit," Jeff said, scowling.

Aware of his precarious position, Arlis said nothing. But his look could've cut stone.

Jusson aimed his disapproval at Laurel. "You had to ask him, didn't you?"

"The Lady spoke to him in the last vision he had," Laurel protested, "and I thought perhaps She did once more, perhaps even giving him wisdom on how to defeat the demon. I certainly didn't expect him to blurt out that he'd seen our deaths."

"Not our deaths," I corrected, my face flushing. My rune gave a weak tingle and I hurriedly added, "Not as a given. Only if we fail here."

"Oh," Thadro said. "That's different. If we *fail*. No worries there."

At that most opportune moment Chadde reappeared with some of her Watch, slipping through the ranks towards us. I gave a silent sigh of relief at the distraction.

"Well, here comes my Keeper of the Peace," Jusson said. "Perhaps she has better news than that we're all going to die."

"We've scouted ahead, Your Majesty," Chadde said as she joined us. "Helto and his band are in the town hall." The peacemaker frowned, looking more disturbed than I'd ever seen her. "Sire, the square looks as though it is in the middle of winter. Everything is frozen."

Jusson sighed aloud. "Then again, perhaps not."

Looking around at the halted army, the king took Chadde's arm and moved to the front again. "Come walk with me, Peacekeeper. Tell me everything you saw." Thadro and Wyln immediately followed after them, as did I, the King's Own, the nobles and their armsmen. After a moment's hesitation, everyone else starting walking again—and if their eyes drifted wistfully to side streets and alleys, at least they were moving in the right direction. Reaching the main avenue, we turned and came into view of the square. A gasp went up and eyes that had been lingering on avenues of escape were now rounded as they stared ahead.

"Like an ice cave in some bloody children's tale," Jeff whispered.

"Yeah," Arlis whispered back. "And we're about to face off with the witch of winter."

There was a sharp line of demarcation—on one side was the mellow gold of autumn and on the other was the glittering white of deep winter. Icicles sparkled as they dripped off eaves, ledges and windowsills, while rime formed patterns on windowpanes and gave the trees a silver sheen. The water in the fountain was frozen solid, with ice droplets from the fountain's spray spread about on the ground, and our boots crunched through them as we walked past, leaving behind powdery crystals on the paving stones.

And burning above it all was the column of fire from the charnel house, the flames spearing up into sky.

"*Cyhn?*" I asked, my hand going to my side.

"I've noticed," Wyln said, pulling my hand away from the quarrel wound. "And no, I don't know what it means."

It's not winter yet.

I turned to Laurel. The Faena's head was tipped back as

he considered the column, his face thoughtful. "What?" I asked.

Laurel lowered his gaze to me. "What what?" he asked back.

"Rebels *and* horse thieves," Jusson said, before I could respond. I faced forward again to see a makeshift corral beside the town hall steps, containing what did look like all the king's horses. Of the royal groomers there was no sign. I frowned at the corral's light guard, and the skin at the back of my neck prickled as I thought on how easily we had gotten this far.

"They're bait, sire," I said to Jusson. "To lure us in." My eyes went up to the town hall rooftop; though steeply sloped like the others to discourage snow accumulation, some forward thinker included a crenelated parapet, just in case folks decided to storm the hall. As we were doing now. However, the parapet was empty.

"So it seems," Jusson said. "But as soneone once said, it is better to spring the trap at our choosing, than have it sprung on us at theirs."

Nothing like having your words tossed back at you. My gloved hand crept back to my side, and this time Laurel pulled it away.

"Kenelm," Jeff said, scowling at one of the two corral guards. "Now we know where he went. Turncoat."

So we did. I glanced around to see the peacekeeper's reaction at the desertion of her man, but Chadde had slipped off once more.

"Who?" Ranulf asked, turning his head to follow Jeff's gaze.

"The watchman who disappeared after discovering the beaten guards in the charnel house courtyard," Beollan said. He nodded at the corral. "He has now reappeared as one of Helto's men."

"Are you surprised?" Thadro asked. "The guards' beating was a warning to those who had been involved in Helto's schemes and then thought that they could just walk away when it was no longer convenient. Right, Guardsman Arlis?"

Arlis remained silent, though Jeff did mutter something under his breath about goateed idiots. I also said nothing, looking at my sometimes drinking partner from the Watch. Kenelm gave me a flat stare back, his mouth tight.

"If so, it doesn't seem to have made that big of an impression," an aristo said. "Whoever might have joined Helto, it seems that many more have joined us."

"That remains to be seen," Jusson murmured.

I jerked my head around to stare at the king in horror, the thought of the throngs behind us rising up in a surprise attack streaking across my mind. But before I could say anything, the door to the town hall opened and a small crowd stepped outside, all dressed in warm winter clothes. Some were Menck's cronies and other bottom feeders. However, the rest were those prominent citizens and town officials who hadn't come with us to the king's residence. Apparently they hadn't been as impressed with the defeat of the revenant as they had been with whatever hold Helto had over them.

Then the mob of Freston's citizenry shifted and the taverner himself appeared, Gawell and Ednoth on his heels.

Jusson stopped about twenty paces from the hall steps and our ad hoc army spread out behind us, the archers taking up positions that allowed them to cover those guarding the horses and the armed men with Helto. Helto's men responded in turn by readying their own weapons. Separating from the crowed on the portico, Helto stepped to the fore, shaking his head. "I'd hoped that it wouldn't have to come to this, Your Majesty," he began, his face sorrowful. "So uncivilized—"

"Mayor Gawell," Jusson interrupted, "and Master Ednoth. Where is she?"

His honor and the head merchant joined Helto at the front of the steps. And a muffled gasp rose up as mouths fell open.

The last I'd seen Gawell, he was plainly dressed in coat and trousers. After escaping from the royal guards, though, he must've found time to change, for he now had on a fur-lined and -trimmed, dark gray woolen cloak, the fur on the hood framing his jowly face and matching the cuffs of his black leather gloves. Unexceptional, even if very fine for a small-town mayor. But the cloak gaped open over his stomach, revealing underneath a blue velvet robe decorated with silver embroidery intertwined with tiny diamonds twinkling in the cold light. The silver and diamonds competed with the mayor's chain of office, the starburst medallion resting on the upper curve of his velvet-clad belly. Between the jewels, silver and gold, Gawell was a blinding sight and I found myself squinting to cut down the glare.

Gawell had inhaled mightily, swelling in outrage as he drew in air to speak. However, Jusson's question threw him off stride and he sputtered it all out again. "Where is who?" he asked.

"Master Rodolfo is dead," Jusson said, "and Mistress Gwynedd is lost. That leaves Rosea. Where is she?"

Master Ednoth pushed to stand next to Gawell. His simple merchant's dress was made drab by the mayor's sartorial glory, the only shine about him the gleam of his balding head. His hand came up to rest on Gawell's shoulder and his honor obediently shut his gaping mouth.

"We've been beset by magicals and witchcraft, and you're asking after a street player?" Ednoth asked, incredulous.

"Yes," Jusson said. "Where is she?"

"You are a fool!" Gawell declared. "No wonder there was a rebellion last spring. Well, this time we will sweep you and your inept House from the throne—"

"*I* am a fool?" Jusson's brow raised. "You accosted me at my dinner two nights ago, exclaiming about how our cousin had harmed your people, your town." The king waved a hand about the square. "Behold your people, behold your town! Your church desecrated, your jailer slain, your churchmen killed by someone possessed by hell itself. And here, in the very heart of the town you claim as your own, frozen death. Look! Life has fled from this place. Listen! Where is the pulse beat of your town?"

Both Gawell and Ednoth tried to interrupt Jusson, but the king had much more experience talking over opposition and rolled right over them. Those who had aligned themselves with Helto, Gawell and Ednoth had shifted uneasily as Jusson spoke, their eyes darting to the church standing desolate on the other side of the square, then down to the scorch marks left from the funeral pyres, before flicking over the ice that lay over everything. Now, as Jusson fell silent and the swaddling, muffling, stifling silence flooded back in, they slid glances at the mayor and head merchant, their faces very unhappy.

"Freezing is normal," Gawell said, contemptuous. "It happens every winter—"

Ednoth's fingers abruptly dug into Gawell's shoulder, the head merchant's knuckles turning white, and the mayor yelped.

Not winter yet.

I looked around to see who spoke. But everyone near me was intent on the drama happening on the steps.

"Freezing weather does happen every year," Jusson agreed. "Usually *after* the harvest is gathered in—"

There was a soft gurgle of laughter and those on the portico parted, most shrinking away with their unhappy looks

turning into ones of terror. Gawell and Ednoth also fell
back, the mayor smirking as a small figure in a green gown
emerged to stand at the front of the portico.

"Very eloquent, King Jusson," Rosea said. "And evoca-
tive! You would've done well treading the boards."

Thirty-seven

Arlis had been right; Rosea had drastically changed. Her once fiery hair was now a dark red, as were her lips. Her skin was the glowing white of snow under a full moon, and her eyes glittered emerald green. As I stared up into them I thought I could hear the pounding sea.

Rosea sketched a curtsey. "Lord Rabbit. It is so good to see you again. But you've lost weight. Are you ill?"

Before I could respond, Thadro signaled and I was surrounded by the Own. At the same time, Jusson shifted, planting himself directly in front of me. "This is the infamous player?" His gaze shifted to Gawell and Ednoth, now standing behind Rosea. "This is who has made strong men foresake their oaths and plot against their king? *This?*" Jusson shook his head. "Open your eyes and see! Look at what she is! Hell's darkness wrapped in the paleness of death."

"Oh, bravo!" Rosea said, clapping her hands.

"No, Mistress Rosea," Gawell said. "'Twas poorly played." He sneered down at the king. "Open *our* eyes and see?" The mayor nodded at Helto, who gave his own signal and suddenly men with crossbows sprang up on the parapet of the town hall roof. "*We* haven't blithely walked into a trap," the mayor continued. "Ednoth is right; you are a fool!"

Unlike those at the corral and on the portico steps, the

parapet bowmen weren't townspeople held by threats and beatings. Nor were they Menck's former henchmen and town bullies. Some looked an awful lot like the bandits that the Mountain Patrol had been chasing for the last five years. Others I recognized from the barroom brawl at the Copper Pig yesterday morning—including the tapster, Bram. Their faces were hard and a little bored as they easily aimed their crossbows down at us. Bram had his pointed straight at Jusson.

"What he is, is a funny man!" Rosea moved closer to the portico's top step, her green eyes a-glitter as she looked down on Jusson. "But you're not a man, are you, Jusson of the House of Iver? While Rabbit is handsome, even with his silly braid and feather, you are beautiful in the way of elves. Just like the fire enchanter is." Her tongue, startlingly red and agile, darted out and licked her lips as she allowed her gaze to drift over Wyln. "Such delicacies. I am sure we will enjoy ourselves together."

It was Jusson's turn to show unconcern. He nodded at Thadro, who again signaled, and two royal guards immediately came forward carrying between them a familiar chest, followed by another carrying a small table. They quickly set the table in the clearing in front of the town hall steps, spreading a silk cloth over it and placing the chest of blessings on top. Dyfrig, standing by himself, went very still.

Jusson had laid his own ambushments.

Rosea clapped her hands again. "Oh, are we going to have an exorcism? How exciting! But wait, didn't you say that your holy men were killed?"

Dyfrig slowly walked to the impromptu altar, the bells on his Staff of Office softly chiming. Gawell's jowls wobbled as he goggled and Ednoth stood gape-mouthed, while Helto's suavity disappeared and Rosea's white face went blank.

"Dyfrig?" Ednoth asked. "Is that you?"

"Contrary to your plans," Jusson said, "he survived."

Gawell found his indignation. "You accuse *us* of attacking *our* church?"

"Yes," Jusson said.

"How *dare* you," Gawell said, his voice full of outrage. "Your *witch* called the revenant forth. Just as he killed Menck. Four murders in the space of two days, just as he returned from that godforsaken place—"

Rosea's shocked gasp cut across Gawell's accusations. "Rabbit a witch? Oh, no, no! This cannot be true! He is a good son of the Church."

"Lord Rabbit is steeped in the dark arts, dear lady," Helto said. He'd regained his suavity and he now again shook his head in sorrow. "He couldn't even go into the church last night but was struck down in a fit as he neared its doors. And as he fell, the revenant came rushing out at its master's cries."

"The revenant came out to protect its master? Only to have the master destroy it? What a tragic figure, even in death!" Rosea mimicked the flourishing of a cape, her green gaze all of a sudden dark and knowing. "Poor Rodolfo. His greatest role and he wasn't there."

Our ad hoc army had remained quiet during the give and take between Jusson and those on the portico. But now a roar went up at Helto and Rosea's words, townspeople shouting, the unnatural hush unable to mute their grief and anger. Many shouted at those who stood on the portico; however, others aimed their anger at me, and cries of "murderers" and "turncoats" mingled with those of "witch." Jeff and Arlis drew closer to me, as did the King's Own, their faces worried as they watched the crowd. However, I wasn't paying attention to the muffled bellows and shaking fists. Instead I was once more staring up at Rosea, the hair rising up on the back of my neck as she smiled down at me with the dead master player's eyes. Outside my ring of the Own,

Laurel snarled and raised his paw, but nothing happened. The rune remained dark. Laurel stared at it, his ears flat against his skull.

"Oh, dear," Helto said, raising his voice over the tumult. "What can the matter be, pussycat? No digging for the truth?"

Laurel, growling, lowered his paw. As he did, though, I brought my hand up in blessing, and Rosea rocked back a bit, blinking. Then her face quickly smoothed over and she smiled again. However, her eyes were once more icy green.

Not winter—

Dyfrig hit his Staff of Office against the ground, causing the bells to jangle, and the roaring diminished. "Did you send that abomination to the church, Ednoth, Gawell?" he asked.

Ednoth shook his head while Gawell drew himself up, his belly thrusting out. "Of course not!" the mayor declared. "It was the witch—"

Dyfrig's mouth was suddenly bracketed by lines of pain—I supposed after knowing them all his life, he could tell when Gawell and Ednoth lied. Shaking his head slowly, the doyen held his staff out to me and, keeping an eye on Rosea, I slipped out from among the Own to join him at the altar. Shifting my own ashwood staff to my other hand, I took the Staff of Office from the doyen and felt the warmth of it through my glove. And Gawell and Ednoth's protestations of innocence died, as did their plans to foist everything on the hellmongering magicals.

"It's a trick," Gawell stuttered. "A false staff and an equally false doyen. Look at him! Unnaturally young—"

The lines deepened around Dyfrig's mouth. "Rabbit didn't stop the revenant." He opened the chest of blessings. "I did. With that Staff of Office as I called on God."

And with a little help from both Wyln and the air aspect. However, I wasn't going to point that out.

Jusson, though, had no problem giving credit where credit was due. "Lord Wyln fought the revenant, Gawell, and His Reverence delivered the grace stroke. Which, apparently, your informants hadn't passed on." A wing brow rose. "Amazing. I wonder why?"

The last of the roar from our ad hoc army faded. It was replaced with a growl, low and full of the rage of betrayal.

"Ah," Jusson said. "It seems that there is some doubt as to your goodwill."

"Our goodwill, beautiful elf-king?" Rosea asked before Gawell could respond. "We have all the goodwill in the world." She tilted her head to the side. "What about you, Priest? Do you?"

Dyfrig ignored the player as he set out the implements of blessing, gently placing them on the altar cloth. Those at the corral and on the portico watched him, their faces yearning. It seemed that it was one thing to be at odds with one's sovereign and risk a hanging; it was another to align oneself with a creature from hell and thereby risk one's soul. Still, I moved closer to the doyen, shifting both staves to one hand to leave my sword arm free, just in case any decided that their orthodoxy was a suitable sacrifice for keeping their neck out of the hangman's noose.

"I'm sure the doyen is full of goodness and light," Helto said to Rosea.

"Is he?" Rosea asked. "His hands too? Are they full of goodness? Or are they stained with blood?"

Dyfrig suddenly faltered, the bell slipping from his hand to hit the table with a clang.

"Your Reverence?" I asked, and the low, growling rumble around us changed, rising on a questioning note.

Rosea came down a step. "What about it, Priest? Are your hands clean?"

For a long moment Dyfrig didn't move, then his shoulders slumped, and I reached out to him, taking his arm. Instead of the frail bones of yesterday morning, I could feel solid muscle and sinew, but he was tight, as if braced against a blow. The questioning rumble faded until there was nothing left but the stifling hush.

Rosea laughed and descended another step, her head turning to Wyln. "What do you think, Enchanter? Has the young-again priest soiled his hands?"

Wyln was standing with Thadro at Jusson's back. And like Thadro he kept his attention on the player. "Did you kill someone, Elder Dyfrig?" he asked without turning around, sounding more intrigued than condemning.

Dyfrig shook his head. "No," he said, his voice cracking. "My sin is one of omission—"

"Omission!" Rosea said. "Was it an omission to turn away from a hand stretched out in supplication?"

"You watched someone murdered and did nothing?" I asked, my concern turning to disbelief. I felt Dyfrig's arm jerk as he flinched.

"Oh, yes, my little rabbit," Rosea said. "But was it a 'someone'? That's the question, isn't it?"

My fingers tightened, digging into Dyfrig's arm. "One of the People was here? In the valley?"

"Up in the mountains," Rosea said. "A holdover from when they roamed freely." She did a dance step, spinning in a pirouette—and I could see that her feet were bare on the icy stone, a twist of pearls twined around one dead-white ankle. "Did it horrify you, dear priest? Or were you filled with joy as you watched the magical's life drain into the ground?"

Dyfrig closed his eyes, his face so drawn that he nearly looked his age.

"Liked it, didn't you, sweetling?" Rosea crooned. "But then, they should all die, shouldn't they? Every single beastly one burned in the fire. After all, look what they did to your father."

"Your father fought in the war, Elder Dyfrig?" Laurel asked. He had given up glaring at his blocked rune to focus on the doyen. However, the Faena's regard was gentle.

Rosea descended another step. "Yes, he did," she said. "He was a fine, upstanding man, answering his liege lord's summons with no thought of himself. But that's not the way he came back, did he, dear heart? Broken in so many places. And his nightmares." She licked her lips again, her voice turning sibilant. "Nightmares that lasted into waking—"

Dyfrig swayed and I tightened my grip more, casting an anguished look at Jusson. But the king was watching the descending player.

"So the very thing you hated you have become, honored elder," Wyln said. "What are you going to do about it?"

"What can he do?" Rosea asked, her voice lilting, her frozen gaze avid. "He's like an old, forgotten barrow. Green, grassy slopes on the outside, but inside full of dead men's bones. Will his prayers be heard? Or is he anathema? What do *you* believe, Priest?"

"That's the question," Dyfrig whispered. "What do I believe?" He looked at me. "The world dying, Rabbit?" he asked.

"Yes, Your Reverence," I said. "If we fail."

Dyfrig nodded, his face grim. Then, pulling from my grasp, he picked up the bell from the altar and rang it. Hard. Unlike all the other sounds, this was bright and strong, the peal cracking around the square like the sound of great ice floes breaking. On the hall steps Rosea went very still. Dyfrig took a deep breath, then his baritone filled the humming silence.

"Hear all who will, my confession of sin. In the second year of my doyenship, I watched a person slain and did nothing—"

"No!" Rosea flew down the rest of the steps, her snow-white hands stretched out for Dyfrig. I quickly moved in front of the altar, bringing the Staff of Office before me and the player abruptly halted, snarling. Out the corner of my eye, I saw Jusson come up on her flank, Thadro and Wyln with him, while Beollan and Ranulf closed in on her other side. I tapped the staff against the ground, causing the bells to jangle.

"By the Holy God and His Saints," I said, Arlis and Jeff joining me.

Seeing Rosea trapped against the steps, Helto lifted an arm, calling out: "Shoot!" On the parapet, Bram and the others immediately loosed their bolts. Thadro quickly raised the shield over the king and, at the same time, a flight of arrows arose from the archers in the square, causing the bravos on the rooftop to duck behind the parapet's merlons, while Gawell, Ednoth and the others on the portico went down, the mayor with a visible bounce. Only Helto remained standing, but before the arrows could reach him, they shattered in midflight, those on the town hall steps crying out as frozen slivers rained down on them. The taverner didn't bother to flinch as he snatched a crossbow from a cowering henchman and aimed it at Jusson. But Thadro kept the shield over the king, its device blazing in the cold light, while the Own formed a turtle around them both. Our archers swiftly nocked arrows, loosing another volley, and our ad hoc army surged forward, parting on either side of Dyfrig as they passed the altar, swords and various other weapons raised. However, the second volley was destroyed midflight like the first, and those on the portico steps rose up to to meet them with a muted clash of arms. And in the muffled background, like a surreal dream, the horses in the corral screamed and kicked at the fence slats, maddened by the sights and sounds of battle.

As Dyfrig continued to confess of his decades-old sin, I took another step towards Rosea, Jeff and Arlis at my back, Laurel joining us. The Own lowered their shields and moved aside to allow Jusson to emerge, the king's sword in his hand, his gaze fixed on the player. Thadro and Wyln stayed with him, the enchanter outlined in blue fire. On the other side, Beollan and Ranulf continued their flanking approach; Beollan also with sword, Ranulf with his battleaxe. Rosea's eyes darted first to the Staff of Office I held. She then glanced at Laurel with his fangs bared and his own staff. She finally turned, but not to flee back up the steps. As the near-silent battle raged around us, the player smiled at Beollan and Ranulf, her hands clasped demurely before her.

"My lords. It is good to see you too."

Beollan's silver eyes overwhelmed his narrow face. "It's over, Rosea," he said. "Let us take you home."

My gaze snapped to the Marcher Lord, but just as quickly I looked back at the player. Rosea hadn't moved. Hands still clasped, she shook her head, the pearls woven into her hair shimmering. "It's *not* over, Uncle. There are still plot twists and turns to uncover. Why, we are just at the scene about the Lord of Bainswyr and his curious relic from the last Border war. A keepsake that has been passed from father to son." Rosea's smile stretched wide, her eyes triangular holes that glittered green as she looked at Ranulf.

"That's your cue, my brother. Change for me."

Thirty-eight

Ranulf screamed, his battleaxe falling with a clatter as he dropped to his hands and knees. His clothes began to rip and tear, the leather ties on his armor snapping, his boots splitting, all of it falling away. Fur appeared, rippling over his body and sprouting on his contorting face, and he screamed again, pointing an elongating muzzle to the sky, muscle and bone shifting under his thickening pelt. The fighting faltered, all involuntarily stopping to watch the translating Marcher Lord.

"Ranulf!" Beollan reached down, but Ranulf swiped out a mutating hand, knocking Beollan against the stone steps.

"Bones and bloody ashes!" Jeff's eyes were wide. "We didn't change like that, Rabbit."

I made a shocked sound of assent. The translations in the embassy and later in the Border had happened easily, in a blink of an eye. They were not pain-wracked and prolonged. Ranulf screamed once more, his voice deeper, wilder.

Rosea turned her too-stretched smile on us. "Sometimes you just can't believe your eyes, Jeffen, son of Corbin."

Suddenly one of our archers shrieked—and Magistrate Ordgar fell, an arrow sticking out of his back. Then a bowman on the roof also gave a muted cry and shot one of his fellows. There were more cries and the bully boys and henchmen's swords flashed out at each other, while around us our ad hoc army disintegrated into small battling groups, pitting walking sticks against carving knives. Gawell and Ednoth, still cowering on the portico step, hurriedly got to their feet, the mayor gaping at the madness spreading before them while the head merchant turned a frightened eye on the mayhem happening behind.

Rosea's agile tongue once more darted out to lick her lips. "And sometimes you can."

"Illusion!" Laurel bellowed. "You are seeing things that aren't there!" He raised his staff and rushed at Rosea, but Helto shot his crossbow even more quickly. The quarrel spun Laurel around, his staff falling to the paving stones with a rattle and clatter.

"Laurel!" The staves I held fell as pain bloomed in my chest. I caught the cat, but his weight bore me to the ground. Letting go of the spent crossbow, Helto grabbed another and aimed it at Jusson. The Own had started to lift their shields over the king once more, but they wavered and then broke apart, one crying out that he was on fire, another beating about himself as he screamed about snakes. The other guards, swamped with nightmares only they could see, attacked each other or dropped, curling in on themselves in terror. There was a clash of arms behind me as Jeff and Arlis fought people rushing the altar. At first I thought my personal guards had escaped the madness, but then Jeff started shouting about giant Pale Deaths while Arlis moaned about being buried alive.

Ranulf gave a roar that sounded like nothing human. An archer rose up, her eyes wild as she aimed at the Marcher Lord, but before she could shoot, someone grabbed her by her hair and dragged her back into the roiling fray.

The Own disintegrating about them, Thadro once more shoved in front of Jusson, but before he could lift the king's shield in place, he too went down with a bolt in him. Helto, smiling, picked up another crossbow and aimed it at Jusson. The king snatched up his shield from Thadro's slackened grasp and, stepping over his Lord Commander's body, started running up the steps, Wyln with him. Just then, however, a wave of people from the square flowed up, engulfing king and enchanter in a deadened clangor of swords against swords and shields.

Ranulf bellowed a final time. Except it wasn't Ranulf anymore but a bear, its eyes red and feral, its frame gaunt, its fur matted. It stood up on its hind legs, towering over those around it, its great shaggy head turning, scanning. It then dropped to all fours and quickly shambled to Dyfrig, its long claws clicking on the paving stones as it bowled over any in its path.

"No!" Beollan shouted. Gathering himself, he rose and hurried after the bear. "Ranulf!"

"Wait!" Gawell cried out at the same time, all righteous indignation gone as he watched his townspeople destroy each other. Moving around Ednoth, he shoved Helto aside as he tried to go down the steps to Rosea. "You said just the king and his men—"

Without looking, Rosea waved her hand and Gawell flew back to crash against the front of the town hall. "I lied," she said. Raising her other hand, she spread her white arms out as if embracing the square, her eyes closed, her lips parted. After a moment, though, a line appeared between her brows. Opening her eyes, she looked down at me as I cradled Laurel. Her frown deepened. "Take off the feather, Rabbit."

"Go to hell," I said. The pain had spread to my wounded side and I gasped for breath, my mouth filling with a coppery taste.

"How original." Rosea sighed, dropping her arms. "The Faena has bound you. If you don't take off the feather, you will die with him."

The coppery taste grew stronger and something warm ran out the side of my mouth. I wiped at it with the back of my hand and, looking down, I saw blood smeared on my glove.

"Even now your life is fading," Rosea said. "Remove the feather and live."

Behind me, Dyfrig finished his confession and segued into a prayer of exorcism, a counterpoint to the growls of the bear, Beollan's desperate shouts, and the muffled screams of the terror-ridden and the dying. I latched on to the sound of the doyen's voice, adding my own desperate prayers to his. Mine, though, were for the protection of all the souls of the mortally wounded—especially mine.

Rosea looked over her shoulder at Helto. "Kill the priest."

Helto had regained his balance and now swung the crossbow to Dyfrig. "As you wish, my lady," he said, and loosed the quarrel. I tried to rise up, but I couldn't make my legs work. Someone cried out, but Dyfrig continued praying. Helto had missed, then. Scowling, the taverner began looking for another loaded crossbow. As he did, Ednoth threw off his paralysis and leaped on the taverner. They both slipped, then went down on the ice-slick portico, their struggle fading from view as my eyesight dimmed.

Not winter yet.

My head jerked up to see that Rosea had moved closer, stopping at the staves I'd dropped between us. She held out her hand. "Don't be foolish. Your dying will accomplish nothing. Give me the feather."

I raised my own hand, but instead of reaching up to my braid, I tried to summon air. It did not respond.

Rosea sighed again, exasperated. "A waste of time and effort." Dyfrig rang the bell and her face rippled. It then firmed, this time full of sympathy. "So tired, aren't you sweet chuck?" she said, her voice soft and gentle. "Just one more thing and you can rest."

I moved to fire and got the same damn sickly blue flame. I tried earth. Nothing.

—not winter—

"Why fight it?" Rosea asked. "The feather, Rabbit."

I let my hand flop to my side. Laurel lay unmoving, his blood dripping on me. Or maybe it was my own. It ran down my chin to splash on the cat's fur.

"Sweetling," Rosea crooned, moving closer.

—yet—

There was nothing left to lose. I reached for water and gasped as a bone-chilling cold settled over me, as if I had plunged into a glacier lake in the Upper Reaches.

Rosea laughed, her voice going smooth and melodic. "Do you think that you will defeat me with what is *mine?* I *am* water. Take the damn feather off, stupid man."

I dropped my hand again, my body slumping, my eyes closing. And I found myself standing in the middle of rolling grassland, stretching out as far as the eye could see in all directions, the sun bright and warm in a forever blue sky.

I let out a breath. Yet another vision. I was wearing the same hodgepodge of clothing as I had the last time I'd visited the metaphor that was my soul. This time, though, I carried the Staff of Office, Laurel's cloth-and-bead-decked carved oak staff, and my own plain ashwood staff. The Faena staff's beads softly clacked and the Church staff's small bells faintly chimed in the soft wind that swept over the grass in waves. My feather danced in the breeze, gently brushing against my cheek.

Not winter yet.

Of course it wasn't winter. But I frowned at lush, ankle-high grass. It wasn't spring, either. It was fall, with Harvestide and my Nameday fast approaching.

"Damn," Rosea said. *"I can't reach him, Master."*

I stared about, pondering the confusion of the seasons and caught something shimmering in the grass. Walking over, I saw a lake that hadn't been there before. I moved to a ledge over the water and, looking down, saw my reflection looking back. Except I wasn't looking at me. My mirror image's eyes were fixed above and to the side of my head. I turned, searching to see what had me so entranced.

"The tie's too strong with the Faena," Rosea said. *"He's almost gone."*

There was nothing but sky. I looked back into the water and blinked. Behind my reflection was Laurel, the cat's amber eyes full of light. As I watched, Thadro appeared, his face wondering. Then Magistrate Ordgar and Alderman Geram showed up, followed by several of the King's Own, a couple of aristos, their armsmen, town watchmen and even a few of Helto's henchmen. Ignoring my reflection in front of them, they all looked straight at me. My heart began thundering in my ears.

"He's done something with the others. Bound them to him in their deaths as far as I can tell. They're also beyond my reach."

The lake filled with people—Albe the blacksmith and one of his apprentices, Danny the postilion, Kenelm the turncoat, Alderman Almaric, more watchmen, another aristo, rowdies off the portico, bravos from the rooftops, women still carrying their bows and quivers, men with cleavers and walking sticks. Ranulf pushed his way to the front, his body once more human. But it was wrapped in what looked like caltrops strung on wire, the caltrops' points embedded deep into his flesh. He met my gaze, his habitual scowl on his face.

"Such a rich soul, so full of power and complexities. It'd be a shame to lose it."

There was a ripple and Jeff moved through the crowd to stand between Laurel and Ranulf. Jeff stared about wide-eyed, then also looked up at me. My own reflection, though, remained unaware of all the people behind it. I waved the bundle of staves I held but it didn't change. The thundering grew louder, now seeming to come from the very ground under my feet. Not my heart, came the distant thought. It was the crashing of an enraged sea. The wind increased, bending the grass before it as it softly howled, but the surface of the lake remained placid, my mirror image blindly staring, transfixed by something that wasn't there. I lifted the staves high, those in the lake tracking, Laurel's whiskers lifting in a smile that showed his eyeteeth—

"Wait, Master, something's happening—"

—and I brought them down with all my might. They crashed through the water's surface as if it were made of glass, shards flying up, the entire lake exploding as the sea roared out and swept over me.

I had summoned water once before. Then it had been a joyous filling to completion, as springs, wells, brooks, streams, rivers and oceans all said yes as I invited them in. There was nothing joyful about this. I was violently seized, the waves churning me about until I didn't know where I ended and the aspect began.

Let go, a voice said, full of the roaring ocean.

Let go? I didn't have it. It had me.

Let go, the voice repeated.

My lungs burning as I sought the surface, I wondered if I had a choice.

There is always a choice.

I took fast stock of my options. I could be defiant and drown. Or I could yield and drown. Like Dyfrig, it was a question of what I believed.

All right, I thought.

And something infinitely vaster than the sea brushed by me. Startled, I exhaled, my breath bubbling out from me.

So I drown.

Breathe.

I inhaled, the salty sea filling me. So I don't drown. Maybe.

Open your eyes.

My eyes flew open to find myself staring into Rosea's face. Startled, she abruptly straightened, her gaze shooting down to where water was beading on her hands.

"You're not water." I gently put aside Laurel's body and, gathering up the three staves, I stood. "That is a lie." Rosea took a step back, her gown wet at the hem. Behind me Dyfrig rang the bell, and her face rippled again, a trickle of water appearing on her forehead. I moved towards her, my own clothes soaking wet, the wild smell of the sea rising off of me. "You're just damned."

Rosea's mouth hung open for a moment, then she spun around and ran up the steps, her gown now wet to her knees. Having thrown off Ednoth, Helto shifted to make room for the player, the loaded crossbow still in the taverner's hands. Rosea pointed at me, the trickle now twin rivulets flowing down both sides of her face. "Shoot him!"

Helto quickly loosed the bolt. I just as quickly twisted to the side and the bolt ripped my tabard, skimming along my hauberk before striking the ground. And where it struck the frost melted, the thaw spreading out in rapid concentric waves over the paving stones to travel up walls, across ledges and eaves and anything else in its path. Icicles' drip-drip joined that falling from trees and lampposts, from the ribbons, garlands and wreaths of Harvestide that festooned the square. The people still caught up in their hushed madness started slipping and splashing in the forming puddles.

"This too is a lie," I said.

Dyfrig rang the bell a third time and the melee slowed, then stopped as the illusions dissipated with the frost. The wave of fighting that had washed over Jusson and Wyln ebbed away again, leaving the king and the elfin enchanter

standing back-to-back, the blades of their swords red with
blood. Sprawled around them on the ground were armsmen,
aristos, townspeople, and royal guards—but that was true of
the entire square. Realizing that they'd been battling friends
and family, the townsfolk still standing dropped their
weapons and, heedless of the wet ground, fell to their knees
to gather the wounded, the dying and the dead in their arms.
A keening wail rose, the sound muted, stifled.

"All illusion," I said, moving towards the portico steps.
"Mist and mirrors."

Jusson lowered his sword, his shoulders slumping.
Wyln, though, swiftly walked towards me, strain finely
drawn on his face as he stepped around Laurel's body. Jusson followed, not looking down at where Thadro lay, staring unseeing at the sky.

Fresh out of loaded crossbows, Helto reached into a belt
sheath and produced a knife, throwing it with deadly accuracy. I knocked it aside with the bundle of staves I held,
sending it skidding along the ground to fetch up against
Jeff, lying so pale and still in front of the altar. Wyln, Jusson and I started climbing the steps, Wyln's gaze resting on
my face for a moment before dropping to the pools of saltwater forming in my footprints. The pools overflowed and
spilled down the portico steps.

"Is it truly an illusion, Rabbit?" Jusson asked. "The
death and destruction look very real."

Arlis, down on one knee, raised his head to stare at the
knife resting against Jeff's body, then his red-rimmed gaze
went first to the taverner, then to Ednoth, who was slowly
and painfully getting to his feet.

"It's by trickery and misdirection, sire," I said, my voice
taking on a basso rumble. "This has been nothing but an
elaborate shell game."

Folks who were whole enough set down their wounded
and dead and picked up their weapons, moving behind us

like a slow, rolling wave. Seeing what was coming at him, Ednoth gave a yelp and quickly limped for the town hall door. He paused briefly, revealing that his storklike frame was stronger than it looked by yanking Gawell to his feet. They both disappeared into the hall, the mayor wobbling, with blood running down his face from his encounter with the building wall.

"Stop him!" Rosea gasped, and Helto pulled and threw another knife. I knocked that one aside also, causing it to land against the body of the bear. Beollan kicked it away and, helping Arlis to his feet, they both moved up the steps to fall in at our backs, tears rolling unheeded down the Marcher Lord's face.

"A shell game?" Wyln asked, his thoughtful gaze returning to my face. "Who then is the thimblerigger? The House Master?"

"Not him, honored *Cyhn*," I said, the rumble deepening. "He doesn't have the talent. Neither does Rosea."

Rosea's skin had become sallow and red streaks appeared in the whites of her eyes. "Help me, Master," she whimpered as she began to shake.

Facing us, Helto drew a long knife and a sword. Down below in the square, Dyfrig poured salt on the altar, encircling the ceremonial bowl and the unlit candle—and the smell of the sea grew stronger.

"So what are they?" Jusson asked as we reached the top step, Beollan and Arlis on our heels, the townspeople right behind them.

Shaking harder, Rosea backed up, her hair coming down in straggly clumps to plaster against her face and neck. A pearl strand fell, the string breaking and the pearls scattering along the stone porch.

"Tools, Your Majesty," I and the sea said. "They're both tools."

"If so," Wyln said, now considering Rosea, "then they're

also fools who've not counted the cost of serving their masters. Then again, those who'd parley with the dark aren't usually very wise to begin with."

Helto also backed up, but it was to give himself sword room. "You're wrong, magical. It's not we who'll pay the price here today. Right, my lady?" He smirked at Rosea, only to have it disappear as he got a good look at the player. Horror flashed over his face.

"Master," Rosea gasped. She stood with her hands straining at her sides, her eyes wide, the cords in her neck standing out. "Help me. Please—"

"The game has ended," Jusson said, moving in a loose, swordsman's stalk towards Helto. "The shells overturned and all shown to be empty."

"Sodding hell," Helto whispered. He broke and ran, dodging bodies to flee into the town hall. But there was a clash and the clatter of falling weaponry, and Helto backed out again, his hands raised high as Peacekeeper Chadde and several of the Watch exited the doorway. Of the mayor and head merchant, though, there was no sign.

Dyfrig picked up the vessel of blessed water and poured it into the ceremonial bowl. The square fountain burst into fluid life, and through the portico step I could feel a distant rumbling.

"I beg pardon for our delay, Your Majesty," Chadde said. Her and her watchmen's faces were pale and some were swallowing hard, as if to keep their gorge from rising. "We'd become a little disoriented going through the side streets and then, when we found our way clear, we discovered—" Chadde stopped abruptly as she took in the carnage in the square.

"Chaddie Laddie," Helto said, his breath coming in short pants. "While I'd love to discuss how uncivilized it is to come through the back door, there are more demanding issues at hand." He cast a wild glance at Rosea. "We really should leave. Right away."

"God damn and blast your civilness," Chadde said, all calmness gone. "We discovered your missing guards and groomers inside, sire. What's left of them."

"Those did have the talent," the sea and I said as we stood in front of Rosea. "Air, fire, water, or earth, they had it in various measures, and so were given to the demon. Others were devoured just because they were yours, sire."

"Mine," Jusson said, the blood still wet upon his sword. "Stay your hand, Peacekeeper. This foolish tool is also mine."

Dyfrig dipped a sprig of hyssop into the blessed water and sprinkled it on the altar. A bird chirped, then another, and another, and suddenly the graveyard silence tore away like rotted cloth. The distant rumbling became abruptly louder; it was the sound of horses' hooves against cobblestones. A lot of horses, all moving very fast.

"Yes, of course, Your Majesty," Helto said to Jusson. He held his hands out, pressed together at the wrists. "I'm guilty as charged. Take me prisoner and let's leave. *Now*—"

"What's wrong with Rosea?" Arlis interrupted.

"She is losing control of the demon," Wyln said.

"Jaban's Waste," Jusson said. "And now Jusson's." He started to turn his head to Rosea, but on the way got a good look at me—and his detachment fell away. "*Cousin?*"

Sweat rolling down his face, Dyfrig held his hands over the unlit candle.

"And Two Trees'son has become an avatar of an aspect turned elemental," Wyln said.

The roar of the sea filling me completely, I planted the bundle of staves against the portico step, waiting.

Rosea gave a faint moan, all of her color fading—except for her pupils. They were still a bright, glittering green.

"When giants fight, the grass is crushed." Chadde

pushed through to the front step. For a terrible moment her gaze rested on Thadro before going across the square. "Perhaps we can find refuge in the church." Everyone turned to look at the church—and its blasted front—and many fell to their knees, commending their souls to God.

Rosea moaned again, this one growing louder until she was screaming, her head thrown back. She went up on her toes, her body impossibly stretched in her extremity. She then slowly came back down on her feet and lowered her head, bringing those glittering, hate-filled eyes to me. "Free," she said, her voice melodic.

Taking advantage of our distraction, Helto shoved through the wall of watchmen and disappeared into the town hall doors. Those not praying (and several who were) emulated the taverner and broke and ran, jostling Dyfrig as the doyen desperately chanted. Jusson, Wyln, Chadde, Beollan and I remained in a loose circle around the player, Arlis standing behind me. Jusson hefted his sword and took a step towards the player, but Wyln shot out an arm.

"*Bei*," Wyln said, his eyes on me. "*Jos dosni*."

Stop, no closer, in the mode of elder to child. Beollan, however, either didn't know elvin or didn't care, as he did come closer. "Rosea," he said. "Ranulf's dead. There's just you. Please, let me take you home."

The demon smiled, showing even white teeth. "Rosea doesn't live here anymore, Warlord. She was evicted for failure to pay her debts."

"Another lie," we said, our voice echoing in the square.

The demon's smile widened. "I was invited in, little bunny. Would you now cast me out? Please, do try."

Yes, the sea roared, and it exploded through me to crest in a long, towering moment before crashing down. But even with the force of the wave, the demon remained standing. Still smiling, it held out its hand and a sphere began to form, white shards of ice shooting through it. However, instead of resting on the palm, the sphere engulfed it. Startled, the demon tried to shake the sphere off, but the rapidly expanding orb swelled until it swallowed the demon whole. The sphere began to spin, slowly at first, then faster and faster with the demon's arms stretching out from the force, its red hair streaming about it. Faces suddenly appeared, swirling past me before disappearing—Rodolfo, Keeve, Tyle, the slain royal guards, groomers. The demon disgorging its prey. The sphere spun faster, the arms now pressed above its head, its throat bulging out, its mouth opening impossibly wide. An outline of a hand and arm thrust out, followed by a suggestion of a head, then a body, more a disturbance in the spinning water than anything obviously corporeal.

The demon escaping.

Waiting until it was almost out, I swung the staves—the Faena's, the Church's, and mine together—a wake of bubbles trailing behind them as they sliced through the whirling sphere. They connected with a solid thump that shook my teeth, and the demon went flying. The spinning sphere immediately split in two, the first part remaining with Rosea while the second engulfed the demon, swiftly narrowing until it was a thin line. There was a flash of glittering, hating eyes, just as the line winked out, and then the sea ebbed, leaving nothing behind but glistening foam and a scattering of pearls on the portico steps.

"Gone," Beollan whispered, tears once more rolling down his face. "Both gone." Where the tears struck the portico step they sparkled. Shivering with cold and wet, I looked down. Diamonds.

Miraculously getting a spark from his wet tinderbox, Dyfrig lit the candle. He then leaned his hands on the altar, his head hanging down in weariness.

"Immersed in water yet we don't drown," Chadde said, dripping. "What *are* you?"

"What he always has been," Jusson said, his voice cracking as he pushed his wet hair back. "Mine. God help us."

"Ours," Wyln corrected, wiping seawater from his face.
He sounded his normal self, but his hands were trembling
once again. "And someone who did by himself what had
taken ten masters working in tandem to accomplish. What
did you do, Rabbit?"

"Nothing," I said, my own voice breaking. Drained, I
leaned against the staves. "It was the aspect, taking back
what was taken in the first place." I hesitated, then decided
to say nothing about metaphors and visions. I wasn't sure I
wanted to talk to myself about them, let alone with others.
Thinking about what lay on the wet ground behind me, I
closed my eyes. A tear leaked out anyway, warm against my
cold face. It remained saltwater as it splashed against the
stone step.

"Kind of left that to the last moment, Rabbit," Jeff said.

"Don't stop now," Laurel said, "we're not finished."

Just then, the cavalry arrived, with troopers and armsmen bursting into the square.

Thirty-nine

I spun around, my eyes wide, my mouth hanging open. *"Jeff?"*

I wasn't the only one gaping. Folks were jumping and shrieking and snorting all over the place—some at the sudden appearance of the garrison horsemen, but many, many more at how those who, just a moment ago, were dead or dying, were now splashing to their feet. However, Jusson proved that he was king material by quickly grasping what was happening. Hastily resheathing his sword, he ran down, with Chadde at his heels, to where Thadro and the King's Own were rising with wondering faces, with more than one aiming their gazes at me with a sort of dazed recognition.

Wyln's gaze, though, was narrowed on Laurel—there were tales of earth masters returning from the dead as something other than their normal, fun-loving selves. Something even darker than necromancers. But before Wyln could speak, he was shoved out of the way by Beollan. Shouting, "Ranulf!" the Lord of Fellmark rushed down the steps to the altar where his newly revealed nephew was also getting to his feet. Ranulf was completely human again. He was also completely naked, wearing nothing but wet beard and skin. Swinging his cloak off, Beollan wrapped it around the burly Marcher Lord, but it wasn't wide enough and gaped in the middle, framing all of the

bear lord's attributes. Neither seemed to care as they
pounded on each other's backs, Ranulf's face still gaunt, his
eyes sunk deep into his head even as he grinned like a ma-
niac.

But then, Jeff and I weren't exactly shining examples of
restraint and decorum. Giving my own shout, I leapt, slamming into Jeff, and we hung onto each other, laughing as we
teetered and swayed, Jeff's sopping uniform squelching
under my hands, the bundle of staves I held fluttering,
clacking and ringing. I felt a steadying arm and, looking up,
saw Arlis encircling us both. Heedless of soaked tabards, he
rested his forehead against my shoulder, his body shaking
hard. Wyln, though, remained where he was, his eyes still
narrowed at Laurel.

"Where were you, Faena?" Wyln asked over the tumult.

"Someplace safe," Laurel said, his wet fur dark brown,
his feathers plastered against his head. He took his staff
back from me. "Where none of us who were, hrmm, vulnerable could be reached."

Unable to ride any further in the press of the crowd,
Commander Ebner had the troopers dismount, and he and
his senior officers pushed their way to where Jusson stood
with his alive-again Lord Commander and royal guards.
Captain Suiden and the Mountain Patrol worked through
the square towards the portico steps, with the butterflies
fluttering above the captain. Apparently Queen Mab's
faeries had made it to the garrison.

"One moment I was fighting for my life against giant
spiders," Jeff said, shuddering. "The next— There was this
lady, Lord Wyln."

Wyln relaxed—somewhat. "Was there now, Corbin'son.
What did she look like?"

Jeff's brow wrinkled. "I don't know. She kept changing.
But she took me to this lake that was full of people—"

I blinked at Jeff. Maybe the vision I had of my soul hadn't been quite so metaphorical after all.

"Reminisce later," Laurel said. He jogged down the steps, the wooden beads in his ears damply clacking. "We're not done yet."

The rush that had me leaping about was fading fast, leaving my legs trembling. Arlis took my arm, but he seemed in just as much danger of imminent collapse as I was. As was Jeff. The three of us sort of leaned on each other as we followed Laurel, stupid grins on our faces. The sky was a perfect autumn blue and we were alive to see it. Wyln, though, placed himself between us and the Faena. It seemed that he hadn't relaxed that much.

"What's not done?" I asked around the enchanter.

"There is still the sorcerer," Laurel said. He pushed his way towards where Jusson and Thadro stood in a knot of royal guards, garrison officers, aristos and even some of the town elders from both sides.

I frowned. "What sorcerer?"

"The one who started all this," Laurel said. "Remember the attempt to bind you?"

Oh, that sorcerer. My frown deepening, I looked about, trying to see if anyone looked like an evil mage, but though there was plenty of laughing and crying, no one was off chortling to himself while favoring a broken wrist. Dyfrig was still at the impromptu altar, packing the implements of blessing. He met my gaze and, putting the last away, came to join us. He was hindered, though, by townsfolk who gently mobbed him, wanting blessings and prayers.

Beollan and Ranulf saw us on the move and also started our way. They had no trouble getting through—nothing blazed a trail faster than a naked man carrying a battleaxe. The crowd parted for Chadde too, though the peacekeeper was fully clothed and carried only her ceremonial truncheon. Sidetracked from Thadro, she and her watchmen had

been quietly separating out those who had aligned themselves with Helto. However, none seemed to mind being
rounded up and more than one of the town rowdies and
turncoats were sitting on the ground amid the puddles, quietly bawling. And more than one watched me go by with
the same wide-eyed stare.

However, Bram was missing, as were Helto, Gawell and
Ednoth. And Rosea had disappeared with the sea. I pushed
away the image of her, forever spinning, her red hair
streaming about her.

"What's wrong?" Chadde asked, arriving at the same
time as Dyfrig, Beollan and Ranulf.

"I don't know," Dyfrig said. He reached over and
plucked the Staff of Office from my grasp. I was once again
down to one—my own. As far as I was concerned, that was
plenty.

"They look as though they're going on a mission," Beollan said.

"As if the one we just had wasn't enough," Ranulf put in,
his scowl back on his face.

"Laurel says the sorcerer is still out there, my lords," Jeff
began. Then he and Arlis stiffened into a sort of walking attention as Suiden and the Mountain Patrol reached us. I
tried but damned near got my legs tangled up.

"Sir!" we three said in unison. The butterflies dancing
about Suiden flitted over and landed on my shoulder. And
they immediately sprung up again at discovering my tabard
was soaking wet.

"What wizard?" Suiden demanded. "The same you
talked about earlier, Sro Wyln? Why do I smell the sea? Did
this wizard raise a storm? Is that why you're all wet?" The
captain's gaze passed Dyfrig, then snapped back in shock.
"Your Reverence?" he asked, a rare look of astonishment
washing over his dark face. He then saw Ranulf and his
mouth dropped open. "What the hell have you been doing?"

Wyln's amused smile briefly flickered. "We've had a rather busy time since we last spoke, Your Highness," he said, keeping his eyes on Laurel.

"And the ones who kept things hopping are missing," Chadde said. "On your way here, Suiden, did you happen to see—" A scream rent the air and she closed her eyes, rubbing her forehead. "Never mind, I think they've been found."

There was another scream, as high-pitched as the first. All eyes turned to the small side street that led to the charnel house and everyone gave a collective sigh.

"I really want this day to end," Jusson said as he watched Laurel stride towards him. He then watched Laurel stride past him. "Master Cat?" the king asked, his brows knitting.

Laurel's ears flicked back, but he didn't slow down.

"What's this about, Captain?" Thadro asked Suiden. Ebner, standing beside Thadro, saw Ranulf and blinked, the garrison commander's mustache points rising in surprise. Captain Javes, on the other side of Ebner, merely raised his quiz glass. He then turned it on Jeff, Arlis and me, his wolf yellow eyes gleaming behind the magnifying lens.

"I don't know, sir," Suiden said. "Sro Faena said that there's a dark wizard still running loose."

"The one that started everything by attacking Rabbit, sir," Jeff added helpfully.

"Oh?" Jusson turned to Laurel, who'd halted a little ways from the alleyway. Beyond him, blazing over the rooftops, was the column of fire, but it might as well have been burning on the backside of the moon. Shivering in my wet clothes, I tried for fire and got the sickly blue flicker. Noting my efforts, Wyln tried himself, and got the same result. Despite the banishment of the demon, we were still blocked—at least in that aspect. I didn't bother with either earth or air. Nor did I try water, afraid that I'd evoke a tidal wave.

The screams echoed nearer as Jusson walked to Laurel's side. "The sorcerer that attacked Rabbit during the play?" he asked the Faena.

"His minions, honored king," Laurel replied, flexing his claws.

"Minions," Jusson repeated. "Coming down that alleyway?"

"Even as we speak."

"Good," Jusson said. "I want to meet them. Badly."

Under Thadro and Ebner's direction, royal guards and troopers moved in front, creating a barrier that was three and four bodies thick. I remained behind them, more than happy to let others be first in line. Jeff and Arlis stayed with me, as did several from the Mountain Patrol. All hell had broken loose the last time Suiden let me out of his sight and I figured that he wasn't about to do so again. Beollan and Ranulf also seemed to have had enough excitement and took up stances next to us, the space around the naked lord and his uncle widening. Wyln stayed with me too, though it seemed that was more because he was still distrustful of Laurel than because of any desire for a peaceful life. However, both Dyfrig and Chadde went to the front, the peacekeeper also deploying her watchmen, bunching them up near the street's mouth.

The screams grew louder and a moment later Gawell and Ednoth careened out of the alleyway.

Jusson sighed. "Why am I not surprised?"

Ebner's mustache points rose further. "*They're* sorcerers?" he asked, incredulous.

"Stooges, honored commander," Laurel said. "Though Gawell does have the talent in some measure."

The mayor and head merchant showed more wear and tear than when they'd left the town hall portico: Ednoth's coat was torn and his trousers were ripped at one knee, while several of the tiny jewels were missing from Gawell's

smeared and stained robe. The mayor still wore the sun-
burst medallion, though, and it bounced on his belly as he
ran. They both came to a halt as they saw us, their terror
changing to bone-melting relief, the drying blood on
Gawell's face crusty red against the pallor of his skin.

"Oh, thank God," Gawell said, blubbering. He ran to
Dyfrig, his wet and begrimed shoes slapping against the
paving stones, his gloved hands clutching at the doyen's
robes. "Thank God you're here!"

Dyfrig gently pushed Gawell away. "Why? Didn't you
declare me a false doyen?"

"We were wrong," Ednoth said, also grabbing at the
doyen. "Where's your chest of blessings? We need blessed
water. That'll stop it. Or fire. Light the holy fire, quick!"

"Stop what?" Jusson asked, mildly curious.

There was a sound of uneven footsteps approaching and
something flashed white in the shadowed alleyway opening. Then the head jailer, Menck, lurched into view.

"That," Laurel said over the gasps of the troopers and the
tired groans of everyone else.

The banishment of the demon hadn't affected whatever
animated the dead man and, recalling the faces I'd seen in
the sea, I realized Menck's hadn't been one of them. The
jailer's corpse was still naked and the ritual wounds on its
chest were frozen, glittering bright red against its fish-
belly-white skin and the thin burn lines from the wardings.
It paused for a moment, its head jerkily turning until it
found Gawell and Ednoth, and it resumed its leering lurch
towards the merchant and the mayor.

Crying out, Ednoth and Gawell did their best to dive into
the crowd, but none were in the mood to let either hide behind them, and the thin merchant bounced just as far off the
solid wall of bodies as the rotund mayor did. Both stumbled
back into the small clearing with the dead jailer staggering
towards them.

"But neither of them can be the sorcerer," I said from where I stood with Wyln and my mates. "I broke the wrist of the one that tried to bind me."

"They're stooges, Rabbit," Laurel repeated. "Remember? Tools?"

I scowled at the Faena. Even dead he'd been eavesdropping on on my conversations.

"They already have the entire valley in their pocket," Ebner said as he watched Gawell and Ednoth skitter around the clearing, the revenant on their tails. "And most of the mountain villages too. Why risk excommunication and a witch's death?"

"The same reason why anyone does, honored commander," Laurel said. "They wanted more. In their case, a kingdom was dangled before them."

"And they believed that they could have it?" Jusson asked. "How stupid. Who dangled—"

"Save us!" Gawell screamed, not caring that he interrupted the king.

"You created it, kinslayer," Laurel growled as the mayor and head merchant once again dodged the corpse. "You get rid of it."

"I *see*," Jusson said into the sudden silence.

"Menck always was an embarrassment to his cousin the mayor, sire," Chadde said, "even as the mayor found Menck's uncouth connections useful."

"It wasn't me," Ednoth said, quickly separating himself from his life-long friend. "I had nothing to do with killing Menck."

"You had everything to do with it, buyer and seller of lives," Laurel said. "You helped lure the jailer to the warehouse, you stood by as he was murdered and you directed the disposal of the body afterwards."

"Laurel suddenly knows much about events he took no part in," Wyln murmured to me, a line between his brows.

"Probably eavesdropped on them," I muttered back.

"He *chose* to dump it in their cohort's backyard?" Thadro asked, watching the corpse waver between Gawell and Ednoth. "That wasn't wise."

"Who would associate the mayor and the head merchant with the owner of a seedy tavern?" Chadde asked back.

"You did, Keeper of my Peace," Jusson pointed out.

"But no one was paying any attention to me, sire," Chadde said. "Ednoth and friends probably thought that it would be assumed that Menck fell afoul of the Pig's equally seedy patrons. Which it would have, if Master Laurel Faena hadn't been here to examine the corpse."

"The best-laid plans going sideways," Jusson remarked. "Still, we cannot allow this abomination to kill people while we watch, no matter how despicable they are."

"I don't see why not, honored king," Laurel said. "In the Border we let those who engage in the dark arts reap the consequences of their actions. As a salutary lesson."

His mustache now flat against his cheeks, Ebner muttered something about how Gawell should reap the whole blooming harvest and eat it too, while Javes, Suiden and the rest of the troopers watched bright-eyed as Menck chose to lurch after the mayor. The garrison didn't seem any more inclined to help his honor than the townspeople were.

That was left to the king. "This is not the Border," Jusson said, drawing his sword. "And however poetic it might be to let Gawell and Ednoth suffer justice from one they betrayed and murdered, heaven knows who it'll go after next. It's better to destroy it now while it's focused on one of them. Then we can focus on who has been so free and easy with my kingdom."

Thadro also drew his sword. "You heard His Majesty, people. Let's go—not you, Rabbit," he added as I began to move towards the clearing. His face briefly flickered before smoothing out. "You've done enough."

Faced with a direct command, the garrison troopers followed the Own and Thadro towards the revenant. Not to be left out, so did the aristos and their armsmen, though Beollan headed in a slightly different direction. Slipping around Menck, he went to the sobbing Gawell.

"This way, Mayor," Beollan said, taking Gawell's arm. But he immediately snatched his hand back, his silver eyes wide. "What the flaming hell is *that?*"

Gawell's pale face flushed purple, the hue clashing with the dried blood, and he backed away. "I don't know what you're talking about—"

Beollan jerked aside Gawell's once fine cloak to reveal a large, heavy-looking purse hanging from the mayor's long-suffering belt. Before Gawell could stop him, he yanked the purse off, juggled it a moment as if it were hot, then flung it away, the Marcher Lord's face twisting in disgust. The purse bounced once, twice, then burst open to scatter jewels, gold coins, and a red silk drawstring bag that slid along the paving stones to come to rest at the edge of the clearing by the alleyway mouth. I stared at the bag shimmering in the sunlight, and an itch started between my shoulder blades.

"Well, well, well," Jusson said in the returning silence. "So that's where Menck's hoard went."

"The head jailer had a hoard?" Suiden asked, looking at the twinkling loot. He frowned, the clan markings on his face suddenly standing out. "What's wrong with it?"

"It's cursed," Thadro said. Some townspeople and even a few soldiers had reached down to the gemstones and coins. At the Lord Commander's words they all snapped upright again, one trooper wiping his hand on his trouser leg. "It appears that we've discovered who put Rodolfo's body in the morgue," Thadro continued, "if not who actually killed the master player."

The itch grew stronger, snaking down my spine, and I

slipped away from Wyln, working my way through the crowd.

"Helto," Gawell wailed. "He killed Rodolfo. To feed the demon." His desperate gaze lit on Ednoth creeping towards the alley. "But it was Ednoth's idea to raise the revenant in the church."

At the abrupt focus of attention, Ednoth broke into a sprint—and was tackled by watchmen and garrison soldiers. "That's not true!" the head merchant declared as he struggled. "Gawell raised Rodolfo, just as he raised Menck—"

"No, I didn't!" Gawell said as he circled away from the still-approaching dead jailer. "Menck didn't work, not at first—" Realizing what he'd just admitted, he broke off. "I mean—"

"The wards we placed on the house of the dead held," Laurel said, "and the demon had to help you break them in order to retrieve the unfortunate jailer. The demon's price was a life—which gave you another victim to play with, one you turned loose on Elder Dyfrig."

"So you *were* trying to kill me," Dyfrig said. "As you killed Keeve and Tyle."

Gawell frantically shook his head. "No! Rodolfo wasn't supposed to hurt anyone. Just wreck the church so we could blame it on Rabbit and the magicals. The demon promised."

"The demon lied," Laurel said.

"I was tricked!" Gawell cried.

"Murderer! Kinslayer!" Dyfrig thundered. "Trafficker in hell!"

"I repent!" Gawell shrieked. "Save me!"

"No matter how despicable," Jusson sighed. "Perhaps a little fire, Lord Wyln?"

Wyln shook his head. "I'm still blocked, Iver'son," he said, holding up his palm with pale blue flame weakly burning in it. He turned to ask me—and discovered that I was no longer at his side. He started scanning the crowd, Jeff, Arlis and the Mountain Patrollers joining him.

"Blast and rot it." Jusson said. "Does anyone have any rope? Perhaps we can tie the damn thing down and let His Reverence deal with it."

Reaching the clearing edge, I steadied myself with my staff and, resting my haunches on my heels, studied the red silk bag. Finely drawn sigils of containment covered it, keeping whatever was inside, inside. I hesitated, then picked up the bag. It was warm against my skin, with a hum coming from within, more felt than heard. The itch crawling over my body, I undid the bag's drawstrings and peered in. It was a knife.

"The jailer is turning around," Thadro called out.

A familiar knife, small enough to fit into a boot sheath. Mine.

"Is it going to Ednoth?" Jusson asked. "Everyone stand away."

"No!" Ednoth cried. "I repent too!"

It was the boot knife that I'd lost in Elanwryfindyll. Here, in the mayor's purse, many leagues from the Fyrst's court. I upended the bag and it slid into my palm. The hum grew louder and my rune, quiescent for so long, twinged.

"It's not going for Ednoth," Chadde said.

But when I'd lost it, the knife had been plain with nothing remarkable about it. It now had symbols etched into the blade on both sides. Curious, the butterflies fluttering above me landed on my hand. But they took off again, frantic. There was a quick intake of breath and I glanced up to see Wyln standing over my shoulder, Jeff, Arlis and the Mountain Patrollers with him.

"Did you also know this, Faena?" Wyln hissed at Laurel.

Laurel turned his head to look over his shoulder at us, then down at what I held. The rest of him quickly turned and he strode over to where I crouched down, his pupils expanding as he stared at the knife. "No," he rumbled. "The Lady told me about the mayor's treason, sorcery and murders when She escorted me to the lake, but She said nothing about *this*—"

"Rabbit!" Ranulf shouted. "The revenant is going for Rabbit!"

Laurel, Wyln and I all looked up to see Menck slowly lurching towards us. Gawell stumbled to a halt and bent as far as he could, gasping for air. "See?" he wheezed, forever quick to foist blame elsewhere. "I *told* you he was a witch—"

"Gawell," the townspeople said. "Shut up."

A couple of troopers appeared carrying coils of rope from their saddles and two of the Own ran up with the doyen's chest of blessings. As Dyfrig knelt at the chest and opened it, lassos flew out. The loops dropped over Menck's head and the troopers hauled back, but the rope around its neck had no effect and the dead jailer still pressed forward, dragging them with it. More troopers and guards joined the two holding the lassos, while others showed up with additional rope, darting in to quickly circle it around the revenant's waist and legs.

"What have you there, cousin?" Jusson asked, he and Thadro joining me.

"It's my knife," I said. "My bloody boot knife." I picked out the symbols for earth and water on one side of the blade, flipping it over to see fire and air on the other. "What the sodding hell did they do to it?"

Wyln turned ancient, rage-filled eyes on Gawell. "Talent thief," the enchanter breathed. "Dream robber. Stealer of life."

Everyone once more went still—except for Menck. Although wrapped from head to toe in rope, Menck's corpse took a dragging step. Townsfolk joined the Own and troopers, adding their strength to those pulling back on the ropes.

"*What?*" Jusson asked.

Laurel flicked a claw at the knife. "It's sympathetic enchantment, honored king, where personal effects like hair or nail clippings, or an object worn close to the body, like a ring, is used to create a gateway to all that person is, even to their very soul."

"I had this knife from when I started in the army until I lost it at the Fyrst's court," I said.

"They must've used it to kill the unfortunate jailer and summon the demon," Laurel said. "Which is probably why the revenant followed Gawell and is trying to come at you."

"All of them feeding on Rabbit's talent," Wyln said, full of rage. "On him! No wonder he has been wasting away—"

"Majesty!" one of the Own cried out.

Jusson and Thadro turned, shifting in time for me to see Menck shove through the crowed that surrounded it. More guards, troopers and townspeople jumped on the revenant, but they were easily flung off. The dead jailer rapidly lurched towards us trailing rope.

"Damn," Thadro said. He moved in front of Jusson and tried to thrust his sword through Menck, but it rebounded off the dead man's frozen belly. Before he could recover, the revenant grabbed and threw him into Suiden and others rushing towards it. They all went down under the Lord Commander's weight. Jusson spun out of its path, bringing his sword against the dead jailer's neck. However, that was just as frozen as the rest of the corpse, and the sword rebounded. With a shove, Menck sent Jusson flying into Laurel, and they both fell, taking Wyln with them. Now moving so fast it was almost a blur, it swung its arm like a club, knocking Arlis and Jeff into Javes, Beollan and Ranulf, all of them going down with a clatter of swords, battleaxe and armor. Then the revenant was on me. I'd risen, bringing my staff around, but it was snatched away and the revenant encircled my throat with its icy hand, its leer filling my vision.

Except it wasn't a leer any longer. The smile on the dead man's face had smoothed out, stretching from ear to ear in a too-wide grin, its eyes flashing a bright green in the sunlight.

The demon had returned.

Roaring filled my ears, but it wasn't the sea. It was my own life being squeezed out of me. Clawing at the fingers clamped around my throat with one hand, I stabbed at the demon-possessed revenant with the only weapon I had at hand—my boot knife—all the while dimly despairing that it would have no effect on a dead man able to disregard swords. But the small dagger slid into the frozen flesh as if it were butter—and the humming abruptly expanded, resonating both through me and the corpse. The demon and I stared at each other, its green eyes widening, its face contorting, its mouth gaping open in what looked like a silent scream of agony. As the demon's hand spasmed away from my neck, behind it I could see Ranulf stand and rush towards us, his arm muscles contracting as he swung his battleaxe, the axe blade describing a silver arc in the sun.

Then there was a blinding flash and I found myself looking into a familiar room. One I'd seen in my dreams: the council chamber. However, this time, instead of being inside, I was at a window, looking in. Or maybe not a window. Pressing my forehead against the glass, I could just see the edges of a gilt frame. It was the cloudy mirror that hung on the wall.

Catching movement, I looked back into the room to see four people standing at the table with the alabaster half globe. They were all wearing dark, hooded robes that left their faces shadowed, but though I couldn't see their expressions, their body stances showed worry as they stared down at the half globe. Instead of the steady, constant light of before, the globe's glow was erratic, dimming down to almost nothing, then flaring bright, then dimming again.

Cracks zigzagged through the alabaster, spreading with each pulse.

"Kan!"

Blinking, I looked away from the globe to see one of the robed figures pointing at me. I frowned. His voice sounded familiar, as was the curve of his face just visible in the shadow of his hood. The others spun around, one reaching for what looked like a carved bone lying on the table. As he did, his sleeve fell back—and my eyes fastened on the splint and bandage on his wrist.

The effing sorcerer who started it all.

A low rumble filling my chest, I shoved against the glass, feeling it give. The sorcerer lifted the carved bone and aimed it at me. But the light contracted one more time, then the half globe exploded, sending alabaster shards flying. Everything seemed to slow. Those standing around the table were bowled over, their hoods falling back to reveal a blur of features—the bloated pudginess of the sorcerer, the gray hair of a woman, the firm, rounded chin of a younger woman, the twisting scar down the side of the familiar man's face. Then he lifted his head and I saw blue eyes, as mild and inoffensive as the spring sky. Slevoic ibn Dru.

"Vicious!" I howled, shoving harder at the looking glass, but just then the explosion hit me, lifting me off my feet and flinging me back, the hum in my body growing in strength until I felt as though I was being shaken apart. I tried to scream, but I couldn't get enough breath.

"Rabbit!"

My eyes flew open to see Menck's face. It was some distance away where its head had rolled near the the alleyway mouth. I lay across the rest of the dead man's body and I could feel a spreading wetness as if it were finally thawing. I tried to spring up, but fell over and sprawled on my back, holding one hand to my bruised throat as I gasped painful breaths. Folks crowded around, including Ranulf, the

Marcher Lord leaning on his battleaxe. But he and most of the rest were turned away, their gazes raised over the rooftops to the mountains. A paw batted my face and I looked up to see Laurel bending over me, his mouth moving. I couldn't hear, though, as roaring still filled my ears. But it wasn't the aftereffects of being strangled. It was the wind. It sounded like a massive rock slide—a rumbling, grinding, furious torrent growing louder as it rushed towards us. It burst over the square, blowing most about like dolls while pulling others into its fury. Dyfrig hung in midair, half wind half man, the Staff of Office clenched in one hand as he fought against being consumed. The wind swirled into a funnel and slammed into my body, its hurricane howl raging through me.

There was another rumbling, this one underground. Hands pressed down on my shoulders. Wyln. "Contain it, Rabbit," he shouted.

Contain what? I tried to say, but I only managed a croak. The rumbling increased and the ground began to shake, making the still-scattered coins and jewels dance. A moment later fire erupted out of the cracks of the paving stones, shooting up over buildings, sheets spreading across the sky, flaming tongues spearing those with the talent. Albe the blacksmith, Kresyl the baker, Wyln, Jusson, others were engulfed. I could just see Jusson amid the fire, holding his sword in a two-handed grip before him, his head bowed.

"Ah, effing hell!" Jeff shouted over sudden screams. The column of fire that had been burning over the charnel house floated out of the side street. Those that had been holding Ednoth captive scattered, fleeing before it as it passed over the coins and jewels to where to I lay. The world went yellow and white as it poured into me.

The roar of the fire died down and in its place arose the quietude of forests. But not the half-tamed Weald of my childhood. This was the quiet of a forest of ancient trees, secret glens and hidden grottos sheltering sacred pools. A wild and holy place.

"Dear God," Arlis whispered, blessing himself. "Cover us and keep us safe."

An enormous white stag stepped into the square, his rack of antlers spread wide and high. He walked to where I lay on the ground, the butterflies alighting on his horns, Laurel bowing low in reverence before him. The Stag lowered his head and breathed into my face. Looking into eyes the color of the night sky tinged with moonlight, I drew in the earth—birthing, living, growing, dying. He then lifted his head and bounded away with a clatter of hooves.

There was another moment of stillness before a bellow rent the cathedral quiet. A dragon, obsidian with gold-shot wings, rose in the heat created by the still-burning buildings. Suiden. But another bellow sounded and a second dragon sprang into the air, this one with silver eyes. It banked, its white scales shimmering purple in the sunlight. They soared around each other, spiraling higher and higher in the blue sky.

"Beollan!" shouted Ranulf. But his shout turned into a bear's roar, which was then drowned out by other animal cries. A hawk glided overhead, lower than the dragons, but still circling up as he too rode the heat, his wings outspread. Griffins, one with blue-gray eyes, spread their own feathered wings, but remained on the ground, surrounding the torch that was the king. Chadde strode by, her ceremonial truncheon in one hand, balance scales outlined in light held in the other, a gray wolf with yellow eyes pacing by her side. The peacekeeper tackled Gawell, who was doing his best to steal away, while Captain Javes took off running and, with a skittering of claws, leapt, landing on the back of the fleeing Ednoth.

And the bear, it—*he* was on his hind legs, his eyes wide,

the red light in them fading, the barbed wire that had been wrapped so tightly around him coiling away, faster and faster, following the Stag, as if the Lady's Consort had snagged a loose end on an antler point. Ranulf sat down with a plop, studying his paws as if he'd never seen them before.

Laurel stood in the middle of the pandemonium, his face lifted in worship, his own paw raised with the truth rune blazing in white light. He then lowered his head and looked down at me with wild eyes, his whiskers swept back in a smile that showed an awful lot of fang. "The Lady is calling out, and the human kingdom has answered, fiat!"

"Uh, yes," I rasped as Jeff, well, scampered up to me, the blaze on the badger's forehead white against the black of his fur. I struggled to sit up—and away from the ice melt from Menck's rapidly thawing body. "So are air and fire too. Calling out." I heard the murmur of waves lapping against a sandy shore. "And then there's water."

Some of his wildness eased as Laurel's gaze turned speculative. "So there is." He reached down and helped me to my feet, handing me my staff. "Which I don't see here."

"It had already—reestablished itself," I said. There was a high, piercing cry and the hawk swooped down. I staggered under its weight as it landed on my shoulder, its talons clutching hard (I was very glad for my chainmail). Placing a black paw on my knee for balance, Jeff sat up on his haunches, trying to see beyond the forest of shins and knees.

"And thank the Lady for that," Wyln said. "We do not need another aspect rampaging through the town." His body was flame-free—apparently centuries of practice helped him to subdue the aspect flooding back into him. At least on the outside. His eyes were no longer dark and blind, but were like lightning strikes on dry tinder, and he gave a gentle smile that was every bit as scary as Laurel's feral one.

"This has been exhilarating, Faena, but it's time to call a halt, before those drunk on their power set the entire valley aflame. Or blow it down. Or trample it. I think I can control fire."

"You're right," Laurel said, with a small sigh of regret. "I'll take earth." He raised his staff. "Rabbit, if you'd take air—"

I lifted my hand and Dyfrig reformed out of the whirlwind to drop lightly to his feet, the bells on his Church staff jingling. At the same time the burning buildings flickered and then went out, as did the flames wrapping those in the fire aspect. Jusson swayed, his eyes damn near crossing. And all those translated once more stood as their human selves, Arlis fortunately leaping up from my shoulder before changing back. That is, all changed except for Suiden and Beollan. The two dragons perched on either side of the town square, Suiden on the church while Beollan alit on the town hall roof. The Marcher Lord spread his wings to the sun, causing them to flash green, then a delicate pink.

Wyln and Laurel looked around the suddenly normal—well, more normal—town square, and Laurel slowly lowered his staff. The Faena then gently took my hand that had held my boot knife. "Let us see," he asked and I opened it. And blinked. Etched into my palm were the symbols for the aspects—fire and air on one side of the rune, and earth and water on the other side.

Wyln let out a breath. "The tool they thought they made has become a weapon against them."

"Them? Who's them?" Jusson asked, his voice a bit slurred, his battle crown slightly askew. He started to move to where we stood, but stumbled over Menck, Thadro catching him before he fell. The dead jailer's headless body finally looked like a three-day-old corpse—its wounds oozing and a ripe, sweetish stink starting to rise from it. Imbedded in the corpse's chest was my boot knife, in the same place as the death wound. Holding my breath, I bent down and pulled the small dagger out.

"What the pox-rotted hell happened?" Jusson asked.

"What was stolen was returned," Laurel said. He ran a paw over his dry head fur as he stared at the dead jailer. "The sorcerer was only a thief, using Rabbit's own talent not only in his dark arts, but to attack Rabbit as well, even in his dreams." He sighed. "As Wyln said, it's no wonder that Rabbit was wasting away before our eyes."

"No," I corrected Laurel. Seeing nothing to wipe my knife with, I held it with a two-fingered grasp. "It *was* a powerful sorcerer. Or, rather, it was four working together." My mouth twisted. "And Slevoic was one of them."

Suiden glided down from the church roof, the dragon landing noiselessly on the ground. The next moment the man was striding to where I stood, his green eyes ablaze. But then, so were other eyes much closer to me, including the king's. Beollan, though, remained where and as he was, turning his great dragon head to look over his shoulder.

Jusson grabbed my arm, pulling me to face him. "Slevoic's not dead?"

"No, sire," I said as Suiden pushed through the knot of people to me. "He's very much alive—" I stopped, instinctively ducking as Beollan dived off the town hall, swooping low over us.

"Damn and blast!" Jusson said, also ducking. "What the bloody hell is he doing?"

"Sire," Thadro said, pointing at the alleyway mouth, and we all turned to see Rosea emerging. The player was still wearing the green gown and her feet were still bare. However, her hair, free of pearl ropes and elaborate coifs, had returned to its original fiery brilliance and her complexion was once more a flawless peaches-and-cream. Or maybe not so flawless. As Rosea stepped out of the shadow of the alley, the sun highlighted the freckles scattered across her nose and a smudge across her cheek. Her hair hung snarled and tangled, and peeping out from her gown's somewhat tattered hem were her dirty toes, curling away from the cold ground.

Rosea gave us a tentative smile, twisting her fingers together. "I know it sounds silly, but there was this lady riding an enormous white deer. She told me that someone was waiting here for me—" The player broke off as she caught sight of Ranulf and Beollan pushing their way to her, their faces full of stunned hope. Her eyes widened and her gentle pink lips parted, showing that one of her front teeth was a little crooked. "Dearest brother," she asked, astonished, "what on earth have you done with your clothes?"

Forty

We burned Menck's body right where it lay, not bothering with wood or rags soaked in oil. No one wanted to wait long enough to get them. But then, fuel wasn't needed. For the first time I saw Wyln gesture as he summoned fire—a small movement of a forefinger—and Menck went up in flames so intense that we had to shield our faces from the heat and light. There were no complaints though, and even Dyfrig looked grimly satisfied when the fire died and only ashes remained. They were placed into an earthen jar, with Dyfrig pouring salt on top of them and Jusson sealing the jar lid shut with the royal seal. Then the doyen sprinkled more salt over where the body had been burned, just in case any trace of the dead jailer remained. Only then did everyone watching sigh in relief.

"I will do purification rites here, in the charnel house, at the warehouse and wherever else needed," Dyfrig said, casting a tired glance at the battered church facade. He then turned to the town hall, where the retrieval of the bodies of the groomers and guards was being overseen by Thadro and Commander Ebner. Unlike those killed in the square, they had not risen—probably because they'd been taken by the demon. Fighting a vague sense of failure, I turned away, only to have my gaze fall on Gawell and Ednoth, sitting on the ground with their hands tied behind their backs. They

were surrounded by a company of soldiers, Own, watchmen, armsmen and townsfolk. All looking as if they hoped
the felonious duo would make an escape attempt.

Rosea was standing between Beollan and Ranulf, her
eyes on the jar that held Menck's ashes. She glanced up
once at the bodies lined up on the paving stones, then down
again, her tangled hair falling forward to shield her face.

"Are we going to burn those poor boys too?" Dyfrig
asked, his voice breaking.

Jusson looked at Laurel. "Must we, Master Cat?"

Having cleaned my boot knife on Gawell's cloak, Laurel
and Wyln had been closely examining the blade, muttering
at each other. At Jusson's question, the Faena raised his
head to look at the row of bodies; Captain Javes had joined
Ebner and Thadro and was now helping lay shrouds over
them. Javes' face was bleak, and I realized that the captain,
having come from the Royal City, would've known most if
not all of the dead. "It would be wise, honored king," Laurel said.

"All right." Jusson sighed. "But not like refuse in a
garbage dump. They shall have a proper funeral with full
rites."

There was some discussion about putting the cursed jewels and coins into the jar with Menck's ashes and burying it
all. But Jusson, exercising his royal prerogative, nixed it,
stating that while we could be reasonably assured of the
dead jailer's ashes remaining undisturbed, the same could
not be said about his ill-fated loot. "Tales abound of idiots
who, despite every warning given, take what they shouldn't
and bring destruction down on themselves and everyone
around them," he said, glaring at the hoard still scattered on
the ground. He transferred his glare to Gawell and Ednoth.
"Like these two."

"Aye, Your Majesty," agreed one of the townspeople.
"And there's no problem burying Menck, for he passed

through the fire. Nothing left but ashes, see? But do we want to put yon noisome plunder in the ground where it can leach into the soil and God knows what else?"

We decided we didn't. A stout wooden box was found and the gold and gemstones were swept up and shoveled into it. Again Dyfrig was ready with the salt, adding a little holy water besides. As he did, steam rose up from the dully gleaming hoard with a faint hiss.

"Right," Jusson said. "What the pox-rotted hell am I suppose to do with that?"

"As water cursed them, sire, give them back to water," I said absently. "Throw them in the Banson and let it carry them to the Southern Sea." There was silence. I looked up to see folks staring at me. "Uh—"

"That's actually not a bad idea," Laurel said.

"Right," Jusson said again.

The jar of ashes and the box of cursed treasure were loaded on a cart and taken back to the king's residence. The bodies of the guards and groomers were also loaded on carts. The funeral cortege wound its way through the streets, and though many folks split off and headed home along the way, there was still a sizable crowd that remained as we reached the king's residence. Jusson didn't stop any from coming—officials, elders and regular townspeople, aristos and their armsmen, garrison officers and troopers—they all trudged with the king up the front steps, everyone's shoulders sagging with weariness, even Jusson's. Even Wyln's. The only one who seemed the same as always was Chadde. She'd winnowed out those who'd joined Helto under duress from the taverner's rowdies and henchmen, sending the latter to the town jail with an escort of watchmen. Though, by their demeanor, the peacekeeper could've just handed them the jail keys and be confident that they'd go—and lock the cell door behind them when they got there.

However, Gawell and Ednoth were kept close at hand. Still surrounded by a mishmash of guards, the head merchant and mayor were marched up the steps, the chain of office bobbing on Gawell's stomach as he climbed.

Cais' wonderfully impassive face was a welcome sight as he opened the door and bowed us in. We didn't get to savor it, though, as Jusson swept us to a familiar place—his study. At Thadro's direction, Gawell and Ednoth were taken elsewhere by their enthusiastic crowd of Own and soldiers, led by Captain Javes and Chadde, but the rest of us crammed inside, including Beollan, Rosea and Ranulf, the Lord of Bainswyr still naked under his borrowed cloak. Cais appeared a few moments later, leading the king's servants pushing tea carts and the bear lord's servant carrying clothes.

Jusson went behind his desk, sighing as he dropped into his chair, while Thadro moved to his usual place behind the king. The afternoon light slanting in from the windows showed shadows under both of their eyes. "How is Gwynedd?" Jusson asked Cais.

"She came to, Your Majesty," Cais said. "Just after the wind started howling and all the fires in the hearths shot up the chimneys. However, her mind is like a little child's."

"I see," Jusson said, his gaze resting on Rosea, seated between her uncle and her newly dressed brother. Both Beollan and Ranulf stared back, half anxious, half defiant. Rosea, though, kept her eyes on her hands, in her lap.

"Chadde told me that she sent watchmen to gather the rest of the players, Majesty," Thadro said. "If they haven't already fled."

Jusson nodded, then, settling back, thrust his feet out and folded his hands over his stomach. "So, cousin. Tell me about Slevoic."

I'd been watching with resignation as Laurel dumped some of his never-ending supply of vile tea in a teapot, but at the king's demand, I launched into the happenings in the council room. When I got to the banner that hung on one wall, though, Suiden stopped me, his dark face grim.

"We won't be able to get to Slevoic or the rest anytime soon, Your Majesty," he said. "He's in Ryadnii, a principality of the Turalian Empire."

"The Amir is involved in this?" Jusson asked, his eyes narrowing in thought.

"Not necessarily," Suiden said. "Ryadnii was a country long before it was joined to the Empire, and the current satrap is a descendant of the suzerains that ruled when it was independent. The Amir could very well be ignorant of what's happening there. In fact, since Ryadnii's liege states are almost autonomous as far as local affairs are concerned, the satrap herself could also have no knowledge. Or so she and the Amir could both plausibly argue."

"This is the second time that Tural's shadow has fallen across a plot against us," Thadro put in. "I have a hard time believing that the Amir doesn't know about either."

"It does boggle the mind," Jusson said, still thoughtful. "The Empire's involvement will be a question for the new Turalian ambassador, when one is appointed."

"Do you think he will tell you, Your Majesty?" I asked.

"Nonanswers can be just as illuminating as direct ones," Jusson said. "It will be very interesting to see how the ambassador responds."

"But Slevoic," Commander Ebner said, entering the conversation. "If he is conspiring in Ryadnii, so far away, how did he communicate with Gawell and Ednoth?"

"Another question," Jusson said. "Perhaps something our royal questioners can discover from Gawell and Ednoth—"

"There's a mirror in Gawell's home, Your Majesty," Rosea said. Her gaze was still on her twisting fingers in her lap, but she glanced up briefly, a flash of moss green behind a tangle of red hair. "In his library, covered with a cloth. The mirror is cloudy but when Gawell worked a spell, it would clear and we could see and talk to the people on the other side. And after the—after I was filled, I could travel through the mirror."

"Illusion and the mirror image," Wyln said. "The mayor must have the water aspect too."

"Along with my knife," I said. Having retrieved my boot dagger from Laurel, I held it in my hand. I didn't have a sheath to place it in and I was unwilling to set it down. "Does he have my sword too?"

"No, my lord," Rosea whispered. "It was taken through the mirror to the others." There was another flash of green, this time at me. "Even with the knife and the globe we weren't able to breach your wards, not completely. You were still able to withstand us, and the water aspect was strangely resistent to our working."

"Globe?" Jusson asked, and I described the glowing alabaster half sphere, and how it had cracked, then shattered.

"An *amplifien*," Laurel rumbled, walking to where I sat and handing me a full teacup. "Used to augment the power of their working. It helped you to enter his dreams, no? Dreams you were able to access because of the knife. But Rabbit regaining the knife must have created a backlash that destroyed the globe."

Wyln stirred in his seat, murmuring something that sounded suspiciously like "Good."

"We thought the knife would be enough at first," Rosea said, "since we used it to kill Menck and raise the demon, binding both the demon and Mencke's death to Lord Rabbit through it. It wasn't, though, so we used the globe. Even that wasn't enough, so we bespelled the crossbow bolts used in the ambush to give us access to you." Rosea's eyes flashed to me again. "You are very strong, my lord."

"So I heard," I said. A thought occurred to me. "But how

was the sorcerer able to attempt to bind me in the first place? If he's in Ryandii, there's no way he could do line of sight."

"We used Gawell's mirror," Rosea said. "It was on the stage, next to Lady Alys' daybed, already spelled so they could see clearly. As it would've been each performance until you came by. We were fortunate that you appeared in the audience so quickly."

"Very fortunate," Wyln said, his voice lilting, his eyes ablaze. "With a sorcerous object placed out in the open and not only a Faena and enchanter in town, but also faeries and a king who has a feel for the talent."

"Yes, my lord," Rosea whispered. "But they wanted Lord Rabbit so badly that they were willing to take the risk. Especially Slevoic." I received another flash of moss green eyes. "He is jealous of you, my lord. He wants what you have, all of your talent, all of everything. The others wouldn't let him bind you, though he desperately wanted to. They said that it was because he wasn't strong enough to hold you—which is true. But it was also because they were afraid that he wouldn't share."

I nodded tiredly; after three years of dodging the Vicious' attentions in the garrison, his "wants" weren't a great surprise. "Who is he?" I asked. "The sorcerer who did try to bind me? Slevoic called him Kan."

"That's an honorific," Suiden said. "It means 'lord' or 'master.' "

"Kan Sikas," Rosea said. "He was very careful not to let me know his family name. The others were also careful. Nor did they let me see their faces—including Slevoic." She took a deep, shuddering breath, and let it out. "Is my life forfeit?"

"Sire," Beollan began, protesting.

"Majesty," Ranulf said at the same time.

Jusson raised his hand and they fell silent. "You tell me,

Lady Rosea," the king said. "Sorcery, necromancy, treason, rebellion, murder. Not to mention the just-confessed assaults upon my heir. What do you think?"

Rosea's head bowed, her knuckles white as her hands knotted together in her lap.

"Mercy, Majesty," Ranulf said. "My sister is mad."

"Oh?" Jusson's brow rose. "She seems remarkably coherent to me."

"Not all who are mad babble to themselves or howl at the moon, Your Majesty," Beollan said. "Rosea's insanity is more subtle than that. Her world has became narrower and narrower, turning in on itself until it contains nothing and no one but herself."

I'd half expected Jusson to make some quip about most folks' worlds being like that, but he went quiet. "That would be very subtle," the king finally said. "I would imagine that it would also be very frightening."

"Yes, sire," Ranulf said. "It was. We didn't know who she'd harm, or why, or how. Our old nurse—" He broke off for a moment, his mouth tight. "This is something that came upon our family from the Border war. The males of our House were cursed as you saw me, turning into ravening, unreasoning beasts at each full moon—

"It's not full now," an aristo remarked, looking nervous. "Yet you changed."

"The demon called forth the bear, despite the Consort not being in phase," Laurel said. He cast a significant glance at my teacup and, sighing, I drained it, shuddering at the lukewarm bitterness. But he only poured me more. "It is an ability of earth, to cause translations, and the demon had taken someone with that aspect," Laurel added.

"If you say so," Ranulf said. "Usually we're able to achieve some sort of control, if only by counting the days and making sure we're locked up on certain nights."

"Your father controlled it very successfully," Jusson said. "I'd no idea he struggled with this."

"He was very adept at counting, sire," Ranulf said. "But our women don't change. Instead, they descend into madness, some screaming, others fading and still others with pieces missing, like Rosea, whom we had to confine. A little over a year ago, though, she escaped and we were unable to find her. Then we received word she was traveling with this acting troupe and we managed to track them here."

"So your arrival in Freston had nothing to do with wanting to reconcile with your king?" Jusson asked, his voice mild.

Ranulf rubbed his beard. "I—" he began, then stopped. When Jusson just waited, he sighed while Beollan closed his silver eyes. "You knew, Your Majesty?"

"That you were involved in Flavan's plots and schemes?" Jusson shrugged. "Of course. Consider who Teram surrounded himself with. As soon as the rebellion failed, they all came running to me, spilling every secret they ever had."

"My father was ailing, Your Majesty," Ranulf said tiredly, "my sister had been missing for several months by then and it seemed that I was getting worse. I was angry— at just about everything. But especially the Border. I was very angry at the Border. And there were Flavan and Dru, whispering about your Border cousin and how you planned to turn us over to the magicals."

"So we did meet at Teram's nightmare masque," I said.

"I didn't know what he planned," Ranulf said.

"How convenient," I said.

"Truth, Rabbit," Ranulf said. "On my House, I swear it. I didn't know until after you came back inside and told about the attack in the garden on you and Lord Esclaur. I argued with Teram and Gherat later. How could we claim honor when we act dishonorably? To invite a man—a kins-man—to your home and then try to kill him on the sly—"

"There's a lot of that going around," Jusson remarked.

"I broke with them right then," Ranulf said. "And at first light the next morning I was on the road home."

"Missing the rebellion?" I asked. "Also convenient."

"I was very angry," Ranulf repeated.

"And you're not now?" Jusson asked, his voice still mild.

Ranulf's face changed, his deep-set brown eyes filling with a bright light. "Oh, no, sire. Not only did I get my sister back, I got *me* back. And my children. And my children's children. The curse is gone, lifted off of me and mine. I could feel its going. It is a miracle."

"Ah, yes," Jusson said. "Miracles. Like everyone dying, then coming back to life. What *did* happen?"

"We went someplace safe, sire," Thadro said. Others in the room began nodding.

"Yes," a southern aristo said. "You see, sire, this lady took us to this lake and there was ibn Chause—"

"Except it wasn't really him," a northern lord broke in. "The *real* Lord Rabbit was standing outside the lake, look-ing in."

"Out of uniform, sire," Thadro said. "But we'd seen him wear that once before."

"Had you?" still another aristo butted in. "It was a hodgepodge of clothes, whatever it was. He also had the Faena cat's, the doyen's, and his staff all bundled together."

"Yeah," Ranulf said. "He stood at the edge of the lake and crashed the staves down into the water—"

"Freeing us—" a townsman piped up.

Jusson remained silent as he listened to everyone inter-rupt each other as they described what it was like to flow up out of the lake and into the sea, before crashing down in the wave that sent them back into their bodies.

"I could see me lying there," Alderman Geram said, "the

blood soaking my clothes from my death wound." He touched a rent in his shirt, the fabric around it still tinged a faint red. "Then, next I knew, I was sitting up and looking around, my wound gone. Lord Bainswyr is right, Your Majesty. It was a miracle."

"Was it?" Jusson asked, turning his head to look at Dyfrig, sitting on the other side of Laurel. "Was it truly, Your Reverence?"

"I don't know, Your Majesty," Dyfrig said, the troubled expression back on his face. "There are so many things that I don't know, things that I was once so sure of."

"I think I died," Rosea whispered. "I was in the charnel house, lying on one of the slabs when the Lady and the White Stag woke me—" She raised her head from her contemplation of her hands, a puzzled expression on her face. "Though how they fit inside such a small space, and then walking with me out the door without the Lady dismounting . . ."

"Magic has returned to Iversterre," Thadro said. "With a vengeance."

"It had never left," Jusson said back. "It just went underground." He turned his head to Beollan. "Like you, Fellmark. If I remember correctly, the last marriage between your House and Ranulf's was just before the last conflict with the Border, when a daughter of Fellmark wed the heir of Bainswyr. You three should be rather distant cousins. Yet Rosea called you 'Uncle.' "

"Dragons do live a long time, honored king," Laurel put in.

A faint smile passed over Beollan's thin face. "Do they? Well, it must be true as it was my sister who married Dougan the Younger of Bainswyr." His smile faded. "And it was I who brought Dougie's body home to my sister after our defeat in the Border war—only to see the devastation wrought on those who remained behind. Those who were innocent." He rubbed his mouth, his silver eyes distant. "My sister was the first to go mad, her insanity a creeping, deepening darkness that drained all light until she was nothing but shadow. At the end she killed herself."

There was a shifting about as folks made surreptitious warding signs at Beollan's sister's suicide.

"I fortunately did not have a wife or children at the time," Beollan said, "so I was spared at least the horror of seeing my own succumb. But I also dared not marry, not knowing what would happen to my spouse or what we'd birth."

"I know," murmured a pale-haired, fair-skinned northern lord. "Dear God, how I know that one. The head of our House also refused to marry—only to have what he sought to avoid show up in the collateral line. Mine."

"So I've seen and so I've heard," Beollan said. "However, it didn't matter that I didn't produce an heir as I did not age—which meant that I was able to watch the sufferings of the House of Bainswyr increase, watch each attempt to break the curse fail." He turned to Wyln, his eyes overlarge in his thin face. "I remember you, elf. From the war. And how you smiled as you directed flaming bolts down on what remained of my men—after the Faena and their damned rune were finished with them."

"I remember you too, Beollan Wulfgar'son," Wyln said. "As I remember many of the Houses here, not only from that battle, but from previous ones as well. Perhaps one day I'll tell you about the first battle between fae and human— and what kind of mercy Iver Bloody-Hand showed my wife, children, and all the other women and children taking refuge in the palace seraglio."

In the silence I could hear the fireplace flames. They had regained their voice, but instead of the usual merry crackle, they were soft and subdued.

"A discussion for another time," Jusson said tiredly into

the quiet. "Right now we have another issue at hand." He settled back again in his chair, turning his head to the former player. "I asked you a question, Lady Rosea. Notwithstanding your kinsmen's claims of madness, I think you can distinguish right from wrong, if only as an academic exercise. Yet you have contravened the laws of both the kingdom and the Church on sorcery. You have attacked my cousin and heir. You have conspired with the enemies of my throne. And even with the miracles of curses lifting and folks coming back to life, there are those who are still dead—Menck, Keeve and Tyle, Rodolfo, my groomers and guardsmen slain in the town hall, to feed a demon you willingly invited in. Why should I spare you?"

"There is no reason, Majesty," Rosea whispered.

"No," Jusson agreed. "There is not."

"Mercy, sire," Ranulf pleaded. "Please."

"Mercy," Jusson repeated. He looked at me. "What do you say, cousin? Most of the harm done by and through Rosea was aimed at you. Should there be mercy?"

I jumped, startled at Jusson seeking my opinion. Despite the new uniform, as far as I was concerned I was still just a farm boy turned horse soldier. Besides, except for Slevoic, everything that had been aimed at me was not because of who I was, but because of who claimed me as kin—King Jusson of Iversterre. Even Rosea's seduction assault had been impersonal, like she'd been reading lines from a play. The former player was back to watching her fingers twist in her lap. Beollan and Ranulf were looking at me—and though the Lord of Bainswyr had claimed innocence, I remembered the brooding malevolence of my cousin Teram's poisonous masque where I had to fight against five assassins while Lord Esclaur lay crumpled in a heap behind me. I also remembered Ranulf's hostility when we met again here in Freston, and his attempts to drive a wedge between me and Jusson, between me and the Church, between me and my home.

However, in the middle of my remembering, I became aware of the susurration of the sea—and other images arose: of Ranulf wrapped tightly in the caltrops-strung wire, the spikes digging deep into his flesh. Of the lines of pain that scored his face and the agony of his translation. And how he looked when his House's curse had been lifted. How he looked now with his eyes full of light, even as he fought not to show worry.

And a different thought crossed my mind on the nature of second chances in all their guises. I also thought that my water aspect was going to be more trouble than my truth rune.

I let out a hard sigh. "Have Rosea go through purification and then have Dyfrig and Laurel examine her. If His Reverence finds no part of hell, she can go home. And if Laurel finds no madness, she can go home without chains."

Everyone stirred: Suiden turning to me in surprise, Thadro and Dyfrig blinking, and Laurel's ears shifting back, his beads softly clacking. Wyln, though, remained as he was.

"The judge," Wyln began.

"I know," Jusson interrupted. "Another characteristic of some poxy aspect." He eyed me. "Are you going to do that from now on? Pop out profoundly simple solutions to complex problems without any warning?"

"I—" I broke off, just stopping myself from shrugging, feeling color flood my face. "It just occurred to me, sire."

"And more reasoned than much of the advice I've received during the course of my rule," Jusson said. He waved a hand. "Yes, well. What my cousin said, I so decree."

Ranulf gave a shout of gladness while a tear rolled down Beollan's cheek to fall on his hands, folded in his lap, where it sparkled. Apparently grief wasn't the only way to get diamonds from a dragon. "Thank you, sire," Beollan said softly. "Thank you."

"You're welcome," Jusson said, his black eyes with their gold ring reflecting the fireplace's fire. Or, considering all the revelations of today, maybe it wasn't a reflection. "Now," the king asked, "does anyone want to intercede for Gawell and Ednoth?"

Laughter exploded, dark and rough. Or maybe it was a growl. There were plenty of bared teeth. Including my own.

"I'll take that as a no." Without going through Thadro, Jusson spoke to the guards standing on either side of the open doorway. "Bring them in."

One of the guards hurried off and a few moments later returned with Peacekeeper Chadde and Captain Javes, followed by the same mob of guards escorting Gawell and Ednoth. The mayor and head merchant were shoved in front of Jusson. Javes and Chadde must've prevented folks from pounding on them for they pretty much looked as they did previously—no new scrapes or bruises anywhere. However, Gawell was no longer wearing the chain of office; it instead hung from Chadde's hand. With a small bow, the peacekeeper set it on Jusson's desk.

"It's not cursed, Your Majesty," Chadde said, her face its usual calm. "We asked Cais."

"Ah," Jusson said. He picked up the chain, holding it to the light.

"Is Cais also a mage, sire?" an aristo asked, his voice tentative.

"No," Jusson said. "He is the keeper of my hearth."

Keeper of the hearth? I jerked around in my chair and met Cais' gaze. He gave me a dry smile, his eyes flashing purple in the afternoon sun coming through the study windows.

"You've never seen a hob before, Rabbit?" Wyln asked, sounding amused.

"Another discussion for another time," Jusson said before I could respond. Once more settling back into his chair, Jusson again folded his hands over his stomach, the mayor's chain looped on his fingers, and thrust his feet out before him, his gaze not on the two before him, but on the town elders.

"All right," the king said. "Start at the beginning and tell me everything."

Forty-one

We buried Menck's ashes along with the rest of the dead on a mountain lea. It wasn't the same meadow where I'd met Laurel six months and a lifetime ago. That was a sunny, open space above the timberline that overlooked the entire valley. This lea, lower in the mountains, was surrounded by trees that, despite the bright fall foliage, made it a dark, secret place. It was where a young doyen had come across men from a nearby village beating to death someone whose only crime was not being human.

And now, several decades later, Dyfrig was back. Garbed in his vestments, he was setting out his implements of blessing on his portable altar. Next to him on the ground was a double row of earthen jars. The graves had already been dug, with neat little mounds of dirt beside each hole, two gravediggers standing by with their shovels to fill them again, their faces properly respectful. The doyen's face, though, was as dark and closed as the lea—as it had been for the last couple of days.

But then, I hadn't been Master Chatty myself.

The lea was crowded with folk: Jusson, Thadro and the royal guards, nobles and their armsmen, a complement of soldiers and senior staff from the garrison, all of the town elders and officials, Peacekeeper Chadde and some of her Watch, and many of the regular townspeople, like Albe the blacksmith and his apprentices. Laurel and Wyln were present too, as were Beollan, Ranulf and Rosea. In her second day of the five-day purification rite, the former player, clad in the white sacking of the penitent, had her hair pulled back into a severe braid, her feet bare and on her forehead the rune of uncovering discernment had been drawn in charcoal by Dyfrig. Despite the trappings of the Church, though, there was a wide space around her, and hands hovered over weapons, ready to pull them at the slightest hint of hell. But Rosea didn't seem aware of the poised violence. Standing sheltered between her brother and great-uncle, she twisted her fingers together as her eyes went to the jars of ashes before traveling to Dyfrig at the altar, then over to me. As soon as she met my gaze, hers went skittering away.

Another person who wouldn't be skipping through the wildflowers singing summer is a-coming anytime soon.

Jusson was also gathering his share of wide space and nervous glances, but that had nothing to do with demon possession. The investigation into Gawell and Ednoth's affairs had started predictably with accounts of petty frauds and malfeasance growing into larger ones as Governor Lord Ormec's health and ability to oversee his territory declined. Jusson at first remained unruffled; it was a familiar story, and one that had played out on a much broader scale last spring, directed by the king's once-close friend, Lord Gherat of Dru. But when the elders got to the part of the closing of Eastgate, Jusson's air of detached interest had evaporated. Fast.

"They had *what?*" he demanded, rising slowing from his chair. The town elders shrank back in theirs. Gawell and Ednoth, though, remained staring sullenly at the floor.

"A letter from you, Your Majesty," Chadde said calmly, though her gray eyes gleamed. "It stated that, due to reports from the garrison of bandit activity, the Eastgate was to be closed and a new gate opened. It had your seal."

"Ebner, were you in on this?" Jusson asked, his voice a harsh whisper.

"No!" Commander Ebner's mustache rose in exclamation points. "The gate was already closed when I arrived, Your Majesty."

"This was before Commander Ebner's time, Your Majesty," Chadde confirmed. "Commander Boschel was in charge. I believe he left the army soon after, though. Came into some money, I understand."

Ednoth had inherited property—including the two buildings where the snipers had waited to ambush us—in what was then the undesirable part of town. Scheming to raise his property values, Ednoth, with the collusion of Gawell and the old garrison commander, forged the letter from the king, closing the old gate while opening a new gate right where Ednoth's property was located. The new gate brought prosperity to Ednoth and his cohorts, while the closure of the old caused that section of town to wither. Those who had suffered decline and loss blamed it on the capricious carelessness of the king, though many of the town elders knew better. They bought property themselves in the soon-to-be-revitalized part of town.

And when Slevoic arrived with his smuggling ring, he found a ready-made coterie that he could slip into like a pair of comfortable slippers, complete with warehouses, stables, safe houses and easy access to and from the new, ironically named Kingsgate.

Remaining on his feet, Jusson had listened to the end of it, the heat of his rage rising off of him in waves. He then walked swiftly for the study door, shouting orders and taking Cais with him. Next we knew, we were on the move. All the way across town to the old posting inn that stood in the shadow of the old gate, where the king personally bargained with the stunned innkeeper for the let of the entire inn for the remainder of the royal stay in Freston.

And Captain Javes led a determined search of Ednoth's properties, turning up all sorts of interesting things, including a small casket. Now, standing with Thadro at Jusson's back, I saw Javes hand Jusson the casket, and the king opened it to stare down at the false royal seal, its gold glittering bright in the gloom of the clearing. Then, closing it with a snap, he gave the casket to Thadro, who carefully placed it in a pocket.

(A search of Gawell's properties caused Dyfrig to place them all under Church edict until he could deal with what had been found in them.)

Captain Javes stepped away from Jusson and, figuring that he was going back to his troop unit, I shifted to let him pass. However, Javes was stopped by me. Turning, he lifted his quiz glass to watch Arlis. Neither Jeff nor Arlis were with me, Thadro having made it very clear that they did not need to guard me as I guarded the king. Arlis had gone back to visit with his old troop mates, looking very dashing with his goatee and Royal Guard tabard against the drabber army uniforms. Beyond him Jeffen stood talking to Captain Suiden and Lieutenant Groskin. Groskin was frowning as he listened, while Suiden was turned slightly away, his gaze fixed on Arlis.

"Interesting choice for a personal guard, what?" Javes murmured very softly. Apparently the captain had no illusion about his former trooper. He didn't wait for a response but dropped his glass and looked at me. "How are you doing, Rabbit?"

"All right, sir."

"You don't sound it," Javes observed. "Or look it either."

"It's been a rough several days," I said.

"So I've heard," Javes said, scanning the entire lea. "You can tell who went through the ordeal and who did not."

The captain was right. More folks had appeared, coming from the surrounding mountain villages to greet their king.

They didn't look as hard-used as their town cousins. They also seemed more inclined to look at me askance than with wide-eyed wonder. As they did my teachers in the talent. Wyln was over by the altar with Dyfrig, the enchanter holding what looked like several small wreathes made of fall grass and colorful leaves. As I watched, Dyfrig nodded and Wyln placed the wreathes on top of the jars of ashes. I'd expected to find Laurel also at the altar, but instead he was standing with Peacekeeper Chadde, holding what looked like an intense discussion.

"Any word on Helto or Bram, sir?" I asked, idly watching the conversing pair.

"No," Javes said, sighing. "The troops searching have found no sign of them. But then, both are familiar with every back path and deer trail. They're probably more than halfway to Gresh by now."

"Very likely, sir—" I stopped, stiffening. Despite the chill, Chadde wasn't wearing gloves and I could see something on her palm. Something that gave a faint glow in the dimness of the clearing. Something that I had etched on the palm of my own hand.

"My word," Javes said, also staring at the peacekeeper. He once more lifted his quiz glass, the better to see the truth rune. "She hadn't had that yesterday." The captain turned to the king, but Jusson had moved a little ways off to meet the villagers. "Does Jusson know—"

Javes broke off as Dyfrig stepped in front of the mobile altar and tapped his Staff of Office on the ground, causing the tiny bells to jingle. All conversations in the lea ceased and we turned to the doyen. At that moment, the sun crested the treetops, bathing Dyfrig and the altar in cool morning light. Perfect timing or something else, I wondered. Then, hearing the lapping of waves against a sandy shore, I decided I didn't want to know.

"Have you noticed lately that every time we leave a place, it's after a funeral?" Javes murmured.

"A mere coincidence, sir," I murmured back, fighting the urge to bless myself.

Dyfrig must've noticed us talking, for he tapped his Staff of Office again, and the captain and I fell silent. The doyen then leaned the staff against the altar and faced us, empty-handed. "A long time ago I came upon a murder happening here. I did nothing to stop it and walked away, feeling no more compunction than if I'd come across a goodwife ridding her house of bugs. I was wrong." He began taking off his vestments, revealing white penitent sacking underneath. "I could preach a week-long sermon on how wrong I was, and how I spread that wrongness to those given into my care." He laid his vestments on the altar. "But a sermon, however well intentioned, is only words." He toed off his shoes, rolled off his hosen, and stood barefoot on the cold ground. "Instead, let our actions speak."

There was silence, then Jusson removed his crown, shed his cloak and also took off his shoes and hosen. Thadro and the Royal Guard followed suit, as did Jusson's nobles and their armsmen, as did Ranulf and Beollan. Rosea, already barefoot, covered her face, tears leaking out the edges of her hands as the townspeople and villagers went shoeless too. Ebner turned to signal his troopers, but they were already taking off their cloaks, some sitting down to have others help pull their boots off. I managed it standing and set them next to my cloak. Wyln considered the doyen for a moment, his head tilted as if he were listening to something only he could hear. Then he too shed cloak and shoes, while Laurel removed his coat and leaned his staff against a tree.

Dyfrig waited until we were facing him once more, some shivering, our breaths misting out before us. "In a few days we will celebrate the gathering in of the harvest," he said. "In the time leading up to Harvestide, though, I declare a holy fast and days of mourning." He turned to the altar, one penitent among many. "Let us pray."

As I recited the prayer of contrition, the butterflies flew from the surrounding trees to land on my shoulder, their weight connecting me to the earth. I turned, expecting to see an antlered shadow in the trees, but no one was there— which meant nothing. Then I felt the ground move under my bare feet and I jumped aside, startled. Thadro, Suiden and Commander Ebner all frowned at me. Javes didn't; he just shook his head. However, he stopped shaking it and raised his quiz glass even as he continued to pray. There, just where I'd been standing, water was welling up—a new spring that carried away the dirt, leaves and other debris as it flowed towards the trees, to wend its way to the mountain cliff beyond.

ABOUT THE AUTHOR

Lorna Freeman started reading fairy tales at an early age in reaction to an ordinary life. Though not a true native, she has lived most of her life in southern California, the land of sunshine and earthquakes.

Lorna Freeman

Covenants
A Borderlands Novel

Rabbit is a trooper on the Border Guards, just another body in the King's army. But when his patrol encounters a Faena—one of the magical guardians of an uneasy ally—Rabbit is thrust into a political and magical intrigue that could start a war. Because Rabbit isn't just another trooper. He is the son of nobility—and a mage who doesn't know his own power...

"Combines drama with whimsy, high fantasy with military action."
—PATRICIA BRIGGS, AUTHOR OF *RAVEN'S STRIKE*

0-451-45980-6

Available wherever books are sold or at penguin.com